# ANOTHER FINE MYTH

# MYTH CONCEPTIONS

# ROBERT ASPRIN

ACE BOOKS, NEW YORK

ANOTHER FINE MYTH/MYTH CONCEPTIONS

An Ace Book / published by arrangement with
Donning Company

PRINTING HISTORY
Ace mass-market edition / May 2002

All rights reserved.
Published by arrangement with Starblaze Editions of
the Donning Company/Publishers.
*Another Fine Myth/Myth Conceptions* copyright © 2002 by
Donning Company.
*Another Fine Myth* copyright © 1978 by Robert L. Asprin.
*Myth Conceptions* copyright © 1980 by Robert L. Asprin.
Cover art by Walter Velez.
Text design by Julie Rogers.

This book, or parts thereof, may not be reproduced in any form without permission. For information address: The Donning Company/Publishers, Inc., 5659 Virginia Beach Blvd., Norfolk, Virginia 23502.

Visit our website at
www.penguinputnam.com
Check out the ACE Science Fiction & Fantasy newsletter!

ISBN: 0-441-00931-X

ACE®
Ace Books are published by The Berkley Publishing Group,
a division of Penguin Putnam Inc.,
375 Hudson Street, New York, New York 10014.
ACE and the "A" design
are trademarks belonging to Penguin Putnam Inc.

PRINTED IN THE UNITED STATES OF AMERICA

10  9  8  7  6  5  4

# ANOTHER FINE MYTH

*This book is dedicated to*

**Bork The Indestructible**
(Known to lesser mortals as George Hunt)

*whose gruff but loyal friendship has seen me through many crises in the past . . . and probably in the future!*

# I:

*"There are things on heaven and earth,
Horatio, Man was not meant to know."*

—HAMLET

One of the few redeeming facets of instructors, I thought, is that occasionally they can be fooled. It was true when my mother taught me to read, it was true when my father tried to teach me to be a farmer, and it's true now when I'm learning magik.

"You haven't been practicing!" Garkin's harsh admonishment interrupted my musings.

"I have too!" I protested. "It's just a difficult exercise."

As if in response, the feather I was levitating began to tremble and wobble in midair.

"You aren't concentrating!" he accused.

"It's the wind," I argued. I wanted to add "from your loud mouth," but didn't dare. Early in our lessons Garkin had demonstrated his lack of appreciation for cheeky apprentices.

"The wind," he sneered, mimicking my voice. "Like this, dolt!"

My mental contact with the object of my concentration

was interrupted as the feather darted suddenly toward the ceiling. It jarred to a halt as if it had become imbedded in something, though it was still a foot from the wooden beams, then slowly rotated to a horizontal plane. Just as slowly it rotated on its axis, then swapped ends and began to glide around an invisible circle like a leaf caught in an eddy.

I risked a glance at Garkin. He was draped over his chair, feet dangling, his entire attention apparently devoted to devouring a leg of roast lizard-bird, a bird I had snared I might add. Concentration indeed!

He looked up suddenly and our eyes met. It was too late to look away so I simply looked back at him.

"Hungry?" His grease-flecked salt-and-pepper beard was suddenly framing a wolfish grin. "Then show me how much you've been practicing."

It took me a heartbeat to realize what he meant; then I looked up desperately. The feather was tumbling floor-ward, a bare shoulder-height from landing. Forcing the sudden tension from my body, I reached out with my mind . . . gently . . . from a pillow . . . don't knock it away. . . .

The feather halted a scant two hand-spans from the floor.

I heard Garkin's low chuckle, but didn't allow it to break my concentration. I hadn't let the feather touch the floor for three years, and it wasn't going to touch now.

Slowly I raised it until it floated at eye level. Wrapping my mind around it, I rotated it on its axis, then enticed it to swap ends. As I led it through the exercise, its movement was not as smooth or sure as when Garkin set his mind to the task, but it did move unerringly in its assigned course.

Although I had not been practicing with the feather, I had been practicing. When Garkin was not about or pre-occupied with his own studies, I devoted most of my time to levitating pieces of metal—keys, to be specific. Each type of levitation had its own inherent problems. Metal was hard to work with because it was an inert material. The feather, having once been part of a living thing, was more responsive . . . too responsive. To lift metal took effort, to maneuver a feather required subtlety. Of the two, I preferred to work with metal. I could see a more direct application of that skill in my chosen profession.

"Good enough, lad. Now put it back in the book."

I smiled to myself. This part I had practiced, not because of its potential applications, but because it was fun.

The book was lying open on the end of the workbench. I brought the feather down in a long lazy spiral, allowing it to pass lightly across the pages of the book and up in a swooping arc, stopped it, and brought it back. As it approached the book the second time, I disengaged part of my mind to dart ahead to the book. As the feather crossed the pages, the book snapped shut like the jaws of a hungry predator, trapping the missile within its grasp.

"Hmmmm . . ." intoned Garkin, "a trifle showy, but effective."

"Just a little something I worked up when I was practicing," I said casually, reaching out with my mind for the other lizard-bird leg. Instead of floating gracefully to my waiting hand, however, it remained on the wooden platter as if it had taken root.

"Not so fast, my little sneak-thief. So you've been practicing, eh?" He stroked his beard thoughtfully with the half-gnawed bone in his hand.

"Certainly. Didn't it show?" It occurred to me that Garkin is not as easy to fool as it sometimes seems.

"In that case, I'd like to see you light your candle. It should be easy if you have been practicing as much as you claim."

"I have no objections to trying, but as you have said yourself so many times, some lessons come easier than others."

Although I sounded confident, my spirits sank as the large candle came floating to the work table in response to Garkin's summons. In four years of trying I was yet to

be successful at this particular exercise. If Garkin was
going to keep me from food until I was successful, I could
go hungry for a long time.

"Say, uh, Garkin, it occurs to me I could probably concentrate better on a full stomach."

"It occurs to me that you're stalling."

"Couldn't I. . . ."

"Now, Skeeve."

There was no swaying him once he used my proper
name. That much I had learned over the years. Lad, Thief,
Idiot, Turnip-Head, though derogatory, as long as he used
one of these, his mind was still open. Once he reverted
to using my proper name, it was hopeless. It is indeed a
sorry state when the sound of your own name becomes a
knell of doom.

Well, if there was no way around it, I'd just have to
give it my best shot. For this there could be no half-effort
or feigned concentration. I would have to use every ounce
of my strength and skill to summon the power.

I studied the candle with a detached mind, momentarily
blanking the effort ahead from my consciousness. The
room, the cluttered workbench, Garkin, even my own
hunger faded from view as I focused on the candle,
though I had long since memorized its every feature.

It was stout, nearly six inches across to stabilize its
ten-inch height. I had carved numerous mystic symbols
into its surface, copied painstakingly from Garkin's books
at his direction, though many of them were partially oblit-
erated by hardened rivulets of wax. The candle had burned
many long hours to light my studies, but it had always
been lit from a taper from the cooking fire and not from
my efforts.

Negative thought. Stop it.

I will light the candle this time. I will light it because
there is no reason I should not.

Consciously deepening my breathing, I began to gather
the power. My world narrowed further until all I was
aware of was the curled, blackened wick of the candle.

I am Skeeve. My father has a farmer's bond with the earth. My mother was an educated woman. My teacher is a master magician. I am Skeeve. I will light this candle.

I could feel myself beginning to grow warm as the energies began to build within me. I focused the heat on the wick.

Like my father, I tap the strength of the earth. The knowledge my mother gave me is like a lens, enabling me to focus what I have gained. The wisdom of my teacher directs my efforts to those points of the universe most likely to yield to my will. I am Skeeve.

The candle remained unlit. There was sweat on my forehead now, and I was beginning to tremble with the effort. No, that was wrong, I should not tense. Relax. Don't try to force it. Tenseness hinders the flow. Let the energies pass freely, serve as a passive conductor. I forced myself to relax, consciously letting the muscles in my face and shoulders go slack as I redoubled my efforts.

The flow was noticeably more intense now. I could almost see the energy streaming from me to my target. I stretched out a finger which focused the energies even more. The candle remained unlit.

I couldn't do it. Negative thought. Stop it. I am Skeeve. I will light the candle. My father. . . . No. Negative thought. Do not rely on others for your strength. I will light the candle because I am Skeeve.

I was rewarded by a sudden surge of energy at the thought. I pursued it, growing heady with power. I am Skeeve. I am stronger than any of them. I escaped my father's attempts to chain me to a plow as he had my brother. My mother died from her idealism, but I used her teachings to survive. My teacher is a gullible fool who took a thief for an apprentice. I have beaten them all. I am Skeeve. I will light the candle.

I was floating now. I realized how my abilities dwarfed those around me. Whether the candle lit or not was inconsequential. I am Skeeve. I am powerful.

Almost contemptuously I reached out with my mind

and touched the wick. A small bright ember appeared as if in answer to my will.

Startled, I sat up and blinked at the candle. As I did, the ember disappeared, leaving a small white plume of smoke to mark its departure. I realized too late I had broken concentration.

"Excellent, Lad!"

Garkin was suddenly beside me pounding my shoulder enthusiastically. How long he had been there I neither knew nor cared.

"It went out," I said plaintively.

"Never you mind that. You lit it. You have the confidence now. Next time it will be easy. By the stars, we'll make a magician of you yet. Here, you must be hungry."

I barely got my hand up in time to intercept the remaining lizard-bird leg before it smacked into my face. It was cold.

"I don't mind admitting I was beginning to despair, lad. What made that lesson so hard? Has it occurred to you you could use that spell to give you extra light when you're picking a lock or even to start a fire to serve as a diversion?"

"I thought about it, but extra light could draw unwanted attention. As for starting a diversion, I'd be afraid of hurting someone. I don't want to hurt anyone, just. . . ."

I stopped, realizing what I was saying, too late. A heavy cuff from Garkin sent me sprawling off my stool.

"I thought so! You're still planning to be a thief. You want to use my magiks to steal!"

He was towering in his rage, but for once I stood my ground.

"What of it?" I snarled. "It beats starving. What's so good about being a magician, anyway? I mean, your lifestyle here gives me so much to look forward to."

I gestured at the cluttered room that was the entirety of the hut.

"Listen to the wolfling complain," Garkin sneered. "It was good enough for you when the winter drove you out

of the woods to steal. 'It beats sleeping under a bush,'
you said."

"And it still does. That's why I'm still here. But I'm
not going to spend the rest of my life here. Hiding in a
little hut in the woods is not my idea of a future to look
forward to. You were living on roots and berries until I
came along and started trapping meat for the fire. Maybe
that's your idea of a wonderful life, Garkin, but it's not
mine!"

We glared at each other for several long moments.
Now that my anger was vented, I was more than a little
afraid. While I had not had extensive experience in the
field, I suspected that sneering at magicians was not the
best way to ensure a long and healthy future.

Surprisingly enough, it was Garkin who gave ground
first. He suddenly dropped his gaze and bowed his head,
giving me a rare view of the unkempt mass of hair atop
it.

"Perhaps you're right, Skeeve," his voice was strangely
soft. "Perhaps I have been showing you all the work of
magik, but not the rewards. I constantly forget how sup-
pressed magik is in these lands."

He raised his eyes to meet mine again, and I shivered
at the impact. They were not angry, but deep within them
burned a glow I had never seen before.

"Know you now, Skeeve, that all lands are not like this
one, nor was I always as you see me now. In lands where
magik is recognized instead of feared as it is here, it is
respected and commissioned by those in power. There a
skillful magician who keeps his wits about him can reap
a hundred times the wealth you aspire to as a thief, and
such power that. . . ."

He broke off suddenly and shook his head as if to clear
it. When he opened his eyes again, the glow I had seen
burning earlier had died to an ember.

"But you aren't to be impressed by words, are you,
lad? Come, I'll show you a little demonstration of some

of the power you may one day wield—if you practice your lessons, that is."

The joviality in his voice was forced. I nodded my agreement in answer to that burning gaze. Truth to tell, I needed no demonstration. His soft, brief oration had awed me far more than any angry tirade or demonstration, but I did not wish to contradict him at this time.

I don't believe he actually noticed my response. He was already striding into the large pentagram permanently inscribed in the floor of the hut. As he walked, he gestured absentmindedly and the charred copper brazier scuttled forth from its place in the corner to meet him at the center of the pentagram.

I had time to reflect that perhaps it was that brazier that had first drawn me to Garkin. I remembered the first time I peered through the window of his hut seeking to identify and place objects of value for a later theft. I had seen Garkin as I have seen him so often since, pacing restlessly up and down the room, his nose buried in a book. It was a surprising enough sight as it was, for reading is not a common pastime in this area, but what captured my attention was the brazier. It hobbled about the room, following Garkin like an impatient puppy that was a little too polite to jump up on its master to get his attention. Then Garkin had looked up from his book, stared thoughtfully at his workbench; then, with a nod of decision, gestured. A small pot of unidentified content rose from the clutter and floated to his waiting hand. He caught it, referred to his book again, and poured out a dollop without looking up. Quick as a cat, the brazier scrambled under his hand and caught the dollop before it reached the floor. That had been my introduction to magik.

Something wrenched my attention back to the present. What was it? I checked Garkin's progress. No, he was still at work, half hidden by a floating cloud of vials and jars, mumbling as he occasionally plucked one from the air and added a bit of its contents to the brazier. Whatever he was working on, it promised to be spectacular.

Then I heard it again, a muffled step outside the hut. But that was impossible! Garkin always set the . . . I began to search my memory. I could not recall Garkin setting the protective wards before he started to work. Ridiculous. Caution was the first and most important thing Garkin hammered into me, and part of caution was always setting wards before you started working. He couldn't have forgotten . . . but he had been rather intense and distracted.

I was still trying to decide if I should attempt to interrupt Garkin's work when he suddenly stepped back from the brazier. He fixed me with his gaze, and my warning died in my throat. This was not the time to impose reality on the situation. The glow was back in his eyes, stronger than before.

"Even demonstrations should give a lesson," he intoned. "Control, Skeeve. Control is the mainstay of magik. Power without control is a disaster. That is why you practice with a feather though you are able to move much larger and heavier objects. Control. Even your meager powers would be dangerous unless controlled, and I will not teach you more until you have learned that control."

He carefully stepped out of the pentagram.

"To demonstrate the value of control, I will now summon forth a demon, a being from another world. He is powerful, cruel, and vicious, and would kill us both if given the chance. Yet despite this, we need not fear him because he will be controlled. He will be unable to harm us or anything else in this world as long as he is contained within that pentagram. Now watch, Skeeve. Watch and learn."

So saying, he turned once more to the brazier. He spread his hands, and as he did, the five candles at the points of the pentagram sprang to life and the lines of the pentagram began to glow with an eerie blue light. Silence reigned for several minutes, then he began to chant in a low mumble. A thread of smoke appeared from the brazier, but instead of rising to the ceiling, it poured onto the floor and began to form a small cloud that seethed and pulsed. Garkin's chanting was louder now, and the cloud grew and darkened. The brazier was almost obscured from view, but there . . . in the depths of the cloud . . . something was taking shape. . . .

"Isstvan sends his greetings, Garkin!"

I nearly jumped out of my skin at the words. They came from inside the hut, but not inside the pentagram! I whirled toward their source. A figure was standing just inside the door, blinding in a glowing gold cloak. For a mad moment I thought it was the demon answering Garkin's summons. Then I saw the crossbow. It was a man, alright, but the crossbow, cocked and loaded in his hand, did little for my peace of mind.

Garkin did not even turn to look.

"Not now, you fool!" he snarled.

"It has been a long hunt, Garkin," the man continued as if he hadn't heard. "You've hidden yourself well, but did you really hope to escape. . . ."

"You dare!?!" Garkin spun from his work, towering in his rage.

The man saw Garkin's face now, saw the eyes, and his face contorted in a grotesque mask of fear. Reflexively, he loosed the bolt from his crossbow, but too late. I did not see what Garkin did, things were happening too fast, but the man suddenly disappeared in a sheet of flame. He shrieked in agony and fell to the floor. The flame disappeared as suddenly as it had come, leaving only the smoldering corpse as evidence it had existed at all.

I remained rooted to the spot for several moments before I could move or even speak.

"Garkin," I said at last, "I . . . Garkin!"

Garkin's form was a crumpled lump on the floor. I was at his side in one bound, but I was far too late. The crossbow bolt protruded with silent finality from his chest. Garkin had given me my last lesson.

As I stooped to touch his body, I noticed something that froze my blood in its veins. Half-hidden by his form was the extinguished candle from the north point of the pentagram. The lines were no longer glowing blue. The protective spell was gone.

With agonizing effort, I raised my head and found myself gazing into a pair of yellow eyes, flecked with gold, that were not of this world.

# II:

*"Things are not always as they seem."*

—MANDRAKE

Once, in the woods, I found myself face to face with a snake-cat. On another occasion, I encountered a spider-bear. Now, faced with a demon, I decided to pattern my behavior after that which had saved me in the aforementioned situations. I froze. At least, in hindsight, I like to think it was a deliberate, calculated act.

The demon curled its lips back, revealing a double row of needle-sharp teeth.

I considered changing my chosen course of action; I considered fainting.

The demon ran a purple tongue over his lips and began to slowly extend a taloned hand toward me. That did it! I went backward, not in a catlike graceful bound, but scrabbling on all fours. It's surprising how fast you can move that way when properly inspired. I managed to build up a substantial head of steam before I crashed head-first into the wall.

"Gaahh. . . ." I said. It may not seem like much, but at

the time it was the calmest expression of pain and terror I could think of.

At my outburst, the demon seemed to choke. Several ragged shouts erupted, then he began to laugh. It wasn't a low menacing laugh, but the wholehearted enthusiastic laughter of someone who has just seen something hysterically funny.

I found it both disquieting and annoying. Annoying because I had a growing suspicion I was the source of his amusement; disquieting because . . . well . . . he was a demon and demons are. . . .

"Cold, vicious, and bloodthirsty," the demon gasped as if he had read my thoughts. "You really bought the whole line, didn't you, kid?"

"I beg your pardon?" I said because I couldn't think of anything else to say.

"Something wrong with your ears? I said 'cold, vicious. . . .' "

"I heard you. I meant what did you mean."

"What I meant was that you were scared stiff, by a few well chosen words from my esteemed colleague, I'll wager." He jerked a thumb at Garkin's body. "Sorry for the dramatics. I felt a touch of comic relief was necessary to lighten an otherwise tragic moment."

"Comic relief?"

"Well, actually, I couldn't pass up the opportunity. You should have seen your face."

He chuckled to himself as he strode out of the pentagram and began leisurely inspecting the premises.

"So this is Garkin's new place, huh? What a dump. Who would have thought he'd come to this?"

To say I was perplexed would be an understatement. I wasn't sure how a demon should act, but it wasn't like this.

I could have bolted for the door, but I did not seem to be in immediate danger. Either this strange being meant me no harm, or he was confident of his ability to stop me even if I tried to flee. For the sake of my nervous system, I decided to assume the former.

The demon continued to inspect the hut, while I inspected him. He was humanoid; that is, he had two arms, two legs, and a head. He was short but powerfully built, a bit broader across the shoulders than a man, and heavily muscled, but he wasn't human. I mean, you don't see many hairless humans with dark green scales covering their body and pointed ears lying flat against their head.

I decided to risk a question.

"Ah, excuse me."

"Yeah, kid?"

"Um, you *are* a demon, aren't you?"

"Huh? Oh, yeah, I guess you could say I am."

"Well, if you don't mind my asking, why don't you act like a demon?"

The demon shot me a disgusted look, then turned his head heavenward in a gesture of martyrdom.

"Everybody's a critic. Tell ya what, kid, would you be happier if I tore your throat out with my teeth?"

"Well, no, but. . . ."

"For that matter, who are you, anyway? Are you an innocent bystander, or did you come with the assassin?"

"I'm with him," I hastened to reply, pointing a shaky finger at Garkin's body. That bit about tearing my throat out had me on edge again. "Or at least I was. Garkin. The one who summoned . . . him! . . . I'm . . . I was his student."

"No kiddin'? Garkin's apprentice?" He began advancing toward me, reaching out a hand, "Pleased ta . . . what's wrong?"

As he moved toward me, I had started backing away from him. I tried to do it casually, but he had noticed.

"Well . . . it's . . . you *are* a demon."

"Yeah. So?"

"Um . . . well, demons are supposed to be. . . ."

"Hey, relax, kid. I don't bite. Look, I'm an old buddy of Garkin's."

"I thought you said you were a demon?"

"That's right. I'm from another dimension. A dimension traveler, or demon for short. Get it?"

"What's a dimension?"

The demon scowled.

"Are you sure you're Garkin's apprentice? I mean, he hasn't told you anything at all about dimensions?"

"No," I answered. "I mean, yes, I'm his apprentice, but he never said anything about the demon-suns."

"That's dimensions," he corrected. "Well, a dimension is another world, actually one of several worlds, existing simultaneously with this one, but on different planes. Follow me?"

"No," I admitted.

"Well, just accept that I'm from another world. Now, in that world, I'm a magician just like Garkin. We had an exchange program going where we could summon each other across the barrier to impress our respective apprentices."

"I thought you said you were a demon," I said suspiciously.

"I *am*! Look, kid. In my world, you'd be a demon, but at the current moment I'm in yours, so I'm a demon."

"I thought you said you were a magician."

"I don't believe this!" The demon made his angry appeal to the heavens. "I'm standing here arguing with some twerp of an apprentice. . . . Look, kid."

He fixed me with his gaze again.

"Let me try it this way. Are you going to shake my hand, or am I going to rip your heart out?"

Since he put it that way . . . I mean, for a minute there, when he lost his temper and started shouting, he sounded just like Garkin. It gave credibility to his claim of friendship with my ex-teacher. I took his extended hand and shook it cautiously.

"I'm. . . . My name is Skeeve."

His grip was cold, but firm. So firm in fact that I found

it impossible to reclaim my hand as rapidly as I would have liked.

"Pleased ta meetcha, kid. I'm Aahz."

"Oz?"

"No relation."

"No relation to what?" I asked, but he was examining the room again.

"Well, there's certainly nothing here to arouse the greedy side of his fellow beings. Early primitive, enduring, but not particularly sought after."

"We like it," I said, rather stiffly. Now that I was over being scared, I didn't like the sneer in his voice. The hut wasn't much and I certainly wasn't overly fond of it, but I resented his criticism.

"Don't get your back up, kid." Aahz said easily. "I'm looking for a motive, that's all."

"Motive?"

"A reason for someone to off old Garkin. I'm not big on vengeance, but he was a drinking buddy of mine and it's got my curiosity up."

He broke off his inspection of the room to address me directly.

"How about you, kid? Can you think of anything? Any milkmaids he's seduced or farmers he's cheated? You've got an interest in this too, you know. You might be the next target."

"But the guy who did it is dead." I gestured to the charred lump by the door. "Doesn't that finish it?"

"Wake up, kid. Didn't you see the gold cloak? That was a professional assassin. Somebody hired him, and that somebody would hire another one."

A chill ran down my spine. I hadn't really thought of that. I began to search my memory for a clue.

"Well . . . he said Isstvan sent him."

"What's an Isstvan?"

"I don't . . . wait a minute. What do you mean, I might be the next target?"

"Neat, huh?" Aahz was holding up the gold cloak.

"Lined, and completely reversible. Always wondered how come no one noticed them until they were ready to pounce."

"Aahz. . . ."

"Hmmm? Oh, didn't mean to scare you. It's just if someone's declared open season on magicians in general or Garkin specifically, you might have some. . . . Hello, what's this?"

"What's what?" I asked, trying to get a look at what he had found.

"This," he said, holding his prize aloft. "It seems I'm not the only demon about."

It was a head, apparently the assassin's. It was badly charred, with bone showing in several places. My natural revulsion at the sight was compounded by several obvious features. The chin and ears of the head were unnaturally pointed, and there were two short, blunt, horns protruding from the forehead.

"A devil!" I exclaimed in horror.

"A what? Oh, a Deveel. No, it's not from Deva, it's from Imper. An Imp. Didn't Garkin teach you anything?"

"Come again?" I asked, but Aahz was busy scowling at the head.

"The question is, who would be crass enough to hire an Imp for an assassin? The only one I can think of is Isstvan, but that's impossible."

"But that's who did it. Don't you remember? I told you. . . ."

"I thought you said 'Isstvan.' "

"I did! Wait a minute. What did you say?"

"I said Isstvan. Can't you tell the difference?"

"No," I admitted.

"Hmmm . . . must be too subtle for the human ear to detect. Oh, well. No matter. This changes everything. If Isstvan is up to his old tricks there's no time to lose. Hey! Wait a minute. What's this?"

"It's a crossbow," I observed.

"With heat-seeking armor-piercing quarrels? Is that the norm in this world?"

"Heat-seeking. . . ."

"Never mind, kid. I didn't think so. Well, that tears it. I'd better check this out quick."

He began to stride into the pentagram. I suddenly realized he was preparing to leave.

"Hey! Wait a minute! What's going on?"

"It would take too long to explain, kid. Maybe I'll see you again sometime."

"But you said I might be a target!"

"Yeah, well, that's the way it crumbles. Tell ya what. Start running and maybe they won't find you until it's over."

My head was awhirl. Things were happening far too fast for clear thought. I still didn't know what or who the demon was or if I should trust him, but I did know one thing. He was the nearest thing to an ally I had in a situation where I was clearly outclassed.

"Couldn't you help me?"

"No time. I've got to move."

"Couldn't I come with you?"

"You'd just get in the way, maybe even get me killed."

"But without you, I'll be killed!"

I was getting desperate, but Aahz was unimpressed.

"Probably not. Tell ya what, kid. I've really got to get going, but just to show you I think you'll survive, I'll show you a little trick you might use sometime. You see all this crud Garkin used to bring me across the barrier? Well, it's not necessary. Watch close and I'll show you how we do it when our apprentices aren't watching."

I wanted to shout, to make him stop and listen to me, but he had already started. He spread his arms at shoulder height, looked heavenward, took a deep breath, then clapped his hands.

Nothing happened.

# III:

*"The only thing more reliable than magik is one's friends!"*

—MACBETH

Aahz scowled and repeated the gesture, a bit quicker this time.

The scene remained unchanged.

I decided something was wrong.

"Is something wrong?" I asked politely.

"You'd better believe there's something wrong," Aahz snarled. "It's not working."

"Are you sure you're doing it right?"

"Yes, I'm sure I'm doing it right, just like I've been sure the last fifty times I did it!"

He was starting to sound annoyed.

"Can you. . . ."

"Look, kid. If I knew what was wrong, I'd have fixed it already. Now, just shut up and let me think!"

He sank down to sit cross-legged in the center of the pentagram where he began sketching vague patterns in the floor as he mumbled darkly to himself. I wasn't sure if he was trying some alternate incantation or was simply thinking hard, but decided it would be unwise to ask. Instead, I used the time to organize my scrambled thoughts.

I still wasn't sure if Aahz was a threat to me or if he was my only possible salvation from a greater threat. I mean, by this time I was pretty sure he was kidding about ripping my heart out, but that's the sort of thing one wants to be very sure of. One thing I had learned for certain, there was more to this magik stuff than floating feathers around.

"That's got to be it!"

Aahz was on his feet again, glaring at Garkin's body.

"That ill-begot son of a wombat!"

"What's a wombat?" I asked, then immediately wished I hadn't. The mental image that sprang into my mind was so horrifying I was sure I didn't want details. I needn't have worried. Aahz was not about to take time to answer me.

"Well, it's a pretty crummy joke. That's all I have to say."

"Um. . . . What are you talking about, Aahz?"

"I'm talking about Garkin! He did this to me. If I thought it would go this far, I would have turned him into a goat-fish when I had the chance."

"Aahz. . . . I still don't. . . ."

I stopped. He had ceased his ranting and was looking at me. I shrank back reflexively before I recognized the snarl as his smile. I liked it better when he was raving.

"I'm sorry, Skeeve," he purred. "I guess I haven't been very clear."

I was growing more uneasy by the minute. I wasn't used to having people, much less demons, being nice to me.

"Um. . . . That's okay. I was just wondering. . . ."

"You see, the situation is this. Garkin and I have been . . . playing little jokes on each other for some time now. It started one time when we were drinking and he stiffed me with the bill. Well, the next time I summoned him, I brought him in over a lake and he had to do his demon act armpit deep in water. He got even by . . . well, I won't bore you with details, but we've gotten in the habit of putting each other in awkward or embarrassing situations. It's really very childish, but quite harmless. But this time. . . ." Aahz's eyes started to narrow, "But this time the old frog-kisser's gone too . . . I mean, it seems to have gotten a little out of hand. Don't you agree?"

He bared his fangs at me again in a smile. I wanted very badly to agree with him, but I didn't have the foggiest idea what he was talking about.

"You still haven't told me what's wrong."

"What's wrong is that stinking slime-monger took away my powers!" he roared, forgetting his composure. "I'm blocked! I can't do a flaming thing unless he removes his stupid prankish spell and he can't 'cause he's dead! Now do you understand me, fly-bait?"

I made up my mind. Savior or not, I'd rather he went back where he came from.

"Well, if there was anything I could do. . . ."

"There is, Skeeve, my boy." Aahz was suddenly all purrs and teeth again. "All you have to do is fire up the old cauldron or whatever and remove this spell. Then we can each go our separate ways and. . . ."

"I can't do that."

"Okay, kid," his smile was a little more forced. "I'll stick around until you're on your feet. I mean, what are friends for?"

"That's not it."

"What do you want? Blood?" Aahz was no longer smiling. "If you're trying to hold me up, I'll. . . ."

"You don't understand!" I interrupted desperately. "I can't do it because I can't do it! I don't know how!"

That stopped him.

"Hmm. That could be a problem. Well, tell you what. Instead of pulling the spell here, what say you just pop me back to my own dimension and I'll get someone there to take it off."

"I can't do that either. Remember, I told you I'd never
even heard of. . . ."

"Well, what *can* you do?!"

"I can levitate objects . . . well, small objects."

"And. . . ." he encouraged.

"And . . . um . . . I can light a candle."

"Light a candle?"

"Well . . . almost."

Aahz sank heavily into a chair and hid his face in his
hands for several minutes. I waited for him to think of
something.

"Kid, have you got anything in this dump to drink?"
he asked finally.

"I'll get you some water."

"I said something to drink, not something to wash in!"

"Oh. Yessir!"

I hastened to bring him a goblet of wine from the small
keg Garkin kept, hoping he wouldn't notice the vessel
wasn't particularly clean.

"What will this do? Will it help you put your powers
back?"

"No. But it might make me feel a little better." He
tossed the wine down in one swallow, and studied the
goblet disdainfully. "Is this the biggest container you've
got?"

I cast about the room desperately, but Aahz was way
ahead of me.

He rose, strode into the pentagram, and picked up the
brazier. I knew from past experience it was deceptively
heavy, but he carried it to the keg as if it were weightless.
Not bothering to empty out Garkin's concoction, he filled
it to the brim and took a deep draught.

"Aah! That's better." He sighed.

I felt a little queasy.

"Well, kid," he said, sweeping me with an appraising
stare, "it looks like we're stuck with each other. The setup
isn't ideal, but it's what we've got. Time to bite the bullet

and play the cards we're dealt. You do know what cards are, don't you?"

"Of course," I said, slightly wounded.

"Good."

"What's a bullet?"

Aahz closed his eyes as if struggling against some inner turmoil.

"Kid," he said at last, "there's a good chance this partnership is going to drive one of us crazy. I would guess it will be me unless you can knock off the dum-dum questions every other sentence."

"But I can't understand half of what you're saying."

"Hmm. Tell ya what. Try to save up the questions and ask me all at one time once a day. Okay?"

"I'll try."

"Right. Now here's the situation as I see it. If Isstvan is hiring Imps for assassins. . . ."

"What's an Imp?"

"Kid, will you give me a break?"

"I'm sorry, Aahz. Keep going."

"Right. Well . . . umm. . . . It's happening!" he made his appeal to the heavens. "I can't remember what I was saying!"

"Imps," I prompted.

"Oh! Right. Well, if he's hiring Imps and arming them with non-spec weapons, it can only mean he's up to his old tricks. Now since I don't have my powers, I can't get out of here to sound the alarm. That's where you come in, kid. . . . Kid?"

He was looking at me expectantly. I found I could contain my misery no longer.

"I'm sorry, Aahz," I said in a small, pitiful voice I hardly recognized as my own. "I don't understand a single thing you've said."

I suddenly realized I was about to cry, and turned away hurriedly so he wouldn't see. I sat there, with tears trickling down my cheeks, alternately fighting the urge to wipe them away and wondering why I was concerned over whether or not a demon saw me crying. I don't know how long I stayed that way, but I was brought back to reality by a gentle hand on my shoulder, a cold, gentle hand.

"Hey, kid. Don't beat on yourself," Aahz's voice was surprisingly sympathetic. "It's not your fault if Garkin was tight with his secrets. Nobody expects you to have learned something you were never taught, so there's no reason you should expect it either."

"I just feel so stupid," I said, not turning. "I'm not used to feeling stupid."

"You aren't stupid, kid. That much I know. Garkin wouldn't have taken you for an apprentice if you were stupid. If anybody here's stupid, it's me. I got so carried away with the situation, I forgot myself and tried talking to an apprentice as if he were a full-blown magician. Now that's stupid."

I still couldn't bring myself to respond.

"Heck, kid." He gave my shoulder a gentle shake. "Right now you can do more magik than I can."

"But you know more."

"But I can't use it. You know, kid, that gives me an idea. With old Garkin dead there, you're kind of cut off. What say you sign on as my apprentice for a while. We'll take it from the top with me teaching you as if you were a new student who didn't know a thing. We'll take it step by step from the beginning. What da ya say?"

In spite of my gloom I felt my spirits lift. Like he said, I'm not stupid. I could recognize a golden opportunity when I saw one.

"Gee, that sounds great, Aahz."

"Then it's a deal?"

"It's a deal," I answered and stuck out my hand.

"What's that?" he snarled. "Isn't my word good enough for you?"

"But you said. . . ."

"That's right. You're my apprentice now, and I don't go around shaking apprentices' hands."

I withdrew my hand. It occurred to me this alliance might not be all roses and song.

"Now as I was saying, here's what we've got to do about the current situation. . . ."

"But I haven't had any lessons yet!"

"That's right. Here's your first lesson. When a crisis shapes up, you don't waste energy wishing for information or skills you haven't got. You dig in and handle it as best you can with what you've got. Now shut up while I fill you in on the situation . . . apprentice."

I shut up and listened. He studied me for a moment, then gave a small satisfied nod, took another gulp from the brazier and began.

"Now, you have a vague idea about other dimensions because I told you about them earlier. You also have first-hand experience that magicians can open passages in the barriers between those dimensions. Well, different magicians use that power in different ways. Some of them, like Garkin, only use it to impress the yokels; summon a demon, visions of other worlds, that kind of schtick. But there are others whose motives are not so pure."

He paused to take another gulp of wine. Surprisingly, I felt no urge to interrupt with questions.

"Technology in different dimensions has progressed at different rates, as has magik. Some magicians use this to their own advantage. They aren't showmen, they're smugglers, buying and selling technology across the barriers for profit and power. Most of the inventors in any dimension are actually closet magicians."

I must have frowned without realizing it, but Aahz noted it and acknowledged it with a wink and a smirk.

"I know what you're thinking, Skeeve. It all sounds a little dishonest and unscrupulous. Actually, they're a fairly ethical bunch. There's a set of unwritten rules called the Smugglers Code they adhere to pretty closely."

"Smugglers Code?" I asked, forgetting myself for a moment. Aahz didn't seem to mind this time.

"It's like the Mercenaries Code, but less violent and

more profitable. Anyway, as an example, one item in that
code states you cannot bring an 'invention' into a dimension that is too far in advance of that dimension's technology, like bringing guided missiles into a longbow
culture or lasers into a flint and powder era."

I kept my silence with great difficulty.

"As I've said, most magicians adhere to the code fairly
closely, but once in a while a bad one crops up. That
brings us to Isstvan."

I got a sudden chill at the sound of that name. Maybe
there *was* something different in the way Aahz pronounced it.

"Some say Isstvan isn't playing with a full deck. I
think he's been playing with his wand too much. But
whatever the reason, somewhere he's gotten it into his
head he wants to rule the dimensions, all of them. He's
tried it before, but we got wind of it in time and a bunch
of us teamed up to teach him a lesson in manners. As a
matter of fact, that's when I first met Garkin there."

He gestured with the brazier and slopped a bit of wine
on the floor. I began to doubt his sobriety, but his voice
seemed steady enough as he continued.

"I thought he had given the thing up after his last drub-
bing. We even gave him a few souvenirs to be sure he
didn't forget. Then this thing pops up. If he's hiring cross-
dimension help and arming them with advance technology
weapons, he's probably trying to do it again."

"Do what?"

"I just told you. Take over the dimensions."

"I know, but how? I mean, how does what he does in
this dimension help him rule the others?"

"Oh, that. Well, each dimension has a certain amount
of power that can be channeled or converted into magik.
Different dimensions have different amounts, and each dimension's power is divided up or shared by the magicians
of that dimension. If he can succeed in controlling or killing the other magicians in this dimension, he can use its
entire magical energy to attack another dimension. If he

succeeds in winning there, he has the power from two dimensions to attack a third, and so on. As you can see, the longer he keeps his plot moving, the stronger he gets and the harder he'll be to stop."

"I understand now," I said, genuinely pleased and enthusiastic.

"Good. Then you understand why we've got to stop him."

I stopped being pleased and enthusiastic.

"We? You mean us? You and me?"

"I know it's not much of a force, kid, but like I said, it's all we've got."

"I think I'd like a little of that wine now."

"None of that, kid. You're in training now. You're going to need all the practice time you can get if we're going to stop Isstvan. Bonkers or not, he's no slouch when it comes to magik."

"Aahz," I said slowly, not looking up. "Tell me the truth. Do you think there's a chance you can teach me enough magik that we'll have a chance of stopping him?"

"Of course, kid. I wouldn't even try if we didn't have a chance. Trust me."

I wasn't convinced, and from the sound of his voice, neither was he.

# IV:

*"Careful planning is the key to safe and swift travel."*

—ULYSSES

"**H**mmm . . . Well, it's not a tailored jump-suit, but it will have to do."

We had been trying to outfit Aahz in a set of clothes and he was surveying the results in a small dark mirror we had found, turning it this way and that to catch his reflection piecemeal.

"Maybe if we could find some other color than this terrible brown."

"That's all we've got."

"Are you sure?"

"Positive. I have two shirts, both brown. You're wearing one, and I'm wearing the other."

"Hmmm. . ." he said, studying me carefully. "Maybe I would look better in the lighter brown. Oh, well, we can argue that out later."

I was curious as to his attention to his appearance. I mean, he couldn't be planning on meeting anyone. The sight of a green, scaly demon would upset most of the locals no matter what he was wearing. For the time being, however, I deemed it wisest to keep quiet and humor him in his efforts.

Actually, the clothes fit him fairly well. The shirt was a bit short in the sleeves due to the length of his arms, but not too because I was taller than him, which made up for most of the difference. We had had to cut off some of the trouser legs to cover for his shorter legs, but they, like the body of the shirt, were not too tight. I had made the clothes myself originally, and they tended to be a bit baggy, or at least they were on me. Tailoring is not my forte.

He was also wearing Garkin's boots, which fitted him surprisingly well. I had raised minor protest at this, until he pointed out Garkin had no further use for them but we did. Pragmatism, he called it. Situational ethics. He said it would come in handy if I was serious about becoming a magician.

"Hey, kid!" Aahz's voice interrupted my thoughts. He seemed to be occupied rummaging through the various chests and cupboards of the hut. "Don't you have anything here in the way of weapons?"

"Weapons?"

"Yeah, you know, the things that killed old Garkin there. Swords, knives, bows, stuff like that."

"I know what they are. I just wasn't expecting you to be interested in them, that's all."

"Why not?"

'Well . . . I thought you said you were a magician."

"We aren't going to go through *that* again, are we, kid? Besides, what's that got to do with weapons?"

"It's just that I've never known a magician who used weapons other than his powers."

"Really? How many magicians have you known?"

"One," I admitted.

"Terrific. Look, kid, if old Garkin didn't want to use weapons, that's his problem. Me, I want some. If you'll notice, Garkin is dead."

It was hard to argue with logic like that.

"Besides," he continued, "do you really want to take on Isstvan and his pack with nothing but your magik and my agility going for us?"

"I'll help you look."

We went to work rummaging for weapons, but aside from the crossbow that had killed Garkin, we didn't find much. One of the chests yielded a sword with a jewel-encrusted handle, and we discovered two knives, one white handled and one black handled, on Garkin's workbench. Aside from those, there was nothing even remotely resembling a fighting utensil in the hut. Aahz was not overjoyed.

"I don't believe this. A sword with a cruddy blade, bad balance, and phony jewels in the handle and two knives that haven't been sharpened since they were made. Anybody who keeps weapons like this should be skewered."

"He was."

"True enough. Well, if that's all we've got, that's what we'll have to use."

He slung the sword on his hip and tucked the white-handled knife into his belt. I thought he would give me the other knife, but instead he stooped down and secured it in his boot.

"Don't I get one?"

"Can you use it?"

"Well. . . ."

He resumed his task. I had a small knife I used to skin small game tucked in my own belt inside my shirt. Even to my inexperienced eye it was of better quality than the two Aahz had just appropriated. I decided not to bring it to his attention.

"Okay, kid. Where did the old man keep his money?"

I showed him. One of the stones in the fireplace was loose and there was a small leather pouch hidden behind it. He peered at the coins suspiciously as they poured into his palm.

"Check me on this, kid. Copper and silver aren't worth much in this dimension, right?"

"Well, silver's sorta valuable, but it's not worth as much as gold."

"Then what's with this chicken-feed? Where's the real money?"

"We never really had much."

"Come off it . . . I haven't met a magician yet who didn't have a bundle socked away. Just because he never spent any of it doesn't mean he doesn't have it. Now think. Haven't you ever seen anything around that was gold or had gems?"

"Well, there are a few items, but they're protected by curses."

"Kid, think for a minute. If you were a doddering old wreck who couldn't fight your way out of a paper bag, how would you protect your treasures?"

"I don't know."

"Terrific. I'll explain while we gather it up."

In short order we had a modest heap of loot on the table, most of it items I had long held in awe. There was a gold statue of a man with the head of a lion, the Three Pearls of Kraul, a gold pendant in the shape of the sun with three of its rays missing, and a ring with a large jewel we took from Garkin's hand. Aahz held up the sun pendant.

"Now this is an example of what I mean. I suppose there's a story about what happened to the missing three rays?"

"Well," I began, "there was a lost tribe that worshipped a huge snake toad. . . ."

"Skip it. It's an old dodge. What you do is take your gold to a craftsman and have him fashion it into something with a lot of small out-juttings like fingers or arms or . . ." He held up the pendant. ". . . rays of sun. It gives you the best of two worlds.

"First, you have something mystical and supernatural, add a ghost story and no one will dare to touch it. Second, it has the advantage that if you need a little ready cash, you just break off a ray or an arm and sell it for the value of the gold. Instead of losing value, the price of the remaining item increases because of its mystical history, the strange circumstances under which it was torn asunder, purely fictional, of course."

Strangely enough, I was not surprised. I was beginning to wonder if anything Garkin had told me was true.

"Then none of these things have any real magical powers or curses?"

"Now, I didn't say that. Occasionally, you stumble across a real item, but they're usually few and far between."

"But how can you tell the real thing from a fake?"

"I take it that Garkin didn't teach you to see auras. Well, that figures. Probably was afraid you'd take his treasure and run. Okay, kid. Time for your first lesson. Have you ever daydreamed? You know, just stared at something and let your mind wander?"

I nodded.

"Okay, here's what I want you to do. Scoot down in your chair until your head is almost level with the table. That's right. Comfortable? Fine. Now I want you to look across the table at the wall. Don't focus on it, just stare at it and let your mind wander."

I did as he said. It was hard not focusing on a specific point, so I set my mind to wandering. What to think about? Well, what was I thinking about when the candle almost lit. Oh yes. I am Skeeve. I am powerful and my power is growing daily. I smiled to myself. With the demon's aid, I would soon become a knowledgeable sorcerer. And that would just be the start. After that. . .

'Hey!" I said, sitting upright.

"What did you see?"

"It was . . . well, nothing, I guess."

"Don't give me a hard time, kid. What did you see?"

"Well, for a second there I thought I saw sort of a red

glow around the ring, but when I looked at it squarely, it disappeared."

"The ring, eh? It figures. Well, that's it. The rest of the stuff should be okay."

He scraped the rest of the loot into a sack, leaving the ring on the table.

"What was it?"

"What? Oh, what you saw? That was an aura. Most people have them. Some places do, but it's a sure test to check if an item is truly magical. I'd be willing to bet that the ring is what old Garkin used to fry the assassin."

"Aren't we going to take it with us?"

"Do you know how to control it?"

"Well. . . no."

"Neither do I. The last thing we need is to carry around a ring that shoots fire. Particularly if we don't know how to activate it. Leave it. Maybe the others will find it and turn it on themselves."

He tucked the sack into his waistband.

"What others?" I prompted.

"Hmmm? Oh, the other assassins."

"What other assassins?" I was trying to be calm, but I was slipping.

"That's right. This is the first time you've tangled with them, isn't it? I would have thought Garkin. . . ."

"Aahz, could you just tell me?"

"Oh! Sure, kid. Assassins never work alone. That's why they never miss. They work in groups of two to eight. There's probably a back-up team around somewhere. Realizing Isstvan's respect for Garkin, I'd guess he wouldn't send less than six out on an assignment like this, maybe even two teams."

"You mean all this time you've been fooling around with clothes and swords, there's been more assassins on the way?"

"Relax, kid. That's the back-up team. They'll be waiting a ways off and won't move until tomorrow at the earliest. It's professional courtesy. They want to give this bozo room to maneuver. Besides, it's tradition that the assassin who actually does the deed gets first pick of any random booty lying around before the others show up to take even shares. Everyone does it, but it's considered polite to not notice some of the loot has been pocketed before the official split."

"How do you know so much about assassins, Aahz?"

"Went with one for a while . . . lovely lass, but she couldn't keep her mouth shut, even in bed. Sometimes I wonder if any profession really guards its secrets as closely as they claim."

"What happened?"

"With what?"

"With your assassin?"

"None of your business, kid." Aahz was suddenly brusque again. "We've got work to do."

"What are we going to do?"

"Well, first we bury the Imp. Maybe it will throw the others off our trail. With any luck, they'll think he grabbed all the loot and disappeared. It wouldn't be the first time."

"No, I mean after that. We're getting ready to travel, but where are we going?"

"Kid, sometimes you worry me. That isn't even magik. It's common sense military action. First, we find Isstvan. Second, we appraise his strength. Third, we make our plans, and fourth, we execute them, and hopefully him."

"Um . . . Aahz, could we back up to one for a minute? Where are we going to find Isstvan?"

That stopped him.

"Don't you know where he is?"

"I never even heard his name before today."

We sat in silence staring at each other for a long time.

# V:

*"Only constant and conscientious practice in the Martial Arts will ensure a long and happy life."*

—B. LEE

"**I** think I've got it figured out, kid."

As Aahz spoke, he paused in honing his sword to inspect the edge. Ever since our trek began he had seized every opportunity to work on his weapons. Even when we simply paused to rest by a stream he busied himself working their edges or adjusting their balance. I felt I had learned more about weapons in the last week just watching him tinker than I had in my entire previous life.

"Figured what out?"

"Why people in this world are trained in weapons or magik, but not both!"

"How's that?"

"Well, two reasons I can see just offhand. First off, it's a matter of conditioning. Reflexes. You'll react the way you're trained. If you've been trained with weapons, you'll react to crisis with a weapon. If you're trained in magik, you'll react with magik. The problem is, if you're trained both ways, you'll hesitate, trying to make up your

mind which to use, and probably get clobbered in the
process. So to keep things simple, Garkin only trained you
in magik. It's probably all he had been trained in himself."

I thought about it.

"That makes sense. What's the other reason?"

He grinned at me.

"Learning curve. If what you told me about life ex-
pectancy in this world is even vaguely accurate, and if
you're any example of how fast people in this world learn,
you only have time to learn one or the other."

"I think I prefer the first explanation."

He chortled to himself and went back to sharpening his
sword.

Once his needling would have bothered me, but now I
took it in stride. It seemed to be his habit to be critical of
everything in our world, and me in particular. After a
week of constant exposure to him, the only way I would
worry is if he stopped complaining.

Actually I was quite pleased with my progress in magik. Under Aahz's tutelage, my powers were growing
daily. One of the most valuable lessons I had learned was
to draw strength directly from the earth. It was a matter
of envisioning energy as a tangible force, like water, and
drawing new energy up one leg and into my mind while
releasing exhausted energy down the other leg and back
into the earth. Already, I could completely recharge myself even after a hard day's walking just by standing motionless with my eyes closed for several minutes and
effecting this energy exchange. Aahz, as always, was unimpressed. According to him, I should have been able to
do the energy exchange while we were walking, but I
didn't let his grumbling dampen my enthusiasm. I was
learning, and at a faster pace than I had dreamed possible.

"Hey, kid. Fetch me a piece of wood, will you?"

I smiled to myself and looked around. About ten feet
away was a small branch of deadwood about two feet
long. I leisurely stretched out a finger and it took flight,

floating gently across the clearing to hover in the air in front of Aahz.

"Not bad, kid," he acknowledged. Then his sword flashed out, cutting the branch into two pieces which dropped to the ground. He picked up one of the pieces and inspected the cut.

"Hmmm . . . there may be hope for this sword yet. Why did you let them fall?"

This last was directed at me.

"I don't know. I guess you startled me when you swung the sword."

"Oh, really?"

Suddenly he threw the stick at me. I yelped and tried to duck out of the way, but it bounced painfully off my shoulder.

"Hey! What was that for?"

"Call it an object lesson. You know you can control the stick because you just did it when you fetched it for me. So why did you duck out of the way? Why not just stop it with your magik?"

"I guess it never occurred to me. You didn't give me much time to think."

"Okay, so think! This time you know it's coming."

He picked up the second piece of wood and waited, grinning evilly, which with pointed teeth is easy. I ignored him, letting my mind settle; then I nodded that I was ready.

The stick struck me squarely in the chest.

"Ow!!" I commented.

"And there, my young friend, is the difference between classroom and field. Classroom is fine to let you know that things can be done and that you can do them, but in actual practice you will never be allowed the luxury of leisurely gathering your power, and seldom will you have a stationary target."

"Say, uh, Aahz. If you're really trying to build up my self-confidence, how come you always cut my legs out from under me every time I start thinking I'm getting someplace?"

He stood up, sheathing his sword.

"Self-confidence is a wonderful thing, kid, but not if it isn't justified. Someday we'll be staking one or both of our lives on your abilities, and it won't do us any good if you've been kidding yourself along. Now let's get down to work!"

"Um . . . have we got the time?"

"Relax, kid. Imps are tenacious, but they travel slow."

Our strategy upon leaving the hut had been simple. Lacking a specific direction for our search, we would trace the force lines of the world until we either found Isstvan or located another magician who would be able to steer us to him.

One might ask what force lines are. I did. Force lines, as Aahz explained them, are those paths of a world along which its energies flow most freely. In many ways, they are not unlike magnetic lines.

One might ask what magnetic lines are. I did. I will not quote Aahz's answer to that, but it was not information.

Anyway, force lines are a magician's ally and enemy. Those who would tap the energies of those lines usually set up residence on or near one of those lines. This makes it easier for them to draw upon the energies. It also makes it easier for their enemies to find them.

It was Aahz's theory that searching the force lines was how Garkin was located. It was therefore logical that we should be able to find Isstvan the same way.

Of course, I knew nothing of force lines or how to follow them, at least until Aahz taught me. It was not a difficult technique, which was fortunate as I had my hands full trying to absorb all the other lessons Aahz was deluging me with.

One simply closes one's eyes and relaxes, trying to envision a two-pointed spear in glowing yellows and reds suspended in midair. The intensity of the glow indicates the nearness to a force line; the direction of the points shows the flow of energies. Rather like the needle of a compass, whatever that is.

Once we had determined that Garkin had set up shop directly on a force line, as Aahz had suspected, and established direction of the flow of energies, we had another problem. Which way did we follow it?

The decision was doubly important as, if Aahz was correct, there would be a team of Imp assassins waiting in one direction, very probably in the direction we wanted to go.

We solved the problem by traveling one day's journey perpendicular to the force line, then for two days parallel to the line in our chosen direction, then returning to the line before continuing our journey. We hoped this would bypass the assassins entirely.

It worked, and it didn't.

It worked in that we didn't walk into an ambush. It didn't work in that now it seemed they were on our trail, though whether they were actually tracking us or merely following the force line back to Isstvan was unknown.

"I keep telling you, kid," Aahz insisted, "it's a good sign. It means we've chosen the right direction, and that we'll reach Isstvan ahead of his assassins' report."

"What if we're heading in the wrong direction?" I argued. "What if they're really following us? How long do we travel in this direction before we give up and admit it?"

"How long do you figure it will take for you to learn enough magik to stand up to a pack of Imp assassins armed with off-dimension weapons?"

"Let's get to work," I said firmly.

He looked around, and pointed to a gnarled fruit tree strewn round with windfalls across the clearing.

"Okay. Here's what I want you to do. Stare at the sky or contemplate your navel or something. Then when I give the word, use your power to grab one of those fruits and toss it to me."

I don't know how many hours we spent on that drill. It's more difficult than it sounds, mustering one's powers from a standing start. Just when I thought I had it down pat, Aahz switched tactics. He would engage in a conversation, deliberately leading me on, then would interrupt me in mid-sentence with his signal. Needless to say, I failed miserably.

"Relax, kid. Look, try it this way. Instead of mustering your power from scratch each time, create a small space inside yourself and store up some energy there. Just habitually keep that reserve squirreled away and ready to cover for you while you get set to level your big guns."

"What's a gun?"

"Never mind. Just build that reserve and we'll try it again."

With this extra bit of advice at my disposal the drill went noticeably better. Finally Aahz broke off the practice session and put me to work helping him with his knife practice. Actually I rather enjoyed this task. It entailed my using my powers to levitate one of the fruits and send it flying around the clearing until Aahz pegged a knife into it. As an extra touch of finesse, I would then extract the knife and float it back to him for another try. The exercise was monotonous, but I never tired of it. It seemed almost supernatural the way the shimmering, somersaulting sliver of steel would dart out to intercept the fruit as Aahz practiced first overhand, then underhand, now backhand.

"Stop it, Skeeve!"

Aahz's shout jolted me out of my reverie. Without thinking, I reached out with my mind and . . . and the knife stopped in midair! I blinked, but held it there, floating a foot from the fruit which also hung suspended in place.

"Hel-lo! That's the stuff, Skeeve! Now there's something to have confidence in!"

"I did it!" I said, disbelieving my own eyes.

"You sure did! That little piece of magik will save your life someday."

Out of habit, I floated the knife back to him. He plucked it from the air and started to tuck it in his belt, then halted, cocking his head to one side.

"In the nick of time, too. Someone's coming."

"How can you tell?"

"Nothing special. My hearing's a bit better than yours is all. Don't panic. It isn't the Imps. Hooved beast from the sound of it. No wild animal moves in that straight a line, or that obviously."

"What did you mean, 'in the nick of time'? Aren't we going to hide?"

"Not this time." He grinned at me. "You're developing fast. It's about time you learned a new spell. We have a few days before whoever it is gets here."

"Days?"

Aahz was adapting rapidly to our dimension, but units of time still gave him trouble.

"Run through those time measurements again," he grumbled.

"In seconds, minutes, hours. . . ."

"Minutes! We've got a few minutes."

"Minutes! I can't learn a new spell in a few minutes!"

"Sure you can. This one's easy. All you've got to do is disguise my features to look like a man."

"How do I do that?"

"The same way you do everything else, with your mind. First, close your eyes . . . close 'em . . . okay, now picture another face. . . ."

All I could think of was Garkin, so I pictured the two faces side by side.

"Now move the new face over mine . . . and melt away or build up the necessary features. Like clay . . . just keep that in the back of your mind and open your eyes."

I looked, and was disappointed.

"It didn't work!"

"Sure it did."

He was looking in the dark mirror which he had fished from his belt pouch.

"But you haven't changed!"

"Yes I have. You can't see it because you cast the spell. It's an illusion, and since your mind knows the truth, it isn't fooled, but anyone else will be. Garkin, huh? Well, it'll do for now."

His identification of the new face took me aback.

"You can really see Garkin's face?"

"Sure, want to look?"

He offered the mirror and grinned. It was a bad joke. One of the first things we discovered about his dubious status in this world was that while he could see himself in mirrors, nobody from our world could. At least I couldn't.

I could now hear the sounds of the rider coming.

"Aahz, are you sure. . . ."

"Trust me, kid. There's nothing to worry about."

I was worried. The rider was in view now. He was a tall muscular man with the look of a warrior about him. This was reinforced by the massive war unicorn he was riding, laden with weapons and armor.

"Hey, Aahz. Shouldn't we. . . ."

"Relax, kid. Watch this."

He stepped forward, raising his arm.

"Hello, stranger! How far to the next town?"

The man veered his mount toward us. He half raised his arm in greeting, then suddenly stiffened. Heaving forward, he squinted at Aahz, then drew back in terror.

"By the Gods! A demon!"

# VI:

*"Attention to detail is the watchword for gleaning information from an unsuspecting witness."*

—INSP. CLOUSEAU

The warrior's terror did not immobilize him long. In fact, it didn't immobilize him at all! No sooner did he make his discovery than he took action. Strangely enough, the action was to lean back in his saddle and begin rummaging frantically through one of his saddlebags, a precarious position at best.

Apparently I was not the only one to notice the instability of his pose. Aahz sprang forward with a yell, waving his arms in the unicorn's face. Being a reasonable creature, the unicorn reared and bolted, dumping the warrior on his head.

"By the Gods!" he bellowed, trying to untangle himself from the ungraceful heap of arms and weapons. "I've killed men for less!"

I decided that if his threat was to be avoided, I should take a personal hand in the matter. Reaching out with my mind, I seized a fist-sized rock and propelled it forcefully against his unhelmeted brow. The man went down like a pole-axed steer.

For a long moment Aahz and I considered the fallen man, catching our breath.

" 'Relax, Skeeve! This'll be easy, Skeeve! Trust me, Skeeve.' Boy, Aahz, when you miss a call you don't do it small, do you?"

"Shut up, kid!"

He was rummaging through his pouch again.

"I don't want to shut up, I want to know what happened to the 'foolproof' spell you taught me."

"I was kind of wondering that myself." He had produced the mirror again and was peering into it. "Tell you what, kid. Check his aura and watch for anything unusual."

" 'Shut up, kid! Check his aura, kid!' You'd think I was some kind of. . . . Hey!"

"What is it?"

"His aura! It's a sort of a reddish yellow except there's a blue patch on his chest."

"I thought so!!" Aahz was across the clearing in a bound, crouching at the fallen man like a beast of prey.

"Look at this!!"

On a thong around the man's neck was a crude silver charm depicting a salamander with one eye in the center of its forehead.

"What is it?"

"I'm not sure, but I've got a hunch. Now play along with me on this. I want you to remove the shape warp spell."

"What spell?"

"C'mon, kid, wake up! The spell that's changing my face."

"That's what I mean. What spell?"

"Now look, kid! Don't give me a lot of back talk. Just do it! He'll be waking up soon."

With a sigh I shut my eyes and set about the seemingly pointless task. It was easier this time, imagining Garkin's face, then melting away the features until Aahz's face was leering at me in my mind's eye. I opened my eyes and looked at Aahz. He looked like Aahz. Terrific.

"Now what?"

As if in answer, the warrior groaned and sat up. He shook his head as if to clear it and opened his eyes. His gaze fell on Aahz, whereupon he blinked, looked again, and reached for his sword, only to find it missing. Also missing were his dagger and hand-axe. Apparently Aahz had not been idle while I was removing the spell.

Aahz spoke first.

"Relax, stranger. Things are not as they seem."

The man sprang to his feet and struck a fighting stance, fists clenched.

"Beware, demon!" he intoned hollowly. "I am not without defenses."

"Oh yeah? Name three. But like I say, relax. First of all, I'm not a demon."

"Know you, demon, that this charm enables me to look through any spells and see you as you really are."

So that was it! My confidence in my powers came back with a rush.

"Friend, though you may not believe me, the sight of that talisman fills me with joy, for it enables me to prove what I am about to tell you."

"Do not waste your lies on me. Your disguise is penetrated! You are a demon!"

"Right. Could you do me one little favor?" Aahz leisurely sat cross-legged on the ground. "Could you take the charm off for a minute?"

"Take it off?" For a moment the man was puzzled, but he quickly rallied his forces. "Nay, demon. You seek to trick me into removing my charm that you might kill me!"

"Look, dummy. If we wanted to kill you we could have done it while you were knocked out cold!"

For the first time, the man seemed doubtful.

"That is, indeed, a fact."

"Then could you humor me for a moment and take the charm off?"

The warrior hesitated, then slowly removed the charm. He looked hard at Aahz and scowled.

"That's strange. You still look like a demon!"

"Correct, now let me ask you a question. Am I correct in assuming from your words you have some knowledge of demons?"

"I have been a demon hunter for over fifteen years now," he declared proudly.

"Oh, yeah?" For a minute I was afraid Aahz was going to blow the whole gambit, but he got himself back under control and continued.

"Then tell me, friend. In your long experience with demons, have you ever met one who looked like a demon?"

"Of course not! They always use their magik to disguise themselves."

Fat lot he knew about demons!

"Then that should prove my point!"

"What point?"

I thought for a moment Aahz was going to take him by the shoulders and shake him. It occurred to me that perhaps Aahz's subtleties were lost on this world.

"Let me try, Aahz. Look, sir. What he's trying to say is that if he were a demon he wouldn't look like a demon, but he does so he isn't."

"Oh!" said the man with sudden understanding.

"Now you've lost me," grumbled Aahz.

"But if you aren't a demon, why do you look like one?"

"Ahh . . . ," Aahz sighed, "therein lies the story. You see, I'm accursed!"

"Accursed?"

"Yes. You see, I am a demon hunter like yourself. A rather successful one, actually. Established quite a name for myself in the field."

"I never heard of you," grumbled the man.

"Well, we've never heard of you either," I chimed in.

"You don't even know my name!"

"Oh, I'm sorry." I remembered my manners. "I'm
Skeeve, and this . . . demon hunter is Aahz."

"Pleased to meet you. I am known as Quigley."

"If I could continue. . . ."

"Sorry, Aahz."

"As I was saying, I had achieved a certain renown
among the demons due to my unprecedented success. At
times it was rather bothersome, as when it was learned I
was coming, most demons would either flee the territory
or kill themselves."

"Does he always brag this much?"

"He's just getting started."

"Anyway . . . one day I was closing with a demon, a
particularly ugly brute, when he startled me by addressing
me by name. 'Aahz!' says he, 'Before you strike, you
should know your career is at an end!' Of course I
laughed at him, for I had slain demons more fierce than
he, sometimes in pairs. 'Laugh if you will,' he boomed,
'but a conclave of demons empowered me to deal with
you. Whether you kill me or not, you are doomed to suffer
the same end you have visited on so many of us.' I killed
him of course, assuming he was bluffing, but my life has
not been the same ever since."

"Why not?"

"Because of the curse! When I returned to my horse,
my faithful squire here took one look at me and fainted
dead away."

"I did no such thing! I mean . . . it was the heat."

"Of course, Skeeve." Aahz winked slyly at Quigley.

"At any rate, I soon discovered to my horror that the
demon had worked a spell on me before he expired, causing me to take on the appearance of a demon to all who
beheld me."

"Fiendish. Clever, but fiendish."

"You see the subtlety of their plan! That I, fiercest of
demon hunters, am now hunted in turn by my fellow humans. I am forced to hide like an animal with only my
son here for companionship."

"I thought you said he was your squire."

"That, too. Oh, the irony of it all."

"Gee, that's tough. I wish I could do something to help."

"Maybe you can," Aahz smiled winningly.

Quigley recoiled. I found it reassuring that someone else shared my reaction to Aahz's smile.

"Um . . . how? I mean, I'm just a demon hunter."

"Precisely how you might be of assistance. You see, at the moment we happen to have several demons following us. It occurs to me we might be of mutual service to each other. We can provide you with targets, and you in turn can rid us of a bloody nuisance."

"They're bloody?" Quigley was horrified.

"Just an expression. Well, what do you say? Is it a deal?"

"I dunno. I'm already on a mission and I don't usually take on a new job until the last one's complete. The mis-informed might think I was quitting or had been scared off or something. That sort of thing is bad for the reputation."

"It'd be no trouble at all," Aahz persisted. "It's not like you'll have to go out of your way. Just wait right here and they'll be along."

"Why are they following you, anyway?"

"A vile magician sent them after us after I was foolish enough to seek his aid. The curse, you know."

"Of course . . . wait a minute. Was that magician's name Garkin by any chance?"

"As a matter of fact it was. Why? Do you know him?"

"Why, he's my mission! That's the man I'm going to kill."

"Why?" I interrupted. "Garkin's no demon."

"But he consorts with demons, lad." Aahz scowled warningly at me. "That's enough for any demon hunter. Right, Quigley?"

"Right. Remember that, lad."

I nodded vigorously at him, feeling suddenly very nervous about this whole encounter.

"Where did you hear about Garkin anyway, Quigley?" Aahz asked casually.

"Strangely enough, from an innkeeper . . . Isstvan, I think he said his name was . . . a bit strange, but a sincere enough fellow. About three weeks ride back . . . , but we were talking about your problem. Why did he send demons after you?"

"Well, as I said, I sought him out to try to get him to remove any curse. What I did not realize was that he was actually in league with demons himself. He had heard of me, and flatly refused me aid. What is more, after we left he set some of his demons on our trail."

"I see. How many of them did you say there were?"

"Just two," Aahz assured him. "We've caught glimpses of them occasionally."

"Very well," concluded Quigley. "I'll do it. I'll assist you in your battle."

"That's fine except for one thing. We won't be here."

"Why not? I should think that as a demon hunter you'd welcome the chance once the odds were even."

"If I were here there would be no fight," Aahz stated grandly. "As I have said, I have a certain reputation among demons. If they saw me here they would simply flee."

"I frankly find that hard to believe," commented Quigley.

I was inclined to agree with him, but kept my silence.

"Well, I must admit their fear of my charmed sword has a bit to do with their reluctance to do battle."

"Charmed sword?"

"Yes." Aahz patted the sword at his side. "This weapon once belonged to the famous demon hunter Alfans De Clario."

"Never heard of him."

"Never heard of him? Are you sure you're a demon hunter? Why the man killed over two hundred demons

with this sword. They say it is charmed such that whomever wields it cannot be killed by a demon."

"How did he die?"

"Knifed by an exotic dancer. Terrible."

"Yes, they're nasty that way. But about the sword, does
it work?"

"It works as well as any sword, a little point-heavy,
maybe, but. . . ."

"No. I mean the charm. Does it work?"

"I can testify that I haven't been killed by a demon
since I started using it."

"And demons actually recognize it and flee from its
owner?"

"Exactly. Of course, I haven't had occasion to use it
for years. Been too busy trying to get this curse removed.
Sometimes I've thought about selling it, but if I ever get
back into business it would be a big help in . . . um . . .
reestablishing my reputation."

I suddenly realized what Aahz was up to. Quigley rose
to the bait like a hungry pike-turtle.

"Hmm. . ." he said. "Tell you what. Just to give a hand
to a fellow demon hunter who's down on his luck, I'll
take it off your hands for five gold pieces."

"Five gold pieces! You must be joking. I paid three
hundred for it. I couldn't possibly let it go for less than
two hundred."

"Oh, well, that counts me out. I only have about fifty
gold pieces on me."

"Fifty?"

"Yes, I never travel with more than. . . ."

"But then again, times have been hard, and seeing as
how you would be using it to do battle against the fiends
who put the curse on me. . . . Yes, I think I could let you
have it for fifty gold pieces."

"But that's all the money I have."

"Yes, but what good is a fat purse if you're torn asunder by a demon?"

"True enough. Let me see it."

He took the blade and hefted, giving it a few experimental swings.

"Crummy balance." He grimaced.

"You get used to it."

"Lousy steel," he declared, squinting at the blade.

"Nice edge on it, though."

"Well, my trainer always told me 'If you take care of your sword, it will take care of you!' "

"We must have had the same trainer."

The two of them smiled at each other. I felt slightly ill.

"Still, I dunno. Fifty pieces of gold is a lot."

"Just look at those stones in the handle."

"I did. They're fake."

"Aha! They're made to look fake. It hides their value."

"Sure did a nice job. What kind of stones are they?"

"Blarney stones."

"Blarney stones?"

"Yes. They're said to ensure your popularity with the ladies, if you know what I mean."

"But fifty gold pieces is all the money I have."

"Tell you what. Make it forty-five gold pieces and throw in your sword."

"My sword?"

"Of course. This beauty will take care of you, and your sword will keep my squire and I from being defenseless in this heathen land."

"Hmm. That seems fair enough. Yes, I believe you have made a deal, my friend."

They shook hands ceremoniously and began effecting the trade. I seized the opportunity to interrupt.

"Gee, it's a shame we have to part so soon."

"Why so soon?" The warrior was puzzled.

"No need to rush off," Aahz assured him, giving me a solid elbow in the ribs.

"But Aahz, we wanted to travel more before sundown and Quigley has to prepare for battle."

"What preparations?" asked Quigley.

"Your unicorn," I continued doggedly. "Don't you want to catch your unicorn?"

"My unicorn! All of my armor is on that animal!"

"Surely it won't wander far. . . ." Aahz growled.

"There are bandits about who would like nothing better than to get their hands on a good war unicorn." Quigley heaved himself to his feet. "And I want him at my side to help me fight the demons. Yes, I must be off. I thank you for your assistance, my friends. Safe journey until we meet again."

With a vague wave of his hand, he disappeared into the woods whistling for his mount.

"Now what was all that about?" Aahz exploded angrily.

"What, Aahz?"

"The big rush to get rid of him. As gullible as he was, I could have traded him out of his pants or anything else vaguely valuable he might have had on him. I specifically wanted to get my hands on that charm."

"Basically I wanted to see him on his way before he caught on to the flaw in your little tale."

"What, the son-nephew slip? He wouldn't have. . . ."

"No, the other thing."

"What other thing?"

I sighed.

"Look, he saw through your disguise because that pendant lets him see through spells, right?"

"Right, and I explained it away saying I was the victim of a demon's curse. . . ."

". . . that changed your appearance with a spell. But if he could see through spells, he should be able to see through that spell to see you as a normal man. Right?"

"Hmm. . . Maybe we'd better be on our way now that we know where Isstvan is."

But I was unwilling to let my little triumph go so easily.

"Tell me, Aahz. What would you do if we encountered a demon hunter as smart as me?"

"That's easy." He smiled, patting the crossbow. "I'd kill him. Think about it."

I did.

# VII:

*"Is there anything in the universe more beautiful and protective than the simple complexity of a spider's web?"*

—CHARLOTTE

I closed my eyes for concentration. This was more difficult than drawing energies from the force line directly into my body. I pointed a finger for focus, pointing at a spot some five yards distant from me.

The idea of drawing energies from a distant location and controlling them would have seemed impossible to me, until Aahz pointed out it was the same as the candle-lighting exercise I had already mastered. Now it did not seem impossible, merely difficult.

Confidently, I narrowed my concentration, and in my mind's eye saw a gleaming blue light appear at the designated point. Without breaking my concentration, I moved my finger overhead in a slow arc. The light followed the lead, etching a glowing blue trail in the air behind it. As it touched the ground again, or where I sensed the ground to be, I moved my finger again, moving the light into the second arc of the protective pentagram.

It occurred to me that what I was doing was not unlike

forming the normal flat pentagram Garkin had used at the
hut. The only difference being that instead of being inscribed on the floor, this was etched overhead with its
points dipping downward to touch the earth. It was more
an umbrella than a border.

The other major difference, I thought as I completed
the task, was that I was doing it. Me. Skeeve. What I had
once watched with awe, I was now performing as routine.

I touched the light down in its original place, completing the pentagram. Quietly pleased, I stood for a moment, eyes closed, studying the glowing blue lines etched
in my mind's eye.

"Terrific, kid," came Aahz's voice. "Now what say you
damp it down a bit before we draw every peasant and
demon hunter in the country."

Surprised, I opened my eyes.

The pentagram was still there! Not imagined in my
mind, but actually glowing overhead. Its cold blue light
gave an eerie illumination to the scene that negated the
warmth of our little campfire.

"Sorry, Aahz." I quickly eased my control on the energy and watched as the lines of the pentagram faded to
invisibility. They were still there. I could feel their presence in the night air above me. Now, however, they could
not be seen by normal vision.

More for the joy of it than out of any lack of confidence, I closed my eyes again and looked at them. They
glowed there in shimmering beauty, a cooler, reassuring
presence to counter the impatience of the redgold glow of
the force-line spear pointing doggedly toward tomorrow's
path.

"Sit down, kid, and finish your lizard-bird."

We were out of the forest proper now, but despite the
presence of the nearby road, game was still plentiful and
fell ready victim to my snares. Aahz still refused to join
me in the meals, insisting alcohol was the only thing in
this dimension worth consuming, but I dined frequently
and royally.

"You know, kid," he said, looking up from his endless sword-sharpening. "You're really coming along pretty well with your studies."

"What do you mean?" I mumbled through a bone, hoping he would elaborate.

"You're a lot more confident with your magik. You'd better watch your controls, though. You had enough energy in that pentagram to fry anything that bumped against it."

"I guess I'm still a bit worried about the assassins."

"Relax, kid. It's been three days since we set 'em up in that ambush of Quigley's. Even if he didn't stop 'em, they'll never catch up with us now."

"Did I really summon up that much power?" I urged, eager for praise.

"Unless you're actually engaged in magical battle, wards are used as a warning signal only. If you put too much energy into them it can have two potentially bad side effects. First, you can draw unnecessary attention to yourself by jarring or burning an innocent bystander who blunders into it. Second, if it actually reaches a magical opponent, it probably won't stop him; just alert him that he has a potentially dangerous foe in the area."

"I thought it was a good thing if I could summon up lots of power."

"Look, kid. This isn't a game. You're tapping into some very powerful forces here. The idea is to strengthen your control, not see how much you can liberate. If you get too careless with experimenting, you could end up helpless when the actual crunch comes."

"Oh," I said, unconvinced.

"Really, kid. You've got to learn this. Let me try an example. Suppose for a minute you're a soldier assigned to guard a pass. Your superiors put you on the post and give you a stack of ten-pound rocks. All you have to do is watch to see if anyone comes, and if they do, drop a rock on their head. Are you with me so far?"

"I guess so."

"Fine. Now it's a long, boring duty, and you have lots of time to think. You're very proud of your muscles, and decide it's a bit insulting that you were only given ten-pound rocks. Twenty-pound rocks would be more effective, and you think you could handle them as easily as the ten-pound variety. Logical?"

I nodded vaguely, still not sure what he was driving at.

"Just to prove the point to yourself, you heft a twenty-pound rock, and, sure enough, you can handle it. Then it occurs to you if you can handle a twenty-pounder, you should be able to handle a forty-pounder, or even a fifty-pounder. So you try. Then it happens."

He was getting so worked up I felt no need to respond.

"You drop it on your foot, or you pull a muscle, or you keel over from heat exhaustion, or any one of a hundred other things. Then where are you?"

He leveled an accusing finger at me.

"The enemy strolls through the pass you're supposed to be guarding and you can't even lift the original ten-pound rock to stop them. All because you indulged in needless testing of idiotic muscle power!"

I was impressed, and gave the matter serious thought before replying.

"I see what you're saying, Aahz, but there's one flaw in your example. The keyword is 'needless.' Now in my case, it's not a matter of having a stack of ten-pound rocks that would do the job. I have a handful of gravel. I'm trying to scrounge around for a rock big enough to do some damage."

"True enough," Aahz retorted, "but the fact remains if you overextend yourself you won't be able to use what you already have. Even gravel can be effective if used at the right time. Don't underrate what you've got or what you're doing. Right now you're keeping the finder spear going, maintaining the wards, and keeping my disguise intact. That's a lot for someone of your abilities to be doing simultaneously. If something happened right now, which would you drop first?"

"Um. . . ."

"Too late! We're already dead. You won't have time to ponder energy problems. That's why you always have to hold some back to deal with immediate situations while you rally your energies from other activities. Now do you see?"

"I think so, Aahz," I said haltingly. "I'm a bit tired."

"Well, think about it. It's important. In the meantime get some sleep and try to store up your energies. Incidentally, let the finder spear go for now. You can summon it up again in the morning. Right now, it's just a needless drain."

"Okay, Aahz. How about your disguise?"

"Hmm . . . better keep that. It'll be good practice for you to maintain both that and the wards in your sleep. Speaking of which. . . ."

"Right, Aahz."

I drew my acquired assassin's cloak about me for warmth and curled up. Despite his gruff manner, Aahz was persistent that I get enough sleep as well as food.

Sleep did not come easily, however. I found I was still a bit wound up over casting the wards.

"Aahz?"

"Yeah, kid?"

"How would you say my powers right now stack up against the devils?"

"What devils?"

"The assassins that were following us."

"I keep telling you, kid. Those weren't Deveels, those were Imps."

"What's the difference?"

"I told you before. Imps are from Imper, and Deveels. . . ."

". . . are from Deva," I finished for him. "But what does that mean? I mean, are their powers different or something?"

"You'd better believe it, kid." Aahz snorted. "Deveels are some of the meanest characters you'd ever not want to tangle with. They're some of the most feared and respected characters in the dimensions."

"Are they warriors? Mercenaries?"

Aahz shook his head.

"Worse!" he answered. "They're merchants."

"Merchants?"

"Don't sneer, kid. Maybe merchants is too sedate a phrase to describe them. Traders Supreme is more like it."

"Tell me more, Aahz."

"Well, history was never my forte, but as near as I can tell, at one time the entire dimension Deva faced economic ruin. The lands suffered a plague that affected the elements. Fish could not live in its oceans, plants could not grow in the soil. Those plants that did grow were twisted and changed and poisoned the animals. The dimension was no longer able to support the life of its citizenry."

I lay, staring up at the stars as Aahz continued his tale.

"Dimension travel, once a frivolous pastime, now became the key to survival. Many left Deva, migrating singly or in groups to other dimensions. Their tales of their barren, miserable homeland served as a prototype for many religious groups' concept of an afterworld for evil souls.

"The ones who stayed, however, decided to use the power of dimension travel in a different way. They established themselves as traders, traveling the dimensions buying and selling wonders. What is common in one dimension is frequently rare in another. As the practice grew, they became rich and powerful . . . also the shrewdest hagglers in all the dimensions. Their techniques for driving a hard bargain have been passed down from generation to generation and polished until now they are without equal. They are scattered through the dimensions, returning to Deva only occasionally to visit the Bazaar."

"The Bazaar?" I prompted.

"No one can travel extensively in all the dimensions in one lifetime. The Bazaar on Deva is the place the Deveels meet to trade with each other. An off-dimension visitor there will be sore pressed to not lose o'er much, much less hold his own. It's said if you make a deal with a Deveel, you'd be wise to count your fingers afterward . . . then your arms and legs, then your relatives. . . ."

"I get the picture. Now how about the Imps?"

"The Imps." Aahz said the word as if it tasted bad. "The Imps are inferior to the Deveels in every way."

"How so?"

"They're cheap imitations. Their dimension, Imper, lies close to Deva, and the Deveels bargain with them so often they're almost bankrupt from the irresistible 'fair deals.' To hold their own, they've taken to aping the Deveels, attempting to peddle wonders through the dimensions. To the uneducated, they may seem clever and powerful; in fact, occasionally they try to pass themselves off as Deveels. Compared to the masters, however, they're bungling incompetents."

He trailed off into silence. I pondered his words, and they prompted another question.

"Say, Aahz?"

"Hmm? Yeah, kid?"

"What dimension do you come from?"

"Perv."

"Does that make you a Pervert?"

"No. That makes me a Pervect. Now shut up!"

I assumed he wanted me to go to sleep, and maintained silence for several minutes. There was just one more question I had to ask, however, if I was going to get any sleep at all.

"Aahz?"

"Keep it down, kid."

"What dimension is this?"

"Hmmm? This is Klah, kid. Now for the last time, shut up."

"What does that make me, Aahz?"

There was no answer.

"Aahz?"

I rolled over to look at him. He was staring out into the darkness and listening intently.

"What is it?"

"I think we've got company, kid."

As if in response to his words, I felt a tremor in the wards as something came through.

I bounded to my feet as two figures appeared at the edge of the firelight. The light was dimming, but was sufficient to reveal the fact that both figures were wearing the hooded cloaks of assassins, and the gold side was out!

# VIII:

*"In times of crisis, it is of utmost importance not to lose one's head."*

—M. ANTOINETTE

The four of us stood in frozen tableau for several minutes studying each other. My mind was racing, but could not focus on the definite course of action. I decided to follow Aahz's lead and simply stood regarding the two figures cooly, trying to ignore the two crossbows leveled steadily on us.

Finally, one of our visitors broke the silence.

"Well, Throckwoddle? Aren't you going to invite your friends to sit down?"

Surprisingly, this was addressed to me!

"Ummm . . ." I said.

"Yes, Throckwoddle," Aahz drawled, turning to me. "And aren't you going to introduce me to your colleagues?"

"Um . . ." I repeated.

"Perhaps he doesn't remember us," the second figure injected sarcastically.

"Nonsense," responded the first with equal sarcasm.

"His two oldest friends? Brockhurst and Higgens? How could he possibly not remember our names? Just because he forgot to share the loot doesn't mean he'd forget our names. Be fair, Higgens."

"Frankly, Brockhurst," responded the other. "I'd rather he remembered the loot and forgot our names."

Their words were stuffy and casual, but the crossbows never wavered.

I was beginning to get the picture. Apparently these were the two Imps Aahz had assured me couldn't overtake us. Fortunately, it seemed they thought I was the Imp who had killed Garkin . . . at least I thought it was fortunate.

"Gentlemen," Aahz exclaimed, stepping forward. "Let me say what a great pleasure it is to. . . ."

He stopped as Brockhurst's crossbow leapt to his shoulder in one smooth move.

"I'm not sure who you are," he intoned. "But I'd advise you to stay out of this. This is a private matter between the three of us."

"Brockhurst," interrupted Higgens. "It occurs to me we may be being a bit hasty in our actions."

"Thank you, Higgens," I said, greatly relieved.

"Now that we've established contact," he continued, favoring me with an icy glare, "I feel we should perhaps secure our traveling companion before we continue this . . . discussion."

"I suppose you're right, Higgens," Brockhurst admitted grudgingly. "Be a good fellow and fetch him along while I watch these two."

"I feel that would be ill-advised on two counts. First, I refuse to approach that beast alone, and second, that would leave you alone facing two to one odds, if you get my point."

"Quite. Well, what do you suggest?"

"That we both fetch our traveling companion and return without delay."

"And what is to keep these two from making a hasty departure?"

"The fact that we'll be watching them from somewhere in the darkness with crossbows. I believe that should be sufficient to discourage them from making . . . ah . . . any movements which might be subject to misinterpretation."

"Very well," Brockhurst yielded grudgingly. "Throckwoddle, I would strongly suggest you not attempt to avoid us further. While I don't believe we could be any more upset with you than we already are, that might actually succeed in provoking us further."

With that, the two figures faded back into darkness.

"What are we going to do, Aahz?" I whispered frantically.

He seemed not to hear me.

"Imps!" he chortled, rubbing his hands together gleefully. "What a stroke of luck!"

"Aahz! They're going to kill me!"

"Hm? Relax, kid. Like I said, Imps are gullible. If they were really thinking, they would have shot us down without talking. I haven't met an Imp yet I couldn't talk circles around."

He cocked his head, listening.

"They're coming back now. Just follow my lead. Oh yes . . . I almost forgot. Drop the disguise on my features when I give you the cue."

"But you said they couldn't catch. . . ."

I broke off as the two Imps reappeared. They were leading a war unicorn between them. The hoods of the cloaks were back now, revealing their features. I was moderately surprised to see they looked human, seedy perhaps, but human nonetheless. Then I saw Quigley.

He was sitting woodenly astride the unicorn, lurching back and forth with the beast's stride. His eyes were staring fixedly straight ahead and his right arm was raised as if in salutation. The light of the fire reflected off his face as if it were glass, and I realized with horror he was no longer alive, but a statue of some unidentified substance.

Any confidence I might have gained from Aahz's assurances left me in a rush. Gullible or not, the Imps played

for keeps, and any mistake we made would in all likeli-
hood be our last.

"Who's that?" Aahz asked, interrupting my thoughts.

I realized I had been dangerously close to showing a
betraying sign of recognition of the statue.

"There will be time for that later, if indeed there is a
later," said Higgens, grimly dropping the unicorn's reins
and raising his crossbow.

"Yes," echoed Brockhurst, imitating Higgens's move
with his own weapon. "First there is a matter of an explanation to be settled. Throckwoddle?"

"Gentlemen, gentlemen," said Aahz soothingly, stepping between me and the crossbows. "Before you proceed
I must insist on introducing myself properly. If you will
but allow me a moment while I remove my disguise."

The sight of the two weapons had rattled me so badly
I almost missed my cue. Fortunately, I managed to gather
my scattered senses and closed my eyes, shakily executing
the change features spell to convert Aahz back to his normal dubious appearance.

I'm not sure what reaction I had expected from the
Imps at the transformation, but the one I got surpassed
any possible expectations.

"By the Gods below!" gasped Brockhurst.

"A Pervert!" gasped Higgens.

"That's Pervect!" smiled Aahz, showing all his pointed
teeth. "And don't ever forget it, friend Imps."

"Yessir!" they chorused in unison.

They were both standing in slack-jawed amazement,
crossbows dangling forgotten in their hands. From their
terrified reactions, I began to suspect that despite all his
bragging, Aahz had perhaps not told me everything about
his dimension or the reputation of its inhabitants.

Aahz ignored their stares and plopped down again at
his place by the fire.

"Now that that's established, why don't you put away
those silly crossbows and sit down so we can chat like
civilized folk, eh?"

He gestured impatiently and they hastened to comply. I also resumed a sitting position, not wishing to be the only one left standing.

"But . . . what are . . . why are you here . . . sir . . . if you don't mind my asking?" Brockhurst finally managed to get the whole question out.

However incompetent he might be as a demon, he sure knew how to grovel.

"Ah!" smiled Aahz. "Therein lies the story."

I settled back. This could take a while.

"I was summoned across the dimensions barrier by one Garkin, a magician I have never cared much for. It seems he was expecting some trouble from a rival and was eager to enlist my aid for the upcoming fracas. Now, as I said before, I had never been fond of Garkin and was not particularly wild about joining him. He began growing unpleasant in his insistence to the point that I considered swaying from my normal easygoing nature to take action against him, when who should appear but Throckwoddle here who did me the favor of putting a quarrel into the old slime-stirrer."

Aahz acknowledged me with an airy wave. I tried to look modest.

"Naturally we fell to chatting afterward, and he mentioned he was in the employment of one Isstvan and that his action against Garkin had been part of an assignment."

"You answered questions about an assignment?" Higgens turned to me aghast.

"Yes I did," I snarled at him. "Wouldn't you, considering the circumstances?"

"Oh, yes . . . of course . . ." He darted a nervous glance at Aahz and lapsed into respectful silence again.

"Anyway," Aahz continued, "it occurred to me I owed this fellow Isstvan a favor for ridding me of a nagging nuisance, so I suggested I accompany Throckwoddle back to his employer that I might offer him my services, on a limited basis, of course."

"You could have waited for us." Brockhurst glowered at me.

"Well . . . I wanted . . . you see . . . I . . ."

"I insisted," Aahz smiled. "You see, my time is quite valuable and I had no desire to waste it waiting around."

"Oh," said Brockhurst.

Higgens was not so easily swayed.

"You could have left us a message," he muttered.

"We did," Aahz replied. "My ring, in full view on the table. I see you found it."

He pointed an accusing finger at Brockhurst. I noticed for the first time the Imp was wearing Garkin's ring.

"This ring?" Brockhurst started. "Is it yours? I thought it was part of Garkin's loot that had been overlooked."

"Yes, it's mine." Aahz bared his teeth. "I'm surprised you didn't recognize it. But now that we're united, you will, of course, return it."

"Certainly!" the Imp fumbled in his haste to remove the ring.

"Careful there," Aahz cautioned. "You know how to operate it, don't you? It can be dangerous in ignorant hands."

"Of course I know how to operate it," Brockhurst replied in an injured tone. "You press against the ring with the fingers on either side of it. I saw one like it at the Bazaar on Deva once."

He tossed the ring to Aahz who caught it neatly and slipped it on his finger. Fortunately it fit. I made a mental note to ask Aahz to let me try using the ring sometime, now that we knew how it worked.

"Now that I've explained about me, how about answering my question," Aahz said, leveling a finger at the Quigley statue. "Who is that?"

"We aren't sure ourselves," Higgens admitted.

"It's all quite puzzling, really," Brockhurst added.

"Would you care to elaborate on that?" Aahz prompted.

"Well, it happened about three days back. We were

following your trail to . . . um . . . with hopes of reuniting
our group. Suddenly this warrior gallops out of the brush
ahead of us and bars our path. It was as if he knew we
were coming and was waiting for us. 'Isstvan was right!'
he shouts, 'This region *does* abound with demons!' "

"Isstvan?" I said, doing my best to look puzzled.

"That's what he said. It surprised us, too. I mean, here
we are working for Isstvan, and were set upon by a man
claiming to be sent by the same employer. Anyway, then
he says, 'Behold the weapon of your doom!' and draws
a sword."

"What kind of sword was it?" Aahz asked innocently.

"Nothing special. Actually a little substandard from all
we could see. Well, it put us in a predicament. We had
to defend ourselves, but were afraid to harm him on the
off-chance he really was working for Isstvan."

"What did you do?" I asked.

"Frankly, we said 'to heck with it' and took the easy
way out. Higgens here bounced one of his stone balls off
the guy's forehead and froze him in place. We've been
dragging him along ever since. We figure we'll dump him
in Isstvan's lap and let him sort it out."

"A wise solution," commented Aahz.

They inclined their heads graciously at the compliment.

"One question I'd like to ask," I interjected. "How
were you able to overtake us, encumbered as you were?"

"Well, it was no small problem. We had little hope of
overtaking you as it was, and with our new burden, it
appeared it would be impossible," Brockhurst began.

"We were naturally quite eager to . . . ah . . . join you,
so we resorted to desperate measures," Higgens continued. "We took a side trip to Twixt and sought the aid of
the Deveel there. It cost us a pretty penny, but he finally
agreed to teleport our group to the trail ahead of you,
allowing us to make our desired contact."

"Deveel? What Deveel?" Aahz interrupted.

"Frumple. The Deveel at Twixt. The one who. . . ."

Brockhurst broke off suddenly, his eyes narrowing suspiciously. He shot a dark glance at Higgens, who was casually reaching for his crossbow.

"I'm surprised Throckwoddle hasn't mentioned Frumple to you," Higgens purred. "After all, he's the one who told us about him."

# IX:

*"To function efficiently, any group of
people or employees must have faith in
their leader."*

—CAPT. BLIGH (RET.)

"Yes, Throckwoddle." If anything, Aahz's voice was
even more menacing than the Imp's. "Why didn't
you tell me about the Deveel?"

"It . . . ah . . . must have slipped my mind," I mumbled.

With a massive exertion of self-control, I shot my most
withering glare at the Imps, forcing myself to ignore the
menace of the crossbows. I was rewarded by seeing them
actually look guilty and avoid my gaze.

"Slipped your mind! More likely you were trying to
hold back a bit of information from me," Aahz said ac-
cusingly. "Well, now that it's out, let's have the rest of
it. What about this Deveel?"

"Ask Brockhurst," I grumbled. "He seems to be eager
to talk about it."

"Well, Brockhurst?" Aahz turned to him.

The Imp gave me an apologetic shrug as he started.

"Well, I guess I've already told you most of it. There's
a Deveel, Frumple, in residence in Twixt. He goes under

the cover of Abdul the Rug Merchant, but he actually
maintains a thriving trade in the usual Deva manner, buying and selling across the dimensions."

"What's he doing in Klah?" Aahz interrupted. "I mean
there's not much business here. Isn't it a little slow for a
Deveel's taste?"

"Well, Throckwoddle said. . . ." Brockhurst broke off
and shot me a look.

"Go on, tell him." I tried to sound resigned.

"Well," the Imp continued, "rumor has it that he was
exiled from Deva and is in hiding here, ashamed to show
his face in a major dimension."

"Barred from Deva? Why? What did he do?"

I was glad Aahz asked. It would have sounded strange
coming from me.

"Throckwoddle wouldn't tell us. Said Frumple was
sensitive on the subject and we shouldn't bring it up."

"Well, Throckwoddle?" Aahz turned to me.

I was so caught up in the story it took me a few beats
before I remembered that I really didn't know.

"Um . . . I can't tell you," I said.

"What?" Aahz scowled.

I began to wonder how much he was caught up in the
story and had lost track of the realities of the situation.

"I learned his secret by accident and hold it as a personal confidence," I said haughtily. "During our travels
these last few days, I've learned some rather interesting
items about you and hold them in the same esteem. I trust
you will respect my silence on the matter of Frumple as
I expect others to respect my silence about those matters
pertaining to you."

"Okay, okay. You've made your point," Aahz conceded.

"Say . . . um . . . Throckwoddle," Higgens interrupted.
"I would suggest we all shed our disguises like our friend
Perver . . . um, Pervect here has. No sense in using up our
energies keeping up false faces among friends."

His tone was casual, but he sounded suspicious. I noticed he had not taken his hand off his crossbow.

"Why?" argued Brockhurst. "I prefer to keep my disguise on at all times when in another dimension. Lessens the chance of forgetting to put it on at a crucial moment."

"I think Higgens is right," Aahz stated before I could support Brockhurst. "I for one like to see the true faces of the people I'm talking to."

"Well," grumbled Brockhurst, "if everyone is going to insist."

He closed his eyes in concentration, and his features began to shimmer and melt.

I didn't watch the whole process. My mind was racing desperately back to Garkin's hut, when Aahz held up the charred face of the assassin. I hastily envisioned my own face next to it and began working, making certain obvious modifications to its appearance to repair the fire damage.

When I was done, I snuck a peek out of one eye. The other two had changed already. My attention was immediately drawn to their complexion. Theirs was a pinkish red, while mine wasn't. I hastily re-closed my eye and made the adjustment.

Satisfied now, I opened my eyes and looked about me. The other two Imps now showed the apparently characteristic pointed ears and chins. Aahz looked like Aahz. The situation had completely reversed since the Imps had arrived. Instead of being normal surrounded by three disguised demons, I was now surrounded by three demons while I was disguised. Terrific.

"Ahh. That's better," chortled Aahz.

"You know, Throckwoddle," Higgens said, cocking a head at me. "For a moment there in the firelight you looked different. In fact. . . ."

"Come, come, gentlemen," Aahz interrupted. "We have serious matters to discuss. Does Isstvan know about Frumple's existence?"

"I don't believe so," answered Brockhurst. "If he did, he would have either enlisted him or had him assassinated."

"Good," exclaimed Aahz. "He could very well be the key to our plot."

"What plot?" I asked.

"Our plot against Isstvan, of course."

"What?" exclaimed Higgens, completely distracted from me now. "Are you insane?"

"No," retorted Aahz. "But Isstvan is. I mean, think! Has he been acting particularly stable?"

"No," admitted Brockhurst. "But then neither has any other magician I've met, present company included."

"Besides," Higgens interrupted, "I thought you were on your way to help him."

"That's before I heard your story," Aahz pointed out. "I'm not particularly eager to work for a magician who pits his own employees against each other."

"When did he do that?" Higgens asked.

Aahz made an exasperated gesture.

"Think, gentlemen! Have you forgotten our stony-faced friend there?" He jerked a thumb at the figure on the unicorn. "If you recall your tale correctly, his words seemed to imply he had been sent by Isstvan to intercept you."

"That's right," said Brockhurst. "So?"

"What do you mean, 'So?'" Aahz exploded. "That's it! Isstvan sent him to kill you. Either he was trying to cut his overhead by assassinating his assassins before payday, or he's so unstable mentally he's lashing out blindly at everyone, including his own allies. Either way he doesn't sound like the most benevolent of employers."

"You know, I believe he has a point there," I observed, determined to be of some assistance in this deception.

"But if that's true, what are we to do?" asked Higgens.

"Well, I don't have a firm plan of action," Aahz admitted. "But I have some general ideas that might help."

"Such as?" prompted Brockhurst.

"You go back to Isstvan. Say nothing at all of your suspicions. If you do, he might consider you dangerous and move against you immediately. What's more, refuse

any new assignments. Find some pretext to stay as close
to him as possible. Learn all about his habits and weak-
nesses, but don't do anything until we get there."

"Where are you going?" asked Higgens.

"We are going to have a little chat with Frumple. If
we're going to move against Isstvan, the support of a Deveel could be invaluable."

"And probably unobtainable," grumbled Brockhurst.
"I've never known a Deveel yet to take sides in a fight.
They prefer being in a position to sell to both sides."

"What do you mean 'we'?" asked Higgens. "Isn't
Throckwoddle coming with us?"

"No. I've developed a fondness for his company. Besides, if he doesn't agree to help us, it would come in
handy to have an assassin close by. Frumple's too powerful to run the risk of leaving him unallied to help Isstvan."

As Aahz was speaking, Brockhurst casually leaned
back out of his line of vision and silently mouthed the
word "Pervert" at Higgens. Higgens quietly nodded his
agreement, and they both shot me sympathetic glances.

"Well, what do you think?" Aahz asked in conclusion.

"Hmm . . . what do we do with him?" Higgens indicated the Quigley statue with a jerk of his head.

"We'll take him with us," I chimed in hastily.

"Of course!" agreed Aahz, shooting me a black look.
"If you two took him back to Isstvan, he might guess you
suspected his treachery."

"Besides," I added, "maybe we can revive him and
convince him to join us in our battle."

"I suppose you'll be wanting the antidote then." Higgens sighed, fishing a small vial from inside his cloak and
tossing it to me. "Just sprinkle a little on him and he'll
return to normal in a few minutes. Watch yourself,
though. There's something strange about him. He seemed
to be able to see right through our disguises."

"Where's the sword you were talking about?" Aahz
asked.

"It's in his pack. Believe me, it's junk. The only reason we brought it along was that he seemed to put so much stock in it. It'll be curious to find out what he thought it was when we revive him."

"Well, I believe that just about covers everything," Brockhurst sighed. "I suggest we get some sleep and start on our respective journeys first thing in the morning."

"I suggest you start on your journey now," Aahz said pointedly.

"Now?" Brockhurst exclaimed.

"But it's the middle of the night," Higgens pointed out.

"Might I remind you gentlemen that the longer you are away from Isstvan, the greater the chances are he'll send another assassin after you."

"He's right, you know," I said thoughtfully.

"I suppose so," grumbled Higgens.

"Well," said Brockhurst, rising to his feet, "I guess we'll be on our way then as soon as we divide Garkin's loot."

"On the contrary," stated Aahz. "Not only do we not divide the loot, I would suggest you give us whatever funds you have at your disposal."

"What?" they chorused, their crossbows instantly in their hands again.

"Think, gentlemen," Aahz said soothingly. "We'd be trying to bargain with a Deveel for his support. As you yourselves have pointed out, they are notoriously unreasonable in their prices. I would hate to think we might fail in our negotiations for a lack of funds."

There was a pregnant silence as the Imps sought to find a hole in his logic.

"Oh, very well," Brockhurst conceded at last, lowering his crossbow and reaching for his purse.

"I still don't think it will do any good," Higgens grumbled, imitating Brockhurst's move. "You probably couldn't buy off a Deveel if you had the Gnomes themselves backing you."

They passed the purses over to Aahz, who hefted them

judiciously before tucking them into his own waistband.

"Trust me, gentlemen." Aahz smiled. "We Pervects have methods of persuasion that are effective even on Deveels."

The Imps shuddered at this and began edging away.

"Well . . . umm . . . I guess we'll see you later," Higgens mumbled. "Watch yourself, Throckwoddle."

"Yes," added Brockhurst. "And be sure when you're done, the Deveel is either with us or dead."

I tried to think of something to say in return, but before anything occurred to me they were gone.

Aahz cocked an eyebrow at me and I held up a restraining hand until I felt them pass through the wards. I signaled him with a nod.

"They've gone," I said.

"Beautiful!" exclaimed Aahz gleefully. "Didn't I tell you they were gullible?"

For once I had to admit he was right.

"Well, get some sleep now, kid. Like I said before, tomorrow's going to be a busy day, and all of a sudden it looks like it's going to be even busier."

I complied, but one question kept nagging at me.

"Aahz?"

"Yeah, kid."

"What dimension do the Gnomes come from?"

"Zoorik," he answered.

On that note, I went to sleep.

# X:

*"Man shall never reach his full capacity while chained to the earth. We must take wing and conquer the heavens."*

—ICARUS

"Are you sure we're up to handling a Deveel, Aahz?" I was aware I had asked the question countless times in the last few days, but I still needed reassurance.

"Will you relax, kid?" Aahz growled. "I was right about the Imps, wasn't I?"

"I suppose so," I admitted hesitantly.

I didn't want to tell Aahz, but I wasn't that happy with the Imp incident. It had been a little too close for my peace of mind. Since the meeting, I had been having recurring nightmares involving Imps and crossbows.

"Look at it this way, kid. With any luck this Frumple character will be able to restore my powers. That'd take you off the hotseat."

"I guess so," I said without enthusiasm.

He had raised this point several times since learning about Frumple. Each time he did, it gave me the same feeling of discomfort.

"Something bothering you, kid?" Aahz asked, cocking his head at me.

"Well . . . it's . . . Aahz, if you do get your powers back, will you still want me as an apprentice?"

"Is that what's been eating at you?" he seemed genuinely surprised. "Of course I'll still want you. What kind of a magician do you think I am? I don't choose my apprentices lightly."

"You wouldn't feel I was a burden?"

"Maybe at first, but not now. You were in at the start of this Isstvan thing; you earned the right to be in on the end of it."

Truth to tell, I wasn't all that eager to be there when Aahz confronted Isstvan, but that seemed to be the price I would have to pay if I was going to continue my association with Aahz.

"Um . . . Aahz?"

"Yeah, kid?"

"Just one more question?"

"Promise?"

"How's that?"

"Nothing. What's the question, kid?"

"If you get your powers back, and I'm still your apprentice, which dimension will we live in?"

"Hmm. To be honest, kid, I hadn't really given it much thought. Tell ya what, we'll burn that bridge when we come to it, okay?"

"Okay, Aahz."

I tried to get my mind off the question. Maybe Aahz was right. No sense worrying about the problem until we knew for sure it existed. Maybe he wouldn't get his powers back. Maybe I'd get to be the one to fight Isstvan after all. Terrific.

"Hey! Watch the beast, kid!"

Aahz's voice broke my train of thought. We were leading the war unicorn between us, and the beast chose this moment to act up.

It nickered and half-reared, then planted its feet and tossed its head.

"Steady . . . ow!"

Aahz extended a hand trying to seize its bridle and received a solid rap on the forearm from the unicorn's horn for his trouble.

"Easy, Buttercup," I said soothingly. "There's a good boy."

The beast responded to my coaxings, first by settling down, pawing the ground nervously, then finally by rubbing his muzzle against me.

Though definitely a friendly gesture, this is not the safest thing to have a unicorn do to you. I ducked nimbly under his swinging horn and cast about me quickly. Snatching an orange flower from a nearby bush, I fed it to him at an arm's length. He accepted the offering and began to munch it contentedly.

"I don't think that beast likes demons," Aahz grumbled sullenly, rubbing his bruised arm.

"It stands to reason," I retorted. "I mean, he was a demon hunter's mount, you know."

"Seems to take readily enough to you, though," Aahz observed. "Are you sure you're not a virgin?"

"Certainly not," I replied in my most injured tones.

Actually I was, but I would have rather been fed to vampire-slugs than admit it to Aahz.

"Speaking of demon hunters, you'd better check on our friend there," Aahz suggested. "It could get a bit grisly if an arm or something broke off before we got around to restoring him."

I hastened to comply. We had rigged a drag-litter for the Quigley-statue to avoid having to load and unload him each night, not to mention escaping the chore of saddling and unsaddling the war unicorn. The bulk of the gear and armor was sharing the drag-litter with the Quigley-statue, a fact which seemed to make the unicorn immensely happy. Apparently it was far easier to drag all that weight than to carry it on one's back.

"He seems to be okay, Aahz," I reported.

"Good," he sneered. "I'd hate to think of anything happening to him, accidental-like."

Aahz was still not happy with our traveling companions. He had only grudgingly given in to my logic for bringing them along as opposed to leaving them behind. I had argued that they could be of potential assistance in dealing with the Deveel, or at least when we had our final showdown with Isstvan.

In actuality, that wasn't my reasoning at all. I felt a bit guilty about having set Quigley up to get clobbered by the Imps and didn't want to see any harm befall him because of it.

"It would make traveling a lot easier if we restored him," I suggested hopefully.

"Forget it, kid."

"But Aahz. . . ."

"I said forget it! In case you've forgotten, that particular gentleman's major pastime seems to consist of seeking out and killing demons. Now I'm aware my winning personality may have duped you into overlooking the fact, but I am a demon. As such, I am not about to accept a living, breathing, and most importantly, functioning demon hunter as a traveling companion."

"We fooled him before!" I argued.

"Not on a permanent basis. Besides, when would you practice your magik if he was restored? Until we meet with the Deveel, you're still our best bet against Isstvan."

I wished he would stop mentioning that. It made me incredibly uncomfortable when he did. Besides, I couldn't think of a good argument to it.

"I guess you're right, Aahz," I admitted.

"You'd better believe I'm right. Incidentally, since we seem to be stopped anyway, this is as good a time as any for your next lesson."

My spirits lifted. Besides my natural eagerness to extend my magical abilities, Aahz's offer contained an implied statement that he was pleased with my progress so far in earlier lessons.

"Okay, Aahz," I said, looping the unicorn's reins around a nearby bush. "I'm ready."

"Good," smiled Aahz, rubbing his hands together. "Today we're going to teach you to fly."

My spirits fell again.

"Fly?" I asked.

"That's what I said, kid. Fly. Exciting, isn't it?"

"Why?"

"Whadya mean, why? Ever since we first cast jealous eyes on the creatures of the air we've wanted to fly. Now you're getting a chance to learn. That's why it's exciting!"

"I meant, why should I want to learn to fly?"

"Well . . . because everybody wants to fly."

"I don't," I said emphatically.

"Why not?"

"I'm afraid of heights, for one thing," I answered.

"That isn't enough reason to not learn," Aahz scowled.

"Well, I haven't heard any reasons yet as to why I should." I scowled back at him.

"Look, kid," Aahz began coaxingly, "It isn't so much flying as floating on air."

"The distinction escapes me," I said dryly.

"Okay, kid. Let me put it to you this way. You're my apprentice, right?"

"Right," I agreed suspiciously.

"Well, I'm not going to have an apprentice that can't fly! Get me!?" he roared.

"All right, Aahz. How does it work?" I knew when I was beaten.

"That's better. Actually it doesn't involve anything you don't already know. You know how to levitate objects, right?"

I nodded slowly, puzzled.

"Well, all flying is is levitating yourself."

"How's that again?"

"Instead of standing firm on the ground and lifting an object, you push against the ground with your will and lift yourself."

"But if I'm not touching the ground, where do I draw my power from?"

"From the air! C'mon, kid, you're a magician, not an elemental."

"What's an elemental?"

"Forget it. What I meant was you aren't bound to any of the four elements, you're a magician. You control them, or at least influence them and draw your power from them. When you're flying, all you have to do is draw your power from the air instead of the ground."

"If you say so, Aahz," I said doubtfully.

"Okay, first locate a force line."

"But we left it when we started off to see the Deveel," I argued.

"Kid, there are lots of force lines. Just because we left one of the ground force lines doesn't mean we're completely out of touch. Check for a force line in the air."

"In the air?"

"Believe me, kid. Check."

I sighed and closed my eyes. Turning my face skyward, I tried to picture the two-headed spear. At first I couldn't do it, then realized with a start I was seeing a spear, but a different spear. It wasn't as bright as the last spear had been, but glowed softly with icy blues and whites.

"I think I've got one, Aahz!" I gasped.

"It's blue and white, right?" Aahz sneered sarcastically.

"Yes, but it's not as bright as the last one."

"It's probably further away. Oh well, it's close enough for you to draw energy from. Well, give it a try, kid. Hook into that force line and push the ground away. Slowly now."

I did as I was instructed, reaching out with my mind to tap the energies of that icy vision. The surge of power I felt was unlike any I had experienced before. Whereas before when I summoned the power I felt warm and swollen with power, this time I felt cool and relaxed. The power flow actually made me feel lighter.

"Push away, kid," came Aahz's voice. "Gently!"

Lazily I touched the ground with my mind, only casually aware of the curious sensation of not physically feeling anything with my feet.

"Open your eyes, kid! Adjust your trim."

Aahz's voice came to me from a strange location this time. Surprised, my eyes popped open.

I was floating some ten feet above the ground at an angle that was rapidly drifting toward a horizontal position. I was flying!

The ground came at me in a rush. I had one moment of dazed puzzlement before it slammed into me with jarring reality.

I lay there for a moment forcing air back into my lungs and wondering if I had broken anything.

"Are you okay, kid?" Aahz was suddenly looming over me. "What happened anyway?"

"I . . . I was flying!" I forced the words at last.

"Yeah, so? Oh, I get it. You were so surprised you forgot to maintain the energy flow, right?"

I nodded, unable to speak.

"Of all the dumb . . . look, kid, when I tell you you're going to fly, believe it!"

"But. . . ."

"Don't 'but' me! Either you believe in me as a teacher or you don't! There's no buts about it!"

"I'm sorry, Aahz." I was getting my breath back again.

"Ahh . . . didn't mean to jump on you like that, kid, but you half scared me to death with that fall. You've got to understand we're starting to get into some pretty powerful magik now. You've got to expect them to work. A surprise-break like that last one with the wrong thing could get you killed, or me for that matter."

"I'll try to remember, Aahz. Shall I try it again?"

"Just take it easy for a few minutes, kid. Flying can take a lot out of you, even without the fall."

I closed my eyes and waited for my head to stop whirling.

"Aahz?" I said finally.

"Yeah, kid?"

"Tell me about Perv."

"What about it?"

"It just occurred to me, those Imps seemed scared to death when they realized you were a Pervect. What kind of a reputation does your dimension have?"

"Well," he began, "Perv is a self-sufficient, standoffish dimension. We may not have the best fighters, but they're close enough that other dimension travelers give them lots of room. Technology and magik exist side by side and are intertwined with each other. All in all it makes a pretty powerful little package."

"But why should anyone be afraid of that?"

"As I said, Perv has a lot going for it. One of the side effects of success is an abundance of hangers-on. There was a time when we were close to being swamped with refugees and immigrants from other dimensions. When they got to be too much of a nuisance, we put a stop to it."

"How?" I pushed.

"First, we took the non-contributing outsiders and ran 'em out. Then, for an added measure of insurance, we encouraged the circulation of rumors of certain anti-social attitudes of Pervects toward those from other dimensions."

"What kind of rumors?"

"Oh, the usual. That we eat our enemies, torture folks for amusement and have sexual practices that are considered dubious by any dimension's standards. Folks aren't sure how much is truth and how much is exaggeration, but they're none too eager to find out firsthand."

"How much of it is true, Aahz?" I asked propping myself up on one elbow.

He grinned evilly at me.

"Enough to keep 'em honest."

I was going to ask what it took to be considered a contributing immigrant, but decided to let it pass for a while.

# XI:

*"One of the joys of travel is visiting new
towns and meeting new people."*

—G. KHAN

"Ah! What a shining example of civilization!" chortled
Aahz exuberantly as he peered about him, delighted
as a child on his first outing.

We were sauntering casually down one of the lesser
used streets of Twixt. Garbage and beggars were strewn
casually about while beady rodent eyes, human and in-
human, studied us from the darkened doors and windows.
It was a cluster of buildings crouched around an army
outpost which was manned more from habit than neces-
sity. The soldiers we occasionally encountered had de-
generated enough from the crisp recruiting poster model
that it was frequently difficult to tell which seemed more
menacing and unsavory, the guards or the obviously crim-
inal types they were watching.

"If you ask me, it looks more like mankind at its
worst!" I mumbled darkly.

"That's what I said, a shining example of civilization!"

There wasn't much I could say to that, not feeling like

getting baited into another one of Aahz's philosophical lectures.

"Aahz, is it my imagination or are people staring at us?"

"Relax, kid. In a town like this the citizens will always instinctively size up a stranger. They're trying to guess if we're victims or victimizers. Our job is to make sure they think we're in the second category."

To illustrate his point he suddenly whirled and crouched like a cat, glaring back down the street with a hand on his sword hilt.

There was sudden movement at the windows and doorways as roughly a dozen half-seen forms melted back into the darkness.

One figure didn't move. A trollop leaning on a windowsill, her arms folded to display her ill-covered breasts, smiled invitingly at him. He smiled and waved. She ran an insolent tongue tip slowly around her lip and winked broadly.

"Um . . . Aahz?"

"Yeah, kid?" he replied, without taking his eyes from the girl.

"I hate to interrupt, but you're supposed to be a doddering old man, remember?"

Aahz was still disguised as Garkin, a fact which seemed to have momentarily slipped his mind.

"Hmm? Oh, yeah. I guess you're right, kid. It doesn't seem to bother anybody else though. Maybe they're used to feisty old men in this town."

"Well, could you at least stop going for your sword? That's supposed to be our surprise weapon."

Aahz was wearing the assassin's cloak now, which he quickly pulled forward again to hide his sword.

"Will you get off my back, kid? Like I said, nobody seems to be paying any attention."

"Nobody?" I jerked my head pointedly toward the girl in the window.

"Her? She's not paying any more attention to us than she is anyone else on the street."

"Really?"

"Well, if she is, it's more because of you than because of me."

"Me? C'mon, Aahz."

"Don't forget, kid, you're a pretty impressive person now."

I blinked. That hadn't occurred to me. I had forgotten I was disguised as Quigley now.

We had hidden the demon hunter just outside of town . . . well, actually we buried him. I had been shocked by the suggestion at first, but as Aahz pointed out, the statue didn't need any air and it was the only surefire way we had of ensuring he wouldn't be found by anyone else.

Even the war unicorn following us, now fully saddled and armored, did not help me keep my new identity in mind. We had been traveling together too long now.

I suppose I should have gotten some satisfaction from the fact I could now maintain not only one, but two disguises without consciously thinking about it. I didn't. I found it unnerving that I had to remember other people were seeing me differently than I was seeing myself.

I shot a glance at the trollop. As our eyes met, her smile broadened noticeably. She displayed her increased enthusiasm by leaning further out of the window until I began to worry about her falling out . . . of the window or her dress.

"What did I tell you, kid!" Aahz slapped me enthusiastically on the shoulder and winked lewdly.

"I'd rather she was attracted to me for me as I really am," I grumbled darkly.

"The price of success, kid," Aahz responded philosophically. "Well, no matter. We're here on business, remember?"

"Right," I said firmly.

I turned to continue our progress, and succeeded only in whacking Aahz soundly in the leg with my sword.

"Hey! Watch it, kid!"

It seemed there was more to this sword-carrying than met the casual eye.

"Sorry, Aahz," I apologized. "This thing's a bit point-heavy."

"Yeah? How would you know?" my comrade retorted.

"Well . . . you said. . . ."

"I said? That won't do it, kid. What's point-heavy for me may not be point-heavy for you. Weapon balance is a personal thing."

"Well . . . I guess I'm just not used to wearing a sword," I admitted.

"It's easy. Just forget you're wearing it. Think of it as part of you."

"I did. That's when I hit you."

"Hmm . . . we'll go into it more later."

Out of the corner of my eye, I could still see the trollop. She clapped her hands in silent applause and blew me a kiss. I suddenly realized she thought I had deliberately hit Aahz, a premeditated act to quell a rival. What's more, she approved of the gesture.

I looked at her again, more closely this time. Maybe later I would give Aahz the slip for a while and. . . .

"We've got to find Frumple." Aahz's voice interrupted my wandering thoughts

"Hmm . . . ? Oh. How, Aahz?"

"Through guile and cunning. Watch this, kid."

So saying, he shot a quick glance up and down the street. A pack of three urchins had just rounded the corner, busily engaged in a game of keep-away with one of the group's hat.

"Hey!" Aahz hailed them. "Where can I find the shop of Abdul the Rug Dealer?"

"Two streets up and five to the left," they called back, pointing the direction.

"See, kid? That wasn't hard."

"Terrific," I responded, unimpressed.

"Now what's wrong, kid?"

"I thought we were trying to avoid unnecessary attention."

"Don't worry, kid."

"Don't worry!? We're on our way to meet a Deveel on a supposedly secret mission, and you seem to be determined to make sure everybody we see notices us and knows where we're going."

"Look, kid, how does a person normally act when they come into a new town?"

"I don't know," I admitted. "I haven't been in that many towns."

"Well, let me sketch it out for you. They want to be noticed. They carry on and make lots of noise. They stare at the women and wave at people they've never seen before."

"But that's what we've been doing."

"Right! Now do you understand?"

"No."

Aahz heaved an exasperated sigh.

"C'mon, kid. Think a minute, even if it hurts. We're acting like anyone else would walking into a strange town, so nobody will look at us twice. They won't pay any more attention to us than they would any other newcomer. Now if we followed your suggestion and came skulking into town, not talking to anyone or looking at anything, and tried real hard not to be noticed, then everyone and his kid brother would zero in on us trying to figure out what we were up to. Now do you understand?"

"I . . . I think so."

"Good . . . cause there's our target."

I blinked and looked in the direction of his pointing finger. There squatting between a blacksmith's forge and a leatherworker's displays was the shop. As I said, I was new to city life, but I would have recognized it as a rug merchant's shop even if it was not adorned with a large sign proclaiming it such. The entire front of the shop was lavishly decorated with colorful geometric patterns apparently meant to emulate the patterns of the rugs inside. I guess it was intended to look rich and prosperous. I found it unforgivably gaudy.

I had been so engrossed in our conversation, I had momentarily forgotten our mission. With the shop now confronting us at close range, however, my nervousness came back in a rush.

"What are we going to do, Aahz?"

"Well, first of all I think I'm going to get a drink."

"A drink?"

"Right. If you think I'm going to match wits with a Deveel on an empty stomach, you've got another think coming."

"A drink?" I repeated, but Aahz was gone, striding purposefully toward a nearby tavern. There was little for me to do but follow, leading the unicorn.

The tavern was a dingy affair, even to my rustic eye. A faded awning sullenly provided shade for a small cluster of scarred wooden tables. Flies buzzed around a cat sleeping on one of the tables . . . at least I like to assume it was asleep.

As I tied the unicorn to one of the awning supports, I could hear Aahz bellowing at the innkeep for two of his largest flagons of wine. I sighed, beginning to despair that Aahz would never fully adapt to his old-man disguise. The innkeep did not seem to notice any irregularity between Aahz's appearance and his drinking habits, however. It occurred to me that Aahz might be right in his theories of how to go unnoticed. City people seemed to be accustomed to loud rude individuals of any age.

"Sit down, kid," Aahz commanded. "You're making me nervous hovering around like that."

"I thought we were going to talk with the Deveel," I grumbled, sinking into a chair.

"Relax, kid. A few minutes one way or the other won't make that much difference. Besides, look!"

A young, well-dressed couple was entering the rug shop.

"See? We couldn't have done any business anyway. At

least not until they left. The kind of talk we're going to have can't be done in front of witnesses. Ahh!"

The innkeeper had arrived, clinking the two flagons of wine down on the table in a lackluster manner.

"About time!" Aahz commented, seizing a flagon in each hand and immediately draining one. "Aren't you going to have anything, kid?"

A toss of his head and the second flagon was gone.

"While my friend here makes up his mind, bring me two more . . . and make them decent sizes this time if you have to use a bucket!"

The innkeep retreated, visibly shaken. I wasn't. I had already witnessed Aahz's capacity for alcohol, astounding in an era noted for heavy drinkers. What did vex me a bit was that the man had departed without taking my order.

I did eventually get my flagon of wine, only to find my stomach was too nervous to readily accept it. As a result, I wound up sipping it slowly. Not so Aahz. He continued to belt them down at an alarming rate. For quite some time he drank. In fact, we sat for nearly an hour, and there was still no sign of the couple who had entered the shop.

Finally, even Aahz began to grow impatient.

"I wonder what's taking them so long," he grumbled.

"Maybe they're having trouble making up their mind," I suggested.

"C'mon, kid. The shop's not that big. He can't have too large a selection."

He downed the last of his wine and stood up.

"We've waited long enough," he declared. "Let's get this show on the road."

"But what about the couple?" I reminded him.

"We'll just have to inspire them to conclude their business with a bit more speed."

That had a vaguely ominous ring to it, and Aahz's toothy grin was additional evidence that something unpleasant was about to happen.

I was about to try to dissuade him, but he started across

the street with a purposeful stride that left me standing
alone.

I hurried to catch up with him, leaving the unicorn
behind in my haste. Even so, I was unable to overtake
him before he had entered the shop.

I plunged after him, fearing the worst. I needn't have
worried. Except for the proprietor, the shop was empty.
There was no sign of the couple anywhere.

# XII:

*"First impressions are of major impor-
tance in business matters."*

—J. Pierpont Finch

"**M**ay I help you, gentlemen?"
The proprietor's rich robes did not successfully
hide his thinness. I am not particularly muscular . . . as
Skeeve, that is . . . but I had the impression that if I struck
this man, he wouldn't bruise, he'd shatter. I mean, I've
seen skinny men before, but he seemed to be a skeleton
with a too-small skin stretched over the bones.

"We'd like to talk with Abdul," Aahz said loftily.

"I am he, and he is I," recited the proprietor. "You see
before you Abdul, a mere shadow of a man, pushed to
the brink of starvation by his clever customers."

"You seem to be doing all right for yourself," I murmured, looking about me.

The shop was well stocked, and even my untraveled
eye could readily detect the undeniable signs of wealth
about. The rugs were delicately woven in soft fabrics un-
familiar to me, and gold and silver shone from the depths
of their designs. Obviously these rugs were intended for

the wealthy, and it seemed doubtful their current owner would be suffering from a lack of comfort.

"Ahh. Therein lies the tale of my foolishness," cried the proprietor wringing his hands. "In my blind confidence, I sank my entire holdings into my inventory. As a result, I starve in the midst of plenty. My customers know this and rob me in my vulnerable times. I lose money on every sale, but a man must eat."

"Actually," Aahz interrupted, "we're looking for something in a deep shag wall-to-wall carpet."

"What's that? . . . I mean, do not confuse poor Abdul so, my humble business. . . ."

"Come off it, Abdul . . . or should I say Frumple." Aahz grinned his widest grin. "We know who you are and what you are. We're here to do a little business."

At his words, the proprietor moved with a swiftness I would not have suspected him capable of. He was at the door in a bound, throwing a bolt and lowering a curtain which seemed to be of a substance even more strange than that of his rugs.

"Where'd you learn your manners!" he snarled back over his shoulder in a voice quite unlike the one used by the whiney proprietor. "I've got to live in this town, you know."

"Sorry," Aahz said, but he didn't sound at all apologetic.

"Well, watch it next time you come barging in and start throwing my name around. People here are not particularly tolerant of strange beings or happenings."

He seemed to be merely grumbling to himself, so I seized the opportunity to whisper to Aahz.

"Psst. Aahz. What's a wall-to-wall. . . ."

"Later, kid."

"You!" The proprietor seemed to see me for the first time. "You're the statue! I didn't recognize you moving."

"Well . . . I . . ."

"I should have known," he raved on. "Deal with Imps and you invite trouble. Next thing you know every. . . ."

He broke off suddenly and eyed us suspiciously. His hand disappeared into the folds and emerged with a clear crystal. He held it up and looked through it like an eye glass, scrutinizing us each in turn.

"I should have known," he spat. "Would you be so kind as to remove your disguises? I like to know who I'm doing business with."

I glanced at Aahz who nodded in agreement.

Closing my eyes, I began to effect the change to our normal appearance. I had enough time to wonder if Frumple would wonder about my transformation, if he realized I was actually a different person than the statue he had seen earlier. I needn't have worried.

"A Pervert!" Frumple managed to make the word sound slimy.

"That's Pervect if you want to do business with us," Aahz corrected.

"It's Pervert until I see the color of your money," Frumple sneered back.

I was suddenly aware he was studying me carefully.

"Say, you wouldn't by any chance be an Imp named Throckwoddle, would you?"

"Me? No! I . . . I'm. . . ."

But he was already squinting at me through the crystal again.

"Hmph," he grunted, tucking his viewer back in his robe. "I guess you're okay. I'd love to get my hands on that Throckwoddle, though. He's been awfully free spreading my name around lately."

"Say, Frumple," Aahz interjected. "You aren't the only one who likes to see who he's doing business with, you know."

"Hm? Oh! Very well, if you insist."

I expected him to close his eyes and go to work, but instead he dipped a hand into his robe again. This time he produced what looked like a small hand mirror with some sort of a dial on the back. Peering into the mirror, he began to gently turn the dial with his fingers.

The result was immediate and startling. Not merely his face, but his whole body began to change, filling out, and taking on a definite reddish hue. As I watched, his brows thickened and grew closer together, his beard line crept up his face as if it were alive, and his eyes narrowed cruelly. Almost as an afterthought, I noted that his feet were now shiny cloven hooves and the tip of a pointed tail appeared at the bottom hem of his robe.

In an impressively short period of time, he had transformed into a . . . well, a devil!

Despite all my preparations, I felt the prickle of superstitious fear as he put away the mirror and turned to us again.

"Are you happy now?" he grumbled at Aahz.

"It's a start," Aahz conceded.

"Enough banter," Frumple was suddenly animated again. "What brings a Pervert to Klah? Slumming? And where does the kid fit in?"

"He's my apprentice," Aahz informed him.

"Really?" Frumple swept me with a sympathetic gaze. "Are things really that tough, kid? Maybe we could work something out."

"He's quite happy with the situation," interrupted Aahz. "Now let's get to our problem."

"You want me to cure the kid's insanity?"

"Huh? No. C'mon, Frumple. We came here on business. Let's declare a truce for a while, okay?"

"If you insist. It'll seem strange, though; Perverts and Deveels have never really gotten along."

"That's Pervects!"

"See what I mean?"

"Aahz!" I interrupted. "Could you just tell him?"

"Hmm? Oh. Right, kid. Look, Frumple. We've got a problem we were hoping you could help us with. You see, I've lost my powers."

"What!?" exploded Frumple. "You came here without the magical ability to protect yourself against being followed? That tears it. I spend seven years building a comfortable front here, and some idiot comes along and. . . ."

"Look, Frumple. We told you the kid here's my apprentice. He knows more than enough to cover us."

"A half-trained apprentice! He's trusting my life and security to a half-trained apprentice!"

"You seem to be overlooking the fact we're already here. If anything was going to happen it would have happened already."

"Every minute you two are here you're threatening my existence."

". . . which is all the more reason for you to deal with our problem immediately and stop this pointless breast-beating!"

The two of them glared at each other for a few moments, while I tried to be very quiet and unnoticeable. Frumple did not seem to be the right choice for someone to pin our hopes on.

"Oh, all right!" Frumple grumbled at last. "Since I probably won't be rid of you any other way."

He strode to the wall and produced what looked like a length of rope from behind one of the rugs.

"That's more like it," Aahz said triumphantly.

"Sid down and shut up," ordered our host.

Aahz did as he was bid, and Frumple proceeded to circle him. As he moved, the Deveel held the rope first this way, then that, sometimes looped in a circle, other times hanging limp. All the while he stared intently at the ceiling as if reading a message written there in fine print.

I didn't have the faintest idea what he was doing, but it was strangely enjoyable to watch someone order Aahz about and get away with it.

"Hmm . . ." the Deveel said at last. "Yes, I think we can say that your powers are definitely gone."

"Terrific!" Aahz growled. "Look, Frumple. We didn't come all this way to be told something we already knew. You Deveels are supposed to be able to do anything. Well, do something!"

"It's not that easy, Pervert!" Frumple snapped back. "I

need information. How did you lose your powers, anyway?"

"I don't know for sure," Aahz admitted. "I was summoned to Klah by a magician and when I arrived they were gone."

"A magician? Which one?"

"Garkin."

"Garkin? He's a mean one to cross. Why don't you just get him to restore your powers instead of getting me involved?"

"Because he's dead. Is that reason enough for you?"

"Hmm . . . that makes it difficult."

"Are you saying you can't do anything?" Aahz sneered. "I should have known. I always thought the reputation of the Deveels was overrated."

"Look, Pervert! Do you want my help or not? I didn't say I couldn't do anything, just that it would be difficult."

"That's more like it," Aahz chortled. "Let's get started."

"Not so fast," interrupted Frumple. "I didn't say I would help you, just that I could."

"I see," sneered Aahz. "Here it comes, kid. The price tag. I told you they were shake-down artists."

"Actually," the Deveel said dryly, "I was thinking of the time factor. It would take a while for me to make my preparations, and I believe I've made my feelings quite clear about you staying here longer than is absolutely necessary."

"In that case," smiled Aahz, "I suggest you get started. I believe I've made *my* feelings quite clear that we intend to stay here until the cure is effected."

"In that case," the Deveel smiled back at him, "I believe *you* raised the matter of cost. How much do you have with you?"

"Well, we have. . . ." I began.

"*That* strikes me as being unimportant," Aahz glared warningly at me. "Suppose you tell us how much you feel is a fair price for your services."

Frumple graced him with one withering glare before sinking thoughtfully into his calculations.

"Hmm . . . material cost is up . . . and of course, there's my time . . . and you did call without an appointment . . . let's say it would cost you, just as a rough estimate, mind you, oh, in the neighborhood of . . . Say!"

He suddenly brightened and smiled at us.

"Maybe you'd be willing to work this as a trade. I cure you, and you do me a little favor."

"What kind of a favor?" Aahz asked suspiciously.

For once I was in complete agreement with him. Something in Frumple's voice did not inspire confidence.

"A small thing, really," the Deveel purred. "Sort of a decoy mission."

"We'd rather pay cash," I asserted firmly.

"Shut up, kid," Aahz advised. "What kind of a decoy mission, Frumple?"

"You may have noticed the young couple who entered my shop ahead of you. You did! Good. Then you have doubtless noticed they are not on the premises currently."

"How did they leave?" I asked curiously.

"I'll get to that in a moment," Frumple smiled. "Anyway, theirs is an interesting if common story. I'll spare you the details, but in short, they're young lovers kept apart by their families. In their desperation, they turned to me for assistance. I obliged them by sending them to another dimension where they can be happy free of their respective family's intervention."

"For a fee, of course," Aahz commented dryly.

"Of course," Frumple smiled.

"C'mon, Aahz," I chided. "It sounds like a decent thing to do, even if he was paid for it."

"Quite so!" beamed the Deveel. "You're quite perceptive for one so young. Anyway, my generosity has left me in a rather precarious position. As you have no doubt noticed, I am quite concerned with my image in this town. There is a chance that image may be threatened if the

couple's relatives succeed in tracking them to my shop
and no farther."

"That must have been some fee," Aahz mumbled.

"Now my proposition is this: in exchange for my assistance, I would ask that you two disguise yourselves as
that couple and lay a false trail away from my shop."

"How much of a false trail?" I asked.

"Oh, it needn't be anything elaborate. Just be seen
leaving town by enough townspeople to ensure that attention will be drawn away from my shop. Once out of sight
of town, you can change to any disguise you like and
return here. By that time, my preparations for your cure
should be complete. Well, what do you say? Is it a deal?"

# XIII:

*"The secret to winning the support of large groups of people is positive thinking."*

—N. BONAPARTE

"**P**eople are staring at us, Aahz."

"Relax, kid. They're supposed to be staring at us."

To illustrate his point, he nodded and waved to a knot of glowering locals. They didn't wave back.

"I don't see why I have to be the girl," I grumbled.

"We went through that before, kid. You walk more like a girl than I do."

"That's what you and Frumple decided. I don't think I walk like a girl at all!"

"Well, let's say I walk less like a girl than you do."

It was hard to argue with logic like that, so I changed subjects.

"Couldn't we at least travel by less populated streets?" I asked.

"Why?" countered Aahz.

"Well, I'm not too wild about having a lot of people seeing me when I'm masquerading as a girl."

"C'mon, kid. The whole idea is that no one would

recognize you. Besides, you don't know anybody in this town. Why should you care what they think of you?"

"I just don't like it, that's all," I grumbled.

"Not good enough," Aahz asserted firmly. "Being seen is part of our deal with Frumple. If you had any objections you should have said so before we closed the negotiations."

"I never got a chance," I pointed out. "But since the subject's come up, I do have a few questions."

"Such as?"

"Such as what are we doing?"

"Weren't you paying attention, kid? We're laying a false trail for. . . ."

"I know that," I interrupted. "What I mean is, why are we doing what we're doing? Why are we doing Frumple a favor instead of just paying his price?"

"You wouldn't ask that if you'd ever dealt with a Deveel before," Aahz snorted. "Their prices are sky-high, especially in a case like ours when they know the customer is desperate. Just be thankful we got such a good deal."

"That's what I mean, Aahz. Are we *sure* we've gotten a good deal?"

"What do you mean?"

"Well, from what I've been told, if you think you've gotten a good deal from a Deveel, it usually means you've overlooked something."

"Of course you speak from a wide range of experience," Aahz sneered sarcastically. "Who told you so much about dealing with Deveels?"

"You did," I said pointedly.

"Hmmm. You're right, kid. Maybe I have been a little hasty."

Normally I would have been ecstatic over having Aahz admit I was right. Somehow, however, in the current situation, it only made me feel that much more uncomfortable.

"So what are we going to do?" I asked.

"Well, normally I deal honestly unless I think I'm being double-crossed. This time, however, you've raised sufficient doubt in my mind that I think we should bend the rules a little."

"Situational ethics again?"

"Right!"

"So what do we do?"

"Start looking for a relatively private place where we can dump these disguises without being noticed."

I began scanning the streets and alleys ahead of us. My uneasiness was growing into panic, and it lent intensity to my search.

"I wish we had our weapons along," I muttered.

"Listen to him," Aahz jeered. "It wasn't that long ago you were telling me all about how magicians don't need weapons. C'mon, kid. What would you do with a weapon if you had one?"

"If you want to get specific," I said dryly, "I was wishing *you* had a weapon."

"Oh! Good point. Say ... ah ... kid? Are you still looking for a private place?"

"Yeah, I've got a couple possibles spotted."

"Well, forget it. Start looking for something wide open with a lot of exits."

"Why the change in strategy?" I asked.

"Take a look over your shoulder ... casual like."

I did as I was bid, though it was not as casual as it might have been. It turned out my acting ability was the least of our worries.

There was a crowd of people following us. They glared at us darkly and muttered to themselves. I wanted very badly to believe we were not the focus of their attention, but it was obvious that was not the case. They were clearly following us, and gathering members as they went.

"We're being followed, Aahz!" I whispered.

"Hey, kid. I pointed them out to you, remember?"

"But why are they following us? What do they want?"

"Well, I don't know for sure, of course, but I'd guess it has something to do with our disguises."

I snuck another glance at the crowd. The interest in us did not seem to be lessening at all. If anything, the crowd was even bigger and looked even angrier. Terrific.

"Say, Aahz?" I whispered.

"Yeah, kid?"

"If they're after us because of our disguises, why don't we just change back?"

"Bad plan, kid. I'd rather run the risk of them having some kind of grudge against the people we're impersonating than facing up to the consequences if they found out we were magicians."

"So what do we do?"

"We keep walking and hope we run into a patrol of soldiers that can offer us some protection."

A fist-sized rock thudded into the street ahead of us, presumably thrown by one of the people following us.

"... or ..." Aahz revised hastily, "we can stop right now and find out what this is all about."

"We could run," I suggested hopefully, but Aahz was already acting on his earlier suggestion.

He stopped abruptly and spun on his heel to face the crowd.

"What is the meaning of this?" he roared at the advancing multitude.

The crowd lurched to a halt before the direct address, those in the rear colliding with those in front who had already stopped. They seemed a bit taken aback by Aahz's action and milled about without direction.

I was pleasantly surprised at the success of my companion's maneuver, but Aahz was never one to leave well enough alone.

"Well?" he demanded, advancing on them. "I'm waiting for an explanation."

For a moment the crowd gave ground before his approach. Then an angry voice rang out from somewhere in the back.

"We want to know about our money!"

That opened the door.

"Yeah! What about our money?!"

The cry was taken up by several other voices, and the crowd began to growl and move forward again.

Aahz stood his ground and held up a hand commanding silence.

"What about your money?" he demanded haughtily.

"Oh, no, you don't," came a particularly menacing voice. "You aren't going to talk your way out of it this time!"

A massive bald man brandishing a butcher's cleaver shouldered his way through the crowd to confront Aahz.

"My good man," Aahz sniffed. "If you're implying. . . ."

"I'm implying nothing!" The man growled. "I'm saying it flat out. You and that trollop of yours are crooks!"

"Now, aren't you being just a bit hasty in. . . ."

"Hasty!" the man bellowed. "Hasty! Mister, we've already been too patient with you. We should have run you out of town when you first showed up with your phony anti-demon charms. That's right, I said phony! Some of us knew it from the start. Anyone with a little education knows there's no such things as demons."

For a moment I was tempted to let Aahz's disguise drop. Then I looked at the crowd again and decided against it. It wasn't a group to joke with.

"Now, some folks bought the charms because they were gullible, some as a gag, some of us because . . . well, because everyone else was buying them. But we all bought them, just like we bought your story that they had to be individually made and you needed the money in advance."

"That was all explained at the time," Aahz protested.

"Sure it was. You're great at explanations. You explained it just like you explained away those two times we caught you trying to leave town."

"Well . . . we . . . uh," Aahz began.

"Actually," I interrupted, "we were only. . . ."

"Well, we've had enough of your explanations. That's what we told you three days ago when we gave you two days to either come up with the charms or give us our money back."

"But these things take time. . . ."

"You've used up that excuse. Your time was up yesterday. Now do we get our money, or. . . ."

"Certainly, certainly," Aahz raised his hands soothingly.

"Just give me a moment to speak with my colleague."

He smiled at the crowd as he took me by the arm and drew me away.

"What are we going to do, Aahz?"

"*Now* we run," he said calmly.

"Huh?" I asked intelligently.

I was talking to thin air. Aahz was already legging it speedily down the street.

I may be slow at times, but I'm not *that* slow. In a flash I was hot on his heels.

Unfortunately, the crowd figured out what Aahz was up to about the same time I did. With a howl they were after us.

Surprisingly, I overtook Aahz. Either he was holding back so I could catch up, or I was more scared than I thought, which is impossible.

"Now what?" I panted.

"Shut up and keep running, kid," Aahz barked, ducking around a knot of people.

"They're gaining on us," I pointed out.

Actually, the group we had just passed had joined the pursuit, but it had the same effect as if the crowd was gaining.

"Will you knock it off and help me look?" Aahz growled.

"Sure. What are we looking for?"

"A couple dressed roughly like us," he replied.

"What do we do if we see them?"

"Simple," Aahz replied. "We plow into them full tilt, you swap our features for theirs, and we let the mob tear *them* apart."

"That doesn't sound right somehow," I said doubtfully.

"Kid, remember what I told you about situational ethics?"

"Yeah."

"Well, this is one of those situations."

I was convinced, though not so much by Aahz's logic as by the rock that narrowly missed my head. I don't know how the crowd managed to keep its speed and still pick up things to throw, but it did.

I began watching for a couple dressed like us. It's harder than it sounds when you're at a dead run with a mob at your heels.

Unfortunately, there was no one in sight who came close to fitting the bill. Whomever it was we were impersonating seemed to be fairly unique in their dress.

"I wish I had a weapon with me," Aahz complained.

"We've already gone through that," I called back. "And besides, what would you do if you had one? The only thing we've got that might stop them is the fire ring."

"Hey! I'd forgotten about that," Aahz gasped. "I've still got it on."

"So what?" I asked. "We can't use it."

"Oh, yeah? Why not?"

"Because then they'd know we're magicians."

"That won't make any difference if they're dead."

Situational ethics or not, my stomach turned at the thought of killing that many people.

"Wait, Aahz!" I shouted.

"Watch this, kid." He grinned and pointed his hand at them.

Nothing happened.

# XIV:

*"A little help at the right time is better
than a lot of help at the wrong time."*

—TEVYE

"C'mon, Aahz!" I shouted desperately, overturning a
fruit stand in the path of the crowd.

Now that it seemed my fellow-humans were safe from
Aahz, my concern returned to making sure he was safe
from them.

"I don't believe it!" Aahz shouted, as he darted past.

"What?" I called, sprinting after him.

"In one day I believed both a Deveel and an Imp. Tell
you what, kid. If we get out of this, I give you my permission to kick me hard. Right in the rump, twice."

"It's a deal!" I panted.

This running was starting to tax my stamina. Unfortunately, the crowd didn't seem tired at all. That was
enough to keep me running.

"Look, kid!" Aahz was pointing excitedly. "We're
saved."

I followed his finger. A uniformed patrol was marching . . . well, sauntering down the street ahead of us.

"It's about time," I grumbled, but I was relieved none-theless.

The crowd saw the soldiers, too. Their cries increased in volume as they redoubled their efforts to reach us.

"C'mon, kid! Step on it!" Aahz called. "We're not safe yet."

"Step on what?" I asked, passing him.

Our approach to the patrol was noisy enough that by the time we got there, the soldiers had all stopped moving and were watching the chase. One of them, a bit less un-kempt than the others, had shouldered his way to the front of the group and stood sneering at us with folded arms. From his manners, I guessed he was an officer. There was no other explanation for the others allowing him to act the way he was.

I skidded to a stop in front of him.

"We're being chased!" I panted.

"Really?" he smiled.

"Let me handle this, kid," Aahz mumbled, brushing me aside. "Are you the officer in charge, sir?"

"I am," the man replied.

"Well, it seems that these . . . citizens," he pointed dis-dainfully at our pursuers, "intend us bodily harm. A bla-tant disregard for your authority . . . sir!"

The mob was some ten feet distant and stood glaring alternately at us and the soldiers. I was gratified to observe that at least some of them were breathing hard.

"I suppose you're right," the officer yawned. "We should take a hand in this."

"Watch this, kid," Aahz whispered, nudging me in the ribs as the officer stepped forward to address the crowd.

"All right. You all know it is against the law for citi-zens to inflict injuries on each other," he began.

The crowd began to grumble darkly, but the officer waved them into silence as he continued.

"I know, I know. We don't like it either. If it were up to us we'd let you settle your own differences and spend our time drinking. But it's not up to us. We have to follow

the laws the same way you do, and the laws say only the
military can judge and punish the citizenry."

"See?" I whispered. "There are some advantages to
civilization."

"Shut up, kid," Aahz hissed back.

"So even though I know you'd love to beat these two
to a bloody pulp, we can't let you do it. They must be
hanged in accordance with the law!"

"What?"

I'm not sure if I said it, or Aahz, or if we cried out in
unison. Whichever it was, it was nearly drowned out in
the enthusiastic roar of the crowd.

A soldier seized my wrists and twisted them painfully
behind my back. Looking about, I saw the same thing had
happened to Aahz. Needless to say, this was not the support we had been hoping for.

"What did you expect?" the officer sneered at us. "If
you wanted help from the military, you shouldn't have
included us on your list of customers. If we had had our
way, we would have strung you up a week ago. The only
reason we held back was these yokels had given you extra
time and we were afraid of a riot if we tried anything."

Our wrists were secured by thongs now. We were
slowly being herded toward a lone tree in front of one of
the open-air restaurants.

"Has anyone got some rope?" the officer called to the
crowd.

Just our luck, somebody did. It was passed rapidly to
the officer, who began ceremoniously tying nooses.

"Psst! kid!" Aahz whispered.

"What now?" I mumbled bitterly.

My faith in Aahz's advice was at an all-time low.

"When they go to hang you, fly!"

"What?"

Despite myself, I was seized with new hope.

"C'mon, kid. Wake up! Fly. Like I taught you on the
trail."

"They'd just shoot me down."

"Not fly away, dummy. Just fly. Hover at the end of the rope and twitch. They'll think you're hanging."

I thought about it . . . hard. It might work, but . . . I noticed they were tossing the nooses over a lower limb of the tree.

"Aahz! I can't do it. I can't levitate us both. I'm not that good yet."

"Not both of us, kid. Just you. Don't worry about me."

"But . . . Aahz . . ."

"Keep my disguise up, though. If they figure out I'm a demon they'll burn the bodies . . . both of them."

"But Aahz . . ."

We were out of time. Rough hands shoved us forward and started fitting the nooses over our heads.

I realized with a start I had no time to think about Aahz. I'd need all my concentration to save myself, if there was even time for that!

I closed my eyes and sought desperately for a force line in the air. There was one there . . . faint, but there. I began to focus on it.

The noose tightened around my neck and I felt my feet leave the ground. I felt panic rising in me and forced it down.

Actually it was better this way. They should feel weight on the rope as they raised me. I concentrated on the force line again . . . focus . . . draw the energies . . . redirect them.

I felt a slight loosening of the noose. Remembering Aahz's lectures on control, I held the energies right there and tried an experimental breath. I could get air! Not much, it was true, but enough to survive.

What else did I have to do? Oh yes, I had to twitch. I thought back to how a squirrel-badger acted when caught in a snare.

I kicked my legs slightly and tried an experimental tremor. It had the overall effect of tightening the noose. I decided to try another tactic. I let my head loll to one side and extended my tongue out of the corner of my mouth.

It worked. There was a sudden increase in the volume of the catcalls from the crowd to reward my efforts.

I held that pose.

My tongue was rapidly drying out, but I forced my mind away from it. To avoid involuntarily swallowing, I tried to think of other things.

Poor Aahz. For all his gruff criticism and claims of not caring for anyone else but himself, his last act had been to think of my welfare. I promised myself that when I got down from here. . . .

What would happen when I got down from here? What do they do with bodies in this town? Do they bury them? It occurred to me it might be better to hang than be buried alive.

"The law says they're supposed to hang there until they rot!"

The officer's voice seemed to answer my thoughts and brought my mind back to the present.

"Well, they aren't hanging in front of the law's restaurant!" came an angry voice in response.

"Tell you what. We'll come back at sundown and cut them down."

"Sundown? Do you realize how much money I could lose before sundown? Nobody wants to eat at a place where a corpse dangles its toes in his soup. I've already lost most of the lunch rush!"

"Hmm . . . It occurs to me that if the day's business means that much to you, you should be willing to share a little of the profit."

"So that's the way it is, is it? Oh, very well. Here . . . for your troubles."

There was the sound of coins being counted out.

"That isn't very much. I have to share with my men, you know."

"You drive a hard bargain! I didn't know bandits had officers."

More coins were counted, accompanied by the officer's chuckle. It occurred to me that instead of studying magik,

I should be devoting my time to bribes and graft. It seemed to work better.

"Men!" the officer called. "Cut this carrion down and haul it out of town. Leave it at the city limits as a warning to anyone else who would seek to cheat the citizens of Twixt."

"You're too considerate." The restaurant owner's voice was edged with sarcasm.

"Think nothing of it, citizen," the officer sneered.

I barely remembered to stop flying before they cut the rope. I bit my tongue as I started into the ground, and risked sneaking it back into my mouth. No one noticed.

Unseen hands grabbed me under the armpits and by the ankles, and the journey began to the city limits.

Now that I knew I wasn't going to be buried, my thoughts returned to my future.

First, I would have to do something to Frumple. What, I wasn't sure, but something. I owed Aahz that much. Maybe I could restore Quigley and enlist his aid. He was supposed to be a demon hunter. He was probably better equipped to handle a Deveel than I was. Then again, remembering Quigley, that might not be a valid assumption.

Then there was Isstvan. What was I going to do about him? I wasn't sure I could beat him with Aahz's help. Without it, I wouldn't stand a chance.

"This should be far enough. Shall we hang them again?"

I froze at the suggestion. Fortunately the voice at my feet had different ideas.

"Why bother? I haven't seen an officer yet who'd move a hundred paces from a bar. Let's just dump 'em here."

There was a general chorus of assent, and the next minute I was flying through the air again. I tried to relax for the impact, but the ground knocked the wind out of me again.

If I was going to continue my efforts to master flying, I'd have to devote more time to the art of forced landings.

I lay there motionless. I couldn't hear the soldiers any more, but I didn't want to run the risk of sitting up and betraying the fact I wasn't dead.

"Are you going to lay there all day or are you going to help me get untied?"

My eyes flew open involuntarily. Aahz was sitting there grinning down at me.

There was only one sensible thing to do, and I did it. I fainted.

# XV:

*"Anyone who uses the phrase 'easy as taking candy from a baby' has never tried taking candy from a baby."*

—R. HOOD

"**C**an we move now?" I asked.

"Not yet, kid. Wait until the lights have been out for a full day."

"You mean a full hour."

"Whatever. Now shut up and keep watching."

We were waiting in the dead-end alley across the street from Frumple's shop. Even though we were supposedly secure in our new disguises, I was uneasy being back in the same town where I had been hung. It's a hard feeling to describe to someone who hasn't experienced it. Then too, it was strange being with Aahz after I had gotten used to the idea of him being dead.

Apparently the neck muscles of a Pervect are considerably stronger than those of a human. Aahz had simply tensed those muscles and they provided sufficient support to keep the noose from cutting off his air supply.

As a point of information, Aahz had further informed me that his scales provided better armor than most chain-mail or plate armor available in this dimension. I had heard once that demons could only be destroyed by specially constructed weapons or by burning. It seemed the old legends may have actually had some root in fact.

"Okay, kid," Aahz whispered. "I guess we've waited long enough."

He eased himself out of the alley and led me in a long circle around the shop, stopping again only when we had returned to our original spot by the alley.

"Well, what do you think, kid?"

"Don't know. What were we looking for?"

"Tell me again about how you planned to be a thief," Aahz sighed. "Look, kid. We're looking over a target. Right?"

"Right," I replied, glad to be able to agree with something.

"Okay, how many ways in and out of that shop did you see?"

"Just one. The one across the street there."

"Right. Now how do you figure we're going to get into the shop?"

"I don't know," I said honestly.

"C'mon, kid. If there's only one way in. . . ."

"You mean we're just going to walk in the front door?"

"Why not? We can see from here the door's open."

"Well . . . if you say so, Aahz. I just thought it would be harder than that."

"Whoa! Nobody said it was going to be easy. Just because the door's open doesn't mean the door's open."

"I didn't quite get that, Aahz."

"Think, kid. We're after a Deveel, right? He's got access to all kinds of magic and gimmicks. Now what say you close your eyes and take another look at that door."

I did as I was told. Immediately the image of a glowing cage sprang into my mind, a cage that completely enclosed the shop.

"He's got some kind of ward up, Aahz," I informed my partner.

It occurred to me that a few short weeks ago I would have held such a structure in awe. Now, I accepted it as relatively normal, just another obstacle to be overcome.

"Describe it to me," Aahz hissed.

"Well . . . it's bright . . . whitish purple . . . there's a series of bars and crossbars forming squares about a handspan across. . . ."

"Is it just over the door, or all over the shop?"

"All over the shop. The top's covered, and the bars run right into the ground."

"Hmm, well, we'll just have to go through it. Listen up, kid. Time for a quick lesson."

I opened my eyes and looked at the shop again. The building looked as innocent as it had when we first circled it. It bothered me that I couldn't sense the cage's presence the way I could our own wards.

"What is it, Aahz?" I asked uneasily.

"Hmm? Oh, it's a ward, kind of like the ones we use, but a lot nastier."

"Nastier, how?"

"Well, the kind of wards I taught you to build are an early warning system and not much else. From the sounds of it, the stuff Frumple is using will do considerably more. Not only will it kill you, it'll knock you into pieces smaller than dust. It's called disintegration."

"And we're going to go through it?" I asked, incredulously.

"*After* you've had a quick lesson. Now, remember your feather drills? How you'd wrap your mind around the feather for control?"

"Yeah," I said, puzzled.

"Well, I want you to do the same thing, but without the feather. Pretend you're holding something that isn't there. Form the energies into a tube."

"Then what?"

"Then you insert the tube into one of the squares in the cage and expand it."

"That's all?"

"That's it. C'mon now. Give it a try."

I closed my eyes and reached out with my mind. Choosing a square in the center of the open doorway, I inserted my mental tube and began to expand it. As it touched the bars forming the square, I experienced a tingle and a physical pressure as if I had encountered a tangible object.

"Easy, kid," Aahz said softly. "We just want to bend the bars a bit, not break them."

I expanded the tube. The bars gave way slowly, until they met with the next set. Then I experienced another tingle and additional pressure.

"Remember, kid. Once we're inside, take your time. Wait for your eyes to adjust to the dark. We don't want to tip Frumple off by stumbling around and knocking things over."

I was having to strain now. The tube had reached another set of bars now, making it a total of twelve bars I was forcing outward.

"Have you got it yet?" Aahz's whisper sounded anxious.

"Just a second . . . Yes!"

The tube was now big enough for us to crawl through.

"Are you sure?"

"Yes."

"Okay. Lead the way, kid. I'll be right behind you."

Strangely enough, I felt none of my usual doubts as I strode boldly across the street to the shop. Apparently my confidence in my abilities was growing, for I didn't even hesitate as I began to crawl through the tube. The only bad moment I had was when I suddenly realized I was crawling on thin air about a foot off the ground. Apparently I had set the tube a little too high, but no matter. It held! Next time I would know better.

I eased myself out of the end of the tube and stood in the shop's interior. I could hear the soft sounds of Aahz's passage behind me as I waited for my eyes to adjust to the dark.

"Ease away from the door, kid," came Aahz's whispered advice in my ear as he stood behind me. "You're standing in a patch of moonlight. And you can collapse the tube now."

Properly notified, I shifted away from the moonlight. I was pleased to note, however, that releasing the tube did not make a significant difference in my mental energies. I was progressing to where I could do more difficult feats with less energy than when I started. I was actually starting to feel like a magician.

I heard a slight noise behind me and craned my neck to look. Aahz was quietly drawing the curtains over the door.

I smiled grimly to myself. Good! We don't want witnesses.

My eyes were nearly adjusted now. I could make out shapes and shadows in the darkness. There was a dark lump in the corner that breathed heavily. Frumple!

I felt a hand on my shoulder. Aahz pointed out a lamp on a table and held up four fingers.

I nodded and started counting slowly to four. As I reached the final number, I focused a quick flash of energy at the lamp, and its wick burst into flame, lighting the shop's interior.

Aahz was kneeling beside Frumple, knife in hand. Apparently he had succeeded in finding at least some of our weapons in the dark.

Frumple sat up blinking, then froze in place. Aahz had the point of his knife hovering a hairsbreadth from the Deveel's throat.

"Hello, Frumple," he smiled. "Remember us?"

"You!" gasped the Deveel. "You're supposed to be dead!"

"Dead?" Aahz purred. "How could any harm befall us with our old pal Frumple helping us blend with the citizenry?"

"Gentlemen!" our victim squealed. "There seems to have been a mistake!"

"That's right," I commented. "And you made it."

"You don't understand!" Frumple persisted, "I was surprised and horrified when I heard about your deaths."

"Yeah, we weren't too happy about it ourselves."

"Later, kid. Look, Frumple. Right now we have both the ability and the motive to kill you. Right?"

"But I. . . ."

"Right?"

Aahz moved the knife until the point was indenting the skin on Frumple's throat.

"Right!" the Deveel whispered.

"Okay, then." Aahz withdrew the knife and tucked it back in his waistband. "Now let's talk business."

"I . . . I don't understand," Frumple stammered, rubbing his throat with one hand as if to assure himself that it was still there.

"What it means," Aahz explained, "is that we want your help more than we want revenge. Don't relax too much, though. The choice wasn't that easy."

"I . . . I see. Well, what can I do for you?"

"C'mon, Frumple. You can honor our original deal. You've got to admit we've laid one heck of a false trail for your two fugitives. Now it's your turn. Just restore my powers and we'll be on our way."

The Deveel blanched, or at least he turned from red to pink.

"I can't do that!" he exclaimed.

"What?"

The knife appeared in Aahz's hand again as if by magik.

"Now look, you double-dealing refugee. Either you restore my powers or. . . ."

"You don't understand," Frumple pleaded. "I don't mean I won't restore your powers. I mean I can't. I don't know what's wrong with you or how to counter it. That's why I set you up with the mob. I was afraid if I told you before, you wouldn't believe me. I've spent too much time establishing myself here to risk being exposed by an unsatisfied customer. I'm sorry, I really am, and I know you'll probably kill me, but I can't help you!"

# XVI:

*"Just because something doesn't do what you planned it to do doesn't mean it's useless."*

—T. Edison

"Hmmm," Aahz said thoughtfully. "So you're powerless to restore my powers?"

"Does that mean we can kill him after all?" I asked eagerly. I had been hopeful of having Aahz's powers restored, but in lieu of that, I was still a bit upset over having been hung.

"You're a rather vicious child," Frumple looked at me speculatively. "What's a Pervect doing traveling with a Klahd, anyway?"

"Who's a clod?" I bristled.

"Easy, kid," Aahz said soothingly. "Nothing personal. Everyone who's native to this dimension is a Klahd. Klah . . . Klahds . . . get it?"

"Well, I don't like the sound of it," I grumbled.

"Relax, kid. What's in a name, anyway?"

"Then it doesn't really matter to you if people call you a Pervect or a Pervert?"

"Watch your mouth, kid. Things are going bad enough without you getting cheeky."

"Gentlemen, gentlemen," Frumple interrupted. "If you're going to fight would you mind going outside? I mean, this *is* my shop."

"Can we kill him now, Aahz?"

"Ease up, kid. Just because he can't restore my powers doesn't mean he's totally useless. I'm sure that he'll be more than happy to help us, particularly after he failed to pay up on our last deal. Right, Frumple?"

"Oh, definitely. Anything I can do to make up for the inconvenience I've caused you."

"Inconvenience?" I asked incredulously.

"Steady, kid. Well, Frumple, you could start by returning the stuff we left here when we went off on your little mission."

"Of course. I'll get it for you."

The Deveel started to rise, only to find Aahz's knife threatening him again.

"Don't trouble yourself, Frumple, old boy," Aahz smiled. "Just point out where they are and we'll fetch them ourselves . . . and keep your hands where I can see them."

"The . . . your things are over there . . . in the big chest against the wall," Frumple's eyes never left the knife as he spoke.

"Check it out, kid."

I did and, surprisingly, the items were exactly where the Deveel said they would be. There was, however, an intriguing collection of other strange items in the chest also.

"Hey, Aahz!" I called. "Take a look at this!"

"Sure, kid."

He backed across the shop to join me. As he did, he flipped the knife into what I now recognized as a throwing grip. Apparently Frumple recognized it too, because he stayed frozen in position.

"Well, what have we here?" Aahz chortled.

"Gentlemen," the Deveel called plaintively. "I could probably help you better if I knew what you needed."

"True enough," Aahz responded, reclaiming his weapons.

"Frumple, it occurs to me we haven't been completely open with you. That will have to be corrected if we're going to be allies."

"Wait a minute, Aahz," I interrupted. "What makes you think we can trust him after he's tried so hard to get us killed?"

"Simple, kid. He tried to get us killed to protect himself, right?"

"Well. . . ."

"So once we explain it's in his own self-interest to help us, he should be completely trustworthy."

"Really?" I sneered.

"Well, as trustworthy as any Deveel can be," Aahz admitted.

"I resent the implications of that, Pervert!" Frumple exclaimed. "If you want any help, you'd better. . . ." Aahz's knife flashed through the air and thunked into the wall scant inches from the Deveel's head.

"Shut up and listen, Frumple!" he snarled. "And that's Pervect!"

"What's in a name, Aahz?" I asked innocently.

"Shut up, kid. Okay, Frumple, does the name Isstvan mean anything to you?"

"No. Should it?"

"It should if you want to stay alive. He's a madman magician who's trying to take over the dimensions, starting with this one."

"Why should that concern me?" Frumple frowned. "We Deveels trade with anyone who can pay the price. We don't concern ourselves with analyzing politics or mental stability. If we only dealt with sane beings, it would cut our business by a third . . . maybe more."

"Well, you'd better concern yourself this time. Maybe you didn't hear me. Isstvan is starting with this dimension. He's out to get a monopoly on Klah's energies to use on other dimensions. To do that, he's out to kill anyone else in this dimension who knows how to tap those energies. He's not big on sharing."

"Hmmm. Interesting theory, but where's the proof—I mean, who's he supposed to have killed?"

"Garkin, for one," I said, dryly.

"That's right," Aahz snarled. "You're so eager to know why the two of us are traveling together. Well, Skeeve here was Garkin's apprentice until Isstvan sent his assassins to wipe out the competition."

"Assassins?"

"That's right. You saw two of them, those Imps you teleported about a week back." Aahz flourished the assassin's cloak we had acquired.

"Where did you think we got this? In a rummage sale?"

"Hmmm," Frumple commented thoughtfully.

"And he's arming them with tech weapons. Take a look at this crossbow quarrel."

Aahz lobbed one of the missiles to the Deveel who caught it deftly and examined it closely.

"Hmmm. I didn't notice that before. It's a good camouflage job, but totally unethical."

"Now do you see why enlisting your aid takes priority over the pleasure of slitting your lying throat?"

"I see what you mean," Frumple replied without rancor. "It's most convincing. But what can I do?"

"You tell us. You Deveels are supposed to have wonders for every occasion. What have you got that would give us an edge over a madman who knows his magik?"

Frumple thought for several minutes. Then shrugged. "I can't think of a thing just offhand. I haven't been stocking weapons lately. Not much call for them in this dimension."

"Terrific," I said. "Can we kill him now, Aahz?"

"Say, could you put a muzzle on him?" Frumple said. "What's your gripe anyway, Skeeve?"

"I don't take well to being hung," I snarled.

"Really? Well, you'll get used to it if you keep practicing magik. It's being burned that's really a pain."

"Wait a minute, Frumple," Aahz interrupted. "You're acting awfully casual about hanging for someone who was so surprised to see us alive."

"I was. I underestimated your apprentice's mastery of the energies. If I had thought you could escape, I would have thought of something else. I *was* trying to get you killed, after all."

"He doesn't sound particularly trustworthy," I observed.

"You will notice, my young friend, that I stated my intentions in the past tense. Now that we share a common goal, you'll find me much easier to deal with."

"Which brings us back to our original question," Aahz asserted. "What can you do for us, Frumple?"

"I really don't know," the Deveel admitted. "Unless . . . I know! I can send you to the Bazaar!"

"The Bazaar?" I asked.

"The Bazaar on Deva! If you can't find what you need there, it doesn't exist. Why didn't I think of that before? That's the answer!"

He was on his feet now, moving toward us.

"I know you're in a hurry, so I'll get you started. . . ."

"Not so fast, Frumple."

Aahz had his sword out menacing the Deveel.

"We want a guarantee this is a round trip you're sending us on."

"I . . . I don't understand."

"Simple. You tried to get rid of us once. It occurs to me you might be tempted to send us off to some backwater dimension with no way to get back."

"But I give you my word that. . . ."

"We don't want your word," Aahz grinned. "We want your presence."

"What?"

"Where we go, you go. You're coming with us, just to be extra sure we get back."

"I can't do that!" Frumple seemed honestly terrified.

"I've been banned from Deva! You don't know what they'd do to me if I went back."

"That's too bad. We want a guaranteed return before we budge, and that's you!"

"Wait a minute! I think I've got the answer!"

The Deveel began frantically rummaging through chests. I watched, fascinated, as an astounding array of strange objects emerged as he searched.

"Here it is!" he cried at last, holding his prize aloft.

It appeared to be a metal rod, about eight inches long and two inches in diameter. It had strange markings on its sides, and a button on the end.

"A D-Hopper!" Aahz exclaimed. "I haven't seen one of those in years."

Frumple tossed it to him.

"There you go. Is that guarantee enough?"

"What is it, Aahz?" I asked, craning my neck to see.

He seized the ends of the rod and twisted in opposite directions. Apparently it was constructed of at least two parts, because the symbols began to slide around the rod in opposite directions.

"Depending on where you want to go, you align different symbols. Then you just push the button and. . . ."

"Wait a minute!" Frumple cried. "We haven't settled on a price for that yet!"

"Price?" I asked.

"Yeah, price! Those things don't grow on trees, you know."

"If you will recall," Aahz murmured, "you still owe us from our last deal."

"True enough," Frumple agreed. "But as you yourself pointed out, those D-Hoppers are rare. A real collector's item. It's only fair that our contract be renegotiated at a slightly higher fee."

"Frumple, we're in too much of a hurry to argue," Aahz announced. "I'll say once what we're willing to relinquish over and above our original deal and you can take it or leave it. Fair enough?"

"What did you have in mind?" Frumple asked, rubbing his hands together eagerly.

"Your life."

"My . . . Oh! I see. Yes, that . . . um . . . should be an acceptable price."

"I'm surprised at you, Frumple," I chimed in. "Letting a collector's item go that cheap."

"C'mon, kid." Aahz was adjusting the settings on the D-Hopper. "Let's get moving."

"Just a second, Aahz. I want to get my sword."

"Leave it. We can pick it up on the way back."

"Say, Aahz, how long does it take to travel between dimensions any. . . ."

The walls of Frumple's hut suddenly dissolved in a kaleidoscope of color.

"Not long, kid. In fact, we're there."

And we were.

# XVII:

*"The wonders of the ages assembled for your edification, education, and enjoyment—for a price."*

—P. T. Barnum

While I knew my home dimension wasn't particularly colorful, I never really considered it drab . . . until I first set eyes on the Bazaar at Deva.

Even though both Aahz and Frumple, and even the Imps, had referred to this phenomenon, I had never actually sat back and tried to envision it. It was just as well. Anything I could have fantasized would have been dwarfed by the real thing.

The Bazaar seemed to stretch endlessly in all directions as far as the eye could see. Tents and lean-tos of all designs and colors were gathered in irregular clumps that shoved against each other for more room.

There were thousands of Deveels everywhere of every age and description. Tall Deveels, fat Deveels, lame Deveels, bald Deveels, all moved about until the populace gave the appearance of being one seething mass with multiple heads and tails. There were other beings scattered through the crowd. Some of them looked like nightmares come to life; others I didn't recognize as being alive until they moved, but they all made noise.

The noise! Twixt had seemed noisy to me after my secluded life with Garkin, but the clamor that assailed my ears now defied all description. There were shrieks and dull explosions and strange burbling noises emanating from the depths of the booths around us, competing with the constant din of barter. It seemed no one spoke below a shout. Whether weeping piteously, barking in anger, or displaying bored indifference, all bartering was to be done at the top of your lungs.

"Welcome to Deva, kid," Aahz gestured expansively. "What do you think?"

"It's loud," I observed.

"What?"

"I said, 'it's loud!' " I shouted.

"Oh, well. It's a bit livelier than your average Farmer's Market or Fisherman's Wharf, but there are noisier places to be."

I was about to respond when a passerby careened into me. He, or she, had eyes spaced all around his head and fur-covered tentacles instead of arms.

"Wzklp!" it said, waving a tentacle as it continued on its way.

"Aahz!"

"Yeah, kid?"

"It just occurred to me. What language do they speak on Deva?"

"Hmm? Oh! Don't worry about it, kid. They speak all languages here. No Deveel that's been hatched would let a sale get away just because they couldn't speak the right tongue. Just drop a few sentences on 'em in Klahdish and they'll adapt fast enough."

"Okay, Aahz. Now that we're here, where do we go first?"

There was no answer. I tore my eyes away from the Bazaar and glanced at my partner. He was standing motionless, sniffing the air.

"Aahz?"

"Hey kid, do you smell that?" he asked eagerly.

I sniffed the air.

"Yeah!" I gagged. "What died?"

"C'mon, kid. Follow me."

He plunged off into the crowd, leaving me little choice but to trail after him. Hands plucked at our sleeves as we passed, and various Deveels leaned out of their stalls and tents to call to us as we passed, but Aahz didn't slacken his pace. I couldn't get a clear look at any of the displays as we passed. Keeping up with Aahz demanded most of my concentration. One tent, however, did catch my eye.

"Look, Aahz!" I cried.

"What?"

"It's raining in that tent!"

As if in answer to my words, a boom of thunder and a crackle of lightning erupted from the display.

"Yeah. So?" Aahz dismissed it with a glance.

"What are they selling, rain?"

"Naw. Weather-control devices. They're scattered through the whole Bazaar instead of hanging together in one section. Something about the devices interfering with each other."

"Are all the displays that spectacular?"

"That isn't spectacular, kid. They used to do tornadoes until the other booths complained and they had to limit their demonstrations to the tame stuff. Now hurry up!"

"Where are we going anyway, Aahz? And what *is* that smell?"

The repulsive aroma was growing noticeably stronger.

"That," proclaimed Aahz, coming to a halt in front of a dome-shaped tent, "is the smell of Pervish cooking!"

"Food? We came all this way so you could have a meal?"

"First things first, kid. I haven't had a decent meal since Garkin called me out of the middle of a party and stranded me in your idiot dimension."

"But we're supposed to be looking for something to use against Isstvan."

"Relax, kid. I haggle better on a full stomach. Just wait here. I won't be long."

"Wait here? Can't I go in with you?"

"I don't think you'd like it, kid. To anyone who wasn't born on Perv, the food looks even worse than it smells."

I found that hard to believe, but pursued the argument gamely.

"I'm not all that weak-stomached, you know. When I was living in the woods, I ate some pretty weird things myself."

"I'll tell ya, kid, the main problem with Pervish food is keeping the goo from crawling out of the bowl while you're eating it."

"I'll wait here," I decided.

"Good. Like I say, I won't be long. You can watch the dragons until I get back."

"Dragons?" I said, but he had already disappeared through the tent flap.

I turned slowly and looked at the display behind me.

Dragons!

There was an enormous stall stocked with dragons not fifteen feet from where I was standing. Most of the beasts were tethered at the back wall which kept me from seeing them as we approached, but upon direct viewing there was no doubt they were dragons.

Curiosity made me drift over to join the small crowd in front of the stall. The stench was overwhelming, but after a whiff of Pervish cooking, it seemed almost pleasant.

I had never seen a dragon before, but the specimens in the stall lived up to the expectations of my daydreams. They were huge, easily ten or fifteen feet high at the shoulder and a full thirty feet long. Their necks were long and serpentine, and their clawed feet dug great gouges in the ground as they shifted their weight nervously.

I was surprised to see how many varieties there were.

It had never occurred to me that there might be more than one type of dragon, but here was living proof to the contrary. Besides the green dragons I had always envisioned, there were red, black, gold and blue dragons. There was even one that was mauve. Some were winged and some weren't. Some had wide, massive jaws and others had narrow snouts. Some had eyes that were squinting and slanted, while others had huge moonlike eyes that never seemed to blink. They had two things in common, however: they were all big and they all looked thoroughly nasty.

My attention was drawn to the Deveel running the operation. He was the biggest Deveel I had ever seen, fully eight feet tall with arms like trees. It was difficult to say which was more fearsome in appearance, the dragons or their keeper.

He brought one of the red dragons to the center of the stall and released it with a flourish. The beast raised its head and surveyed the crowd with seething yellow eyes. The crowd fell back a few steps before that gaze. I seriously considered leaving.

The Deveel shouted a few words at the crowd in gibberish I couldn't understand, then picked up a sword from the rack by the wall.

Fast as a cat, the dragon arched his neck and spat a stream of fire at its keeper. By some miracle, the flame parted as it hit the Deveel and passed harmlessly on either side of him.

The keeper smiled and turned to shout a few more words at his audience. As he did, the dragon leapt at him with murderous intent. The Deveel dove to the ground and rolled out from under the attack as the beast landed with an impact that shook the tent. The dragon whirled, but the keeper was on his feet again, holding aloft a pendant before the beast's eyes.

I didn't understand his move, but apparently the dragon did, for it cowered back on its haunches. The Deveel pointed forcefully and it slunk back to its place at the back of the stall.

A small ripple of applause came from the crowd. Apparently they were impressed with the ferocity of the dragon's attack. Me, I was impressed by the pendant.

The keeper acknowledged the applause and launched into another spiel of gibberish, this time punctuated by gestures and exclamations.

I decided it was about time for me to go.

"Gleep!"

There was a tug at my sleeve.

I looked around. There, behind me, was a small dragon! Well, he was about four feet high and ten feet long, but after looking at the other dragons, he seemed small. He was green with big blue eyes and what appeared to be a drooping white mustache.

For a split second I was panicky, but that rapidly gave way to curiosity. He didn't look dangerous. He seemed quite content just standing there chewing on. . . .

My sleeve! The beast was eating a piece of my sleeve! I looked down and confirmed that part of my shirt was indeed missing.

"Gleep," said the dragon again, stretching his neck out for another mouthful.

"Go away!" I said, and cuffed him before I realized what I was doing.

"Gleep?" it said, puzzled.

I started to edge away. I was unsure of what to do if he cut loose with a blast of fire and therefore eager to avoid it.

"Gleep," it said, shuffling after me.

"Gazabkp!" roared a voice behind me.

I spun and found myself looking at a hairy stomach. I followed it up, way up, and saw the dragon keeper's face looming over me.

"I'm sorry," I apologized readily. "I don't speak your language."

"Oh. A Klahd!" The Deveel boomed. "Well, the statement still stands. Pay up!"

"Pay up for what?"

"For the dragon! What do you think, we're giving away samples?"

"Gleep!" said the dragon, pressing his head against my leg.

"There seems to be some mistake," I said hastily.

"I'll say there is," the Deveel scowled. "And you're making it. We don't take kindly to shoplifters on Deva!"

"Gleep!" said the dragon.

Things were rapidly getting out of hand. If I ever needed Aahz's help or advice, it was now. I shot a desperate glance toward the tent he was in, hoping beyond hope to see him emerge.

He wasn't there. In fact, the tent wasn't there! It was gone, vanished into thin air, and so had Aahz!

# XVIII:

*"No matter what the product or service
might be, you can find it somewhere else
cheaper!"*

—E. SCROOGE

"Where did that tent go?" I demanded desperately.

"What tent?" The keeper blinked, looming behind me.

"That tent," I exclaimed, pointing at the now vacant space.

The Deveel frowned, craning his neck, which at his height, gave him considerable visibility.

"There isn't any tent there," he announced with finality.

"I know! That's the point!"

"Hey! Quit trying to change the subject!" The keeper growled, poking me in the chest with an unbelievably large finger. "Are you going to pay for the dragon or not?"

I looked around for support, but no one was watching. Apparently disputes such as this were common on Deva.

"I told you there's been a mistake! I don't want your dragon."

"Gleep!" said the dragon, cocking his head at me.

"Don't give me that!" the keeper boomed. "If you didn't want him, why did you feed him?"

"I didn't feed him! He ate a piece of my sleeve!"

"Gleep!" said the dragon, making another unsuccessful pass at my shirt.

"So you admit he got food from you?"

"Well . . . in a manner of speaking . . . Yeah! So what?" I was getting tired of being shouted at.

"So pay up! He's no good to me anymore."

I surveyed the dragon. He didn't seem to be any the worse for having eaten the shirt.

"What's wrong with him? He looks all right to me."

"Gleep!" said the dragon, and sidled up to me again.

"Oh! He's fine," the keeper sneered. "Except now he's attached. An attached dragon isn't any good except to the person or thing he's attached to."

"Well, who's he attached to?"

"Don't get smart with me! He's attached to you! Has been ever since you fed him."

"Well, feed him again and unattach him! I have pressing matters elsewhere."

"Just like that, huh?" the Deveel said skeptically, towering to new heights. "You know very well it doesn't work that way. Once a dragon's attached, it's attached forever. That's why they're so valuable."

"Forever?" I asked.

"Well . . . until one of you dies. But any fool knows not to feed a dragon unless they want it attached to them. The idiot beasts are too impressionable, especially the young ones like this."

I looked at the dragon again. He was very young. His wings were just beginning to bud, which I took as a sign of immaturity, and his fangs were needle-sharp instead of worn to rounded points like his brethren in the stall. Still, there was strength in the muscles rippling beneath those scales . . . yes, I decided, I'd back my dragon in a fight against any. . . .

"Gleep!" said the dragon, licking both ends of his mustache simultaneously with his forked tongue.

That brought me to my senses. A dragon? What did I want with a dragon?

"Well," I said haughtily, "I guess I'm not just any fool, then. If I had known the consequences of allowing him to eat my sleeve, I would have . . ."

"Look, sonny!" The Deveel snarled, poking my chest again. "If you think you're going to. . . ."

Something inside me snapped. I knocked his hand away with a fury that surprised me.

"The name isn't 'Sonny,' " I hissed in a low voice I didn't recognize as my own. "It's Skeeve! Now lower your voice when you're talking to me and keep your dirty finger to yourself!"

I was shaking, though whether from rage or from fear I couldn't tell. I had spent my entire burst of emotion in that tirade and now found myself wondering if I would survive the aftermath.

Surprisingly, the keeper gave ground a few steps at my tirade, and was now studying me with new puzzlement. I felt a pressure at the back of my legs and risked a glance. The dragon was now crouched behind me, craning his neck to peer around my waist at the keeper.

"I'm sorry." The keeper was suddenly humble and fawning. "I didn't recognize you at first. You said your name was . . . ?"

"Skeeve." I prompted haughtily.

"Skeeve." He frowned thoughtfully. "Strange. I don't remember that name."

I wasn't sure who or what he thought I was, but if I had learned one thing traveling with Aahz, it was to recognize and seize an advantage when I saw one.

"The secrecy surrounding my identity should be a clue in itself, if you know what I mean," I murmured, giving him my best conspiratorial wink.

"Of course," he responded. "I should have realized immediately. . . ."

"No matter," I yawned. "Now then, about the dragon. . . ."

"Yes. Forgive me for losing my temper, but you can see my predicament."

It seemed strange having someone that immense simpering at me, but I rose to the occasion.

"Well, I'm sure we can work something out," I smiled.

As I spoke, a thought flashed through my head. Aahz had all our money! I didn't have a single item of any value on me except. . . .

I reached into my pocket, forcing myself to make the move casual. It was still there! The charm I had taken from Quigley's statue-body that allowed the wearer to see through spells. I had taken it when Aahz wasn't looking and had kept it hidden in case it might be useful in some crisis. Well, this definitely looked like a crisis!

"Here!" I said, tossing the charm to him. "I believe this should settle our accounts."

He caught it deftly and gave it a fast, squinting appraisal.

"This?" he said. "You want to purchase a hatchling dragon for this?"

I had no idea of the charm's relative worth, but bluffing had gotten me this far.

"I do not haggle," I said coldly. "That is my first and final offer. If it is not satisfactory, then return the charm and see if you can get a better price for an attached dragon."

"You drive a hard bargain, Skeeve." The Deveel was still polite, but his smile looked like it hurt. "Very well, it's a deal. Shake on it."

He extended his hand.

There was a sudden hissing noise and my vision was obscured. The dragon had arched his neck forward over my head and was confronting the Deveel eye-to-eye. His attitude was suddenly a miniature version of the ferocity I had seen displayed earlier by his larger brethren. I realized with a start that he was defending me!

Apparently the keeper realized it too, for he jerked back his hand as if he had just stuck it in an open fire.

". . . if you could call off your dragon long enough for us to close the deal?" he suggested with forced politeness.

I wasn't sure just how I was supposed to do this, but I was willing to give it a try.

"He's okay!" I shouted, thumping the dragon on the side of the neck to get his attention.

"Gleep?" said the dragon, turning his head to peer into my face.

I noticed his breath was bad enough to kill an insect in flight.

"It's okay," I repeated, edging out from under his neck.

Since I was already moving, I stepped forward and shook the keeper's hand. He responded absently, never taking his eyes from the dragon.

"Say," I said. "Confidentially, I'm rather new to the dragon game. What does he eat . . . besides shirts, I mean."

"Oh, a little of this and a little of that. They're omnivorous, so they can eat anything, but they're picky eaters. Just let him alone and he'll choose his own diet . . . old clothes, selected leaves, house pets."

"Terrific!" I mumbled.

"Well, if you'll excuse me I've got other customers to talk to."

"Just a minute! Don't I get one of those pendants like you used to control the big dragons?"

"Hmm? What for?"

"Well . . . to control my dragon."

"Those are to control unattached dragons. You don't need one for one that's attached to you and it wouldn't work on a dragon that's attached to someone else."

"Oh," I said, with a wisdom I didn't feel.

"If you want one, though, I have a cousin who has a stall that sells them. It's about three rows up and two rows over. It might be a good investment for you. Could save wear and tear on your dragon if you come up against an unattached dragon. It'd give Junior there a better chance of growing up."

"That brings up another question," I said. "How long does it take?"

"Not long. It's just three rows up and. . . ."

"No. I mean how long until my dragon reaches maturity?"

"Oh, not more than four or five centuries."

"Gleep!"

I'm not sure if the dragon said that or I did.

# XIX:

*"By persevering over all obstacles and distractions, one may unfailingly arrive at his chosen goal or destination."*

—C. COLUMBUS

"C'mon, Gleep," I said.

"Gleep," my dragon responded, falling in behind me.

Now that I was the not-so-proud owner of a permanently immature dragon, I was more eager than ever to find Aahz. At the moment, I was alone in a strange dimension, penniless, and now I had a dragon tagging after me. The only way things could be worse would be if the situation became permanent, which could happen if Aahz decided to return to Klah without me.

The place previously occupied by the Pervish restaurant tent was definitely empty, even at close examination, so I decided to ask the Deveel running the neighboring booth.

"Um . . . excuse me, sir."

I decided I was going to be polite as possible for the duration of my stay on Deva. The last thing I needed was another dispute with a Deveel. It seemed, however, in this situation I needn't have worried.

"No excuses are necessary, young sahr." The proprietor smiled eagerly, displaying an impressive number of teeth.

"You are interested in purchasing a stick?"

"A stick?"

"Of course!" the Deveel gestured grandly around his stall. "The finest sticks in all the dimensions."

"Aah . . . thanks, but we have plenty of sticks in my home dimension."

"Not like these sticks, young sahr. You are from Klah, are you not?"

"Yes, why?"

"I can guarantee you, there are no such sticks as these in all of Klah. They come from a dimension only I have access to and I have not sold them in Klah or to anyone who was going there."

Despite myself, my curiosity was piqued. I looked again at the sticks lining the walls of the stall. They looked like ordinary sticks such as could be found anywhere.

"What do they do?" I asked cautiously.

"Aah! Different ones do different things. Some control animals, others control plants. A few very rare ones allow you to summon an army of warriors from the stones themselves. Some of the most powerful magicians of any dimension wield staffs of the same wood as these sticks, but for most people's purposes the smaller model will suffice."

"Gleep!" said the dragon, sniffing at one of the sticks.

"Leave it alone!" I barked, shoving his head away from the display.

All I needed was to have my dragon eat up the entire stock of one of these super-merchants.

"May I inquire, is that your dragon, young sahr?"

"Well . . . sort of."

"In that case, you might find a particular use for a stick most magicians wouldn't."

"What's that?"

"You could use it to beat your dragon."

"Gleep!" said the dragon, looking at me with his big blue eyes.

"Actually, I'm not really interested in a stick."

I thought I'd better get to my original purpose before this conversation got out of hand.

"Ridiculous, young sahr. Everybody should have a stick."

"The reason I stopped here in the first place is I wondered if you knew what happened to that tent."

"What tent, young sahr?"

I had a vague feeling of having had this conversation before.

"The tent that was right there next to your stall."

"The Pervish restaurant?" The Deveel's voice was tinged with horror.

"Gleep," said the dragon.

"Why would you seek such a place, young sahr? You seem well-bred and educated."

"I had a friend who was inside the tent when it vanished."

"You have a Pervert for a friend?" His voice had lost its friendly tone.

"Well actually . . . um . . . it's a long story."

"I can tell you this much, punk. It didn't disappear, it moved on," the Deveel snarled, without the accent or politeness he had displayed earlier.

"Moved on?"

"Yeah. It's a new ordinance we passed. All places serving Pervish food have to migrate. They cannot be established permanently, or even temporarily at any point in the Bazaar."

"Why?" I asked.

"Have you ever smelled Pervish food? It's enough to make a scavenger nauseous. Would you want to man a stall downwind of that for a whole day? In this heat?"

"I see what you mean," I admitted.

"Either they moved or the Bazaar did, and we have them outnumbered."

"But what exactly do you mean, move?"

"The tents! All that's involved is a simple spell or two. Either they constantly move at a slow pace, or they stay in one place for a short period and then scuttle off to a new location, but they all move."

"How does anyone find one, then, if they keep moving around?"

"That's easy, just follow your nose."

I sniffed the air experimentally. Sure enough, the unmistakable odor was still lingering in the air.

"Gleep!" the dragon had imitated my action and was now rubbing his nose with one paw.

"Well, thank you . . . for . . . your. . . ."

I was talking to thin air. The Deveel was at the other end of the stall, baring his teeth at another customer. It occurred to me that the citizens of Deva were not particularly concerned with social pleasantries beyond those necessary to transact a sale.

I set out to follow the smell of the Pervish restaurant with the dragon faithfully trailing along behind. Despite my growing desire to reunite with Aahz, my pace was considerably slower than that Aahz had set when we first arrived. I was completely mesmerized by this strange Bazaar and wanted to see as much of it as I could.

Upon more leisurely examination, there did seem to be a vague order to the Bazaar. The various stalls and booths were generally grouped by type of merchandise. This appeared to be more from circumstance than by plan. Apparently, if one Deveel set up a display, say, of invisible cloaks, in no time at all he had a pack of competitors in residence around him, each vying to top the other for quality of goods or prices. Most of the confused babble of voices were disputes between the merchants over the location of their respective stalls or the space occupied by the same.

The smell grew stronger as I wandered through an area specializing in exotic and magical jewelry, which I resisted the temptation to examine more closely. The temp-

tation was even stronger as I traversed an area which
featured weaponry. It occurred to me that I might find a
weapon here we could use against Isstvan, but the smell
of the Pervish food was even stronger now, and I steeled
myself to finish my search. We could look for a weapon
after I found Aahz. From the intensity of the stench, I was
sure we would find our objective soon.

"C'mon, Gleep," I encouraged.

The dragon was hanging back now and didn't respond
except to speed his pace a bit.

I expectantly rounded one last corner and came to an
abrupt halt. I had found the source of the odor.

I was looking at the back of a large display of some
alien livestock. There was a large pile of some moist green
and yellow substance in front of me. As I watched, a
young Deveel emerged from the display holding a shovel
filled with the same substance. He glanced at me quizzically as he heaved the load onto the pile and returned to
the display.

A dung heap! I had been following the smell of a dung
heap!

"Gleep!" said the dragon, looking at me quizzically.

He seemed to be asking me what we were going to do
next. That was a good question.

I stood contemplating my next move. Probably the best
chance would be to retrace our steps back to the stick
seller and try again.

"Spare a girl a little time, handsome?"

I whirled around. A girl was standing there, a girl unlike any I had ever seen before. She was Klahdish in appearance and could have passed for another of my
dimension except for her complexion and hair. Her skin
was a marvelous golden-olive hue, and her head was
crowned with a mane of light green hair that shimmered
in the sun. She was a little taller than me and incredibly
curvaceous, her generous figure straining against the con-
fines of her clothes.

". . . or have you really got a thing about dung heaps?" she concluded.

She had almond cat-eyes that danced with mischief as she talked.

"Um . . . are you talking to me?" I stammered.

"Of course I'm talking to you," she purred, coming close to me and twining her arms around my neck. "I'm certainly not talking to your dragon. I mean, he's cute and all, but my tastes don't run in those directions."

"Gleep!" said the dragon.

I felt my body temperature soar. The touch of her arms caused a tingling sensation which seemed to wreak havoc on my metabolism.

"Um . . . actually I'm looking for a friend," I blurted.

"Well, you've found one," she murmured, moving her body against me.

"Aah . . . I . . . um." Suddenly I was having trouble concentrating. "What is it you want?"

"Hmm," she said thoughtfully, "Even though it's not my normal line, I think I'd like to tell your fortune . . . free."

"Oh?" I said, surprised.

This was the first time since I reached the Bazaar that anyone had offered me anything for free. I didn't know if I should be happy or suspicious.

"You're going to have a fight," she whispered in my ear. "A big one."

"What?" I exclaimed. "When? With who?"

"Easy, handsome," she warned, tightening her grip around my neck. "When is in a very few minutes. With who is the rat pack over my shoulder . . . don't look right at them!"

Her final sharp warning checked my reflexive glance. Moving more cautiously, I snuck a peek out of the corner of my eye.

Lounging against a shop wall, watching us closely, were a dozen or so of the ugliest, nastiest-looking characters I had ever seen.

"Them? I mean, all of them?" I asked.

"Uh-huh!" she confirmed, snuggling into my chest.

"Why?" I demanded.

"I probably shouldn't tell you this," she smiled, "but because of me."

Only her firm grip on me kept me from dislodging her with a shove.

"You? What about you?"

"Well, they're an awfully greedy bunch. One way or another, they're going to make some money from this encounter. Normally, you'd give the money to me and I'd cut them in for a share. In the unlikely event that doesn't work, they'll pretend to be defending my honor and beat it out of you."

"But you don't understand! I don't have any money."

"I know that. That's why you're going to get into a fight, see?"

"If you knew I didn't have any money, why did you. . . ."

"Oh, I didn't know when I first stopped you. I found out just now when I searched you."

"Searched me?"

"Oh, come on, handsome. There's more ways to search a person than with your hands," she winked knowingly at me.

"Well, can't you tell them I don't have any money?"

"They wouldn't believe me. The only way they'd be convinced is searching you themselves."

"I'd be willing to let them if that's what it takes to convince them."

"I don't think you would," she smiled, stroking my face with her hand. "One of the things they'll look for is if you swallowed your money."

"Oh!" I said, "I see what you mean. But I can't fight them. I don't have any weapons."

"You have that little knife under your shirt at the small of your back," she pointed out.

I had forgotten about my skinning knife. I started to believe in her no-hands frisking technique.

"But I've never been in a fight before."

"Well, I think you're about to learn."

"Say, why are you telling me all this, anyway?" I asked.

"I don't know," she shrugged. "I like your act. That's why I singled you out in the first place. Then again, I feel a little guilty about having gotten you into this."

"Will you help me?"

"I don't feel *that* guilty, handsome," she smiled. "But there is one more thing I can do for you."

She started to pull me toward her.

"Wait a minute," I protested. "Won't that. . . ."

"Relax, handsome," she purred. "You're about to get pounded for offending my honor. You might as well get a little of the sweet along with the bitter."

Before I could protest further, she kissed me. Long and warm and sweet, she kissed me.

I had never been kissed by anyone except my mother. This was different! The fight, the dragon, Aahz, everything faded from my mind. I was lost in the wonder of that moment.

"Hey!"

A rough hand fell on my shoulder and pulled us apart.

"Is this shrimp bothering you, lady?"

The person on the other end of that hand was no taller than I was, but he was twice as broad and had short, twisted tusks protruding from his mouth. His cronies had fanned out behind him, effectively boxing me in against the dung heap.

I looked at the girl. She shrugged and backed away.

It looked like I was going to have to fight all of them. Me and the dragon. Terrific.

I remembered my skinning knife. It wasn't much, but it was all I had. As casually as I could, I reached behind me and tugged at my shirt, trying to pull it up so I could get at the knife. The knife promptly fell down inside my pants.

The wrecking crew started forward.

# XX:

*"With the proper consideration in choice of allies, victory may be guaranteed in any conflict."*

—B. ARNOLD

"Get 'em, Gleep!" I barked.

The dragon bounded into action, a move which I think surprised me more than it did my assailants.

It leaped between me and the advancing rat pack and crouched there, hissing menacingly. His tail gave a mighty lash which neatly swept the legs out from under two of the flanking members of the party. Somehow, he seemed much bigger when he was mad.

"Watch out! He's got a dragon!" the leader called.

"Thanks for the warning!" one of the fallen men growled, struggling to regain his feet.

"I've got him!" came a voice from my left.

I turned just in time to see a foot-long dagger flashing through the air at the dragon's neck. My dragon!

Suddenly I was back at the practice sessions. My mind darted out and grabbed at the knife. It jerked to a halt in midair and hovered there.

"Nice move, handsome!" the girl called.

"Hey! The shrimp's a magician!"

The pack fell back a few steps.

"That's right!" I barked. "Skeeve's the name, magik's the game. What kind of clod did you think you were dealing with?"

With that, I brought the dagger down, swooping it back and forth through their formation. I was mad now. One of these louts had tried to kill my dragon!

"A dozen of you isn't enough!" I shouted. "Go back and get some friends . . . if you have any!"

I cast about desperately for something else to throw. My eyes fell on the dung heap. I smiled to myself despite my anger. Why not?

In a moment I had great gobs of dung hurtling through the air at my assailants. My accuracy wasn't the best, but it was good enough as the outraged howls testified.

"Levitation!" the leader bawled. "Quanto! Stop him!"

"Right, boss!"

One of the plug-uglies waved in affirmation and started rummaging through his belt pouch.

He had made a mistake identifying himself. I didn't know what he was about to come up with, but I was sure I didn't want to wait and find out.

"Stop him, Gleep!" I ordered, pointing to the victim.

The dragon raised his head and fixed his gaze on the fumbling brigand. With a sound that might have been a roar if he were older, he shot a stream of flame and charged.

It wasn't much of a stream of flame, and it missed to boot, but it was enough to get the brigand's attention. He looked up to see a mountain of dragon flesh bearing down on him and panicked. Without pausing to call to his comrades, he spun and ran off screaming with the dragon in hot pursuit.

"Okay, shrimp! Let's see you stop this!"

I jerked my attention back to the leader. He was standing now, confidently holding aloft a stick. Yesterday it wouldn't have fazed me, but knowing what I did now, I froze. I didn't know what model it was, but apparently the leader was confident its powers would surpass my own.

He grinned evilly and slowly began to level the stick at me.

I tried desperately to think of a defense, but couldn't. I didn't even know what I was supposed to be defending against!

Suddenly, something flashed across my line of vision and the stick was gone.

I blinked and looked again. The stick was lying on the ground, split by a throwing knife, a black-handled throwing knife.

"Any trouble here, Master Skeeve?" a voice boomed.

I spun toward the source of the voice. Aahz was standing there, cocked crossbow leveled at the pack. He was grinning broadly, which I have mentioned before is not that comforting to anyone who doesn't know him.

"A Pervert!" the leader gasped.

"What?" Aahz swung the crossbow toward him.

"I mean a Pervect!" the leader amended hastily.

"That's better. How about it, Skeeve? You want 'em dead or running?"

I looked at the rat pack. Without breaking their frozen tableau, they pleaded with me with their eyes.

"Um . . . running, I think," I said thoughtfully. "They smell bad enough alive. Dead they might give the Bazaar a bad name."

"You heard him," Aahz growled. "Move!"

They disappeared like they had melted into the ground.

"Aahz!"

The girl came flying forward to throw her arms around him.

"Tanda!" Aahz exclaimed, lowering the crossbow. "Are you mixed up with that pack?"

"Are you kidding? I'm the bait!" she winked bawdily.

"Little low class for you, isn't it?"

"Aah . . . it's a living."

"Why'd you leave the Assassins?"

"Got tired of paying union dues."

"Um . . . harrumph . . ." I interrupted.

"Hmm?" Aahz looked around. "Oh! Sorry, kid. Say, have you two met?"

"Sort of," the girl acknowledged. "We . . . say, is this the friend you were looking for, handsome?"

"Handsome?" Aahz wrinkled his nose.

"Well, yes," I admitted. "We got separated back by the. . . ."

"Handsome?" Aahz repeated.

"Oh, hush!" the girl commanded, slapping his stomach playfully. "I like him. He's got style."

"Actually, I don't believe we've met formally," I said, giving my most winning smile. "My name is Skeeve."

"Well, la-de-dah!" Aahz grumbled.

"Ignore him. I'm Tananda, but call me Tanda."

"Love to," I leered.

"If you two are quite through. . . ." Aahz interrupted, "I have a couple questions. . . ."

"Gleep!" said the dragon, prancing up to our assemblage.

"What's that?" Aahz demanded.

"It's a dragon," I said helpfully.

Tanda giggled rudely.

"I know that," Aahz barked. "I mean what is he doing here?"

Suddenly I was hesitant to supply the whole story.

"There are lots of dragons at the Bazaar, Aahz," I mumbled, not looking at him. "In fact, there's a stall just down the way that. . . ."

"What is *that* dragon doing *here*?"

"Gleep!" said the dragon, rubbing his head against my chest.

"Um . . . he's mine," I admitted.

"Yours?" Aahz bellowed. "I told you to look at the dragons, not buy one!"

"But Aahz. . . ."

"What are we going to do with a dragon?"

"I got a good deal on him," I chimed hopefully.

"What did you say, kid?"

"I said I got a good deal. . . ."

"From a Deveel?"

"Oh. I see what you mean."

"C'mon. Let's have it. What were the terms of this fantastic deal?"

"Well . . . I . . . that is . . ."

"Out with it!"

"I traded Quigley's pendant for him."

"Quigley's pendant? The one that sees through spells? You traded a good magical pendant for a half-grown dragon?"

"Oh, give him a break, Aahz," Tanda interrupted. "What do you expect letting him wander off alone that way? You're lucky he didn't get stuck with half the tourist crud on Deva! Where were you all this time, anyway?"

"Well . . . I was . . . um . . ."

"Don't tell me," she said, holding up a hand. "If I know you, you were either chasing a girl or stuffing your face, right?"

"She's got you there, Aahz," I commented.

"Shut up, kid."

". . . so don't get down on Skeeve here. Compared to what could have happened to him, he didn't do half bad. How did you find us, anyway?"

"I listened for the sounds of a fight and followed it," Aahz admitted.

"See! You were expecting him to get into trouble. Might I point out he was doing just fine before you barged in. He and his dragon had those thugs treed all by themselves. He's pretty handy with that magik, you know."

"I know," Aahz responded proudly. "I taught him."

"Gee, thanks, Aahz."

"Shut up, kid."

"Gleep," said the dragon, craning his neck around to look at Aahz upside down.

"A dragon, huh?" Aahz said, studying the dragon more thoughtfully.

"He might help us against Isstvan," I suggested hopefully.

"Isstvan?" Tanda asked quizzically.

"Yeah," Aahz replied. "You remember him, don't you? Well, he's up to his old tricks, this time on Klah."

"So that's what's going on, huh? Well, what are we going to do about it?"

"We?" I asked, surprised.

"Sure," she smiled. "This racket is a bit low class, like Aahz says. I might as well tag along with you two for a while . . . if you don't mind, that is."

"Terrific!" I said, and meant it for a change.

"Not so fast, Tanda," Aahz cautioned. "There are a few details you haven't been filled in on yet."

"Such as?"

"Such as I've lost my powers."

"No fooling? Gee, that's tough."

"That means we'll be relying on the kid here to give us cover in the magik department."

"All the more reason for me to come along. I've picked up a few tricks myself."

"I know," Aahz leered.

"Not like that," she said, punching him in the side. "I mean magik tricks."

"Even so, it's not going to be easy."

"C'mon, Aahz," Tanda chided. "Are you trying to say it wouldn't be helpful having a trained Assassin on your side?"

"Well . . . it could give us a bit of an advantage," Aahz admitted.

"Good! Then it's settled. What do we do first?"

"There're some stalls just around the corner that carry weapons," I suggested. "We could. . . ."

"Relax, kid. I've already taken care of that."

"You have?" I asked, surprised.

"Yeah. I found just what we need over in the practical

jokes section. I was just looking for you before we headed back."

"Then we're ready to go?" Tanda asked.

"Yep," Aahz nodded, fishing the D-Hopper out of his shirt.

"What about my dragon?"

"What about him?"

"Are we going to take him with us?"

"Of course we're going to take him with us. We don't leave anything of value behind."

"Gleep!" said the dragon.

". . . and he must be valuable to someone!" Aahz finished, glaring at the dragon.

He pressed the button on the D-Hopper. The Bazaar wavered and faded . . . and we were back in Frumple's shop . . . sort of.

"Interesting place you've got here," Tanda commented dryly. "Did you do the decor?"

All that was left of Frumple's shop was a burnt-out shell.

# XXI:

*"One must deal openly and fairly with one's forces if maximum effectiveness is to be achieved."*

—D. VADER

"What happened?" I demanded of Aahz.

"Hey, kid. I was on Deva, too. Remember?"

"Um . . . hey, guys. I hate to interrupt," Tanda interrupted, "but shouldn't something be done about disguises?"

She was right. Being on Deva had made me forget the mundane necessities of our existence. I ignored Aahz's sarcastic reply and set to work.

Aahz returned to his now traditional Garkin disguise. Tanda was fine once I changed her complexion and the color of her hair. After a bit of thought, I disguised Gleep as the war unicorn. It was a bit risky, but it would do as long as he kept his mouth shut. Me, I left as myself. I mean, what the heck. Tanda liked my looks the way they were.

Fortunately the sun wasn't up yet, so there weren't any people about to witness the transformation.

"Say, handsome," Tanda commented, observing the results of my work, "you're a pretty handy guy to have around."

"His name's Skeeve," Aahz grumbled.

"Whatever," Tanda murmured. "He's got style."

She snuggled up to me.

"Gleep!" said the dragon, pressing his head against my other side.

I was starting to feel awfully popular.

"If you can spare a few minutes, kid," Aahz commented dryly, "we do have a mission, remember?"

"That's right," I said, forcing my attention away from Tanda's advances. "What do you think happened to Frumple?"

"Either the citizens of Twixt got wise to him, or he's off to tell Isstvan we're coming, would be my two guesses."

"Who's Frumple?" Tanda asked.

"Hmm? Oh, he's the resident Deveel," Aahz said. "He's the one who helped us get to the Bazaar."

". . . at sword point," I added sarcastically.

"What's a Deveel doing here?"

"All we know is that rumor has it he was barred from Deva," I told her.

"Hmm . . . sounds like a bit of a nasty character."

"Well, he won't win any popularity contests."

"It occurs to me," Aahz interrupted, "that if either of my two guesses are correct, we'd best be on our way. Time seems to be running out."

"Right," agreed Tanda. "Which way is Isstvan?"

"First, we've got to pick up Quigley," I inserted.

"Why?" asked Aahz. "Oh, I suppose you're right, kid. We're going to need all the help we can muster."

"Who's Quigley?" Tanda asked.

"Later, Tanda," Aahz insisted. "First help us see if there's anything here worth salvaging."

Unfortunately, there wasn't. In fact, there weren't even the charred remains of anything left for our discovery.

Even the garish sword I had left behind seemed to have vanished.

"That settles it," Aahz commented grimly as we completed our search. "He's on his way to Isstvan."

"The natives might have taken the sword after they burned the place," I suggested hopefully.

"No way, kid. Even yokels like these wouldn't bother with a crummy sword like that."

"It was that bad?" Tanda asked.

"It was that bad," Aahz assured her firmly.

"If it was that worthless, why would Frumple take it with him?" I asked.

"For the same reason we've been lugging it around," Aahz said pointedly. "There's always some sucker to unload it on for a profit. Remember Quigley?"

"Who's Quigley?" Tanda insisted.

"Well," sighed Aahz, "at the moment he's a statue, but in duller times he's a demon hunter."

"Swell," she commented sarcastically. "Just what we need."

"Wait until you meet him," Aahz rolled his eyes and sighed. "Oh well, let's go."

Our departure from Twixt was blissfully uneventful. On the road, we rehearsed our story until, by the time we finally dug up Quigley and sprinkled him with the restoring power, we were ready to present a united front.

"Really? Turned to stone, you say?" he said, brushing the dirt from his clothes.

"Yes," Aahz assured him. "They were looting your body when we launched our counterattack. It's lucky for you we decided to come back and fight at your side."

"And they took my magik sword and my amulet?"

I felt a little uneasy on those subjects, but Aahz never batted an eye.

"That's right, the blackguards!" he snarled. "We tried to stop them, but they eluded us."

"Well, at least they didn't get my war unicorn," muttered the demon hunter.

"Um . . ." I said, bracing myself for my part in this charade. "We've got some bad news about that, too."

"Bad news?" Quigley frowned, "I don't understand. I can see the beast with my own eyes and he seems fit enough."

"Oh, he's fine physically," Aahz reassured him, "but before they disappeared, the demons put a spell on him."

"A spell?"

"Yes," I said. "Now he . . . um . . . well . . . he thinks he's a dragon."

"A dragon?" Quigley exclaimed.

"Gleep!" said the dragon.

"And that's not all," Aahz continued. "The beast was so wild at first that only through the continued efforts of my squire here were we able to gentle him at all. Frankly, I was for putting the poor animal out of its misery, but he insisted he could tame it and you see before you the results of his patient teachings."

"That's wonderful!" exclaimed Quigley.

"No. That's terrible," corrected Aahz. "You see, in the process, your animal has formed a strong attachment for my squire . . . stronger, I fear, than his attachment for you."

"Hah! Ridiculous," Quigley proclaimed. "But I do feel I owe you an additional debt of gratitude, lad. If there's ever anything I can . . ."

He began to advance on me with his hand extended. In a flash, Gleep was between us, head down and hissing.

Quigley froze, his eyes bulging with surprise.

"Stop that!" I ordered, cuffing the dragon.

"Gleep!" said the dragon, slinking back to his place behind me.

"See what I mean?" Aahz said pointedly.

"Hmm. . . ." Quigley mumbled thoughtfully. "That's strange, he never defended me that way."

"I guess we'll just have to buy him from you," I said eagerly.

"Buy him?" Quigley turned his attention to me again.

Aahz tried to catch my eye, shaking his head emphatically, but I ignored him.

"That's right," I continued. "He's no good to you this way, and since we're sort of to blame for what happened to him. . . ."

"Think nothing of it, lad." Quigley drew himself up proudly. "I give him to you as a gift. After all, if it weren't for you he'd be dead anyway, and so would I, for that matter."

"But I. . . ."

"No! I will hear nothing more." The demon hunter held up a restraining hand. "The matter is closed. Treat him well, lad. He's a good animal."

"Terrific," muttered Aahz.

"Gleep," said the dragon.

I felt miserable. It had occurred to me that our plans involved taking shameless advantage of Quigley's gullibility. As he was my only fellow Klahd in this adventure, I had wanted to force Aahz into giving him some money under the guise of buying the "war unicorn." It would have salved my conscience a bit, but Quigley's generosity and sense of fair play had ruined my plan. Now I felt worse than before.

"Actually, Quigley," Aahz smiled, "If there's anyone you should thank, it should be Tananda here. If it were not for her, we would be in dire straits indeed."

"It's about time," mumbled Tanda, obviously unimpressed with Aahz's rhetoric.

"Charmed, milady," Quigley smiled, taking her hand to kiss.

"She's a witch," added Aahz casually.

"A witch?" Quigley dropped her hand as if it had bitten him.

"That's right, sugar," Tanda smiled, batting her eyes at him.

"Perhaps I should explain," Aahz interrupted mercifully. "Tananda here has certain powers she has consented to use in support of our war on demons. You already noticed I have regained my normal appearance?"

Another blatant lie. Aahz was currently disguised as Garkin.

"Yes," the demon hunter admitted hesitantly.

"Tananda's work," Aahz confided. "Just as it was her powers that restored you after you had been turned to stone."

"Hmmm . . ." Quigley said, looking at Tanda again.

"Really, you must realize, Quigley, that when one fights demons, sometimes it is helpful to employ a demon's weapons," Aahz admonished gently.

"Tananda here can be a powerful ally . . . and frankly, I find your attitude toward her deplorable and ungrateful."

"Forgive me, milady," Quigley sighed, stepping up to her again. "I did not mean to offend you. It's just that . . . well . . . I've had some bad experiences with those who associate with demons."

"Think nothing of it, sugar," said Tanda the demon, taking his hand, "And call me Tanda."

While they were occupied with each other, I seized the opportunity and snagged Aahz's arm.

"Hm? What is it, kid?"

"Give him back his sword!" I hissed.

"What? No way, kid. By my count he's still got five pieces of gold left. I'll sell it to him."

"But he gave us his unicorn."

"He gave us a dragon . . . your dragon! I fail to see anything benevolent in that."

"Look, Aahz. Either you give him that sword or you can work your own magik! Get me?"

"Talk about ingratitude! Look kid, if you. . . ."

"Aahz!" Tanda's voice interrupted our dispute. "Come help me convince Quigley to join our mission."

"Would that I could, milady," Quigley sighed, "but I would be of little help. This late misfortune has left me afoot, weaponless, and penniless."

"Actually," Aahz chimed, "you still have five. . . ."

I interrupted him with an elbow in his ribs.

"What was that, Aahz?" Quigley asked.

"Aah . . . my . . . um . . . squire and I were just discussing that and we have reached a decision. So . . . um . . . so fine a warrior should not be left so destitute, so . . . um . . . we. . . ."

"We've decided to give you back your sword," I announced proudly.

"Really?" Quigley's face lit up.

"I didn't know you had it in you, Aahz," Tanda smiled sweetly.

"I say, this is comradeship indeed." Quigley was obviously beside himself with joy. "How can I ever repay you?"

"By never mentioning this to anyone," Aahz growled.

"How's that again?"

"I said don't mention it," Aahz amended. "It's the least we can do."

"Believe him," I smiled.

"Now I will gladly assist you on your mission," Quigley answered. "Why, with a weapon and good comrades, what more could a warrior ask for?"

"Money," Aahz said bluntly.

"Oh Aahz." Tanda punched him a little too hard for it to be playful. "You're such a kidder."

"Don't you want to know what the mission is?" I asked Quigley.

"Oh, yes, I suppose you're right, lad. Forgive me. I was carried away by my enthusiasm."

"Tell him, Skeeve," prompted Tanda.

"Actually," I said, with a sudden flash of diplomacy, "Aahz explains it much better than I do."

"It's really quite simple," mumbled Aahz, still sulking a bit. "We're going after Isstvan."

"Isstvan?" Quigley looked puzzled. "The harmless old innkeeper?"

"Harmless? Harmless, did you say?" Aahz took the bait. "Quigley, as one demon hunter to another, you've got a lot to learn."

"I do all right for myself."

"Sure you do. That's why you got turned to stone, remember?"

"I got turned to stone because I put my faith in a magik sword that. . . ."

Things were back to normal.

"Gentlemen, gentlemen," I interrupted. "We were talking about the upcoming mission."

"Right, kid. As I was saying, Quigley, that harmless old innkeeper is working so closely with demons I wouldn't be surprised to learn he was one himself."

"Impossible!" scoffed Quigley. "Why, the man sent me out hunting for demons."

"Ahh!" smiled Aahz. "Therein lies the story."

I caught Tanda's eyes and winked. She smiled back at me and nodded. This might take a while, but as of now Quigley was in the bag!

# XXII:

*"This is another fine myth you've gotten me into!"*

—LOR L. AND HAR D.

There was something there in the shadows. I could sense its presence more than see it. It was dark and serpentine . . . and it was watching me.

I was alone. I didn't know where the others had gone, but I knew they were counting on me.

"Who's there?" I called.

The voice that came back to me out of the darkness echoed hollowly.

"I am Isstvan, Skeeve. I've been waiting for you."

"You know who I am?" I asked, surprised.

"I know all about you and your friends. I've known all along what you're trying to do."

I tried to set wards about me, but I couldn't find a force line. I tried to run, but I was rooted to the spot.

"See how my powers dwarf yours? And you expected to challenge me."

I tried to fight back a wave of despair.

"Wait until the others come," I cried defiantly.

"They already have," the voice boomed. "Look!"

Two objects came rolling at me out of the darkness. I saw with horror that they were heads! Tanda's and Quigley's!

I felt ill, but clung to a shred of hope. There was still no sign of Aahz. If he was still at large, we might. . . .

"Don't look to your Pervert for help," the voice answered my thoughts. "I've dealt with him too."

Aahz appeared, sheathed in fire. He staggered and fell, writhing on the ground as the flames consumed his body.

"Now it's just you and me, Skeeve!" the voice echoed. "You and me."

"I'll go!" I shouted desperately. "You've won. Just let me go."

The darkness was moving closer.

"It's too late. I'm coming for you, Skeeve . . . Skeeve. . . ."

"Skeeve!"

Something was shaking my shoulder. I bolted upright, blinking my eyes as the world swam back into focus.

The camp was asleep. Aahz was kneeling beside me, the glow from the campfire's dying embers revealing the concerned expression on his face.

"Wake up, kid! If you keep thrashing around, you'll end up in the fire."

"It's Isstvan!" I explained desperately. "He knows all about us."

"What?"

"I was talking to him. He came into my dream!"

"Hmmm . . . sounds more like a plain old nightmare," Aahz proclaimed. "I warned you not to let Tanda season the food."

"Are you sure?" I said doubtfully.

"Positive," Aahz insisted. "If Isstvan knew we were coming, he'd hit us with something a lot more powerful than making faces at you in a dream."

I guess that was supposed to reassure me. It didn't. All

it did was remind me I was thoroughly outclassed in the upcoming campaign.

"Aahz, can't you tell me anything about Isstvan? What he looks like, for instance."

"Not a chance, kid," Aahz grinned at me.

"Why not?"

"Because we won't both see him the same way, or at least we wouldn't describe him the same way. If I describe him to you, one of two things will happen when you first see him. If he looks scarier to you than I've described him, you'll freeze. If he looks more harmless than I've described him, you'll relax. Either way, it'll slow your reactions and give him the first move. There's no point in gaining the element of surprise if we aren't going to use it."

"Well," I persisted. "Couldn't you at least tell me about his powers? What can he do?"

"For one thing, it would take too long. Just assume that if you can imagine it, he can do it."

"What's the other?" I asked.

"The other what?"

"You said 'for one thing.' That implies you have at least one other reason."

"Hmm," Aahz pondered. "Well, I'm not sure you'll understand, but to a certain degree what he can do, I mean the whole list, is irrelevant."

"Why?"

"Because we're taking the initiative. That puts him in a reactive instead of an active role."

"You're right," I said thoughtfully. "I don't understand."

"Look kid, if we just sat here and waited for him, he could take his time and choose exactly what he wanted to do and when he wanted to do it. That's an active role and lets him play with his entire list of powers. Right?"

"I guess so."

"But we aren't doing that. We're carrying the attack to him. That should limit him as to what he can do. There are only a certain number of responses he can successfully use to each of our gambits, and he'll have to use them because he can't afford to ignore the attack. Most of all, we'll rob him of time. Instead of leisurely choosing what he's going to do next, he'll have to choose fast. That means he'll go with the option he's surest of, the one he does best."

I considered this for a few moments. It sort of made sense.

"Just one question, Aahz," I asked finally.

"What's that, kid?"

"What if you've guessed wrong?"

"Then we drop back ten and punt," he answered lightly.

"What's a . . ."

"Then we try something else," he amended hastily.

"Like what?"

"Can't tell yet," Aahz shrugged. "Too many variables. We're going with my best guess right now. Beyond that we'll just have to wait and see."

We sat staring into the dying fire for a few minutes, each lost in our own thoughts.

"Say, Aahz?" I said at last.

"Yea, kid?"

"Do you think we'll reach Isstvan before Frumple does?"

"Relax, kid. Frumple's probably drinking wine and pinching bottoms in some other dimension by now."

"But you said. . . ."

"I've had time to think about it since then. The only reason a Deveel does anything is for a profit or out of fear. As far as his sticking his head into this brawl goes, I figure the fear will outweigh the profit. Trying to sell information to a madman is risky at best. My bet is he's lying low until the dust settles."

I reminded myself again of my faith in Aahz's expertise in such matters. It occurred to me, however, there was an awful lot of guesswork in our planning.

"Um, Aahz? Wouldn't it be a little safer if we had invested in a couple of those jazzy weapons back in Deva?"

"We don't need them," he replied firmly. "Besides, they're susceptible to Gremlins. I'd rather go into a fight with a crude but reliable weapon than pin my hopes on a contraption that's liable to malfunction when you need it most."

"Where are Gremlins from?" I asked.

"What?"

"Gremlins. You said. . . ."

"Oh, that. It's just a figure of speech. There are no such things as Gremlins."

I was only listening with half an ear. I suddenly realized that while I could see Quigley's sleeping form, there was no sign of Tanda or Gleep.

"Where's . . . um . . . where's Gleep?" I asked abruptly.

Aahz grinned at me.

"Gleep is standing watch . . . and just in case you're interested, so's Tanda."

I was vaguely annoyed he had seen through me so easily, but was determined not to show it.

"When is . . . um . . . are they coming back?"

"Relax, kid. I told Tanda to leave you alone tonight. You need the sleep for tomorrow."

He jerked his head pointedly toward the assassin's robe I had been using for a pillow. I grudgingly resumed my horizontal position.

"Did I wake you up, Aahz?" I asked apologetically. "With the nightmare, I mean."

"Naw. I was still up. Just making a few last-minute preparations for tomorrow."

"Oh," I said drowsily.

"Say, uh, kid?"

"Yes, Aahz?"

"We probably won't have much time to talk tomorrow when Quigley's awake, so while we've got a few minutes

alone I want to say however it goes tomorrow . . . well . . . •
it's been nice working with you, kid."

"Gee, Aahz. . . ." I said starting to sit up.

A rough hand interrupted me and pushed me back
down.

"Sleep!" Aahz commanded, but there was a gentle note
lurking in his gruff tone.

# XXIII:

*"Since prehistoric man, no battle has ever gone as planned."*

—D. GRAEME

We crouched in a grove of small trees on a knoll overlooking the inn, studying our target. The inn was as Quigley had described it, an isolated two-story building with an attached stable squatting by a road overgrown with weeds. If Isstvan was relying on transients to support his business, he was in trouble, except we knew he was doing no such thing. He was mustering his strength to take over the dimensions, and the isolated inn was a perfect base for him to work from.

"Are you sure there are no wards?" Aahz whispered.

He addressed his question to Tanda. She in turn shot me a glance. I gave a small nod of my head.

"Positive," she whispered back.

It was all part of our plan. As far as Quigley was concerned, Tanda was the only one of our group that had any supernatural powers.

"Good," said the demon hunter. "Demon powers make me uneasy. The less we have to deal with, the better I like it."

"Don't get your hopes up," Aahz commented, not taking his eyes from the inn. "They're there all right. The easier it is to get in, the harder it'll be to get out . . . and they're making it awfully easy for us to get in."

"I don't like it," said Tanda firmly.

"Neither do I," admitted Aahz. "But things aren't going to get any better, so let's get started. You might as well get into disguise now."

"Right, Aahz," she said.

Neither of them looked at me. In fact Aahz stared directly at Tanda. This kept Quigley's attention on her also, though I must admit it helped that she began to writhe and gyrate wildly. Unobserved, I shut my eyes and got to work.

I was getting pretty good at this disguise game, which was fortunate because I was going to be sorely tested today. With a few masterful strokes, I converted Tanda's lovely features into the dubious face of the Imp Higgens . . . or rather Higgens's human disguise. This done, I opened my eyes again.

Tanda was still gyrating. It was a pleasant enough sight that I was tempted to prolong it, but we had work to do. I cleared my throat and Tanda acknowledged the signal by stopping.

"How do I look?" she asked proudly.

"Terrific!" I exclaimed with no trace of modesty.

Aahz shot me a dirty look.

"It's uncanny!" Quigley marveled. "How do you do that?"

"Professional secret." Tanda winked at him.

"Off with you!" Aahz commanded. "And you too, Skeeve."

"But Aahz, couldn't I. . . ."

"No, you can't. We've discussed it before. This mission's far too dangerous for a lad of your inexperience."

"Oh, all right, Aahz," I said, crestfallen.

"Cheer up, lad," Quigley told me. "Your day will come. If we fail, the mission falls to you."

"I suppose so. Well, good luck. . . ."

I turned to Tanda, but she was already gone, vanished as if the ground had swallowed her up.

"I say!" exclaimed Quigley. "She does move quietly, doesn't she?"

"I told you she could handle herself," Aahz said proudly. "Now it's your turn, Skeeve."

"Right, Aahz!"

I turned to the dragon.

"Stay here, Gleep. I'll be back soon, and until then you do what Aahz says. Understand?"

"Gleep?" said the dragon, cocking his head.

For a minute I thought he was going to ruin everything, but then he turned and slunk to Aahz's side and stood there regarding me with mournful blue eyes.

Everything was ready.

"Well, good-bye. Good luck!" I called, and trudged slowly back over the knoll, hopefully a picture of abject misery.

Once out of sight, however, I turned and began to sprint as fast as I could in a wide circle around the inn.

On the surface, our plan was quite simple. Aahz and Quigley were to give Tanda enough time to circle around the inn and enter it over the stable roof. Then they were to boldly enter the front door. Supposedly this would create a diversion, allowing Tanda to attack Isstvan magically from the rear. I was to wait safely on the knoll until the affair was settled.

In actuality, our plan was a bit more complex. Unbeknownst to Quigley, I was also supposed to circle the inn and find a covert entrance. Then, at the appropriate moment, Tanda and I were to create a magical diversion, allowing Aahz to use the secret weapon he had acquired on Deva.

A gully blocked my path. I took to the air without hesitation and flew over it. I had to be in position in time, or Aahz would have no magical support at all.

Actually magik was quite easy here. The inn was sitting squarely on an intersection of two ground force lines, while a force line in the air passed directly overhead. Whatever happened in the upcoming battle of magik, we wouldn't suffer for a lack of energy.

I wished I knew more about Aahz's secret weapon. He had been doggedly mysterious about it, and neither Tanda nor I had been able to pry any information out of him. He had said it had to be used at close range. He had said it couldn't be used while Isstvan was watching him. He had said it was our only hope to beat Isstvan. He had said it was supposed to be a surprise.

Terrific!

Maybe when all this was over I would find a mentor who didn't have a sense of humor.

I slowed my pace. I was coming to the back of the inn now. The brush had grown right up to the wall, which made my approach easy.

I paused and checked for wards again.

Nothing.

Trying to force Aahz's "easy in, hard out" prophecy from my mind, I scanned the upper windows. None of them were open, so I chose the nearest one and levitated to it. Hovering there, I cautiously pushed, then pulled at the frame.

Locked!

Hurriedly, I pulled myself along the wall with my hands to the next window.

Also locked.

It occurred to me it would be ironic if, after all our magical preparations, we were stopped by something as mundane as a locked window.

To my relief, the next window yielded to my pressure, and in a moment I was standing inside the inn, trying to get my heartbeat under control.

The room I was in was furnished, but vacant. Judging from the dust on the bed, it had been vacant for some time.

I wondered for a moment where demons slept, if they

slept at all, then forced the question from my mind. Time was running out and I wasn't in position yet.

I darted silently across the room and tried the door. Unlocked!

Getting down on my hands and knees, I eased the door open and crawled through, pushing it shut behind me.

After studying the inn's interior so often in Quigley's dirt sketches, it seemed strange to actually be here. I was on the long side of an L-shaped mezzanine which gave access to the upper-story rooms. Peering through the bars of the railing that lined the mezzanine, I could look down into the inn proper.

There were three people currently occupying a table below. I recognized the disguised features of Higgens and Brockhurst as two of them. The third was sitting hunched with his back to me and I couldn't make out his face.

I was debating shifting to another position to get a better view, when a fourth figure entered bearing an enormous tray with a huge jug of wine on it as well as an assortment of dirty flagons.

"This round's on the house, boys!" the figure chortled merrily. "Have one on old Isstvan."

Isstvan! That was Isstvan?

The waddling figure below did not seem to display any of the menacing features I had expected in a would-be ruler of the dimensions.

Quickly I checked him for a magical aura. There was none. It wasn't a disguise. He really looked like that. I studied him carefully.

He was tall, but his stoutness kept his height from being imposing. He had long white hair and a longer white beard which nearly covered his chest with its fullness. His bright eyes were set in a face that seemed to be permanently smiling, and his nose and cheeks were flushed, though whether from drink or laughter I couldn't tell.

This was the dark figure of evil I had been dreading all these weeks? He looked to be exactly what Quigley said he was . . . a harmless old innkeeper.

A movement at the far end of the mezzanine caught my eye. Tanda! She was crouched behind the railing as I was on the other side of the stairs, and at first I thought I had just seen the movement of her easing into position. Then she looked my way and cautiously waved her hand again, and I realized she was signaling for my attention.

I waved an acknowledgment, which she must have seen, for she stopped signaling and changed to another set of actions. Glancing furtively at the figures below to be sure she wasn't observed, she began a strange pantomime.

First she made several repeated gestures around her forehead, then pointed urgently behind her.

I didn't understand, and shook my head to convey this.

She repeated the gestures more emphatically, and this time I realized she was actually pointing down and behind her. The stables! Something about the stables. But what about the stables?

I considered her first gesture again. She appeared to be stabbing herself in the forehead. Something had hit her in the stables? She had killed something in the stables?

I shook my head again. She bared her teeth at me in frustration.

"Innkeep!"

I jumped a foot at the bellow.

Aahz and Quigley had just walked through the door. Whatever Tanda was trying to tell me would just have to wait. Our attack had begun.

"Two flagons of your best wine . . . and send someone to see to my unicorn."

Aahz was doing all the talking, of course. It had been agreed that he would take the lead in the conversation. Quigley hadn't been too happy about that, but in the end had consented to speaking only when absolutely necessary.

Their entrance had had surprisingly little impact on the assemblage below. In fact, Isstvan was the only one to even look in their direction.

"Come in. Come in, gentlemen," he smiled, spreading

his arms wide in welcome. "We've been expecting you!"

"You have?" blurted Quigley, echoing my thoughts.

"Of course, of course. You shouldn't try to fool old Isstvan." He shook a finger at them in mock sternness. "Word was just brought to us by . . . oh, I'm sorry. I haven't introduced you to my new purchasing agent yet."

"We've met," came the voice of the hunched figure as he turned to face them.

Frumple!

That's what Tanda had been trying to tell me! The war unicorn, Quigley's unicorn, was down in the stable. For all our speed, Frumple had gotten here ahead of us.

"Who are you?" asked Quigley, peering at the Deveel.

For some reason this seemed to set Isstvan off into peals of laughter from his eyes. "We are going to have such fun this afternoon!"

He gestured absently and the inn door slammed shut. There was a sudden ripple of dull clunks behind me, and I realized the room doors were locking themselves. We were sealed in! All of us.

"I don't believe I've had such a good time since I made love to my week-dead sister."

Isstvan's voice was still jovial, but it struck an icy note of fear within me. I realized that not only was he a powerful magician, he was quite insane.

# XXIV:

*"Ya gotta be subtle!"*

—M. Hammer

There was a tense, expectant silence as the foursome leaned forward to study their captives. It was as if two songbirds had tried to edge through a crowd of vultures to steal a snack only to find they were the intended meal.

I knelt, watching in frozen horror, fully expecting to witness the immediate demise of my two allies.

"Since Frumple's already announced us," Aahz said smoothly, "I guess there's no need to maintain this disguise."

The confident tone of his voice steadied my shattered nerve. We were in it now, and win or lose we'd just have to keep going.

Quickly, I shut my eyes and removed Aahz's Garkin disguise.

"Aahz!" cried Isstvan in delight. "I should have known it was you."

"He's the one who. . . ." Brockhurst began.

"Do you two know each other?" Frumple asked, ignoring the Imp.

"Know each other?" Isstvan chortled. "We're *old* enemies. He and a couple other scalawags nearly destroyed me the last time we met."

"Well it's our turn now, right Isstvan?" smiled Higgens, leisurely reaching for his crossbow.

"Now, now!" said Isstvan, picking the Imp up by his head and shaking him gently. "Mustn't rush things."

"Seems to me," Aahz sneered, "that you're having trouble finding decent allies, Isstvan."

"Oh, Aahz," Isstvan laughed. "Still the sharp tongue, eh?"

"Imps?" Aahz's voice was scornful. "C'mon, Isstvan. Even you can do better than that."

Isstvan sighed and dropped Higgens back in his chair.

"Well, one does what one can. Inflation, you know."

He shook his head sadly, then brightened again.

"Oh you don't know how glad I am to see you, Aahz. I thought I was going to have to wait until we conquered Perv before I got my revenge, and here you just walk in. Now don't you dare pop off before we've settled our score."

"I told you before," Frumple interrupted. "He's lost his powers."

"Powers. Hmph! He never had any powers," Quigley chimed in, baited from his frightened silence at the insult of having been ignored.

"Well, who do we have here?" Isstvan smiled, looking at Quigley for the first time. "Have we met?"

"Say Isstvan," interrupted Aahz. "Mind if I have some of that wine? No reason to be barbaric about this."

"Certainly, Aahz." Isstvan waved him forward. "Help yourself."

It was eerie listening to the conversation: apparently civilized and friendly, it had a cat-and-mouse undercurrent which belied the casual tones.

"Watch him!" Frumple hissed, glaring at Aahz.

"Oh Frumple! You are such a wart," Isstvan scolded.

"Why, you were the one who assured me that he had lost his powers."

"Well, I think he makes sense," Brockhurst grumbled, rising and backing away as Aahz approached the table. "If you don't mind, Isstvan, I'll watch from over here."

He sat on the bottom steps of the flight of stairs heading up to the mezzanine where Tanda and I were hidden. His tone was conversational, but it was clear he was only waiting for Isstvan's signal to loose him on the helpless pair.

"Oh, you Imps are worse than the Deveels!" Isstvan scowled.

"That's a given," Frumple commented dryly.

"Now look, Frumple. . . ." Higgens began angrily.

"As to who this figure is," Frumple pointed to Quigley, ignoring the Imps. "That is Garkin's apprentice. He's the one who's been handling the magik for our Pervert since he lost his powers."

"Really?" asked Isstvan eagerly. "Can you do the cups and balls trick? I love the cups and balls trick."

"I don't understand," mumbled Quigley vacantly, backing away from the assemblage.

Well, if we were ever going to have a diversion, it would have to be now. Closing my eyes, I changed Quigley's features. The obvious choice for his disguise was . . . me!

"See," said Frumple pointing proudly. "I told you so."

"Throckwoddle!" exclaimed the two Imps simultaneously.

"What?" said Frumple narrowing his eyes suspiciously.

I was ready for them. As the exclamations rose, I changed Quigley again. This time, I gave him Throckwoddle features.

"Why, it *is* Throckwoddle," cried Isstvan. "Oh, that's funny."

"Wait a minute!" Brockhurst hissed. "How could you be Throckwoddle when we turned you into a statue before we caught up with Throckwoddle?"

This set Isstvan off into even greater peals of laughter.

"Stop," he called breathless. "Oh stop. Oh! My ribs hurt. Aahz, you've outdone yourself this time."

"It's nothing really," Aahz acknowledged modestly.

"There's something wrong here!" Frumple declared.

He plunged a hand deep into his robe, never taking his eyes from Quigley. Almost too late I realized what he was doing. He was going for his crystal, the one that let him detect disguises. As the glittering bauble emerged, I swung into action.

A simple levitation, a small flick with my mind, and the crystal popped out of Frumple's grasp and plopped into the wine jug.

"Framitz!" Frumple swore, starting to fish for his possession.

"Get your hands out of the wine, Frumple!" Aahz chided slapping his wrist. "You'll get your toy when we finish the jug!"

As if to illustrate his point, he hefted the jug and began refilling the flagons around the table.

"Enough of this insanity!" Quigley exploded.

I winced at the use of the word "insanity," but Isstvan didn't seem to mind. He merely leaned forward to watch Quigley.

"I am neither Skeeve nor Throckwoddle," Quigley continued, "I am Quigley, demon hunter extraordinaire! Let any dispute who dare, and man or demon I'll show him who I am!"

This proved too much for Isstvan, who actually collapsed in laughter.

"Oh, he's funny, Aahz," he gasped. "Where did you find this funny man?"

"You sent him to me, remember?" Aahz prompted.

"Why, so I did, so I did," Isstvan mused, and even this fact he seemed to find hysterically funny.

The others were not so amused.

"So you're a demon hunter, eh?" Frumple snarled. "What's your gripe anyway?"

"The offenses of demons are too numerous to list," Quigley retorted haughtily.

"We aren't going anywhere for a while," Brockhurst chimed in from the stairs. "And neither are you. List us a few of these offenses."

"Well . . ." began Quigley, "you stole my magik pendant and my magik sword. . . ."

"We don't know anything about a magik pendant." Higgens bristled. "And we gave your so-called magik sword to. . . ."

"What else do demons do?" Frumple interrupted, apparently none too eager to have the discussion turn to swords.

"Well . . . you bewitched my war unicorn into thinking he's a dragon!" Quigley challenged.

"Your war unicorn is currently tethered in the stable," Higgens stated flatly. "Frumple brought him in."

"My unicorn is tethered outside the door!" Quigley insisted. "And he thinks he's a dragon!"

"Your unicorn is tethered in the stable," Higgens barked back. "And we think you're a fruitcake!"

"Gentlemen, gentlemen," Isstvan managed to hold up his hands despite his laughter. "All this is quite amusing, but . . . well, will you look at that!"

This last was said in such a tone of wonder that the attention of everyone in the room was immediately drawn to the spot he was looking at.

Suspended in midair, not two hand-spans from Isstvan's head, was a small red dart with gold and black fletchings.

"An assassin's dart!" Isstvan marveled, gently plucking the missile from where it was hovering. "Now who would be naughty enough to try to poison me from behind?"

His eyes slowly moved to Brockhurst sitting casually on the stairs.

Brockhurst suddenly realized he was the object of everyone's attention. His eyes widened in fright.

"No! I . . . Wait! Isstvan!" he half-rose holding out a

hand as if to ward off a blow. "I didn't . . . No! Don't. Glaag!"

This last was said as his hands suddenly flew to his throat and began choking him violently.

"Glaak . . . eak . . . urk . . ."

He fell back on the stairs and began rolling frantically back and forth.

"Isstvan," Higgens began hesitantly, "normally I wouldn't interfere, but don't you think you should hear what he has to say, first?"

"But I'm not doing anything," Isstvan blinked with hurt innocence.

My eyes flashed to the other end of the mezzanine. Tanda was crouched there, her eyes closed. She seemed to be choking an invisible person on the floor in front of her. With dawning realization, I began to appreciate more and more the subtleties of a trained assassin.

"You aren't doing anything?" Higgens shrilled, "Well, then do something! He's dying!"

I thought for a moment that the ludicrous statement would set Isstvan to laughing again, but not this time.

"Oh," he sighed. "This is all so confusing. Yes, I guess you're right."

He clicked his fingers and Brockhurst stopped thrashing about and began breathing again in long, ragged breaths.

"Here, old boy," said Aahz. "Have some wine."

He offered Brockhurst a brimming flagon which the Imp began to gulp gratefully.

"Aahz," Isstvan said sternly. "I don't think you've been honest with us."

"Me?" Aahz asked innocently.

"Even you couldn't have caused this much havoc without assistance. Now where is it coming from?"

He closed his eyes and turned his face toward the ceiling for a moment.

"Aah!" he suddenly proclaimed. "Here it is."

There was a squawk from the other end of the mezzanine and Tanda was suddenly lifted into view by unseen hands.

"Higgens!" exclaimed Isstvan, "Another one! Well, well, the day is full of surprises."

Tanda held her silence as she was floated down to a chair on a level with the others.

"Now let's see," Isstvan mumbled to himself. "Have we missed anybody?"

I felt the sudden pressure of invisible forces and realized I was next. I tried desperately to think of a disguise, but the only thing that came to mind was Gleep . . . so I tried it.

"A dragon!" cried Brockhurst as I floated into view.

"Gleep!" I said, rolling my eyes desperately.

"Oh now that's too much," Isstvan pouted. "I want to see who I'm dealing with."

He gave a vacant wave of his hand, and the disguises disappeared . . . all of them. I was me, Quigley was Quigley, Tanda was Tanda, the Imps were Imps, and the Deveel was a Deveel. Aahz, of course, was Aahz. Apparently a moratorium had been declared on disguises . . . by a majority of one . . . Isstvan.

I came drifting down to join the others, but my entrance was generally ignored in the other proceedings.

"Tanda!" Isstvan cried enthusiastically. "Well, well. This *is* a reunion, isn't it?"

"Bark at the moon, Isstvan," Tanda snarled defiantly.

Quigley was looking at everyone else with such speed I thought his head would fall off.

"I don't understand!" he whimpered plaintively.

"Shut up, Quigley," Aahz growled. "We'll explain later."

"That's assuming there is a later," Frumple sneered.

I tended to agree with Frumple. The atmosphere in the room no longer had even the semblance of joviality. It was over. We had lost. We were all exposed and captured, and Isstvan was as strong as ever. Whatever Aahz's secret weapon was, it apparently hadn't worked.

"Well, I'm afraid all good things must come to an end," Isstvan sighed, draining his flagon. "Now I'm afraid I'll have to dispose of you."

He sounded genuinely sad, but somehow I couldn't muster any sympathy for his plight.

"Just one question before we begin, Aahz," he asked in surprisingly sane tones.

"What's that?" Aahz responded.

"Why did you do it? I mean, with as feeble a team as this, how did you possibly hope to beat me?"

Isstvan sounded genuinely sincere.

"Well, Isstvan," Aahz drawled, "that's a matter of opinion."

"What's that supposed to mean?" Isstvan asked suspiciously.

"I don't 'hope' we can beat you," Aahz smiled. "I know we can."

"Really?" Isstvan chuckled. "And upon what are you basing your logic?"

"Why, I'm basing it on the fact that we've already won," Aahz blinked innocently. "It's all over, Isstvan, whether you realize it or not."

# XXV:

*"Just because you've beaten a sorcerer, doesn't mean you've beaten a sorcerer."*

—TOTH-AAMON

"Aahz," Isstvan said sternly, "there comes a time when even your humor wears a little thin."

"I'm not kidding, Isstvan," Aahz assured him. "You've lost your powers. Go ahead, try something. Anything!"

Isstvan hesitated. He closed his eyes.

Nothing happened.

"You see?" Aahz shrugged. "You've lost your powers. All of them. And don't look to your associates for help. They're all in the same boat."

"You mean we've really won?" I blurted out, the full impact of what was transpiring finally starting to sink in.

"That's right, kid."

Aahz suddenly leaned forward and clapped Frumple on the shoulder.

"Congratulations, Frumple," he exclaimed. "I've got to admit I didn't think you could do it."

"What?" blinked the Deveel.

"I'm just glad this squares our debt with you," Aahz

continued without pause. "You won't try to back out on it now, will you?"

"Frumple!" Isstvan's voice was dark with menace. "Did you do this to us?"

"I . . . I . . ." Frumple stammered.

"Go ahead, Frumple. Gloat!" Aahz encouraged. "He can't do anything to you now. Besides, you can teleport out of here anytime you want."

"No, he can't!" snarled Higgens, and his arm flashed forward.

I caught a glimpse of a small ball flying through the air before it exploded against Frumple's forehead in a cloud of purple dust.

"But . . ." began Frumple, but it was too late.

In mid-gesture his limbs became rigid and his face froze. We had another statue on our hands.

"Good move, Higgens," applauded Aahz.

"If it wouldn't be too much trouble, Aahz," interrupted Isstvan. "Could you explain what's going on here?"

"Aah!" said Aahz, "therein lies the story."

"This sounds familiar," Quigley mumbled.

I poked him in the ribs with my elbow. We weren't out of this yet.

"It seems that Frumple learned about your plans from Throckwoddle. Apparently he was afraid that if you succeeded in taking over the dimensions, you would implement price controls, thereby putting him out of business as a merchant. You know how those Deveels are."

The Imps snorted. Isstvan nodded thoughtfully.

"Anyway, he decided to try to stop you. To accomplish this, he blackmailed the four of us into assisting him. We were to create a diversion while he effected the actual attack."

"Well, what did he do?" prompted Higgens.

"He drugged the wine!" explained Aahz. "Don't you remember?"

"When?" asked Brockhurst.

"When he dropped that phony crystal into the jug, remember?"

"But he drank from the jug, too!" exclaimed Higgens.

"That's right, but he had taken an antidote in advance," Aahz finished with a flourish.

"So we're stuck here!" Brockhurst spat in disgust.

"You know, Aahz," Isstvan said slowly. "It occurs to me that even if everything happened exactly as you described it, you and your friends here played a fairly large part in the plot."

"You're right, Isstvan," Aahz admitted, "but I'm prepared to offer you a bargain."

"What kind of a bargain?" Isstvan asked suspiciously.

"It's in two parts. First, to clear Tanda and myself from having opposed you in your last bid for power, I can offer transportation for you and your allies out of this dimension."

"Hmm . . ." said Isstvan. "And the second part?"

"For the second part, I can give you the ultimate vengeance to visit on Frumple here. In exchange, I want your promise you'll bear no grudge against the four of us for our part in today's misfortune."

"Pardon for four in exchange for vengeance on one?" Isstvan grunted. "That doesn't sound like much of a deal."

"I think you're overlooking something, Isstvan," Aahz cautioned.

"What's that?"

"You've lost your powers. That makes it four of us against three of you."

"Look at your four," Brockhurst sneered. "A woman, a half-trained apprentice, a broken-down demon hunter, and a Pervert."

"Broken-down?" Quigley scowled.

"Easy, Quigley . . . and you too, Tanda," Aahz ordered. "Your three are nothing to brag about either, Brockhurst. Two Imps who've lost their powers and a fat madman."

Surprisingly, this seemed to revive Isstvan's humor. The Imps were not amused.

"Now look, Aahz," Higgens began, "if you want a fight. . . ."

"You miss the point entirely, gentlemen," Aahz said soothingly. "I'm trying to avoid a fight. I'm merely trying to point out that if this comes to a fight, you'll lose."

"Not necessarily," Brockhurst bristled.

"Inescapably," Aahz insisted. "Look, if we fight and we win, you lose. On the other hand, if we fight and we lose, you lose."

"How do you figure that?" Higgens asked suspiciously.

"Simple!" said Aahz smugly, "If you kill us, you'll have lost your only way to get out of this dimension. You'll be stuck forever on Klah. By my figuring, that's losing."

"We're in agreement there," Brockhurst mumbled.

"Oh, stop this bickering!" Isstvan interrupted with a chuckle. "Aahz is right, as usual. He may have lost a couple of fights, both magical and physical, but I've never heard of anyone out-arguing him."

"Then it's a deal?" Aahz asked.

"It's a deal!" Isstvan said firmly. "As if we had any choice in the matter."

They shook hands ceremoniously.

I noticed the Imps were whispering together and shooting dark glances in our direction. I wondered if a deal with Isstvan was binding on the Imps. I wondered if a handshake was legally binding in a situation such as this. But most of all, I wondered what Aahz had up his sleeve this time.

"Well, Aahz?" Isstvan asked, "Where is this escape clause you promised?"

"Right here!" Aahz said, fishing a familiar object from inside his shirt and tossing it to Isstvan.

"A D-Hopper!" Isstvan cried with delight. "I haven't seen one of these since. . . ."

"What is it?" Higgens interrupted.

Isstvan scowled at him.

"It's our ticket off this dimension," he exclaimed grudgingly.

"How does it work?" Brockhurst asked suspiciously.

"Trust me, gentlemen." Isstvan's distasteful expression gave lie to the joviality of his words. "It works."

He turned to Aahz again.

"Imps!" he mumbled to himself.

"You hired 'em," Aahz commented, unsympathetically.

"So I did. Well, what is this diabolical vengeance you have in mind for Frumple?"

"That's easy," smiled Aahz. "Use the D-Hopper and take him back to Deva."

"Why Deva?" Isstvan asked.

"Because he's been banned from Deva," Higgens answered, the light dawning.

". . . and the Deveels are unequaled at meting out punishment to those who break their laws," Brockhurst finished with an evil smile.

"Why was Frumple banned from Deva?" Tanda whispered to me.

"I don't know," I confided. "Maybe he gave a refund or something."

"I don't believe it," she snorted, "I mean he *is* a Deveel."

"Aahz," Isstvan smiled, regarding the D-Hopper, "I've always admired your sense of humor. It's even nastier than mine."

"What do you expect from a Pervert?" snorted Brockhurst.

"Watch your mouth, Imp," I snarled.

He was starting to get on my nerves.

"Then it's settled!" Isstvan chortled, clapping his hands together gleefully. "Brockhurst! Higgens! Come gather around Frumple here. We're off to Deva."

"Right now?" asked Brockhurst.

"With . . . things here so unsettled?" Higgens added, glancing at us again.

"Oh, we won't be long," Isstvan assured them.

"There's nothing here we can't come back and pick up later."

"That's true," admitted Brockhurst, staring at me thoughtfully.

"Umm . . . Isstvan?"

It was Quigley.

"Are you addressing me?" Isstvan asked with mock formality.

"Yes." Quigley looked uncomfortable. "Am I to understand you are all about to depart for some place completely populated with demons?"

"That is correct," Isstvan nodded.

"Could . . . that is . . . would you mind if I accompanied you?"

"What?" I exclaimed, genuinely startled. "Why?"

"Well . . ." Quigley said hesitantly, "if there is one thing I have learned this day, it's that I really know very little about demons."

"Hear, hear!" mumbled Aahz.

"I am undecided as to whether or not to continue in my chosen profession," Quigley continued, "but in any case it behooves me to learn more about demons. What better place could there be for such study than in a land completely populated with demons?"

"Why should we burden ourselves with a demon hunter of all things?" Brockhurst appealed to Isstvan.

"Maybe we could teach him a few things about demons," Higgens suggested in an overly innocent voice, giving his partner a covert poke in the side.

"What? Hmm . . . You know, you're right, Higgens." Brockhurst was suddenly smiling again.

"Good!" exclaimed Isstvan. "We'll make a party of it."

"In that case," purred Tanda, "you won't mind if I tag along, too."

"What?" exclaimed Brockhurst.

"Why?" challenged Higgens.

"To help, of course," she smiled. "I want to be there when you teach Quigley about demons. Maybe I can help him learn."

"Wonderful, wonderful," Isstvan beamed, overriding the Imps' objections. "The more the merrier. Aahz? Skeeve? Will you be joining us?"

"Not this time, thanks," Aahz replied before I could open my mouth. "The kid here and I have a few things to go over that won't wait."

"Like what?" I asked.

"Shut up, kid," Aahz hissed, then smiled again at the group. "You all run along. We'll be here when you come back."

"We'll be looking forward to it." Brockhurst smiled grimly.

"G'bye, Aahz, Skeeve!" Tanda waved. "I'll look for you next time around."

"But Tanda. . . ." I began.

"Don't worry, lad," Quigley assured me. "I'll make sure nothing happens to her."

Behind him, Tanda shot me a bawdy wink.

"Aahz!" Isstvan chuckled. "I do enjoy your company. We must work together more often."

He adjusted the settings on the D-Hopper and prepared to trigger it.

"Good-bye, Isstvan." Aahz smiled and waved. "Remember me!"

There was a rippling in the air and they were gone. All of them.

"Aahz!" I said urgently. "Did you see how those Imps looked at us?"

"Hmm? Oh. Yeah, kid. I told you they were vicious little creatures."

"But what are we going to do when they get back?"

"Don't worry about it, kid."

"Don't worry about it!" I shrieked. "We've got to. . . ."

". . . because they aren't coming back," Aahz finished.
That stopped me.

"But . . . when they get done on Deva. . . ."

"That's the joke, kid," Aahz grinned at me. "They
aren't going to Deva."

# XXVI:

*"A woman, like a good piece of music,
should have a solid end."*

—F. SCHUBERT

"They aren't going to Deva?"

I was having a rough time dealing with the concept.

"That's right, kid," Aahz said, pouring himself some more wine.

"But Isstvan set the D-Hopper himself."

"Yeah!" Aahz grinned smugly. "But last night I made one extra preparation for this sortie. I changed the markings on the dials."

"Then where are they going?"

"Beats me!" Aahz shrugged, taking a deep draught of the wine. "But I'm betting it'll take 'em a long time to find their way back. There are a lot of settings on a D-Hopper."

"But what about Tanda and Quigley?"

"Tanda can take care of Quigley," Aahz assured me. "Besides, she has the powers to pull them out anytime she wants."

"She does?"

"Sure. But she'll probably have a few laughs just tagging along for a while. Can't say as I blame her. I'd love to see Quigley deal with a few dimensions myself."

He took another generous gulp of the wine.

"Aahz!" I cried in sudden realization. "The wine!"

"What about it? Oh. Don't worry kid," he smiled. "I've already lost my powers, remember? Besides, you don't think I'd drug my own wine, do you?"

"You drugged the wine?"

"Yeah. That was my secret weapon. You didn't really believe all that bunk about Frumple, did you?"

"Ahh . . . of course not," I said, offended.

Actually, even though I knew Frumple hadn't done it, I had completely lost track of actually who had done what and to whom.

"Here, kid." Aahz handed me his flagon and picked up the jug. "Have some yourself. You did pretty good this afternoon."

I took the flagon, but somehow couldn't bring myself to drink any.

"What did you put in the wine, anyway?" I asked.

"Joke powder," Aahz replied. "As near as I can tell, it's the same stuff Garkin used on me. You can put it in a drink, sprinkle it over food, or burn it and have your victim inhale the smoke."

I had a sudden flash recollection of the brazier billowing smoke as Aahz materialized.

"What does it do?"

"Weren't you paying attention, kid?" Aahz cocked his head at me. "It takes away your powers."

"Permanently?"

"Of course not!" Aahz scoffed. "Only for a century."

"What's the antidote?"

"There isn't one . . . at least I couldn't get the stall-proprietor to admit to having one. Maybe when you get a little better with the magik, we'll go back to Deva and beat an answer out of him."

I thought for a few minutes. That seemed to answer all my questions . . . except one.

"Say . . . um, Aahz?"

"Yeah, kid?"

"What do we do now?"

"About what?" Aahz asked.

"I mean, what do we do? We've been spending all the time since we met getting ready to fight Isstvan. Well, it's over. Now what do we do?"

"What *you* do, apprentice," Aahz said sternly, "is devote your time to your magik. You've still got a long way to go before you're even close to Master status. As for me . . . well, I guess most of my time will be spent teaching you."

He poured a little more wine down his throat.

"Actually, we're in pretty good shape," he stated. "We've got a magik crystal courtesy of Frumple . . . and that crummy sword if we search his gear."

"And a malfunctioning fire-ring," I prompted.

"Um . . ." said Aahz. "Actually, I . . . ahh . . . well, I gave the ring to Tanda."

"Gave?" I asked. "You *gave* something away?"

Aahz shrugged.

"I'm a soft touch. Ask anybody."

"Hmm . . ." I said.

"We've, um, also got a war unicorn if we want to go anywhere," Aahz hastened on, "and that stupid dragon of yours."

"Gleep isn't stupid!" I insisted hotly.

"Okay, okay," Aahz amended, ". . . your intelligent, personable dragon."

"That's better," I mumbled.

". . . Even though it beats me why we'd want to go anyplace," Aahz commented, looking around him. "This place seems sound enough. You'd have some good force lines to play with, and the wine cellar will be well stocked if I know Isstvan. We could do lots worse for a base of operations."

Another question occurred to me.

"Say, Aahz?"

"Yeah, kid?"

"A few minutes ago you said you wanted to see Quigley when he visited other dimensions . . . and you seem to have a weak spot for Tanda. . . ."

"Yeah?" Aahz growled. "So?"

"So why didn't you go along with them? You didn't have to get stranded in this dimension."

"Isstvan's a fruitcake," Aahz declared pointedly, "and I don't like Imps. You think I'd like having them for traveling companions?"

"But you said Tanda could travel the dimensions by herself. Couldn't you and she have. . . ."

"All right, all right," interrupted Aahz. "You want me to say it? I stayed here because of you."

"Why?"

"Because you're not up to traveling the dimensions yet. Not until you. . . ."

"I mean, why stay with me at all?"

"Why? Because you're my apprentice! That's why."

Aahz seemed genuinely angry. "We made a deal, remember? You help me against Isstvan and I teach you magik. Well, you did your part and now I'm going to do mine. I'm going to teach you magik if it kills you . . . or me, which is more probable!"

"Yes, Aahz!" I agreed hastily.

"Besides," he mumbled, taking another drink. "I like you."

"Excuse me?" I said. "I didn't quite hear that."

"Then pay attention!" Aahz barked. "I said drink your wine, and give some to that stupid dragon of yours. I will allow you one . . . count it, one . . . night of celebration. Then bright and early tomorrow, we start working in earnest."

"Yes, Aahz," I said obediently.

"And kid," Aahz grinned, "don't worry about it being boring. We don't have to go looking for adventure. In our profession, it usually comes looking for us."

I had an ugly feeling he was right.

# MYTH CONCEPTIONS

*This book is dedicated to*

Laurie Oshrin and Judith Sampson

*a modern day student-teacher team who*
*unwittingly guaranteed the myth-adventures*
*of Aahz and Skeeve would continue to be written!*

# I

*"Life is a series of rude awakenings."*

—R. V. Winkle

Of all the various unpleasant ways to be aroused from a sound sleep, one of the worst is the noise of a dragon and a unicorn playing tag.

I pried one eye open and blearily tried to focus on the room. A chair toppled noisily to the floor, convincing me the blurred images my mind was receiving were due at least in part to the irregular vibrations coming from the floor and walls. One without my vast storehouse of knowledge (hard won and painfully endured) might be inclined to blame the pandemonium on an earthquake. I didn't. The logic behind this conclusion was simple. Earthquakes were extremely uncommon in this area. A dragon and a unicorn playing tag wasn't.

It was starting out as an ordinary day . . . that is, ordinary if you're a junior magician apprenticed to a demon.

If I had been able to predict the future with any degree of accuracy and thus forsee the events to come, I probably would have stayed in bed. I mean, fighting has never been my forte, and the idea of taking on a whole army . . . but I'm getting ahead of myself.

The thud that aroused me shook the building, accompanied by the crash of various dirty dishes shattering on the floor. The second thud was even more spectacular.

I considered doing something. I considered going back to sleep. Then I remembered my mentor's condition when he had gone to bed the night before.

That woke me up fast. The only thing nastier than a demon from Perv is a demon from Perv with a hangover.

I was on my feet and headed for the door in a flash. (My agility was a tribute more to my fear rather than to any inborn talent.) Wrenching the door open, I thrust my head outside and surveyed the terrain. The grounds outside the inn seemed normal. The weeds were totally out of hand, more than chest high in places. Something would have to be done about them someday, but my mentor didn't seem to mind their riotous growth, and since I was the logical candidate to cut them if I raised the point, I decided once again to keep silent on the subject.

Instead, I studied the various flattened patches and newly torn paths in the overgrowth, trying to determine the location or at least the direction of my quarries' movement. I had almost convinced myself that the silence was at least semipermanent and it would be all right to go back to sleep, when the ground began to tremble again. I sighed and shakily drew myself up to my full height, what there was of it, and prepared to meet the onslaught.

The unicorn was the first to come into view, great clumps of dirt flying from beneath his hooves as he ducked around the corner of the inn on my right.

"Buttercup!" I shouted in my most authoritative tone.

A split second later I had to jump back into the shelter of the doorway to avoid being trampled by the speeding beast. Though a bit miffed at his disobedience, I didn't really blame him. He had a dragon chasing him, and dragons are not notoriously agile when it comes to quick stops.

As if acting on a cue from my thoughts, the dragon

burst into view. To be accurate, he didn't really burst, he thudded, shaking the inn as he rebounded off the corner. As I said, dragons are not notoriously agile.

"Gleep!" I shouted. "Stop it this instant!"

He responded by taking an affectionate swipe at me with his tail as he bounded past. Fortunately for me, the gesture went wide of its mark, hitting the inn with another jarring thud instead.

So much for my most authoritative tone. If our two faithful charges were any more obedient, I'd be lucky to escape with my life. Still I had to stop them. Whoever came up with the immortal quote about waking sleeping dragons had obviously never had to contend with a sleeping demon.

I studied the two of them chasing each other through the weeds for a few moments, then decided to handle this the easy way. Closing my eyes, I envisioned both of them, the dragon and the unicorn. Then I superimposed the image of the dragon over that of the unicorn, fleshed it out with a few strokes of my mental paintbrush, then opened my eyes.

To my eyes, the scene was the same, a dragon and a unicorn confronting each other in a field of weeds. But, of course, I had cast the spell, so naturally I wouldn't be taken in. Its true effect could be read in Gleep's reaction.

He cocked his head and peered at Buttercup, first from this angle, then that, stretching his long serpentine neck to its limits. Then he swiveled his head until he was looking backward and repeated the process, scanning the surrounding weeds. Then he looked at Buttercup again.

To his eyes, his playmate had suddenly disappeared, to be replaced by another dragon. It was all very confusing, and he wanted his playmate back.

In my pet's defense, when I speak of his lack of agility, both physically and mentally, I don't mean to imply he is either clumsy or stupid. He's young, which also accounts for his mere ten-foot length and half-formed wings. I fully expect that when he matures—in another four or five hundred years—he will be very deft and wise, which is more than I can say for myself. In the unlikely event I should live that long, all I'll be is old.

"Gleep?"

The dragon was looking at me now. Having stretched his limited mental abilities to their utmost, he turned to me to correct the situation or at least provide an explanation. As the perpetrator of the situation causing his distress, I felt horribly guilty. For a moment, I wavered on the brink of restoring Buttercup's normal appearance.

"If you're *quite* sure you're making enough noise. . . ."

I winced at the deep, sarcastic tones booming close behind me. All my efforts were for naught. Aahz was awake.

I assumed my best hangdog attitude and turned to face him.

Needless to say, he looked terrible.

If, perchance, you think a demon covered with green scales already looks terrible, you've never encountered one with a hangover. The normal gold flecks in his yellow eyes were now copper, accented by a throbbing network of orange veins. His lips were drawn back in a painful grimace which exposed even more of his pointed teeth than his frightening, *reassuring* smile. Looming there, his fists clenched on his hips, he presented a picture terrifying enough to make a spider-bear faint.

I wasn't frightened, however. I had been with Aahz for over a year now, and knew his bark was worse than his bite. Then again, he had never bitten me.

"Gee, Aahz," I said, digging a small hole with my toe. "You're always telling me if I can't sleep through anything, I'm not really tired."

He ignored the barb, as he so frequently does when I catch him on his own quotes. Instead he squinted over my shoulder at the scene outside.

"Kid," he said. "Tell me you're practicing. Tell me you haven't really scrounged up another stupid dragon to make our lives miserable."

"I'm practicing!" I hastened to reassure him.

To prove the point, I quickly restored Buttercup's normal appearance.

"Gleep!" said Gleep happily, and the two of them were off again.

"Really, Aahz," I said innocently to head off his next caustic remark. "Where would I find another dragon in this dimension?"

"If there was one to be found here on Klah, you'd find it," he snarled. "As I recall, you didn't have that much trouble finding this one the first time I turned my back on you. Apprentices!"

He turned and retreated out of the sunlight into the dim interior of the inn.

"If I recall," I commented, following him, "that was at the Bazaar on Deva. I couldn't get another dragon there because you won't teach me how to travel through the dimensions."

"Get off my case, kid!" he moaned. "We've been over it a thousand times. Dimension traveling is dangerous. Look at me! Stranded without my powers in a backassward dimension like Klah, where the lifestyle is barbaric and the food is disgusting."

"You lost your powers because Garkin laced his special effects cauldron with that joke powder and then got killed before he could give you the antidote," I pointed out.

"Watch out how you talk about your old teacher," Aahz warned. "The old slime-monger was inclined to get carried away with practical jokes once in a while, true. But he was a master magician . . . and a friend of mine. If he wasn't, I wouldn't have saddled myself with his mouthy apprentice," he finished, giving me a meaningful look.

"I'm sorry, Aahz," I apologized. "It's just that I—"

"Look, kid," he interrupted wearily, "if I had my powers—which I don't—and if you were ready to learn dimension hopping—which you aren't—we could give it a try. Then, if you miscalculated and dumped us into the wrong dimension, I could get our tails out before anything bad happened. As things stand, trying to teach you dimension hopping would be more dangerous than playing Russian roulette."

"What's russian?" I asked.

The inn shook as Gleep missed the corner turn again.

"When are you going to teach your stupid dragon to play on the other side of the road?" Aahz snarled, craning his neck to glare out a window.

"I'm working on it, Aahz," I insisted soothingly. "Remember, it took me almost a whole year to housebreak him."

"Don't remind me," Aahz grumbled. "If I had my way, we'd . . ."

He broke off suddenly and cocked his head to one side.

"You'd better disguise that dragon, kid," he announced suddenly. "And get ready to do your 'dubious character' bit. We're about to have a visitor."

I didn't contest the information. We had established long ago that Aahz's hearing was much more acute than mine.

"Right, Aahz," I acknowledged and hurried about my task.

The trouble with using an inn for a base of operations, however abandoned or weather-beaten it might be, was that occasionally people would stop here seeking food and lodging. Magik was still outlawed in these lands, and the last thing we wanted was witnesses.

# II:

*"First impressions, being the longest lasting, are of utmost importance."*

—J. CARTER

**A**ahz and I had acquired the inn under rather dubious circumstances. Specifically, we claimed it as our rightful spoils of war after the two of us (with the assistance of a couple of allies, now absent) had routed Isstvan, a maniac magician, and sent him packing into far dimensions along with all his surviving accomplices. The inn had been Isstvan's base of operations. But now it was ours. Who Isstvan had gotten it from and how, I didn't want to know. Despite Aahz's constant assurances, I lived in dread of encountering the inn's rightful owner.

I couldn't help remembering all this as I waited outside the inn for our visitor. As I said, Aahz has very good hearing. When he tells me he hears something "close by," he frequently forgets to mention that "close by" may be over a mile away.

I have also noted, over the course of our friendship, that his hearing is curiously erratic. He can hear a lizard-bird scratching itself half a mile away, but occasionally

seems unable to hear the politest of requests no matter
how loudly I shout them at him.

There was still no sign of our rumored visitor. I considered moving back inside the inn out of the late morning
sun, but decided against it. I had carefully arranged the
scene for our guest's arrival, and I hated to disrupt it for
such a minor thing as personal comfort.

I had used the disguise spell liberally on Buttercup,
Gleep, and myself. Gleep now looked like a unicorn, a
change that did not seem to bother Buttercup in the
slightest. Apparently unicorns are less discriminating
about their playmates than are dragons. I had made them
both considerably more disheveled and unkempt-looking
than they actually were. This was necessary to maintain
the image set forth by my own appearance.

Aahz and I had decided early in our stay that the best
way to handle unwanted guests was not to threaten them
or frighten them away, but rather to be so repulsive that
they left of their own accord. To this end, I had slowly
devised a disguise designed to convince strangers they did
not want to be in the same inn with me, no matter how
large the inn was or how many other people were there.
In this disguise, I would greet wayward travelers as the
proprietor of the inn.

Modestly, I will admit the disguise was a screaming
success. In fact, that was the specific reaction many visitors had to it. Some screamed, some looked ill, others
sketched various religious symbols in the air between
themselves and me. None of them elected to spend the
night.

When I experimented with various physical defects,
Aahz correctly pointed out that many people did not find
any single defect revolting. In fact, in a dimension such
as Klah, most would consider it normal. To guarantee the
desired effect, I adopted many of them.

When disguised, I walked with a painful limp, had a
hump-back, and a deformed hand which was noticeably
diseased. What teeth remained were twisted and stained,

and the focus of one of my eyes had a tendency to wander about independently of the other. My nose—in fact, my entire face—was not symmetrical, and as a masterstroke of my disguise abilities, there appeared to be vicious-looking bugs crawling about my mangy hair and tattered clothes.

The overall effect was horrifying. Even Aahz admitted he found it disquieting, which, considering the things he's seen in his travels through the dimensions, was high praise indeed.

My thoughts were interrupted as our visitor came into view. He sat ramrod-straight astride a huge, flightless riding bird. He carried no visible weapons and wore no uniform, but his bearing marked him as a soldier much more than any outer trappings could have. His eyes were wary, constantly darting suspiciously about as he walked his bird up to the inn in slow, deliberate steps. Surprisingly enough, his gaze passed over me several times without registering my presence. Perhaps he didn't realize I was alive.

I didn't like this. The man seemed more the hunter than the casual traveler. Still, he was here and had to be dealt with. I went into my act.

"Does the noble sahr require a room?"

As I spoke I moved forward in my practical, rolling gait. In case the subtlety of my disguise escaped him, I allowed a large gob of spittle to ooze from the corner of my mouth where it rolled unhindered down to my chin.

For a moment the man's attention was occupied controlling his mount. Flightless or not, the bird was trying to take to the air.

Apparently my disguise had touched a primal chord in the bird's mind that went back prior to its flightless ancestry.

I waited, head cocked curiously, while the man fought the bird to a fidgety standstill. Finally, he turned his attention to me for a moment. Then he averted his eyes and stared carefully at the sky.

"I come seeking the one known as Skeeve the magician," he told me.

Now it was my turn to jump. To the best of my knowledge, no one knew who I was and what I was, much less where I was, except for Aahz and me.

"That's me!" I blurted out, forgetting myself and using my real voice.

The man turned horrified eyes on me, and I remembered my appearance.

"That's me master!" I amended hastily. "You wait . . . I fetch."

I turned and scuttled hastily into the inn. Aahz was waiting inside.

"What is it?" he demanded.

"He's . . . he wants to talk to Skeeve . . . to me!" I babbled nervously.

"So?" he asked pointedly. "What are you doing in here? Go outside and talk to the man."

"Looking like this?"

Aahz rolled his eyes at the ceiling in exasperation.

"Who cares what you look like?" he barked. "C'mon, kid. The man's a total stranger!"

"I care!" I declared, drawing myself up haughtily. "The man asked for Skeeve the magician, and I think—"

"He what?" Aahz interrupted.

"He asked for Skeeve the magician," I repeated, covertly studying the figure waiting outside.

"He looks like a soldier to me," I supplied.

"He looks scared to me," Aahz retorted. "Maybe you should tone down your disguise a bit next time."

"Do you think he's a demon-hunter?" I asked nervously.

Instead of answering my question, Aahz turned abruptly from the window.

"If he wants a magician, we'll give him a magician," he murmured. "Quick, kid, slap the Garkin disguise on me."

As I noted earlier, Garkin was my first magik instructor. An imposing figure with a salt-and-pepper beard, he was one of our favorite and most oft-used disguises. I could do Garkin in my sleep.

"Good enough, kid," Aahz commented, surveying the results of my work. "Now follow close and let me do the talking."

"Like this?" I exclaimed.

"Relax, kid," he reassured me. "For this conversation I'm you. Understand?"

Aahz was already heading out through the door without waiting for my reply, leaving me little choice other than to follow along behind him.

"Who seeks an audience with the great Skeeve?" Aahz bellowed in a resonant bass voice.

The man shot another nervous glance at me, then drew himself up in stiff formality.

"I come as an emissary from his most noble Majesty, Rodrick the Fifth, King of Possiltum, who—"

"Where's Possiltum?" Aahz interrupted.

"I beg your pardon?" the man blinked.

"Possiltum," Aahz repeated. "Where is it?"

"Oh!" the man said with sudden understanding. "It's the kingdom just east of here . . . other side of the Ember River . . . you can't miss it."

"Okay," Aahz nodded. "Go on."

The man took a deep breath, then hesitated, frowning.

"King of Possiltum," I prompted.

"Oh yes! Thanks." The man shot a quick smile, then another quick stare, then continued, "King of Possiltum, who sends his respects and greetings to the one known as Skeeve the magician . . ."

He paused and looked at Aahz expectantly. He was rewarded with a polite nod of the head. Satisfied, the man continued.

"His Majesty extends an invitation to Skeeve the magician to appear before the court of Possiltum that he

might be reviewed for his suitability for the position of
court magician."

"I don't really feel qualified to pass judgment on the
king's suitability as a court magician," Aahz said modestly, eyeing the man carefully. "Isn't he content just to
be king?"

"No, no!" the man corrected hastily. "The king wants
to review *your* suitability."

"Oh!" Aahz said with the appearance of sudden understanding. "That's a different matter entirely. Well,
well. An invitation from . . . who was it again?"

"Rodrick the Fifth," the man announced, lifting his
head haughtily.

"Well," Aahz said, grinning broadly. "I've never been
one to refuse a *fifth!*"

The man blinked and frowned, then glanced at me
quizzically. I shrugged, not understanding the joke myself.

"You may tell His Majesty," Aahz continued, unaware
of our confusion. "I shall be happy to accept his kind
invitation. I shall arrive at his court at my earliest con-
venience."

The man frowned.

"I believe His Majesty requires your immediate presence," he commented darkly.

"Of course," Aahz answered smoothly. "How silly of
me. If you will accept our hospitality for the night, I and
my assistant here will be most pleased to accompany you
in the morning."

I knew a cue when I heard one. I drooled and bared
my teeth at the messenger.

The man shot a horrified look in my direction.

"Actually," he said hastily, "I really must be going. I'll
tell His Majesty you'll be following close behind."

"You're sure you wouldn't like to stay?" Aahz asked
hopefully.

"Positive!" The man nearly shouted his reply as he
began backing the bird away from us.

"Oh, well," Aahz said. "Perhaps we'll catch up with you on the road."

"In that case," the man said, turning his bird, "I'll want a head . . . that is, I'd best be on my way to announce your coming."

I raised my hand to wave good-bye, but he was already moving at a rapid pace, urging his mount to still greater speeds and ignoring me completely.

"Excellent!" Aahz exclaimed, rubbing his hands together gleefully. "A court magician! What a soft job! And the day started out so miserably."

"If I can interrupt," I interrupted. "There's one minor flaw in your plan."

"Hmm? What's that?"

"I don't want to be a court magician!"

As usual, my protest didn't dampen his enthusiasm at all.

"You didn't want to be a magician, either," he reminded me bluntly. "You wanted to be a thief. Well, here's a good compromise for you. As a court magician, you'll be a civil servant . . . and civil servants are thieves on a grander scale than you ever dreamed possible!"

# III:

*"Ninety percent of any business trans-
action is selling yourself to the client."*

—X. HOLLANDER

"**N**ow let me see if I've got this right," I said carefully.
"You're saying they probably *won't* hire me on the
basis of my abilities?"

I couldn't believe I'd interpreted Aahz's lecture correctly, but he beamed enthusiastically.

"That's right, kid," he approved. "Now you've got it."

"No, I don't," I insisted. "That's the craziest thing I've
ever heard!"

Aahz groaned and hid his face in his hand.

It had been like this ever since we left the inn, and
three days of a demon's groaning is a bit much for anyone
to take.

"I'm sorry, Aahz," I said testily, "but I don't believe
it. I've taken a lot of things you've told me on faith, but
this . . . this goes against common sense."

"What does common sense have to do with it?" he
exploded. "We're talking about a job interview!"

At this outburst, Buttercup snorted and tossed his head,

making it necessary for us to duck out of range of his horn.

"Steady, Buttercup!" I admonished soothingly.

Though he still rolled his eyes, the unicorn resumed his stoic plodding, the travois loaded with our equipment dragging along behind him still intact. Despite incidents such as had occurred back at the inn, Buttercup and I got along fairly well, and he usually obeyed me. In contrast, he and Aahz never really hit it off, especially when the latter chose to raise his voice angrily.

"All it takes is a little gentleness," I informed Aahz smugly. "You should try it sometime."

"While you're showing off your dubious rapport with animals," Aahz retorted, "you might call your dragon back. All we need is to have him stirring up the country-side."

I cast a quick glance about. He was right. Gleep had disappeared . . . again.

"Gleep!" I called. "Come here, fella!"

"Gleep!" came an answering cry.

The bushes off to our left parted, and the dragon's head emerged.

"Gleep?" he said, cocking his head.

"Come here!" I repeated.

My pet needed no more encouragement. He bounded into the open and trotted to my side.

"I still say we should have left that stupid dragon back at the inn," Aahz grumbled.

I ignored him, checking to be sure that the gear hung saddlebag fashion over the dragon's back was still secure. Personally, I felt we were carrying far too much in the way of personal belongings, but Aahz had insisted. Gleep tried to nuzzle me affectionately with his head, and I caught a whiff of his breath. For a moment, I wondered if Aahz had been right about leaving the dragon behind.

"What were you saying about job interviews?" I asked, both to change the subject and to hide the fact I was gagging.

"I know it sounds ridiculous, kid," Aahz began with sudden sincerity, "and it is, but a lot of things are ridiculous, particularly in this dimension. That doesn't mean we don't have to deal with them."

That gave me pause to think. To a lot of people, having a demon and a dragon for traveling companions would seem ridiculous. As a matter of fact, if I took time to think it through, it seemed pretty ridiculous to me!

"Okay, Aahz," I said finally, "I can accept the existence of ridiculousness as reality. Now try explaining the court magician thing to me again."

We resumed walking as Aahz organized his thoughts. For a change, Gleep trailed placidly along beside Buttercup instead of taking off on another of his exploratory side trips.

"See if this makes any sense," Aahz said finally. "Court magicians don't do much . . . magically at least. They're primarily kept around for show, as a status symbol to demonstrate a court is advanced enough to rate a magician. It's a rare occasion when they're called upon to do anything. If you were a jester, they'd work your tail off, but not as a magician. Remember, most people are skittish about magik, and use it as seldom as possible."

"If that's the case," I said confidently, "I'm qualified. I'll match my ability to do nothing against any magician on Klah."

"No argument there," Aahz observed dryly. "But it's not quite that easy. To hold the job takes next to no effort at all. Getting the job can be an uphill struggle."

"Oh!" I said, mollified.

"Now to get the job, you'll have to impress the king and probably his advisors," Aahz continued. "You'll have to impress them with *you*, not with your abilities."

"How's that again?" I frowned.

"Look, kid. Like I said, a court magician is window dressing, a showpiece. They'll be looking for someone they want to have hanging around their court, someone who is impressive whether or not he ever does anything.

You'll have to exude confidence. Most important, you'll have to look like a magician . . . or at least, what they think a magician looks like. If you can dress like a magician, talk like a magician, and act like a magician, maybe no one will notice you don't have the abilities of a magician."

"Thanks, Aahz," I grimaced. "You're really doing wonders towards building my confidence."

"Now don't sulk," Aahz admonished. "You know how to levitate reasonably large objects, you can fly after a fashion, and you've got the disguise spell down pat. You're doing pretty well for a rank novice, but don't kid yourself into believing you're anywhere near full magician's status."

He was right, of course, but I was loath to admit it.

"If I'm such a bumbling incompetent," I said stiffly, "why are we on our way to establish me as a court magician?"

Aahz bared his teeth at me in irritation.

"You aren't listening, kid," he snarled. "Holding the job once you've got it will be a breeze. You can handle that now. The tricky part will be getting you hired. Fortunately, with a few minor modifications and a little coaching, I think we can get you ready for polite society."

"Modifications such as what?" I asked, curious despite myself.

Aahz made a big show of surveying me from head to foot.

"For a start," he said, "there's the way you dress."

"What's wrong with the way I dress?" I countered defensively.

"Nothing at all," he replied innocently. "That is, if you want people to see you as a bumpkin peasant with dung on his boots. Of course, if you want to be a court magician, well, that's another story. No respectable magician would be caught dead in an outfit like that."

"But I am a respectable magician!" I argued.

"Really? Respected by who?"

He had me there, so I lapsed into silence.

"That's specifically the reason I had the foresight to bring along a few items from the inn," Aahz continued, indicating Buttercup's burdens with a grand sweep of his hand.

"And here I thought you were just looting the place," I said dryly.

"Watch your mouth, kid," he warned. "This is all for your benefit."

"Really? You aren't expecting anything at all out of this deal?"

My sarcasm, as usual, was lost on him.

"Oh, I'll be around," he acknowledged. "Don't worry about that. Publicly, I'll be your apprentice."

"My apprentice?"

This job was suddenly sounding much better.

"Publicly!" Aahz repeated hastily. "Privately, you'll continue your lessons as normal. Remember that before you start getting frisky with your 'apprentice.' "

"Of course, Aahz," I assured him. "Now, what was it you were saying about changing the way I dress?"

He shot me a sidelong glance, apparently suspicious of my sudden enthusiasm.

"Not that there's anything wrong with me the way I am," I added with a theatrical scowl.

That seemed to ease his doubts.

"Everything's wrong with the way you dress," he growled. "We're lucky those two Imps left most of their wardrobe behind when we sent 'em packing along with Isstvan."

"Higgens and Brockhurst?"

"Yeah, those two," Aahz grinned evilly at the memory. "I'll say one thing for Imps. They may be inferior to Deveels as merchants, but they *are* snappy dressers."

"I find it hard to believe that all that stuff you bundled along is wardrobe," I observed skeptically.

"Of course it isn't," my mentor moaned. "It's special effects gear."

"Special effects?"

"Don't you remember anything, kid?" Aahz scowled.
"I told you all this when we first met. However easy magik is, you can't let it *look* easy. You need a few hand
props, a line of patter . . . you know, like Garkin had."

Garkin's hut, where I had first been introduced to magik, had been full of candles, vials of strange powders,
dusty books . . . now there was a magician's lair! Of
course, I had since discovered most of what he had was
unnecessary for the actual working of magik itself.

I was beginning to see what Aahz meant when he said
I'd have to learn to put on a show.

"We've got a lot of stuff we can work into your presentation," Aahz continued. "Isstvan left a lot of his junk
behind when he left. Oh, and you might find some familiar items when we unload. I think the Imps helped
themselves to some of Garkin's equipment and brought it
back to the inn with them."

"Really?" I said, genuinely interested. "Did they get
Garkin's brazier?"

"Brazier?" My mentor frowned.

"You remember," I prompted. "You used it to drink
wine out of when you first arrived."

"That's right! Yeah, I think I saw it in there. Why?"

"No special reason," I replied innocently. "It was always a favorite of mine, that's all."

From watching Garkin back in my early apprentice
days, I knew there were secrets to that brazier I was dying
to learn. I also knew that, if possible, I wanted to save it
as a surprise for Aahz.

"We're going to have to do something about your
physical appearance, too," Aahz continued thoughtfully.

"What's—"

"You're too young!" he answered, anticipating my
question. "Nobody hires a young magician. They want
one who's been around for a while. If we—"

He broke off suddenly and craned his neck to look
around.

"Kid," he said carefully, studying the sky. "Your dragon's gone again."

I did a fast scan. He was right.

"Gleep!" I called. "Here, fella!"

The dragon's head appeared from the depths of a bush behind us. There was something slimy with legs dangling from his mouth, but before I could manage an exact identification, my pet swallowed and the whatzit disappeared.

"Gleep!" he said proudly, licking his lips with his long forked tongue.

"Stupid dragon," Aahz muttered darkly.

"He's cheap to feed," I countered, playing on what I knew to be Aahz's tight-fisted nature.

As we waited for the dragon to catch up, I had time to reflect that for once I felt no moral or ethical qualms about taking part in one of Aahz's schemes. If the unsuspecting Rodrick the Fifth was taken in by our charade and hired us, I was confident the king would be getting more than he bargained for.

# IV:

*"If the proper preparations have been made and the necessary precautions taken, any staged event is guaranteed success."*

—ETHELRED THE UNREADY

The candle lit at the barest flick from my mind. Delighted, I snuffed it and tried again.

A sidelong glance, a fleeting concentration of my will, and the smoldering wick burst into flame again.

I snuffed the flame and sat smiling at the familiar candle.

This was the first real proof I'd had as to how far my magical powers had developed in the past year. I knew this candle from my years as Garkin's apprentice. In those days, it was my arch nemesis. Even focusing all my energies failed to light it then. But now . . .

I glanced at the wick again, and again it rewarded me with a burst of flame.

I snuffed it and repeated the exercise, my confidence growing as I realized how easily I could now do something I once thought impossible.

"Will you knock it off with the candle!"

I jumped at the sound of Aahz's outburst, nearly upsetting the candle and setting the blanket afire.

"I'm sorry, Aahz," I said, hastily snuffing the candle for the last time. "I just—"

"You're here to audition for court magician," he interrupted. "Not for town Christmas tree!"

I considered asking what a Christmas tree was, but decided against it. Aahz seemed uncommonly irritable and nervous, and I was pretty sure, however I chose to phrase my question, that the answer would be both sarcastic and unproductive.

"Stupid candle blinking on and off," Aahz grumbled half to himself. "Attract the attention of every guard in the castle."

"I thought we were trying to attract their attention," I pointed out, but Aahz ignored me, peering at the castle through the early-morning light.

He didn't have to peer far, as we were camped in the middle of the road just short of the castle's main gates.

As I said, I was under the impression our position was specifically chosen to attract attention to ourselves.

We had crept into position in the dead of night, clumsily picking our way through the sleeping buildings clustered about the main gate. Not wishing to show a light, unpacking had been minimal, but even in the dark, I had recognized Garkin's candle.

All of this had to do with something Aahz called a "dramatic entrance." As near as I could tell, all this meant was we couldn't do anything the easy way.

Our appearance was also carefully designed for effect, with the aid of the Imps' abandoned wardrobe and my disguise spells.

Aahz was outfitted in my now traditional "dubious character" disguise. Gleep was standing placidly beside Buttercup disguised as a unicorn, giving us a matched pair. It was my own appearance, however, which had been the main focus of our attentions.

Both Aahz and I had agreed that the Garkin disguise would be unsuitable for this effort. While my own natural appearance was too young, Garkin's would be too old. Since we could pretty much choose the image we wanted, we decided to field a magician in his mid to late thirties; young without being youthful, experienced without being old, and powerful but still learning.

To achieve this disguise involved a bit more work than normal, as I did not have an image in mind to superimpose over my own. Instead, I closed my eyes and envisioned myself as I appeared normally, then slowly erased the features until I had a blank face to begin on. Then I set to work with Aahz watching carefully and offering suggestions and modifications.

The first thing I changed was my height, adjusting the image until the new figure stood a head and a half taller than my actual diminutive stature. My hair was next and I changed my strawberry-blond thatch to a more sinister black, at the same time darkening my complexion several shades.

The face gave us the most trouble.

"Elongate the chin a little more," Aahz instructed. "Put on a beard . . . not that much, stupid! Just a little goatee! . . . That's better! . . . Now lower the sideburns . . . okay, build up the nose . . . narrow it . . . make the eyebrows bushier . . . no, change 'em back and sink the eyes a little instead . . . for crying out loud change the eye color! Make 'em brown . . . okay, now a couple of frown wrinkles in the middle of the forehead. . . . Good. That should do it."

I stared at the figure in my mind, burning the image into my memory. It was effective, maybe a bit more sinister than I would have designed if left to my own devices, but Aahz was the expert and I had to trust his judgment. I opened my eyes.

"Terrific, kid!" Aahz beamed. "Now put on that black robe with the gold and red trim the Imps left, and you'll cut a figure fit to grace any court."

"Move along there! You're blocking the road!"

The rude order wrenched my thoughts back to the present.

A soldier, resplendent in leather armor and brandishing an evil-looking pike, was angrily approaching our crude encampment. Behind him the gates stood slightly ajar, and I could see the heads of several other soldiers watching us curiously.

Now that the light was improving, I could see the wall better. It wasn't much of a wall, barely ten feet high. That figured. From what we had seen since we crossed the border, it wasn't much of a kingdom, either.

"You deaf or something?" the soldier barked drawing close. "I said move along!"

Aahz scuttled forward and planted himself in the soldier's path.

"Skeeve the Magnificent has arrived," he announced. "And he—"

"I don't care who you are!" the soldier snarled, wasting no time placing his pike between himself and the figure addressing him. "You can't—"

He broke off abruptly as his pike leaped from his grasp and floated horizontally in mid-air until it was forming a barricade between him and Aahz.

The occurrence was my doing, a simple feat of levitation. Regardless of our planned gambit, I felt I should take a direct hand in the proceedings before things got completely out of hand.

"I am Skeeve!" I boomed, forcing my voice into a resonant bass. "And that is my assistant you are attempting to threaten with your feeble weapon. We have come in response to an invitation from Rodrick the Fifth, King of Possiltum!"

"That's right, Bosco!" Aahz leered at the soldier. "Now just run along like a good fellow and pass the word we're here . . . eh?"

As I noted earlier, all this was designed to impress the hell out of the general populace. Apparently the guard hadn't read the script. He did not cower in terror or cringe with fear. If anything, our little act seemed to have the exact opposite effect on him.

MYTH CONCEPTIONS        233

"A magician, eh?" he said with a mocking sneer. "For that I've got standing orders. Go around to the back where the others are."

This took us aback. Well, at least it took *me* aback. According to our plan, we would end up arguing whether we entered the palace to perform in the king's court, or if the king had to bring his court outside to where we were. Being sent to the back door was not an option we had considered.

"To the back?" Aahz glowered. "You dare to suggest a magician of my master's stature go to the back door like a common servant?"

The soldier didn't budge an inch.

"If it were up to me, I'd 'dare to suggest' a far less pleasant activity for you. As it is, I have my orders. You're to go around to the back like all the others."

"Others?" I asked carefully.

"That's right," the guard sneered. "The king is holding an open air court to deal with all you 'miracle workers.' Every hack charm-peddler for eight kingdoms is in town. Some of 'em have been in line since noon yesterday. Now get around to the back and quit blocking the road!"

With that he turned on his heel and marched back to the gate, leaving his pike hanging in mid-air.

For once, Aahz was as speechless as I was. Apparently I wasn't the only one the king had invited to drop by. Apparently we were in big trouble.

# V:

*"... Eye of newt, toe of frog ..."*

—BELIEVED TO BE THE FIRST RECIPE
FOR AN EXPLOSIVE MIXTURE ... THE
FORERUNNER OF GUNPOWDER.

"What are we going to do, Aahz?"

With the guard out of earshot, I could revert to my normal voice and speech patterns, though it was still necessary to keep my physical disguise intact.

"That's easy," he responded. "We pack up our things and go around the back. Weren't you listening, kid?"

"But what are we going to do about ..."

But Aahz was already at work, rebinding the few items we had unpacked.

"Don't do anything, kid," he warned over his shoulder. "We can't let anyone see you doing menial work. It's bad for the image."

"He said there were other magicians here!" I blurted at last.

"Yeah. So?"

"Well, what are we going to do?"

Aahz scowled. "I told you once. We're going to pack our things and—"

"What are we going to do about the other magicians?"

"Do? We aren't going to *do* anything. You aren't up to dueling, you know."

He had finished packing and stepped back to survey his handiwork. Nodding in satisfaction, he turned and shot a glance over my shoulder.

"Do something about the pike, will ya, kid?"

I followed his gaze. The guard's pike was still hanging suspended in mid-air. Even though I hadn't been thinking about it, part of my mind had been keeping it afloat until I decided what to do with it. The question was, what should I do with it?

"Say, Aahz . . ." I began, but Aahz had already started walking along the wall.

For a moment I was immobilized with indecision. The guard had gone so I couldn't return his weapon to him. Still, simply letting it drop to the ground seemed somehow anticlimatic.

Unable to think of anything to do that would have the proper dramatic flair, I decided to postpone the decision. For the time being, I let the pike float along behind me as I hurried after Aahz, first giving it additional elevation so it would not be a danger to Gleep and Buttercup.

"Were you expecting other magicians to be here?" I asked, drawing abreast of my mentor.

"Not really," Aahz admitted. "It was a possibility, of course, but I didn't give it a very high probability rating. Still, it's not all that surprising. A job like this is bound to draw competition out of the woodwork."

He didn't seem particularly upset, so I tried to take this new development in stride.

"Okay," I said calmly. "How does this change our plans?"

"It doesn't. Just do your thing like I showed you and everything should come out fine."

"But if the other magicians—"

Aahz stopped short and turned to face me.

"Look, kid," he said seriously, "just because I keep

telling you you've got a long way to go before you're a master magician doesn't mean you're a hack! I wouldn't have encouraged you to show up for this interview if I didn't think you were good enough to land the job."

"Really, Aahz?"

He turned and started walking again.

"Just remember, as dimensions go, Klah isn't noted for its magicians. You're no master, but masters are few and far between. I'm betting that compared to the competition, you'll look like a real expert."

That made sense. Aahz was quite outspoken in his low opinion of Klah and the Klahds that inhabited it, including me. That last thought made me fish for a bit more reassurance.

"Aahz?"

"Yeah, kid?"

"What's your honest appraisal of my chances?"

There was a moment of silence before he answered.

"Kid, you know how you're always complaining that I keep tearing down your confidence?"

"Yeah?"

"Well, for both our sakes, don't push too hard for my honest appraisal."

I didn't.

Getting through the back gate proved to be no problem . . . mostly because there wasn't a back gate. To my surprise and Aahz's disgust, the wall did not extend completely around the palace. As near as I could see, only the front wall was complete. The two side walls were under construction, and the back wall was nonexistent. I should clarify that. My statement that the side walls were under construction was an assumption based on the presence of scaffolding at the end of the wall rather than by the observation of any activity going on. If there was any work being performed, it was being done carefully enough not to disturb the weeds which abounded throughout the scaffolding.

I was beginning to have grave doubts about the kingdom I was about to ally myself with.

It was difficult to tell if the court was being convened in a garden, or if this was a courtyard losing its fight with the weeds and underbrush which crowded in through the opening where the back wall should have been. (Having grown up on a farm, my basic education in plants was that if it wasn't edible and growing in neat rows, it was a weed.)

As if in answer to my thoughts, Buttercup took a large mouthful of the nearest clump of growth and began chewing enthusiastically. Gleep sniffed the same bush and turned up his nose at it.

All this I noted only as an aside. My main attention was focused on the court itself.

There was a small open-sided pavilion set against the wall of the palace sheltering a seated figure, presumably the king. Standing close beside him on either side were two other men. The crowd, such as it was, was split into two groups. The first was standing in a somewhat orderly line along one side of the garden. I assumed this was the waiting line . . . or rather I hoped it was as that was the group we joined. The second group was standing in a disorganized mob on the far side of the garden watching the proceedings. Whether these were rejected applicants or merely interested hangers-on, I didn't know.

Suddenly, a young couple in the watching group caught my eye. I hadn't expected to encounter any familiar faces here, but these two I had seen before. Not only had I seen them, Aahz and I had impersonated them at one point, a charade which had resulted in our being hanged.

"Aahz!" I whispered urgently. "Do you see those two over there?"

"No," Aahz said bluntly, not even turning his head to look.

"But they're the—"

"Forget 'em," he insisted. "Watch the judges. They're the ones we have to impress."

I had to admit that made a certain amount of sense. Grudgingly, I turned my attention to the figures in the pavilion.

The king was surprisingly young, perhaps in his mid-twenties. His hair was a tumble of shoulder-length curls, which combined with his slight build almost made him look effeminate. Judging from his posture, either the interviews had been going on for some time, or he had mastered the art of looking totally bored.

The man on his left bent and urgently whispered something in the king's ear and was answered by a vague nod.

This man, only slightly older than the king but balding noticeably, was dressed in a tunic and cloak of drab color and conservative cut. Though relaxed in posture and quiet in bearing, there was a watchful brightness to his eyes that reminded me of a feverish weasel.

There was a stirring of the figure on the king's right, which drew my attention in that direction. I had a flash impression of a massive furry lump, then I realized with a start that it was a man. He was tall and broad, his head crowned with thick, black, unkempt curls, his face nearly obscured by a full beard and mustache. This, combined with his heavy fur cloak, gave him an animal-like appearance which had dominated my first impression. He spoke briefly to the king, then recrossed his arms in a gesture of finality and glared at the other advisor. His cloak opened briefly during his oration, giving me a glimpse of a glittering shirt of mail and a massive double-headed hand-axe hung on a belt at his waist. Clearly this was not a man to cross. The balding figure seemed unimpressed, matching his rival's glare with one of his own.

There was a sharp nudge in my ribs.

"Did you see that?" Aahz whispered urgently.

"See what?" I asked.

"The king's advisors. A general and a chancellor unless

I miss my guess. Did you see the gold medallion on the general?"

"I saw his axe!" I whispered back.

The light in the courtyard suddenly dimmed.

Looking up, I saw a mass of clouds forming overhead, blotting out the sun.

"Weather control," Aahz murmured half to himself. "Not bad."

Sure enough, the old man in the red cloak currently before the throne gestured wildly and tossed a cloud of purple powder into the air, and a light drizzle began to fall.

My spirits fell along with the rain. Even with Aahz's coaching on presentation, my magik was not this powerful or impressive.

"Aahz . . ." I whispered urgently.

Instead of responding, he waved me to silence, his eyes riveted on the pavilion.

Following his gaze, I saw the general speaking urgently with the king. The king listened for a moment, then shrugged and said something to the magician.

Whatever he said, the magician didn't like it. Drawing himself up haughtily, he turned to leave, only to be called back by the king. Pointing to the clouds, the king said a few more words and leaned back. The magician hesitated, then shrugged, and began gesturing and chanting once more.

"Turned him down," Aahz said smugly.

"Then what's he doing now?"

"Clearing up the rain before the next act goes on," Aahz informed me.

Sure enough, the drizzle was slowing and the clouds began to scatter, much to the relief of the audience who, unlike the king, had no pavilion to protect them from the storm. This further display of the magician's power, however, did little to bolster my sagging confidence.

"Aahz!" I whispered. "He's a better magician than I am."

"Yeah," Aahz responded. "So?"

"So if they turned him down, I haven't got a chance!"

"Maybe yes, maybe no," came the thoughtful reply. "As near as I can tell, they're looking for something specific. Who knows? Maybe you're it. Remember what I told you, cushy jobs don't always go to the most skillful. In fact, it usually goes the other way."

"Yeah," I said, trying to sound optimistic. "Maybe I'll get lucky."

"It's going to take more than luck," Aahz corrected me sternly. "Now, what have you learned watching the king's advisors?"

"They don't like each other," I observed immediately.

"Right!" Aahz sounded surprised and pleased. "Now that means you probably won't be able to please them both. You'll have to play up to one of them . . . or better still insult one. That'll get the other one on your side faster than anything. Now, which one do you want on your side?"

That was easier than his first question.

"The general," I said firmly.

"Wrong! You want the chancellor."

"The chancellor!" I exclaimed, blurting the words out louder than I had intended. "Did you see the size of that axe the general's carrying?"

"Uh-huh," Aahz replied. "Did you hear what happened to the guy who interviewed before old Red Cloak here got his turn?"

I closed my eyes and controlled my first sharp remark.

"Aahz," I said carefully, "remember me? I'm Skeeve. I'm the one who can't hear whispers a mile away."

As usual Aahz ignored my sarcasm.

"The last guy didn't even get a chance to show his stuff," he informed me. "The chancellor took one look at the crowd he brought with him and asked how many were in his retinue. 'Eight,' the man said. 'Too many!' says the chancellor and the poor fool was dismissed immediately."

"So?" I asked bluntly.

"So the chancellor is the one watching the purse strings," concluded Aahz. "What's more, he has more influence than the general. Look at these silly walls. Do you think a military man would leave walls half-finished if he had the final say? Somebody decided too much money was being spent constructing them and the project was canceled or delayed. I'm betting that somebody was the chancellor."

"Maybe they ran out of stones," I suggested.

"C'mon, kid. From what we've seen since we crossed the border this kingdom's principal crop is stones."

"But the general . . ."

As I spoke, I glanced in the general's direction again. To my surprise and discomfort, he was staring directly at me. It wasn't a friendly stare.

I hesitated for a moment, hoping I was wrong. I wasn't. The general's gaze didn't waver, nor did his expression soften. If anything, it got uglier.

"Aahz," I hissed desperately, unable to tear my eyes from the general.

Now the king and the chancellor were staring in my direction too, their attention drawn by the general's gaze.

"Kid!" Aahz moaned beside me. "I thought I told you to do something about that pike!"

The pike! I had completely forgotten about it!

I pulled my eyes from the general's glare and glanced behind me as casually as I could.

Buttercup and Gleep were still standing patiently to our rear, and floating serenely above them was the guard's pike. I guess it was kind of noticeable.

"You!"

I turned toward the pavilion and the sound of the bellow. The general had stepped forward and was pointing a massive finger at me.

"Yes, you!" he roared as our eyes met once more. "Where did you get that pike? It belongs to the palace guards."

"I think you're about to have your interview, kid,"

Aahz murmured. "Give it your best and knock 'em stiff."

"But—" I protested.

"It beats standing in line!"

With that, Aahz took a long leisurely step backward. The effect was the same as if I had stepped forward, which I definitely hadn't. With the attention of the entire courtyard now centered on me, however, I had no choice but to take the plunge.

# VI:

*"That's entertainment!"*

—VLAD THE IMPALER

Crossing my arms, I moved toward the pavilion, keeping my pace slow and measured.

Aahz had insisted I practice this walk. He said it would make me look confident and self-possessed. Now that I was actually appearing before a king, I found I was using the walk, not as a show of arrogance, but to hide the weakness in my legs.

"Well?" the general rumbled, looming before me. "I asked you a question! Where did you get that pike? You'd best answer before I grow angry!"

Something in me snapped. Any fear I felt of the general and his axe evaporated, replaced by a heady glow of strength.

I had discovered on my first visit to the Bazaar at Deva that I didn't like to be pushed by big, loud Deveels. I discovered now that I also didn't like it any better when the arrogance came from a big, loud fellow Klahd.

So the big man wanted to throw his weight around, did he?

With a twitch of my mind, I summoned the pike. Without turning to look, I brought it arrowing over my shoulder in a course destined to embed it in the general's chest.

The general saw it coming and paled. He took an awkward step backward, realized it was too late for flight, and groped madly for his axe.

I stopped the pike three feet from his chest, floating it in front of him with its point leveled at his heart.

"This pike?" I asked casually.

"Ahh . . ." the general responded, his eyes never leaving the weapon.

"I took this pike from an overly rude soldier. He said he was following orders. Would those orders come from you, by any chance?"

"I . . . um. . . ." The general licked his lips. "I issued orders that my men deal with strangers in an expedient fashion. I said nothing about their being less than polite."

"In that case . . ."

I moved the pike ninety degrees so that it no longer threatened the general.

". . . I return the pike to you so that you might give it back to the guard along with a clarification of your orders. . . ."

The general hesitated, scowling, then extended his hand to grasp the floating pike. Just before he reached it, I let it fall to the ground where it clattered noisily.

". . . and hopefully additional instructions as to how to handle their weapons," I concluded.

The general flushed and started to pick up the pike. Then the chancellor snickered, and the general spun around to glare at him. The chancellor smirked openly and whispered something to the king, who tried to suppress a smile at his words.

The general turned to me again, ignoring the pike, and glared down from his full height.

"Who are you?" he asked in a tone which implied my name would be immediately moved to the head of the list for public execution.

"Who's asking?" I glared back, still not completely over my anger.

"The man you are addressing," the king interceded, "is Hugh Badaxe, Commander of the Royal Armies of Possiltum."

"And I am J. R. Grimble," the chancellor added hastily, afraid of being left out. "First Advisor to His Majesty."

The general shot another black look at Grimble. I decided it was time to get down to business.

"I am the magician known as Skeeve," I began grandly. "I have come in response to a gracious invitation from His Most Noble Majesty, Rodrick the Fifth."

I paused and inclined my head slightly to the king who smiled and nodded in return.

"I have come to determine for myself if I should consider accepting a position at the court of Possiltum."

The phrasing of that last part had been chosen very carefully by Aahz. It was designed to display my confidence by implying the choice was mine rather than theirs.

The subtlety was not lost on the chancellor, who raised a critical eyebrow at my choice of words.

"Now, such a position requires confidence on both sides," I continued. "I must feel that I will be amply rewarded for my services, and His Majesty must be satisfied that my skills are worthy of his sponsorship."

I turned slightly and raised my voice to address the entire court.

"The generosity of the crown of Possiltum is known to all," I declared. "And I have every confidence His Majesty will reward his retainers in proportion to their service to him."

There was a strangled sound behind me, from the general, I think. I ignored it.

"Therefore, all that is required is that I satisfy His Majesty . . . and his advisors . . . that my humble skills will indeed suffice his needs."

I turned to the throne once more, letting the king see my secret smile which belied the humility of my words.

"Your Majesty, my powers are many and varied. However, the essence of power is control. Therefore realizing you are a busy man, rather than waste time with mere commercial trickeries and minor demonstrations such as we have already seen, I shall weave but three spells and trust in your wisdom to perceive the depths behind them."

I turned and stretched forth a finger to point at Buttercup and Gleep.

"Yonder are my prize pair of matched unicorns," I said dramatically. "Would Your Majesty be so kind as to choose one of them?"

The king blinked in surprise at being invited to participate in my demonstration. For a moment he hesitated.

"Umm . . . I choose the one on the left," he said, finally indicating Buttercup.

I bowed slightly.

"Very well, Your Majesty. By your word shall that creature be spared. Observe the other closely."

Actually, that was another little stunt Aahz had taught me. It's called a "magician's force," and allows a performer to offer his audience a choice without really giving them a choice. Had the king chosen Gleep, I would have simply proceeded to work on "the creature he had doomed with a word."

Slowly, I pointed a finger at Gleep and lowered my head slightly.

"*Walla walla Washington!*" I said somberly.

I don't know what the words meant, but Aahz assured me they had historic precedence and would convince people I was actually doing something complex.

"*Alla kazam shazam,*" I continued, raising my other arm. "*Bibbity bobbity . . .*"

I mentally removed Gleep's disguise.

The crowd reacted with a gasp, drowning out my final "*goo-gleep.*"

My dragon heard his name, though, and reacted immediately. His head came up and he lumbered forward to stand docilely at my side. As planned, Aahz immediately shambled forward to a position near Gleep's head and stood watchful and ready.

This was meant to imply that we were prepared to handle any difficulty which might arise with the dragon. The crowd's reaction to him, however, overshadowed their horror at seeing a unicorn transformed to a dragon. I had forgotten how effective the "disreputable character" disguise was. Afraid of losing the momentum of my performance, I hurried on.

"This misshapen wretch is my apprentice Aahz," I announced. "You may wonder if it is within his power to stop the dragon should the beast grow angry. I tell you now . . . it is not!"

The crowd edged back nervously. From the corner of my eye, I saw the general's hand slide to the handle of his axe.

"But it *is* within my power! Now you know that the forces of darkness are no strangers to Skeeve!"

I spun and stabbed a finger at Aahz.

*"Bobbelty gook, crumbs and martyrs!"*

I removed Aahz's disguise.

There was a moment of stunned silence, then Aahz smiled. Aahz's smile has been known to make strong men weak, and there were not many strong men in the crowd.

The audience half trampled each other in their haste to backpedal from the demon, and the sound of screeches was intermixed with hastily chanted protection spells.

I turned to the throne once more. The king and the chancellor seemed to be taking it well. They were composed, though a bit pale. The general was scowling thoughtfully at Aahz.

"As a demon, my apprentice can suppress the dragon if need be . . . nay, ten dragons. Such is my power. Yet power must be tempered with gentleness . . . gentility if you will."

I allowed my expression to grow thoughtful.

"To confuse one's enemies and receive one's allies, you need no open show of power or menace. For occa-

sions such as those, one's powers can be masked until one
is no more conspicuous than . . . than a stripling."

As I spoke the final words, I stripped away my own
disguise and stood in my youthful unsplendor. I probably
should have used some fake magik words, but I had already used up all the ones Aahz had taught me and was
afraid of experimenting with new ones.

The king and the chancellor were staring at me intently
as if trying to penetrate my magical disguise with will-
power alone. The general was performing a similar exercise staring at Aahz, who folded his arms and bared his
teeth in a confident smile.

For a change, I shared his confidence. Let them stare.
It was too late to penetrate my magik because I wasn't
working any more. Though the royal troupe and the entire
audience was convinced they were witnessing a powerful
spell, in actuality all I had done was remove the spells
which had been distorting their vision. At the moment, all
of us, Aahz, Buttercup, Gleep, and myself, were our normal selves, however abnormal we appeared. Even the
most adept magical vision could not penetrate a nonexistent spell.

"As you see, Your Majesty," I concluded. "My powers
are far from ordinary. They can make the gentle fearsome,
or the mighty harmless. They can destroy your enemies
or amuse your court, depending upon your whim. Say the
word, speak your approval, and the powers of Skeeve are
yours to command."

I drew myself up and bowed my head respectfully, and
remained in that position awaiting judgment from the
throne.

Several moments passed without a word. Finally, I
risked a peek at the pavilion.

The chancellor and the general were exchanging heated
whispers over the head of the king, who inclined his head
this way and that as he listened. Realizing this could take
a while, I quietly eased my head to an upright position as
I waited.

"Skeeve!" the king called suddenly, interrupting his advisor's arguments. "That thing you did with the pike. Can you always control weapons so easily?"

"Child's play, Your Majesty," I said modestly. "I hesitate to even acknowledge it as a power."

The king nodded and spoke briefly to his advisors in undertones. When he had finished, the general flushed and, turning on his heel, strode off into the palace. The chancellor looked smug.

I risked a glance at Aahz, who winked at me. Even though he was further away, apparently his acute hearing had given him advance notice of the king's decision.

"Let all here assembled bear witness!" the chancellor's ringing voice announced. "Rodrick the Fifth, King of Possiltum, does hereby commend the magical skill and knowledge of one Skeeve and does formally name him Magician to the Court of Possiltum. Let all applaud the appointment of this master magician . . . and then disperse!"

There was a smattering of halfhearted applause from my vanquished rivals, and more than a few glares. I acknowledged neither as I tried to comprehend the chancellor's words.

I did it! Court Magician! Of the entire selection of magicians from five kingdoms, I had been chosen! Me! Skeeve!

I was suddenly aware of the chancellor beckoning me forward. Trying to be nonchalant, I approached the throne.

"Lord Magician," the chancellor said with a smile. "If you will, might we discuss the matter of your wages?"

"My apprentice handles such matters," I informed him loftily. "I prefer not to distract myself with such mundane matters."

Again, we had agreed that Aahz would handle the wage negotiations, his knowledge of magik being surpassed only by his skill at haggling. I turned and beckoned to him. He responded by hurrying forward, his eavesdropping having forewarned him of the situation.

"That can wait, Grimble," the king interrupted. "There are more pressing matters which command our magician's attention."

"You need only command, Your Majesty," I said, bowing grandly.

"Fine," the king beamed. "Then report to General Bad-axe immediately for your briefing."

"Briefing about what?" I asked, genuinely puzzled.

"Why, your briefing about the invading army, of course," the king replied.

An alarm gong went off in the back of my mind.

"Invading army?" I blurted, forgetting my rehearsed pompous tones. "What invading army?"

"The one which even now approaches our borders," the chancellor supplied. "Why else would we suddenly need a magician?"

# VII:

*"Numerical superiority is of no conse-
quence. In battle, victory will go to the
best tactician."*

—G. A. CUSTER

"Cushy job, he said! Chance to practice, he said! Piece
of cake, he said!"

"Simmer down, kid!" Aahz growled.

"Simmer down? Aahz, weren't you listening? I'm supposed to stop an army! Me!"

"It could be worse," Aahz insisted.

"How?" I asked bluntly.

"You could be doing it without me," he replied. "Think
about it."

I did, and cooled down immediately. Even though my
association with Aahz seemed to land me in an inordinate
amount of trouble, he had also been unfailing in his ability
to get me out . . . so far. The last thing I wanted to do was
drive him away just when I needed him the most.

"What am I going to do, Aahz?" I moaned.

"Since you ask"—Aahz smiled—"my advice would be
to not panic until we get the whole story. Remember, there
are armies and there are armies. For all we know, this one

might be weak enough for us to beat fair and square."

"And if it isn't?" I asked skeptically.

"We'll burn that bridge when we come to it," Aahz sighed. "First, let's hear what old Badaxe has to say."

Not being able to think of anything to say in reply to that, I didn't. Instead, I kept pace with my mentor in gloomy silence as we followed the chancellor's directions through the corridors of the palace.

It would have been easier to accept the offered guide to lead us to our destination, but I had been more than a little eager to speak with Aahz privately. Consequently, we had left Buttercup and Gleep in the courtyard with our equipment and were seeking out the general's chambers on our own.

The palace was honeycombed with corridors to the point where I wondered if there weren't more corridors than rooms. Our trek was made even more difficult by the light, or lack thereof. Though there were numerous mountings for torches set in the walls, it seemed only about one out of every four was being used, and the light shed by those torches was less than adequate for accurate navigation of the labyrinth.

I commented on this to Aahz as further proof of the tightfisted nature of the kingdom. His curt response was that the more money they saved on overhead and maintenance, the more they would have to splurge on luxuries . . . like us.

He was doggedly trying to explain the concept of an "energy crisis" to me, when we rounded a corner and sighted the general's quarters.

They were fairly easy to distinguish, since this was the only door we had encountered which was bracketed by a pair of matching honor guards. Their polished armor gleamed from broad shoulders as they observed our approach through narrowed eyes.

"Are these the quarters of General Badaxe?" I inquired politely.

"Are you the magician called Skeeve?" the guard challenged back.

"The kid asked you a question, soldier!" Aahz interceded. "Now are you going to answer or are you so dumb you don't know what's on the other side of the door you're guarding?"

The guard flushed bright red, and I noticed his partner's knuckles whitening on the pike he was gripping. It occurred to me that now that I had landed the magician's job, it might not be the wisest course to continue antagonizing the military.

"Um, Aahz . . ." I murmured.

"Yes! These are the quarters of General Badaxe . . . sir!" the guard barked suddenly.

Apparently the mention of my colleague's name had confirmed my identity, though I wondered how many strangers could be wandering the halls accompanied by large scaly demons. The final, painful, "sir" was a tribute to my performance in the courtyard. Apparently the guards had been instructed to be polite, at least to me, no matter how much it hurt . . . which it obviously did.

"Thank you, guard," I said loftily, and hammered on the door with my fist.

"Further," the guard observed, "the general left word that you were to go right in."

The fact that he had withheld that bit of information until after I had knocked indicated that the guards hadn't completely abandoned their low regard for magicians. They were simply finding more subtle ways of being annoying.

I realized Aahz was getting ready to start a new round with the guard, so I hastily opened the door and entered, forcing him to follow.

The general was standing at the window, silhouetted by the light streaming in from outside. As we entered, he turned to face us.

"Ah! Come in, gentlemen," he boomed in a mellow tone. "I've been expecting you. Do make yourselves comfortable. Help yourselves to the wine if you wish."

I found his sudden display of friendliness even more disquieting than his earlier show of hostility. Aahz, however, took it all in stride, immediately taking up the indicated jug of wine. For a moment I thought he was going to pour a bit of it into one of the goblets which shared the tray with the jug and pass it to me. Instead, he took a deep drink directly from the jug and kept it, licking his lips in appreciation. In the midst of the chaos my life had suddenly become, it was nice to know some things remained constant.

The general frowned at the display for a moment, then forced his features back into the jovial expression he had first greeted us with.

"Before we begin the briefing," he smiled, "I must apologize for my rude behavior during the interview. Grimble and I have . . . differed in our opinions on the existing situation, and I'm afraid I took it out on you. For that I extend my regrets. Ordinarily, I would have nothing against magicians as a group, or you specifically."

"Whoa! Back up a minute, General," Aahz interrupted. "How does your feud with the chancellor involve us?"

The general's eyes glittered with a fierceness that belied the gentility of his oration.

"It's an extension of our old argument concerning allocation of funds," he said. "When news reached us of the approaching force, my advice to the king was to immediately strengthen our own army that we might adequately perform our sworn duty of defending the realm."

"Sounds like good advice to me," I interjected, hoping to improve my status with the general by agreeing with him.

Badaxe responded by fixing me with a hard glare.

"Strange that you should say that, magician," he observed stonily. "Grimble's advice was to invest the money elsewhere than in the army, specifically in a magician."

It suddenly became clear why we had been received by the guards and the general with something less than open-armed camaraderie. Not only were they getting us instead of reinforcements, our presence was a slap at their abilities.

"Okay, General," Aahz acknowledged. "All that's water under the drawbridge. What are we up against?"

The general glanced back and forth between me and Aahz, apparently surprised that I was allowing my apprentice to take the lead in the briefing. When I failed to rebuke Aahz for his forwardness, the general shrugged and moved to a piece of parchment hanging on the wall.

"I believe the situation is shown clearly by this—" he began.

"What's that?" Aahz interrupted.

The general started to respond sharply, then caught himself. "This," he said evenly, "is a map of the kingdom you are supposed to defend. It's called Possiltum."

"Yes, of course," I nodded. "Continue."

"This line here to the north of our border represents the advancing army you are to deal with."

"Too bad you couldn't get it to scale," Aahz commented. "The way you have it there, the enemy's front is longer than your border."

The general bared his teeth.

"The drawing *is* to scale," he said pointedly. "Perhaps now you will realize the magnitude of the task before you."

My mind balked at accepting his statement.

"Really, General," I chided. "Surely you're overstating the case. There aren't enough fighting men in any kingdom to form a front that long."

"Magician," the general's voice was menacing, "I did not reach my current rank by overstating military situations. The army you are facing is one of the mightiest forces the world has ever seen. It is the striking arm of a rapidly growing empire situated far to the north. They have been advancing for three years now, absorbing smaller kingdoms and crushing any resistance offered. All able-bodied men of conquered lands are conscripted for

military service, swelling their ranks to the size you see
indicated on the map. The only reason they are not advancing faster is that in addition to limitless numbers of
men, they possess massive war machines which, though
effective, are slow to transport."

"Now tell us the bad news," Aahz commented dryly.

The general took him seriously.

"The bad news," he growled, "is that their leader is a
strategist without peer. He rose to power trouncing forces
triple the size of his own numbers, and now that he has
a massive army at his command, he is virtually unbeatable."

"I'm beginning to see why the king put his money into
a magician," my mentor observed. "It doesn't look like
you could have assembled a force large enough to stop
them."

"That wasn't my plan!" the general bristled. "While
we may not have been able to crush the enemy, we could
have made them pay dearly enough for crossing our border that they might have turned aside for weaker lands
easier to conquer."

"You know, Badaxe," Aahz said thoughtfully, "that's
not a bad plan. Working together we might still pull it
off. How many men can you give us for support?"

"None," the general said firmly.

I blinked.

"Excuse me, General," I pressed. "For a moment there,
I thought you said—"

"None," he repeated. "I will not assign a single soldier
of mine to support your campaign."

"That's insane!" Aahz exploded. "How do you expect
us to stop an army like that with just magik?"

"I don't," the general smiled.

"But if we fail," I pointed out, "Possiltum falls."

"That is correct," Badaxe replied calmly.

"But—"

"Allow me to clarify my position," he interrupted. "In
my estimation, there is more at stake here than one king-

dom. If you succeed in your mission, it will establish that magik is more effective than military force in defending a kingdom. Eventually, that could lead to all armies being disbanded in preference to hiring magicians. I will have no part in establishing a precedent such as that. If you want to show that magicians are superior to armies, you will have to do it with magik alone. The military will not lift a finger to assist you."

As he spoke, he took the jug of wine from Aahz's unresisting fingers, a sign in itself that Aahz was as stunned by the general's words as I was.

"My feelings on this subject are very strong, gentlemen," Badaxe continued, pouring himself some wine. "So strong, in fact, I am willing to sacrifice myself and my kingdom to prove the point. What is more, I would strongly suggest that you do the same."

He paused, regarding us with those glittering eyes.

"Because I tell you here and now, should you emerge victorious from the impending battle, you will not live to collect your reward. The king may rule the court, but word of what happens in the kingdom comes to him through my soldiers, and those soldiers will be posted along your return path to the palace, with orders to bring back word of your accidental demise, even if they have to arrange it. Do I make myself clear?"

# VIII:

*"Anything worth doing, is worth doing for a profit."*

—TERESIAS

With a massive effort of self-control, I contained myself not only after we had left the general's quarters, but until we were out of earshot of the honor guard. When I finally spoke, I managed to keep the telltale note of hysteria out of my voice which would have betrayed my true feelings.

"Like you said, Aahz," I commented casually, "there are armies and there are armies. Right?"

Aahz wasn't fooled for a minute.

"Hysterics won't get us anywhere, kid," he observed. "What we need is sound thinking."

"Excuse me," I said pointedly, "but isn't 'sound thinking' what got us into the mess in the first place?"

"Okay, okay!" Aahz grimaced. "I'll admit I made a few oversights when I originally appraised the situation."

"A few oversights?" I echoed incredulously. "Aahz, this 'cushy job' you set me up for doesn't bear even the vaguest resemblance to what you described when you sold me on the idea."

"I know, kid," Aahz sighed. "I definitely owe you an apology. This sounds like it's actually going to be work."

"Work!" I shrieked, losing control slightly. "It's going to be suicide."

Aahz shook his head sadly.

"There you go overreacting again. It doesn't have to be suicide. We've got a choice, you know."

"Sure," I retorted sarcastically. "We can get killed by the invaders or we can get killed by Badaxe's boys. How silly of me not to have realized it. For a moment there I was getting worried."

"Our choice," Aahz corrected sternly, "is to go through with this lame-brained mission, or to take the money and run."

A ray of hope broke through the dismal gloom that had burdened my mind.

"Aahz," I said in genuine awe, "you're a genius. C'mon, let's get going."

"Get going where?" Aahz asked.

"Back to the inn, of course," I replied. "The sooner the better."

"That wasn't one of our options," my mentor sneered.

"But you said—"

"I said 'take the money *and* run' not just 'run,' " he corrected. "We aren't going anywhere until we've seen Grimble."

"But Aahz—"

" 'But Aahz' nothing," he interrupted fiercely. "This little jaunt has cost us a bundle. We're going to at least make it break even, if not show a small profit."

"It hasn't cost us anything," I said bluntly.

"It cost us travel time and time away from your studies," Aahz countered. "That's worth something."

"But—"

"Besides," he continued loftily, "there are more important issues at stake here."

"Like what?" I pressed.

"Well . . . like, um . . ."

"There you are, gentlemen!"

We turned to find Grimble approaching us rapidly from behind.

"I was hoping to catch you after the briefing," the chancellor continued, joining us. "Do you mind if I watch with you? I know you'll be eager to start off on your campaign, but there are certain matters we *must* discuss before you leave."

"Like our wages," Aahz supplied firmly.

Grimble's smile froze.

"Oh! Yes, of course. First, however, there are other things to deal with. I trust the general supplied you with the necessary information for your mission."

"Down to the last gruesome detail," I confirmed.

"Good, good," the chancellor chortled, his enthusiasm undimmed by my sarcasm. "I have every confidence you'll be able to deal with the riffraff from the North. I'll have you know you were my personal choice even before the interviews. In fact, I was the one responsible for sending you the invitation in the first place."

"We'll remember that," Aahz smiled, his eyes narrowing dangerously.

A thought occurred to me.

"Say . . . um, Lord Chancellor," I said casually, "how did you happen to hear of us in the first place?"

"Why do you ask?" Grimble countered.

"No special reason," I assured him. "But as the interview proved so fruitful, I would like to send a token of my gratitude to that person who spoke so highly of me to you."

It was a pretty flimsy story, but the chancellor seemed to accept it.

"Well . . . um, actually it was a wench," he admitted. "Rather comely, but I don't recall her name just offhand. She may have dyed her hair since you met her. It was green at the time we . . . er . . . met. Do you know her?"

Indeed I did. There was only one woman who knew of Aahz and me, much less our whereabouts. Then again, there was only one woman I knew who fit the description of being voluptuous with green hair. Tanda!

I opened my mouth to acknowledge my recognition, when Aahz dug a warning elbow into my rib.

"Glah!" I said intelligently.

"How's that again?" Grimble inquired.

"I . . . um, I can't place the person, just offhand," I lied. "But you know how absentminded we magicians are."

"Of course," the chancellor smiled, for some reason relieved.

"Now that that's settled," Aahz interrupted, "I believe you mentioned something about our wages."

Grimble scowled for a moment, then broke into a good-natured grin.

"I can see why Master Skeeve leaves his business dealings to you, Aahz," he conceded.

"Flattery's nice," Aahz observed, "but you can't spend it. The subject was our wages."

"You must realize we are a humble kingdom," Grimble sighed, "though we try to reward our retainers as best we can. There have been quarters set aside for the court magician which should be spacious enough to accommodate both of you. Your meals will be provided . . . that is, of course, assuming you are on time when they are served. Also, there is a possibility . . . no, I'd go so far as to say it is a certainty that His Majesty's generosity will be extended to include free stable space and food for your unicorns. How does that sound?"

"So far, pretty cheap," Aahz observed bluntly.

"What do you mean, 'cheap?' " the chancellor snarled, losing his composure for a moment.

"What you've offered so far," Aahz sneered, "is a room we won't be sleeping in, meals we won't be eating, and stable space we won't be using because we'll be in the field fighting your war for you. In exchange, you want Skeeve here to use his skills to save your kingdom. By my calculations, that's cheap!"

"Yes, I see your point," Grimble conceded. "Well,

there will, of course, be a small wage paid."

"How small?" Aahz pressed.

"Sufficient to cover your expenses," the chancellor smiled. "Shall we say fifty gold pieces a month?"

"Let's say two hundred," Aahz smiled back?

"Perhaps we could go as high as seventy-five," Grimble countered.

"And we'll come down to two-twenty-five," Aahz offered.

"Considering his skills, we could pay . . . excuse me," the chancellor blinked. "Did you say two-twenty-five?"

"Actually," Aahz conceded, "I misspoke."

"I thought so." Grimble smiled.

"I meant two-fifty."

"Now see here—" the chancellor began.

"Look, Grimble," Aahz met him halfway, "you had three choices. You could double the size of your army, hire a magician, or lose the kingdom. Even at three hundred a month, Skeeve here is your best deal. Don't look at what you're spending, look at what you're saving."

Grimble thought about it for a few moments.

"Very well," he said, grimacing. "Two-fifty it is."

"I believe the figure under discussion was three hundred," I observed pointedly.

That earned me a black look, but I stood my ground and returned his stare levelly.

"Three hundred," he said, forcing the words out through gritted teeth.

"Payable in advance," Aahz added.

"Payable at the end of the pay period," Grimble corrected.

"C'mon, Grimble," Aahz began, but the chancellor interrupted him, holding up his hand.

"No! On that point I must remain inflexible," he insisted. "Everyone in the Royal Retinue is paid at the same time, when the vaults are opened at the end of the pay period. If we break that rule and start allowing exceptions, there will be no end to it."

"Can you at least give us a partial advance?" Aahz pressed. "Something to cover expenses on the upcoming campaign?"

"Definitely not!" Grimble retorted. "If I paid out monies for services not yet rendered, certain people, specifically Hugh Badaxe, would suspect you intended to take the money and flee without entering battle at all!"

That hit uncomfortably close to home, and I found myself averting my eyes for fear of betraying my guilt. Aahz, however, never even blinked.

"What about bribes?" he asked.

Grimble scowled.

"It is unthinkable that one of the king's retainers would accept a bribe, much less count on it as part of his income. Any attempt to bribe you should be reported immediately to His Majesty!"

"Not *taking* bribes, Grimble," Aahz snarled. "*Giving* them. When we give money out to the enemy, does that come out of our wages, or does the kingdom pay for it?"

"I seriously doubt you could buy off the army facing you," the chancellor observed skeptically. "Besides, you're supposed to carry the day with magik. That's what we're paying you for."

"Even magik is aided by accurate information," Aahz replied pointedly. "C'mon Grimble, you know court intrigue. A little advance warning can go a long way in any battle."

"True enough," the chancellor admitted. "Very well, I guess we can give you an allowance for bribes, assuming it will be kept within reason."

"How much in reason?" Aahz inquired.

"Say . . . five gold pieces."

"Twenty-five would—"

"Five!" Grimble said firmly.

Aahz studied his adversary for a moment, then sighed.

"Five," he said, extending his palm.

The chancellor grudgingly dug into his purse and

counted out five gold pieces. In fact, he counted them twice before passing them to Aahz.

"You realize, of course," he warned, "I will require an accounting of those funds after your victory."

"Of course," Aahz smiled, fondling the coins.

"You seem very confident of our victory, Lord Chancellor," I observed.

Grimble regarded me with cocked eyebrow for a moment.

"Of course I am confident, Lord Magician," he said at last. "So confident, I have staked my kingdom, and more importantly, my reputation, on your success. You will note I rate my reputation above the kingdom. That is no accident. Kingdoms rise and fall, but a chancellor can always find employment. That is, of course, providing it was not his advice which brought the kingdom to ruin. Should you fail in your campaign to save Possiltum, my career is finished. If that should happen, gentlemen, your careers fall with mine."

"That has the sound of a threat to it, Grimble," Aahz observed dryly.

"Does it?" the chancellor responded with mock innocence. "That was not my intent. I am not threatening, I am stating a fact. I maintain very close contact with the chancellors of all of the surrounding kingdoms; in fact I am related to several. They are all aware of my position in this magik versus the military issue. Should I prove wrong in my judgment, should you fail in your defense of Possiltum, they will note it. Thereafter, any magician—and you specifically, Skeeve—will be denounced as a fraud and a charlatan should you seek further employment. In fact, as the chancellors frequently control the courts, I would not be surprised if they found an excuse or a trumped-up charge which would allow them to have you put to death as a favor to me. The method of death varies from kingdom to kingdom, but the end result is the same. I trust you will keep that in mind as you plan your campaign."

With that, he turned on his heel and strode away, leaving us standing in silence.

"Well, Aahz," I said finally, "do you have any sound advice on our situation now?"

"Of course," he retorted.

"What?" I asked.

"Now that we've got the whole story," he said solemnly, "now you can panic."

# IX:

*"There is more at stake here than our lives."*

—COL. TRAVIS
ALAMO PEP TALK

**O**n the third night after leaving Possiltum's capital, we camped on a small knoll overlooking the kingdom's main north-south trail.

Actually, I use the phase "north-south" rather loosely in this instance. In three days' travel, our progress was the only northward movement we had observed on this particular strip of beaten dirt. The dearth of northbound traffic was emphasized by the high volume of people bound in the opposite direction.

As we traveled we were constantly encountering small groups and families picking their way steadily toward the capital in that unhurried yet ground-eating pace that typifies people accustomed to traveling without means of transport other than their feet. They did not seem particularly frightened or panicky, but two common characteristics marked them all as being more than casual travelers.

First, the great amount of personal effects they carried was far in excess of that required for a simple pilgrimage.

Whether bound in cumbersome backpacks or heaped in small, hand-pushed carts, it was obvious the southbound travelers were bringing with them as much of their worldly possessions as they could carry or drag.

Second, no one paid us any heed other than a passing glance. This was even more noteworthy than the prior observation.

Currently, our party consisted of three: myself, Aahz, and Gleep. We had left Buttercup at the palace, much to Aahz's disgust. He would have preferred to leave Gleep and bring Buttercup, but the royal orders had been firm on this point. The dragon was not to remain at the palace unless one or both of us also stayed behind to handle him. As a result, we traveled as a trio—a youth, a dragon, and a grumbling demon—not exactly a common sight in these or any other parts. The peasants flowing south, however, barely noticed us other than to give us clear road space when we passed.

Aahz maintained that this was because whatever they were running from inspired such fear that they barely noted anything or anybody in their path. He further surmised that the motivating force for this exodus could only be the very army we were on our way to oppose.

To prove his point, we attempted to question several of the groups when we encountered them. We stopped doing this after the first day due to the similarities of the replies we received. Sample:

Aahz: Hold, stranger! Where are you going?
Answer: To the capital!

Aahz: Why?
Answer: To be as near as possible to the king when he makes his defense against the invaders from the North. He'll have to try to save himself even if he won't defend the outlands.

Aahz: Citizen, you need flee no more. You have underestimated your king's concern for your safety.

You see before you the new court magician, retained by His Majesty specifically for the purpose of defending Possiltum from the invading army. What say you to that?

Answer: One magician?

Aahz: With my own able assistance, of course.
Answer: I'd say you were crazy.

Aahz: Now look—
Answer: No, *you* look, whoever or whatever you are. Meaning no disrespect to this or any other magician, you're fools to oppose that army. Magik may be well and good against an ordinary force, but you aren't going to stop *that* army with one magician . . . or twenty magicians for that matter.

Aahz: We have every confidence—
Answer: Fine, then *you* go north. Me, I'm heading for the capital!

Though this exchange had eventually quelled our efforts to reassure the populace, it had given rise to an argument which was still unresolved as we prepared to sleep on the third night.

"What happened to your plan to take the money and run?" I grumbled.

"Big deal," Aahz shot back. "Five whole gold pieces."

"You said you wanted a profit," I pressed. "Okay! We've got one. So it's small . . . but so was the effort we put into it. Considering we didn't spend anything—"

"What about the unicorn?" Aahz countered. "While they're still holding the unicorn, we've lost money on the deal."

"Aahz," I reminded him. "Buttercup didn't cost us anything, remember? He was a gift from Quigley."

"It would cost money to replace him," Aahz insisted. "That means that we lost money on the deal unless we get him back. I've told you, I want a profit . . . and definitely refuse to accept a loss."

"Gleep?"

Aahz's heated words had awakened my dragon, who raised his head in sleepy inquiry.

"Go back to sleep, Gleep!" I said soothingly. "Everything's all right."

Reassured, he rolled onto his back and laid back his head.

Ridiculous as he looked, lying there with his four legs sticking up in the air, he had reminded me of something.

I pondered the memory for a moment, then decided to change my tactics.

"Aahz," I said thoughtfully, "what's the real reason for your wanting to go through with this?"

"Weren't you listening, kid? I said—"

"I know, I know," I interrupted. "You said it was for the profit. The only thing wrong with that is you tried to leave Gleep behind, who cost us money, instead of Buttercup, who didn't cost us anything! That doesn't ring true if you're trying to show a profit with the least possible effort."

"Um, you know how I feel about that stupid dragon—" Aahz began.

"And you know how I feel about him," I interrupted, "As such, you also know I'd never abandon him to save my own skin, much less for money. For some reason, you wanted to be sure I'd see this thing through . . . and that reason has nothing at all to do with money. Now, what is it?"

It was Aahz's turn to lapse into thoughtful silence.

"You're getting better at figuring things out, kid," he said finally.

Normally, I would have been happy to accept the compliment. This time, however, I saw it as what it was: an attempt to distract me.

"The reason, Aahz," I said firmly.

"There are several reasons, kid," he said with uncharacteristic solemnity. "The main one is that you're not a master magician yet."

"If you don't mind my saying so," I commented dryly, "that doesn't make a whole lot of sense. If I'm short on ability, why are you so eager to shove me into this mission?"

"Hear me out, kid," Aahz said, raising a restraining hand. "I made a mistake, and that mistake has dumped us into a situation that needs a master magician. More than a master magician's abilities, we need a master magician's conscience. Do you follow me?"

"No," I admitted.

"Not surprising," Aahz sighed. "That's why I tried to trick you into completing this mission instead of explaining it. So far, all your training has been on physical abilities without developing your professional conscience."

"You've taught me to keep one eye on the profits," I pointed out defensively.

"That's not what I mean, kid. Look, for a minute forget about profits."

"Are you feeling okay, Aahz?" I asked with genuine concern. "You don't sound like yourself at all."

"Will you get off my back, kid," he snarled. "I'm trying to explain something important!"

I sank into a cowed silence. Still I was reassured. Aahz was definitely Aahz.

"When you were apprenticed to Garkin," Aahz began, "and even when you first met me, you didn't want to be a magician. You wanted to be a thief. To focus your energies behind your lessons, I had to stress how much benefit you could reap from learning magik."

He paused. I didn't say anything. There was nothing to say. He was right, both in his recollections and his interpretation of them.

"Well," he sighed, "there's another side to magik. There's a responsibility . . . a responsibility to your fellow practitioners, and, more importantly, to magik itself. Even though we have rivals and will probably acquire more if we live that long, and even though we may fight with them or beat them out for a job, we are all bound by a common cause. Every magician has a duty to promote magik, to see that its use is respected and reputable. The greater the magician, the greater his sense of duty."

"What's that got to do with our current situation?" I prompted.

"There's an issue at stake here, kid," he answered carefully. "You heard it from Badaxe and Grimble both. More importantly, you heard it from the populace when we talked to the peasants. Rodrick is gambling his entire kingdom on the ability of magik to do a job. Now, no one but a magician can tell how reasonable or unreasonable a task that might be. If we fail, all the laymen will see is that magik failed, and they'll never trust it again. That's why we can't walk away from this mission. We're here representing magik . . . and we've got to give it our best shot."

I thought about that for a few moments.

"But what can we do against a whole army?" I asked finally.

"To be honest with you," Aahz sighed, "I really don't know. I'm hoping we can come up with an idea after we've seen exactly what it is we're up against."

We sat silently together for a long time after that, each lost in his own thoughts of the mission and what was at stake.

# X:

*"One need not fear superior numbers if the opposing force has been properly scouted and appraised."*

—S. BULL

My last vestige of hope was squashed when we finally sighted the army. Reports of its massive size had not been overstated; if anything, they had failed to express the full impact of the force's might.

Our scouting mission had taken us across Possiltum's northern border and several days' journey into its neighbor's interior. The name of this kingdom was inconsequential. If it was not already considered part of the new empire, it would be as soon as the news spread.

We weren't sure if we had just missed the last battle, or if the kingdom had simply surrendered. Whichever the case, there were no defending troops in evidence, just large encampments of the Empire's forces spread out in a rough line which disappeared over the horizon in either direction.

Fortunately, the army was not currently on the move, which made our scouting considerably easier. There were sentries posted at regular intervals all along the front line, but as they were not more than a given distance from the encampments, we simply traversed the line without approaching them too closely, and thus escaped detection.

Periodically, we would creep closer to an encampment or climb a tree to improve our view. Aahz seemed very absorbed in his own thoughts, both when we were actually viewing the troops and as we were traveling to new locations. Since I couldn't get more than an occasional grunt or monosyllable out of him, I occupied myself making my own observations.

The soldiers were clothed roughly the same. Standard equipment seemed to include a leather helmet and breastplate, a rough knee-length cloth tunic, sandals, sword, two javelins, and a large rectangular shield. Apparently they were not planning to move immediately, for they had pitched their tents and spent most of their time sharpening weapons, repairing armor, eating, or simply lolling about. Occasionally, a metal-encrusted soldier, presumably an officer, would appear and shout at the others, whereupon they would listlessly form ranks and drill. Their practice would usually grind to a halt as soon as the officer passed from view.

There were occasional pieces of siege equipment designed to throw large rocks or spears long distances, though we never saw them in operation. The only pieces of equipment that seemed to be used with any regularity were the signal towers. Each encampment had one of these, a rickety affair of lashed-together poles stretching roughly twenty feet in the air and surmounted by a small, square platform. Several times a day, one soldier in each encampment would mount one of these structures, and they would signal to each other with pennants or standards. The towers also did duty as clotheslines, and were periodically draped with drying tunics.

All in all, it looked like an incredibly boring existence. In fact, from my appraisal, the only thing duller than being a soldier of the Empire was spending days on end watching soldiers of the Empire!

I commented on this to Aahz as we lay belly-down on a grassy knoll, surveying yet another encampment.

"You're right, kid," he admitted absently. "Being a soldier is pretty dull work."

"How about us?" I probed, eager to keep him talking. "What we're doing isn't exactly exciting, you know!"

"You want excitement?" he asked, focusing on me for the first time in days. "Tell you what. Why don't you just stroll down there and ask the Officer of the Day for a quick rundown on how their army operates? I bet that'll liven things up for you."

"I'm not *that* bored!" I amended hastily.

"Then what say you just keep quiet and let me do this my way." Aahz smiled and resumed his studies.

"Do what your way?" I persisted. "Exactly what is it we're trying to accomplish anyway?"

Aahz sighed.

"We're scouting the enemy," he explained patiently. "We've got enough going against us on this campaign without rushing in uninformed."

"How much information do we need?" I grumbled. "This encampment doesn't look any different from the last five we looked at."

"That's because you don't know what you're looking for," Aahz scoffed. "What have you learned so far about the opposition?"

I wasn't ready for the question but I gamely rose to the challenge.

"Um . . . there are a lot of them . . . they're well armed . . . um . . . and they have catapults . . ."

"That's all?" Aahz sneered. "Brilliant! You and Bad-axe make a great team of tacticians."

"Okay, so teach me!" I shot back. "What have you learned?"

"You can spend years trying to learn military theory without scratching the surface," my mentor replied sternly. "But I'll try to give you the important parts in a nutshell. To appraise a force, such as we're doing now, remember two words: 'Sam' and 'Doc.' "

" 'Sam' and 'Doc,' " I repeated dutifully.

"Some folks prefer to remember 'Salute' but I like 'Sam' and 'Doc,' " Aahz added as an aside.

"Terrific," I said, grimacing. "Now tell me what it means."

"They're to help you remember an information checklist," Aahz confided. "Salute's stands for Size, Activity, Location, Unit, Time, and Equipment. That's fine as far as it goes, but it assumes no judgmental ability on the part of the scout. I prefer 'Sam' and 'Doc.' That stands for Strength, Armament, Movement, and Deployment, Organization, and Communications."

"Oh," I said, hoping he wasn't expecting me to remember all this.

"Now, using that framework," Aahz continued, "let's summarize what we've seen so far. Size: there are lots of them, enough so it's kind of pointless to try for an exact count. Movement: currently, they're just sitting there."

"I got that far all by myself," I pointed out sarcastically.

"The big key, however," Aahz continued, ignoring me, "is in their Armament and Equipment. When you look at this, consider both what is there and what isn't."

"How's that again?" I asked.

"What there is is a lot of foot-schloggers, infantry, a little artillery in the form of catapults and archers, but nothing even vaguely resembling cavalry. That means they're going to go slow when they move, particularly in battle. We don't have to worry about any fast, flanking moves; it'll be a toe-to-toe slugfest."

"But, Aahz—" I began.

"As to the Deployment and Organization," he pushed on undaunted, "they're strung out all over the place, probably because it's easier to forage for food that way. Then again, it displays a certain confidence on their part that they don't feel it's necessary to mass their forces. I think we're looking at their Organization, a collection of companies or battalions each under the leadership of two or three officers, all under the guidance of a super-leader or general."

"Aahz—" I tried again.

"Communications seems to be their most vulnerable point," Aahz pushed on doggedly. "If an army this size doesn't coordinate its movements, it's in big trouble. If they're really using signal towers and runners to pass messages, we might be able to jinx the works for them."

"All of which means what?" I interrupted finally.

"Hmm? Oh, that's a capsule summary of what we're up against," Aahz replied innocently.

"I know, I know," I sighed. "But for days you've been saying you'll formulate a plan after you've seen what we're up against. Well, you've seen it. What's the plan? How can we beat 'em?"

"There's no way, kid," Aahz admitted heavily. "If I had seen one, I would have told you, but I haven't, and that's why I keep looking."

"Maybe there isn't one," I suggested cautiously.

Aahz sighed.

"I'm starting to think you're right. If so, that means we'll have to do something I really don't want to do."

"You mean give up?" I said, genuinely startled. "After that big speech you gave me about responsibility and—"

"Whoa," Aahz interrupted. "I didn't say anything about giving up. What we're going to do is—"

"Gleep!"

The unmistakable sound came to us from behind, rolling up the hill from the brush-filled gully where we'd left my pet.

"Kid," Aahz moaned, "will you keep that stupid dragon quiet? All we need now is to have him pull the army down our necks."

"Right, Aahz!" I agreed, worming away backward as fast as I could.

As soon as I was clear of the crest of the hill, I rose

to a low crouch and scuttled down the slope in that position. Crawling is neither a fast nor comfortable means of travel for me.

As per our now normal procedure, we had tethered Gleep to a tree . . . a large tree after he had successfully uprooted several small ones. Needless to say, he wasn't wild about the idea, but it was necessary considering the delicate nature of our current work.

"Gleep!"

I could see him now, eagerly straining at the end of his rope. Surprisingly, however, for a change he wasn't trying to get to me. In fact, he was trying his best to get at a large bush which stood some distance from his tree . . . or at something hidden in the bush!

Cold sweat suddenly popped out on my brow. It occurred to me that Gleep might have been discovered by one of the enemy army scouts. That would be bad enough, but even worse was the possibility said scout might still be around.

I hurriedly stepped sideways into the shadow of a tree and reviewed the situation. I hadn't actually *seen* a scout. In fact, there was no movement at all in the indicated bush. I could sneak back and get Aahz, but if I were wrong he wouldn't be very happy over being called to handle a false alarm. I could set Gleep loose and let him find the intruder, but that would mean exposing myself.

As I stood debating my next course of action, someone slipped up behind me and put hands over my eyes.

"Surprise!" came a soft voice in my ear.

# XI:

*"Should old acquaintance be forgot...."*

—Count of Monte Cristo

I jumped!

Perhaps I should clarify. When I say "I jumped," I mean I really jumped. Over a year ago, Aahz had taught me to fly, which is actually controlled hovering caused by reverse levitation.

Whatever it was, I did it. I went straight up in the air about ten feet and stayed there. I didn't know what had snuck up behind me, and didn't want to know. I wanted help! I wanted Aahz!

I drew a mighty breath to express this desire.

"Kinda jumpy, aren't you, handsome?"

That penetrated my panic.

Stifling my shout before it truly began, I looked down on my attacker. From my vantage point, I was treated to a view of a gorgeous golden-olive complexioned face, accented by almond-shaped cat's eyes, framed by a magnificent tumble of light green hair. I could also see a generous expanse of cleavage.

"Tanda!" I crowed with delight, forcing my eyes back to her face.

"Do you mind coming down?" she called. "I can't come up."

I considered swooping down on her dramatically, but decided against it. I'm still not all that good at flying, and the effect would be lost completely if I crashed into her.

Instead, I settled for lowering myself gently to the ground a few paces from her.

"Gee, Tanda, I . . . *glack!*"

The last was squeezed forcefully from me as she swept me into a bone-crushing embrace.

"Gee, it's good to see you, handsome," she murmured happily. "How have you been?"

"I *was* fine," I noted, untangling myself briefly. "What are you doing here?"

The last time I had seen her, Tanda was part of the ill-fated group Aahz and I had seen off to dimensions unknown. Of the whole crowd, she had been the only one I was sorry to see go.

"I'm waiting for you, silly," she teased, slipping an affectionate arm around my waist. "Where's Aahz?"

"He's—" I started to point up the hill when a thought occurred to me. "Say . . . how did you know I had Aahz with me?"

"Oh! Don't get mad," she scolded, giving me a playful shake. "It stands to reason. Even Aahz wouldn't let you face that army alone."

"But how did you—"

"Gleep!"

My dragon had discovered his quarry was no longer hiding behind the bush. As a result, he was now straining at the end of his rope trying to reach us. The tree he was tethered to was swaying dangerously.

"Gleep!" Tanda called in a delighted voice. "How are ya, fella?"

The tree dipped to new lows as my dragon quivered with glee at having been recognized. I was quivering a little myself. Tanda had that effect on males.

Heedless of her own safety, Tanda bounded forward to kneel before the dragon, pulling his whiskers and scratching his nose affectionately.

Gleep loved it. I loved it, too. In addition to her usual soft, calf-high boots, Tanda was wearing a short green tunic which hugged her generous curves and showed off her legs just swell. What's more, when she knelt down like that, the hem rode up until. . . .

"What's wrong with that dragon?" Aahz boomed, bursting out of the brush behind me.

This time I didn't jump . . . much.

"Gee, Aahz," I began. "It's . . ."

I needn't have bothered trying to explain.

Tanda uncoiled and came past me in a bound.

"Aahz!" she exclaimed, flinging herself into his arms.

For a change, my mentor was caught as flat-footed as I had been. For a moment, the tangle of arms teetered on the brink of collapse, then down it went.

They landed with a resounding thump, Aahz on the bottom and therefore soaking up most of the impact.

"Still impulsive, aren't you?" Tanda leered.

"Whoosh . . . hah . . . ah . . ." Aahz responded urbanely.

Tanda rolled to her feet and began rearranging her tunic.

"At least I don't have to ask if you're glad to see me," she observed.

"Tanda!" Aahz gasped at last.

"You remembered?" Tanda beamed.

"She's been waiting for us, Aahz," I supplied brightly.

"That's right!" Aahz scowled. "Grimble said you set us up for this job."

Tanda winced.

"I can explain that," she said apologetically.

"I can hardly wait," Aahz intoned.

"I'm kind of curious about that myself," I added.

"Um . . . this could take a while, guys," she said

thoughtfully. "Got anything around to drink?"

That was easily the most reasonable question asked so far today. We broke out the wine, and in no time were sitting around in a small circle quenching our thirst. Much to Aahz's disgust, I insisted we sit close enough to Gleep that he not be left out. This meant, of course, his rather aromatic breath flavored our discussion, but as I pointed out it was the only way to keep him quiet while we talked.

"What happened after you left?" I prodded. "Where are Isstvan and Brockhurst and Higgins? What happened to Quigley? Did they ever bring Frumple back to life, or is he still a statue?"

"Later, kid," Aahz interrupted. "First things first. You were about to explain about Grimble."

"Grimble," Tanda responded, wrinkling her nose. "Did you ever notice the 'crookeder' a person is, the more possessive he is? He's the main reason I didn't wait for you at Possiltum."

"From the beginning," Aahz instructed.

"From the beginning." Tanda pursed her lips thoughtfully. "Well, I picked him up in a singles bar . . . he's married, but I didn't know that till later."

"What's a singles bar?" I interrupted.

"Shut up, kid," Aahz snarled.

"Well, it wasn't actually a singles bar," Tanda corrected. "It was more of a tavern. I should have known he was married. I mean, nobody that young is *that* bald unless he's got a wife at home."

"Skip the philosophy," Aahz moaned. "Just tell us the story, huh?"

Tanda cocked an eyebrow at him.

"You know, Aahz," she accused, "for someone as long-winded as you are when it comes to telling stories, you're awfully impatient when it comes to listening to someone else."

"She's right, you know," I commented.

"Enough!" Aahz bellowed. "The story!"

"Well, one of the things Grimble mentioned while he

was trying to impress me with how important his job was, was that he was trying to find a court magician. He said he had convinced the king to hire one, but now he couldn't find one and was going to end up looking like an idiot."

"And when he mentioned idiots," I supplied, "naturally you thought of us."

"Now, don't be that way," Tanda scolded. "I thought it was a good way to help out a couple of friends. I knew you two were hanging out in this neck of the woods . . . and everybody knows what a cushy job being a court magician is."

"What did I tell you, kid," Aahz commented.

"We must be talking about different jobs," I retorted.

"Hey," Tanda interrupted, laying a soft hand on my arm. "When I gave him your names, I didn't know about the invading army. Honest!"

My anger melted away at her touch. Right then, she could have told me she had sold my head as a centerpiece and I would have forgiven her.

"Well . . ." I began, but she persisted, which was fine by me.

"As soon as I found out what the real story was, I knew I had gotten you into a tight spot," she said with soft sincerity. "Like I said, I would have waited at Possiltum, but I was afraid what with your disguises and all, that you'd recognize me before I spotted you. If you gave me the kind of greeting I've grown to expect, it could have really queered the deal. Grimble's a jealous twit, and if he thought we were more than nodding acquaintances, he would have held back whatever support he might normally give."

"Big deal," Aahz grumbled. "Five whole gold pieces."

"That much?" Tanda sounded honestly surprised. "Which arm did you break?"

"Aahz always gets us the best possible deal," I said proudly. "At least, monetarily."

"Well," Tanda concluded, "at least I won't dig into

your war funds. When I found out the mess I had gotten you into, I decided I'd work this one for free. Since I got you into it, the least I can do is help get you out."

"That's terrific," I exclaimed.

"It sure is!" Aahz agreed.

Something in his voice annoyed me.

"I meant that she was helping us," I snarled. "Not that she was doing it for free."

"That's what I meant, too, apprentice," Aahz glowered back. "But unlike some, I know what I'm talking about!"

"Boys, boys," Tanda said, separating us with her hands. "We're on the same side. Remember?"

"Gleep!" said the dragon, siding with Tanda.

As I have said, Gleep's breath is powerful enough to stop any conversation, and it was several minutes before the air cleared enough for us to continue.

"Before we were so rudely interrupted," Tanda gasped at last, "you were starting to say something, Aahz. Have you got a plan?"

"Now I do," Aahz smiled, chucking her under the chin. "And believe me, doing it without you would have been rough."

That had an anxious sound to it. Tanda's main calling, at least the only one mentionable in polite company, was Assassin.

"C'mon, Aahz," I chided. "Tanda's good, but she's not good enough to take on a whole army."

"Don't bet on it, handsome," she corrected, winking at me.

I blushed but continued with my argument.

"I still say the job's too big for one person, or three people for that matter," I insisted.

"You're right, kid," Aahz said solemnly.

"We just can't . . . what did you say, Aahz?"

"I said you were right," Aahz repeated.

"I thought so," I marveled. "I just wanted to hear it again."

"You'd *hear* it more often if you were *right* more often," Aahz pointed out.

"C'mon, Aahz," Tanda interrupted. "What's the plan?"

"Like the kid says," Aahz said loftily, "we need more help. We need an army of our own."

"But Aahz," I reminded him, "Badaxe said—"

"Who said anything about Badaxe?" Aahz replied innocently. "We're supposed to win this war with magik, aren't we? Well, fine. With Tanda on our team, we've got a couple of extra skills to draw on. Remember?"

I remembered. I remembered Aahz saying he wasn't worried about Tanda leaving with Isstvan because she could travel the dimensions by herself if things got rough. The light began to dawn.

"You mean . . ."

"That's right, kid," Aahz smiled. "We're going back to Deva. We're going to recruit a little invasionary force of our own!"

# XII:

*"This is no game for old men! Send in the boys!"*

—W. HAYS

I don't know how Tanda transported us from Klah to Deva. If I did, we wouldn't have needed her. All I know is that at the appropriate time she commenced to chant and shift her shoulders (a fascinating process in itself), and we were there.

"There," in this case, was at the Bazaar at Deva. That phrase alone, however, does not begin to describe our new surroundings as they came into focus.

A long time ago, the dimension of Deva had undergone an economic collapse. To survive, the Deveels (who I once knew as devils) used their ability to travel the dimensions and become merchants. Through the process of natural selection, the most successful Deveels were not the best fighters, but the best traders. Now, after countless generations of this process, the Deveels were acknowledged as the best merchants in all the dimensions. They were also acknowledged as being the shrewdest, coldest, most profit-hungry cheats ever to come down the pike.

The Bazaar at Deva was their showcase. It was an all-day, all-night, year-round fair where the Deveels met to haggle with each other over the wares fetched back from the various dimensions. Though it was originally established and maintained by Deveels, it was not unusual to find travelers from many dimensions shopping the endless rows of displays and booths. The rule of thumb was, "If it's to be found anywhere, you'll find it at the Bazaar at Deva."

I had been here once before with Aahz. At the time, we were searching for a surprise weapon to use against Isstvan. What we ended up with was Gleep and Tanda! . . . Distractions abound at the Bazaar.

I mention this in part to explain why, as unusual as our foursome must have appeared, no one paid us the slightest attention as we stood watching the kaleidoscope of activity whirling about us.

Gleep pressed against me for reassurance, momentarily taken aback at the sudden change of surroundings. I ignored him. My first visit to this place had been far too brief for my satisfaction. As such, I was rubbernecking madly, trying to see as much as possible as fast as possible.

Tanda was more businesslike.

"Now that we're here, Aahz," she drawled, "do you know where we're going?"

"No," Aahz admitted. "But I'll find out right now."

Without further warning, he casually reached out and grabbed the arm of the nearest passerby, a short, ugly fellow with tusks. Spinning his chosen victim around, Aahz bent to scowl in his face.

"You!" he snarled. "Do you like to fight?"

For a moment my heart stopped. All we needed now was to get into a brawl.

Fortunately, instead of producing a weapon, the tusker gave ground a step and eyed our party suspiciously.

"Not with a Pervert backed by a dragon, I don't," he retorted cautiously.

"Good!" Aahz smiled. "Then if you wanted to hire someone to do your fighting for you, where would you go?"

"To the Bazaar at Deva," the tusker shrugged.

"I know that!" Aahz snarled. "But *where* at the Bazaar?"

"Oh," the tusker exclaimed with sudden understanding. "About twenty rows in that direction, then turn right for another thirty or so. That's where the mercenaries hang out."

"Twenty, then up thirty," Aahz repeated carefully. "Thanks."

"A finder's fee would be appreciated more than any thanks," the tusker smiled, extending a palm.

"You're right!" Aahz agreed, and turned his back on our benefactor.

The tusker hesitated for a moment, then shrugged and continued on his way. I could have told him that Perverts in general and Aahz specifically are not noted for their generosity. "We go twenty rows that way, then up thirty," Aahz informed us.

"Yeah, we heard," Tanda grimaced. "Why didn't you just ask him flat out?"

"My way is quicker," Aahz replied smugly.

"Is it?" I asked skeptically.

"Look, kid," Aahz scowled. "Do you want to lead us through this zoo?"

"Well . . ." I hesitated.

"Then shut up and let me do it, okay?"

Actually, I was more than willing to let Aahz lead the way to wherever it was we were going. For one thing, it kept him busy navigating a path through the crowd. For another, it left me with next to nothing to do except marvel at the sights of the Bazaar as I followed along in his wake.

Try as I might, though, there was just too much for one set of eyes to see.

In one booth, two Deveels argued with an elephant-headed being over a skull; at least, I think it was a skull. In another, a Deveel was putting on a demonstration for a mixed group of shoppers, summoning clouds of floating green bubbles from a tiny wooden box.

At one point, our path was all but blocked by a booth selling rings which shot bolts of lightning. Between the salesman's demonstrations and the customers trying out their purchases, the way was virtually impassable.

Aahz and Tanda never broke stride, however, confidently maintaining their pace as they walked through the thick of the bolts. Miraculously, they passed through unscathed.

Gritting my teeth, I seized one of Gleep's ears and followed in their footsteps. Again, the bolts of energy failed to find us. Apparently no Deveel would bring injury or allow anyone in his shop to bring injury to a potential customer. It was a handy fact to know.

The lightning rings brought something else to mind, however. The last time we parted company with Tanda, Aahz had given her a ring that shot a heat ray capable of frying a man-sized target on the spot. That's right . . . I said he *gave* it to her. You might think this was proof of the depth of his feelings for her. It's my theory he was sick. Anyway, I was reminded of the ring and curious as to what had become of it.

Increasing my pace slightly, I closed the distance between myself and the pair in the lead, only to find they were already deeply engrossed in conversation. The din that prevails at the Bazaar stymies any attempt at serious eavesdropping, but I managed to catch occasional bits and pieces of the conversation as we walked.

". . . heard . . . awfully expensive, aren't they?" Tanda was saying.

". . . lick their weight in . . ." Aahz replied smugly.

I moved in a little closer, trying to hear better.

". . . makes you think they've got anyone here?" Tanda asked.

"With the number of bars here?" Aahz retorted. "The way I hear it, this is one of their main . . ."

I lost the rest of that argument. A knee-high, tentacled mass suddenly scuttled across my boots and ducked through a tent flap, closely pursued by two very frustrated-looking Deveels.

I ignored the chase and the following screams, hurrying to catch up with Aahz and Tanda again. Apparently they were discussing mercenaries, and I wanted to hear as much as possible, both to further my education, and because I might have to lead them into battle eventually.

". . . find them?" Tanda was asking. "All we have is a general area."

". . . easy," Aahz replied confidently. "Just listen for the singing."

"Singing?" Tanda was skeptical.

"It's their trademark," Aahz pronounced. "It also lands them in most of their . . ."

A Deveel stepped in front of me, proudly displaying a handful of seeds. He threw them on the ground with a flourish, and a dense black thornbush sprang up to block my path. Terrific. Normally, I would have been fascinated, but at the moment I was in a hurry.

Without even pausing to upbraid the Deveel, I took to the air, desperation giving wings to my feet . . . desperation assisted by a little levitation. I cleared the thornbush easily, touched down lightly on the far side, and was practically trampled by Gleep as he burst through the barrier.

"Gleep?" he said, cocking his head at me curiously.

I picked myself up from the dust where I had been knocked by his enthusiasm and cuffed him.

"Watch where you're going next time," I ordered angrily.

He responded by snaking out his long tongue and licking my face. His breath was devastating and his tongue left a trail of slime. Obviously my admonishment had terrified him.

Heaving a deep sigh, I sprinted off after Aahz with Gleep lumbering along in hot pursuit.

I was just overtaking them when Aahz stopped suddenly in his tracks and started to turn. Unable to halt my headlong sprint, I plowed into him, knocking him sprawling.

"In a hurry, handsome?" Tanda asked, eyeing me slyly.

"Gee, Aahz," I stammered, bending over him, "I didn't mean to—"

From a half-sitting position, his hand lashed out in a cuff that spun me halfway around.

"Watch where you're going next time," he growled.

"Gleep!" said the dragon and licked my face.

Either my head was spinning more than I thought, or I had been through this scene before.

"Now quit clowning around and listen, kid."

Aahz was on his feet again, and all business.

"Here's where we part company for a while. You wait here while I go haggle with the mercenaries."

"Gee, Aahz," I whined. "Can't I—"

"No, you can't!" he said firmly. "The crew I'm going after is sharp. All we need is one of your dumb questions in the middle of negotiations and they'll triple their prices."

"But—" I began.

"You will wait here," Aahz ordered. "I repeat, wait. No fights, no window shopping for dragons, just wait!"

"I'll stay here with him, Aahz," Tanda volunteered.

"Good," Aahz nodded. "And try to keep him out of trouble, okay?"

With that, he turned and disappeared into the crowd. Actually, I wasn't too disappointed. I mean, I would have liked to have gone with him, but I liked having some time alone with Tanda even more . . . that is, if you can consider standing in the middle of the Bazaar at Deva being alone with someone.

"Well, Tanda," I said, flashing my brightest smile.

"Later, handsome," she replied briskly. "Right now I've got some errands to run."

"Errands?" I blinked.

"Yeah. Aahz is big on manpower, but I'd just as soon have a few extra tricks up my sleeve in case the going gets rough," she explained. "I'm going to duck over to the special effects section and see what they have in stock."

"Okay," I agreed. "Let's go."

"No, you don't," she said, shaking her head. "I think I'd better go this one alone. The kind of places I have in mind aren't fit for civilized customers. You and the dragon wait here."

"But you're supposed to be keeping me out of trouble!" I argued.

"And that's why I'm not taking you along," she said, smiling. "Now, what do you have along in the way of weaponry?"

"Well . . ." I said hesitantly, "there's a sort of a sword in one of Gleep's packs."

"Fine!" she said. "Get it out and wear it. It'll keep the riffraff at a distance. Then . . . um . . . wait for me in there!"

She pointed at a strange-looking stone structure with a peeling sign on its front.

"What is it?" I asked, peering at it suspiciously.

"It's a 'Yellow Crescent Inn,' " she explained. "It's sort of a restaurant. Get yourself something to eat. The food's unappetizing, but vaguely digestible."

I studied the place for a moment.

"Actually," I decided finally, "I think I'd rather . . ."

Right about there I discovered I was talking to myself. Tanda had disappeared without a trace.

For the second time in my life I was alone in the Bazaar at Deva.

# XIII:

*"Hold the pickles, hold the lettuce."*

—HENRY VIII

Fascinating as the Bazaar is, facing it alone can be rather frightening.

Being particularly susceptible to fear, I decided to follow Tanda's advice and entered the inn.

First, however, I took the precaution of tethering Gleep to the inn's hitching post and unpacking the sword. We had one decent sword. Unfortunately, Aahz was currently wearing it. That left me with Garkin's old sword, a weapon which has been sneered at by demon and demon-hunter alike. Still, its weight was reassuring on my hip, though it might have been more reassuring if I had known anything about how to handle it. Unfortunately, my lessons with Aahz to date had not included swordsmanship. I could only hope it would not be apparent to the casual observer that this was my first time to wear a sword.

Pausing in the door, I surveyed the inn's interior. Unaccustomed as I was to gracious dining, I realized in a flash that this wasn't it.

One of the few pieces of advice my farmer father had given me before I ran away from home was not to trust any inn or restaurant that appeared overly clean. He maintained the cleaner a place was, the more dubious the quality and origin of their food would be. If he were even vaguely right, this inn must be the bottom of the barrel. It was not only clean, it gleamed.

I do not mean that figuratively. Harsh overhead lights glinted off a haphazard arrangement of tiny tables and uncomfortable-looking chairs constructed of shiny metal and a hard white substance I didn't recognize. At the far end of the inn was a counter behind which stood a large stone gargoyle, the only decorative feature in the place. Behind the gargoyle was a door, presumably leading into the kitchen. There was a small window in the door through which I caught glimpses of the food being prepared. Preparation consisted of passing patties of meat over a stove, cramming them into a split roll, slopping a variety of colored pastes on top of the meat, and wrapping the whole mess in a piece of paper.

Watching this process confirmed my earlier fears. I do all the cooking for Aahz and myself, as I did before that for Garkin and myself, and before that just for myself. While I have no delusions as to the high quality of my cooking, I do know that what they were doing to that meat could only yield a meal the consistency and flavor of charred glove leather.

Despite the obvious low quality of the food, the inn seemed nearly full of customers. I noticed this out of the corner of my eye. I also noticed that a high percentage of them were staring at me. It occurred to me that this was probably because I had been standing in the door for some time without entering while working up my courage to go in.

Feeling slightly embarrassed, I stepped inside and let the door swing shut behind me. With fiendish accuracy, the door closed on my sword, pinning it momentarily and forcing me to break stride clumsily as I started forward. So much for my image as a swordsman.

Humiliated, I avoided looking at the other customers and made my way hurriedly to the inn's counter. I wasn't sure what I was going to do once I got there, since I didn't trust the food, but hopefully people would stop staring at me if I went through the motions of ordering.

Still trying to avoid eye contact with anyone, I made a big show of studying the gargoyle. There was a grinding noise, and the statue turned its head to return my stare. It wasn't a statue! They really had a gargoyle tending the counter!

The gargoyle seemed to be made of coarse gray stone, and when he flexed his wings, small pieces of crushed rock and dust showered silently to the floor. His hands were taloned, and there were curved spikes growing out of his elbows. The only redeeming feature I could see was his smile, which in itself was a bit unnerving. Dominating his wrinkled face, the smile seemed permanently etched in place, stretching well past his ears and displaying a set of pointed teeth even longer than Aahz's.

"Take your order?" the gargoyle asked politely, the smile never twitching.

"Um . . ." I said taking a step back. "I'll have to think about it. There's so much to choose from."

In actuality I couldn't read the menu . . . if that's what it was. There was something etched in the wall behind the gargoyle in a language I couldn't decipher. I assume it was a menu because the prices weren't etched in the wall, but written in chalk over many erasures.

The gargoyle shrugged.

"Suit yourself," he said indifferently. "When you make up your mind, just holler. The name's Gus."

"I'll do that . . . Gus," I smiled, backing slowly toward the door.

Though it was my intent to exit quietly and wait outside with Gleep, things didn't work out that way. Before I had taken four steps, a hand fell on my shoulder.

"Skeeve, isn't it?" a voice proclaimed.

I spun around, or started to. I was brought up short when my sword banged into a table leg. My head kept moving, however, and I found myself face to face with an Imp.

"Brockhurst!" I exclaimed, recognizing him immediately.

"I thought I recognized you when you . . . *hey!*" The Imp took a step backward and raised his hands defensively. "Take it easy! I'm not looking for any trouble."

My hand had gone to my sword hilt in an involuntary effort to free it from the table leg. Apparently Brockhurst had interpreted the gesture as an effort to draw my weapon.

That was fine by me. Brockhurst had been one of Isstvan's lieutenants, and we hadn't parted on the best of terms. Having him a little afraid of my "ready sword" was probably a good thing.

"I don't hold any grudges," Brockhurst continued insistently. "That was just a job! Right now I'm between jobs . . . permanently!"

That last was added with a note of bitterness which piqued my curiosity.

"Things haven't been going well?" I asked cautiously.

The Imp grimaced.

"That's an understatement. Come on, sit down. I'll buy you a milkshake and tell you all about it."

I wasn't certain what a milkshake was, but I was sure I didn't want one if they were sold here.

"Um . . . thanks anyway, Brockhurst," I said, forcing a smile, "but I think I'll pass."

The Imp arched an eyebrow at me.

"Still a little suspicious, eh?" he murmured. "Well, can't say as I blame you. Tell you what we'll do."

Before I could stop him, he strolled to the counter.

"Hey, Gus!" he called. "Mind if I take an extra cup?"

"Actually . . ." the gargoyle began.

"Thanks!"

Brockhurst was already on his way back, bearing his prize with him, some kind of a thin-sided, flimsy cannister. Plopping down at a nearby table, he beckoned to me, indicating the seat opposite him with a wave of his hand.

There was no gracious course for me to follow other than to join him, though it would later occur to me I had no real obligation to be gracious. Moving carefully to avoid knocking anything over with my sword, I maneuvered my way to the indicated seat.

Apparently, Brockhurst had been sitting here before, as there was already a cannister on the table identical to the one he had fetched from the counter. The only difference was that the one on the table was three-quarters full of a curious pink liquid.

With great ceremony, the Imp picked up the cannister from the table and poured half its contents into the new vessel. The liquid poured with the consistency of swamp muck.

"Here!" he said, pushing one of the cannisters across the table to me. "Now you don't have to worry about any funny business with the drinks. We're both drinking the same thing."

With that, he raised his vessel in a mock toast and took a healthy swallow from it. Apparently he expected me to do the same. I would have rather sucked blood.

"Um . . . it's hard to believe things aren't going well for you," I stalled. "You look well enough."

For a change, I was actually sincere. Brockhurst looked good . . . even for an Imp. As Aahz had said, Imps are snappy dressers, and Brockhurst was no exception. He was outfitted in a rust-colored velvet jerkin trimmed in gold, which set off his pink complexion and sleek black hair superbly. If he were starving, you couldn't tell it from looking at him. Though still fairly slender, he was as well muscled and adroit as when I had first met him.

"Don't let appearances fool you," Brockhurst insisted, shaking his head. "You see before you an Imp pushed to the wall. I've had to sell everything—my crossbow, my pouch of magic tricks—I couldn't even raise enough money to pay my dues to the Assassins Guild."

"It's that hard to find work?" I sympathized.

"I'll tell you, Skeeve," he whispered confidentially, "I haven't worked since that fiasco with Isstvan."

The sound of that name still sent chills down my back.

"Where is Isstvan, anyway?" I asked casually.

"Don't worry about him," Brochkurst said grimly. "We left him working concession stands on the Isle of Coney, a couple of dimensions from here."

"What happened to the others?"

I was genuinely curious. I hadn't had much of a chance to talk with Tanda since our reunion.

"We left Frumple under a cloud of birds in some park or other . . . figured he looked better as a statue than he did alive. The demon hunter and the girl took off for parts unknown one night while we were asleep. My partner, Higgens, headed back to Imper. He figured his career was over and that he might as well settle down. Me, I've been looking for work ever since, and I'm starting to think Higgens was right."

"Come on, Brockhurst," I chided. "There must be something you can do. I mean, this is the Bazaar."

The Imp heaved a sigh and took another sip of his drink.

"It's nice of you to say that, Skeeve," he smiled. "But I've got to face the facts. There's not a big demand for Imps anyway, and none at all for an Imp with no powers."

I knew what he meant. All the dimension travelers I had met so far—Aahz, Isstvan, Tanda, and even the Deveel Frumple—seemed to regard Imps as inferior beings. The nicest thing I had heard said about them was that they were styleless imitators of the Deveels.

I felt sorry for him. Despite the fact we had first met as enemies, it wasn't that long ago I had been a loser nobody wanted.

"You've got to keep trying," I encouraged.

"Somewhere, there's someone who wants to hire you."

"Not very likely," the Imp grimaced. "The way I am now, *I* wouldn't hire me. Would you?"

"Sure I would," I insisted. "In a minute."

"Oh, well," he sighed. "I shouldn't dwell on myself. How have things been with you? What brings you to the Bazaar?"

Now it was my turn to grimace.

"Aahz and I are in a bad spot," I explained. "We're here trying to recruit a force to help us out."

"You're hiring people?" Brockhurst was suddenly intense.

"Yeah. Why?" I replied.

Too late, I realized what I was saying.

"Then you weren't kidding about hiring me!" Brockhurst was beside himself with glee.

"Um . . ." I said.

"This is great," the Imp chortled, rubbing his hands together. "Believe me, Skeeve, you won't regret this."

I was regretting it already.

"Wait a minute, Brockhurst," I interrupted desperately. "There are a few things you should know about the job."

"Like what?"

"Well . . . for one thing, the odds are bad," I said judiciously. "We're up against an army. That's pretty rough fare considering how low the pay is."

I thought I would touch a nerve with that remark about the pay. I was right.

"How low *is* the pay?" the Imp asked bluntly.

Now I was stuck. I didn't have the vaguest idea how much mercenaries were normally paid.

"We . . . um . . . we couldn't offer you more than one gold piece for the whole job," I shrugged.

"Done!" Brockhurst proclaimed. "With the current state of my finances, I can't turn down an offer like that no matter how dangerous it is."

It occurred to me that sometime I should have Aahz give me a quick course in rates of exchange.

"Um . . . there's one other problem," I murmured thoughtfully.

"What's that?"

"Well, my partner, you remember Aahz?"

The Imp nodded.

"Well, he's out right now trying to hire a force, and he's got the money," I continued. "There's a good chance that if he's successful, and he usually is, there won't be enough money left to hire you."

Brockhurst pursed his lips for a moment, then shrugged.

"Well," he said, "I'll take the chance. I wasn't going anywhere anyway. As I said, they haven't exactly been beating my door down with job offers."

I had run out of excuses.

"Well"—I smiled lamely—"as long as you're aware—"

"Heads up, boss," the Imp's murmur interrupted me. "We've got company."

I'm not sure which worried me more, Brockhurst calling me "boss" or the specterlike character who had just stepped up to our table.

# XIV:

*"We're looking for a few good men."*

—B. CASSIDY

For a moment I thought we were being confronted by a skeleton. Then I looked closer and realized there really *was* skin stretched over the bones, though its dusty-white color made it seem very dead indeed.

The figure's paleness was made even more corpse-like by the blue-black hooded robe that enshrouded it. It wasn't until I noted the wrinkled face with a short, bristly white beard that I realized our visitor was actually a very old man . . . very old.

He looked weak to the point of near collapse, desperately clutching a twisted black walking staff which seemed to be the only thing keeping him erect. Still, his eyes were bright and his smile confident as he stood regarding us.

"Did I hear you boys right?" he asked in a crackling voice.

"I beg your pardon?" Brockhurst scowled at him.

The ancient figure sneered and raised his voice.

"I said, 'Did I hear you boys right?'!" he barked.

"What's the matter? Are you deaf?"

"Um . . . excuse me," I interrupted hastily. "Before we can answer you, we have to know what you thought we said." ·

The old man thought for a minute, then bobbed his head in a sudden nod.

"You know, yer right!" he cackled. "Pretty smart, young fella."

He began to list, but caught himself before he fell.

"Thought I heard you tell Pinko here you were looking for a force to take on an army," he pronounced, jerking a thumb at Brockhurst.

"The name's Brockhurst, not Pinko!" the Imp snarled.

"All right, Bratwurst," the old man nodded. "No need to get your dander up."

"That's Brockhurst!"

"You heard right," I interrupted again, hoping the old man would go away as soon as his curiosity was satisfied.

"Good!" the man declared. "Count me in! Me and Blackie haven't been in a good fight for a long time."

"How long is that in centuries?" Brockhurst sneered.

"Watch your mouth, Bratwurst!" the old man warned. "We may be old, but we can still teach you a thing or two about winnin' wars."

"Who's Blackie?" I asked, cutting off Brockhurst's reply.

In reply, the old man drew himself erect . . . well, nearly erect, and patted his walking staff.

"This is Blackie!" he announced proudly. "The finest bow ever to come from Archiah, and that takes in a lot of fine bows!"

I realized with a start that the walking staff was a bow, unstrung, with its bowstring wrapped around it. It was unlike any bow I had ever seen, lumpy and uneven, but polished to a sheen that seemed to glimmer with a life all its own.

"Wait a minute!" Brockhurst was suddenly attentive. "Did you say you come from Archiah?"

"That I did," the old man grinned. "Ajax's the name, fighting's my game. Ain't seen a war yet that could lay old Ajax low, and I've seen a lot of 'em."

"Um . . . could you excuse us for just a minute, sir?" Brockhurst smiled apologetically.

"Sure, son," Ajax nodded. "Take your time."

I couldn't understand the Imp's sudden change in attitude, but he seemed quite intense as he jerked his head at me, so I leaned close to hear what he had to say.

"Hire him, boss!" he hissed in my ear.

"What?" I gasped, not believing I had heard him right.

"I said hire him!" the Imp repeated. "I may not have much to offer you, but I can give you advice. Right now, my advice is to hire him."

"But he's—"

"He's from Archiah!" Brockhurst interrupted. "Boss, that dimension *invented* archery. You don't find many genuine Archers of any age for hire. If you've really got a war on your hands, hire him. He could tip the balance for us."

"If he's that good," I whispered back, "can we afford him?"

"One gold piece will be adequate," Ajax smiled toothily, adding his head to our conference. "I accept your offer."

"Excellent!" Brockhurst beamed.

"Wait a minute," I shrieked desperately, "I have a partner that—"

"I know, I know," Ajax sighed, holding up a restraining hand. "I heard when you told Bratwurst here."

"That's Brockhurst," the Imp growled, but he did it smiling.

"If your partner can't find help, then we're hired!" the old man laughed, shaking his head. "It's a mite strange, but these are strange times."

"You can say that again," I muttered.

I was beginning to think I had spoken too loud in my conversation with Brockhurst.

"One thing you should know, though, youngster," Ajax murmured confidentially. "I'm bein' followed."

"By who?" I asked.

"Don't rightly know," he admitted. "Haven't figured it out yet. It's the little blue fella in the corner behind me."

I craned my neck to look at the indicated corner. It was empty.

"What fella? I mean, fellow," I corrected myself.

Ajax whipped his head around with a speed that belied his frail appearance.

"Dang it," he cursed. "He did it again. I'm telling you, youngster, that's why I can't figure what he's after!"

"Ah . . . sure, Ajax," I said soothingly. "You'll catch him next time."

Terrific. An Imp with no powers, and now an old Archer who sees things.

My thoughts were interrupted by a gentle tap on my shoulder. I turned to find the gargoyle looming over me.

"Your order's ready, sir," he said through his permasmile.

"My order?"

"Yes, if you'll step this way."

"There must be some mistake," I began, "I didn't . . ."

The gargoyle was already gone, lumbering back to his counter. I considered ignoring him. Then I considered his size and countenance, and decided I should straighten out this misunderstanding in a polite fashion.

"Excuse me," I told my charges. "I'll be right back."

"Don't worry about us, boss," Brockhurst waved.

I wasn't reassured.

I managed to make my way to the counter without banging my sword against anything or anyone, a feat that raised my spirits for the first time that afternoon. Thus bolstered, I approached the gargoyle.

"I . . . um . . . I don't recall ordering anything," I stated politely.

"Don't blame you, either," the gargoyle growled through his smile. "Beats me how anyone or anything can eat the slop they serve here."

"But—"

"That was just to get you away from those two," the gargoyle shrugged. "You see, I'm shy."

"Shy about what?"

"About asking you for a job, of course!"

I decided I would definitely have to keep my voice down in the future. My quiet conversation with Brockhurst seemed to have attracted the attention of half the Bazaar.

"Look . . . um . . ."

"Gus!" the gargoyle supplied.

"Yes, well, ah, Gus, I'm really not hiring—"

"I know. Your partner is," Gus interrupted. "But you're here and he isn't, so I figured I'd make our pitch to you before the second team roster is completely filled."

"Oh!" I said, not knowing what else to say.

"The way I see it," the gargoyle continued, "we could do you a lot of good. You're a Klahd, aren't you?"

"I'm from Klah," I acknowledged stiffly.

"Well, if my memory serves me correctly, warfare in that dimension isn't too far advanced technologically."

"We have crossbows and catapults," I informed him. "At least the other side does."

"That's what I said," Gus agreed. "Primitive. To stop that force, all you need is air support and a little firepower. We can supply both, and we'll work cheap, both of us for one gold piece."

Now I was sure I had underestimated the market value of gold pieces. Still, the price was tempting.

"I dunno, Gus," I said cagily. "Ajax there is supposed to be a pretty good Archer."

"Archers," the gargoyle snorted. "I'm talking about *real* firepower. The kind my partner can give you."

"Who is your partner?" I asked. "He isn't short and blue by any chance, is he?"

"Naw," Gus replied, pointing to the far corner. "That's the Gremlin. He came in with the Archer."

"A Gremlin?" I said, following his finger.

Sure enough, perched on a chair in the corner was a small, elfish character. Mischievous eyes danced in his soft blue face as he nodded to me in silent recognition. Reflexively, I smiled and nodded back. Apparently I owed Ajax an apology.

"I thought Gremlins didn't exist," I commented casually to Gus.

"A lot of folks think that," the gargoyle agreed. "But you can see for yourself, they're real."

I wasn't sure. In the split second I had taken my eyes off the Gremlin to speak with Gus, he had vanished without a trace. I was tempted to go looking for him, but Gus was talking again.

"Just a second and I'll introduce you to my partner," he was saying. "He's here somewhere."

As he spoke, the gargoyle began rummaging about his own body, feeling his armpits and peering into the wrinkles on his skin.

I watched curiously, until my attention was arrested by a small lizard that had crawled out of one of the gargoyle's wing folds and was now regarding me fixedly from Gus's right shoulder. It was only about three inches long, but glowed with a brilliant orange hue. There were blotchy red patterns which seemed to crawl about the lizard's skin with a life of their own. The overall effect was startlingly beautiful.

"Is that your lizard?" I asked.

"There he is!" Gus crowed triumphantly, snatching the reptile from his shoulder and cupping it in his hands. "Meet Berfert. He's the partner I was telling you about."

"Hello, Berfert," I smiled, extending a finger to stroke him.

The gargoyle reacted violently, jerking the lizard back out of my reach.

"Careful, there," he warned. "That's a good way to lose a finger."

"I wasn't going to hurt him," I explained.

"No, he was about to hurt you!" Gus countered. "Berfert's a salamander, a walking firebomb. We get along because I'm one of the few beings around that won't burn to a crisp when I touch him."

"Oh," I said with sudden understanding. "So when you said 'firepower'—"

"I meant *firepower*," Gus finished. "Berfert cleans 'em out on the ground, and I work 'em over from the air. Well, what do you say? Have we got a deal?"

"I'll . . . um . . . have to talk it over with my partner," I countered.

"Fine," Gus beamed. "I'll start packing."

He was gone before I could stop him.

I sagged against the counter, wishing fervently for Aahz's return. As if in answer to my thoughts, my mentor burst through the door, following closely by Tanda.

My greeting died in my throat when I saw his scowl. Aahz was not in a good mood.

"I thought I told you to wait outside," he bellowed at me.

"Calm down, Aahz," Tanda soothed. "I thought he'd be more comfortable waiting in here. Besides, there's no reason to get upset. We're here and he's here. Nothing has gone wrong."

"You haven't been dealing with any Deveels?" Aahz asked suspiciously.

"I haven't even talked with any," I protested.

"Good!" he retorted, slightly mollified. "There's hope for you yet, kid."

"I told you he could stay out of trouble," Tanda smiled triumphantly. "Isn't that right, handsome?"

Try as I might, I couldn't bring myself to answer her.

# XV:

*"I'll worry about it tomorrow."*

—S. O'HARA

"Um . . . are the mercenaries waiting outside?" I asked finally.

"You didn't answer her question, kid," Aahz observed, peering at me with renewed suspicion.

"Don't strain your neck looking for your troops, handsome," Tanda advised me. "There weren't any. It seems our mighty negotiator has met his match."

"Those bandits!" Aahz exploded. "Do you have any idea what it would cost us if I had agreed to pay their bar bill as part of the contract? If that's a nonprofit group, I want to audit their books."

My hopes for salvation sank like a rock.

"You didn't hire them?" I asked.

"No, I didn't," Aahz scowled. "And that moves us back to square one. Now we've got to recruit a force one at a time."

"Did you try—" I began.

"Look, kid," Aahz interrupted with a snarl, "I did the

best I could, and I got nowhere. I'd like to see you do better."

"He already has!" Brockhurst announced, rising from his seat. "While you were wasting time, Skeeve here has hired himself a fighting team."

"He what?" Aahz bellowed, turning on his critic. "Brockhurst! What are you doing here?"

"Waiting for orders in our upcoming campaign," the Imp replied innocently.

"What campaign?" Aahz glowered.

"The one on Klah, of course," Brockhurst blinked. "Haven't you told him yet, boss?"

"Boss?" Aahz roared. "Boss?"

"No need ta shout," Ajax grumbled, turning to face the assemblage. "We hear ya plain enough."

"Ajax!" Tanda exclaimed gleefully.

"Tanda!" the old man yelped back.

She was at him in a bound, but he smoothly interposed his bow between them.

"Easy, girl," he laughed. "None of your athletic greetings. I'm not as young as I used to be, ya know."

"You old fraud!" Tanda teased. "You'll outlive us all."

Ajax shrugged dramatically. "That kinda depends on how good a general the youngster there is," he commented.

"Kid," Aahz growled through gritted teeth, "I want to talk to you! *Now!*"

"I know that temper!" Gus announced, emerging from the back room.

"Gus!" Aahz exclaimed.

"In the stone!" the gargoyle confirmed. "Are you in on this expedition? The boss didn't say anything about working with Perverts."

Instead of replying, Aahz sank heavily into a chair and hid his face in his hands.

"Tanda!" he moaned. "Tell me again about how this kid can stay out of trouble."

"Um . . . Aahz," I said cautiously, "could I talk to you for a minute . . . privately?"

"Why, I think that's an excellent idea . . . boss," he said.

The smile he gave me wasn't pleasant.

"**K**id!" Aahz moaned after I had finished my tale. "How many times do I have to tell you? This is the Bazaar at Deva! You've *got* to be careful what you say and to whom, especially when there's money involved."

"But I told them nothing was definite until we found out if you had hired someone else," I protested.

"But I didn't hire anyone else, so now the deal is final," Aahz sighed.

"Can't we get out of it?" I asked hopefully.

"Back out of a deal on Deva?" Aahz shook his head. "That would get us barred from the Bazaar so fast it would make your head spin. Remember, the Merchants Association runs this dimension."

"Well, you said you wanted outside help," I pointed out.

"I didn't expect to go that far outside," he grimaced. "An Imp, a senile Archer, and a gargoyle."

"And a salamander," I added.

"Gus is still bumming around with Berfert?" Aahz asked, brightening slightly. "That's a plus."

"The only really uncertain factor," I said thoughtfully, "is the Gremlin."

"How do you figure that?" Aahz yawned.

"Well, he's been following Ajax. The question is, why? And will he follow us to Klah?"

"Kid," Aahz said solemnly, "I've told you before. There are no such things as Gremlins."

"But Aahz, I saw him."

"Don't let it bother you, kid," Aahz sympathized. "After a day like you've been through, I wouldn't be surprised if you saw a Jabberwocky."

"What's a—"

"Is everything set?" Tanda asked, joining our conversation.

"About as set as we'll ever be," Aahz sighed. "Though if you want my honest opinion, with a crew like this, we're set more for a zoo than a war."

"Aahz is a bit critical of my choice in recruits," I confided.

"What's your gripe, Aahz?" she asked, cocking her head. "I thought you and Gus were old foxhole buddies."

"I'm not worried about Gus," Aahz put in hastily. "Or Berfert either. That little lizard's terrific under fire."

"Well, I can vouch for Ajax," Tanda informed him. "Don't let his age fool you. I'd rather have him backing my move than a whole company of counterfeit archers."

"Is he really from Archiah?" Aahz asked skeptically.

"That's what he's said as long as I've known him," Tanda shrugged. "And after seeing him shoot, I've got no reason to doubt it. Why?"

"I've never met a genuine Archer before," Aahz said. "For a while I was willing to believe the whole dimension was a legend. Well, if he can shoot half as well as Archers are supposed to, I've got no gripes having him on the team."

I started to feel a little better. Unfortunately, Aahz noticed my smile.

"The Imp is another story," he said grimly. "I'm not wild about working with any Imp, but to hire one without powers is a waste of good money."

"Don't forget he's an Assassin," Tanda pointed out. "Powers or no powers, I'll bet we find a use for him. When we were talking with the Gremlin just now—"

"Now don't you start on that!" Aahz snarled.

"Start on what?" Tanda blinked.

"The Gremlin bit," Aahz scowled. "Any half-wit knows there are no such things as Gremlins."

"Do you want to tell him that?" Tanda smiled. "I'll call him over here and . . . oh, rats! He's gone again."

"If you're quite through," Aahz grumbled, rising from his chair, "we'd best get moving. There's a war waiting for us, you know."

"Oops! That reminds me!" Tanda exclaimed, fishing inside her tunic.

"I know I shouldn't ask," Aahz signed, "but what—"

"Here!" Tanda announced, flipping him a familiar object.

It was a metal rod about eight inches long and two inches in diameter with a button on one end of it.

"A D-Hopper!" I cried, recognizing the device instantly.

"It's the same one you gave Isstvan," Tanda smiled proudly. "I lifted it from him when we parted company. You'll probably want to undo whatever you did to the controls before you use it, though."

"If I can remember for sure," Aahz scowled, staring at the device.

"I thought it might come in handy in case we get separated on this job and you need a fast exit," Tanda shrugged.

"The thought's appreciated," Aahz smiled, putting an arm around her.

"Does this mean you'll be able to teach me how to travel the dimensions?" I asked hopefully.

"Not now I won't," Aahz grimaced. "We've got a war to fight, remember?"

"Oh! Yes, of course."

"Well, get your troops together and let's go," Aahz ordered.

"Okay," I agreed, rising from my chair. "I'll get Gleep and . . . wait a minute! Did you say *my* troops?"

"You hired 'em, you lead 'em," my mentor smiled.

"But you're—"

"I'll be your military advisor, of course," Aahz continued casually. "But the job of Fearless Leader is all yours. You're the court magician, remember?"

I swallowed hard. Somehow this had never entered into my thinking.

"But what do I do?" I asked desperately.

"Well," Aahz drawled. "First, I'd advise you to move 'em outside so we can all head for Klah together . . . that is, unless you're willing to leave your dragon behind."

That didn't even deserve an answer. I turned to face the troops, sweeping them with what I hoped was a masterful gaze which would immediately command their attention.

No one noticed. They were all involved in a jovial conversation.

I cleared my throat noisily.

Nothing.

I considered going over to their table.

"Listen up!" Aahz barked suddenly, scaring me half to death.

The conversation stopped abruptly and all heads swiveled my way.

"Aah . . ." I began confidently. "We're ready to go now. Everybody outside. Wait for me by the dragon."

"Right, boss!" Brockhurst called, starting for the door.

"I'll be a minute, youngster," Ajax wheezed, struggling to rise.

"Here, Gramps," Gus said. "Let me give you a hand."

"Name's not Gramps, it's Ajax!" the Archer scowled.

"Just trying to be helpful," the gargoyle apologized.

"I kin' stand up by myself," Ajax insisted. "Just 'cause I'm old don't mean I'm helpless."

I glanced to Aahz for help, but he and Tanda were already headed out.

As I turned back to Ajax, I thought I caught a glimpse of a small, blue figure slipping out through the door ahead of us. If it was the Gremlin, he was nowhere in sight when I finally reached the street.

# XVI:

*"Myth-conceptions are the major cause
of wars!"*

—A. HITLER

Fortunately, the army had not moved from the position it held when we left for Deva. I say fortunately because Aahz pointed out they might well have renewed their advance in our absence. If that had happened, we would have returned to find ourselves behind the enemy lines, if not actually in the middle of one of their encampments.

Of course, he pointed this out to me after we had arrived back on Klah. Aahz is full of helpful little tidbits of information, but his timing leaves a lot to be desired.

Ajax lost no time upon our arrival. Moving with a briskness that belied his years, he strung his bow and stood squinting at the distant encampments.

"Well, youngster," he asked, never taking his eyes from the enemy's formations, "what's my first batch of targets?"

His eagerness took me aback a bit, but Aahz covered for me neatly.

"First," he said loftily, "we'll have to hold a final planning session."

"We didn't expect to have you along, Ajax," Tanda added. "Having a genuine Archer on our side naturally calls for some drastic revisions of our battle plans."

"Don't bother me none," Ajax shrugged. "Just wanted ta let you know I was ready to earn my keep. Take yer time. Seen too many wars messed up 'cause nobody bothered to do any plannin'! If ya don't mind, though, think I'll take me a little nap. Jes' holler when ya want some shootin' done."

"Ah . . . go ahead, Ajax," I agreed.

Without further conversation, Ajax plopped down and pulled his cloak a bit closer about him. Within a few minutes, he was snoring lightly, but I noticed his bow was still in his grip.

"Now there's a seasoned soldier," Aahz observed. "Gets his sleep when and where he can."

"You want me to do a little scouting, boss?" Gus asked.

"Um . . ." I hesitated, glancing quickly at Aahz.

Aahz caught my look and gave a small nod.

"Sure, Gus," I finished. "We'll wait for you here."

"I'll scout in the other direction," Brockhurst volunteered.

"Okay," I nodded. "Aahz, can you give 'em a quick briefing?"

I was trying to drop the load in Aahz's lap, but he joined the conversation as smoothly as if we had rehearsed it this way.

"There are a couple of things we need specific information on," he said solemnly. "First, we need a battlefield, small with scattered cover. Gus, you check that out. You know what we're going to need. Brockhurst, see what details you can bring back on the three nearest encampments."

Both scouts nodded briskly.

"And both of you, stay out of sight," Aahz warned.

"The information's no good to us if you don't come back."

"C'mon, Aahz," Gus admonished. "What have they got that can put a dent in the old rock?"

He demonstrated by smashing his forearm into a sapling. The tree went down, apparently without affecting the gargoyle's arm in the slightest.

"I don't know," Aahz admitted. "And I don't want to know, yet. You're one of our surprise weapons. No point in giving the enemy an advance warning. Get my meaning?"

"Got it, Aahz," Gus nodded, and lumbered off.

"Be back in a bit," Brockhurst said with a wave of his hand, heading off in the opposite direction.

"Now that we've got a minute," I murmured to Aahz as I returned Brockhurst's wave, "would you mind telling me what our final plan is? I don't even know what the preliminary plans were."

"That's easy," Aahz replied. "We don't have one . . . yet."

"Well, when are we going to form one?" I asked with forced patience.

"Probably on the battlefield," Aahz yawned. "Until then it's pointless. There're too many variables until then."

"Wouldn't it be a good idea to have at least a general idea as to what we're going to do *before* we wander out on the battlefield?" I insisted. "It would do a lot for my peace of mind."

"Oh, I've already got a general idea as to what we'll be doing," Aahz admitted.

"Isn't he sweet?" Tanda grimaced. "Would you mind sharing it with us, Aahz? We've got a stake in this, too."

"Well," he began lazily, "the name of the game is delay and demoralize. The way I figure it, we aren't going to overpower them. We haven't got enough going for us to even try that."

I bit back a sarcastic observation and let him continue.

"Delay and demoralize we should be able to do, though," Aahz smiled. "Right off the bat, we've got two big weapons going for us in that kind of a fight."

"Ajax and Gus," I supplied helpfully.

"Fear and bureaucracy," Aahz corrected.

"How's that again?" Tanda frowned.

"Tanda, my girl," Aahz smiled, "you've been spoiled by your skylarking through the dimensions. You've forgotten how the man on the street thinks. The average person in any dimension doesn't know the first thing about magik, particularly about its limitations. If the kid here tells 'em he can make the sun stop or trees grow upside down, they'll believe him. Particularly if he's got a few strange characters parading around as proof of his power, and I think you'll have to admit, the crew he's got backing him this time around is pretty strange."

"What's bureaucracy?" I asked, finally getting a word in edgewise.

"Red tape . . . the system," Aahz informed me. "The organization to get things done that keeps things from getting done. In this case, it's called the chain-of-command. An army the size of the one we're facing has to function like a well-oiled machine or it starts tripping over its own feet. I'm betting if we toss a couple of handfuls of sand into its gears, they'll spend more time fighting each other than chasing us."

This was one of the first times Aahz had actually clarified something he said. I wished he hadn't. I was more confused than I had been before.

"Um . . . how are we going to do all this?" I asked.

"We'll be able to tell better after you've had your first war council," Aahz shrugged.

"Aren't we having it now?"

"I meant with the enemy," Aahz scowled. "Sometime in the near future, you're going to have to sit down with one of their officers and decide how this war's going to be fought."

"Me?" I blinked.

"You *are* the leader of the defenses, remember?" Aahz grinned at me.

"It's part of the job, handsome," Tanda confirmed.

"Wait a minute," I interrupted. "It just came to me. I think I have a better idea."

"This I've got to hear," Aahz grinned.

"Shut up, Aahz," Tanda ordered, poking him in the ribs. "Whatcha got, handsome?"

"We've got a couple of trained Assassins on our side, don't we?" I observed. "Why don't we just put 'em to work? If enough officers suddenly turn up dead, odds are the army will fall apart. Right?"

"It won't work, kid," Aahz announced bluntly.

"Why not?"

"We can bend the rules, but we can't break 'em," Aahz explained. "Wars are fought between the troops. Killing off the officers without engaging their troops goes against tradition. I doubt if your own force would stand still for it. Old troopers like Ajax would have no part of a scheme like that."

"He's right," Tanda confirmed. "Assassins take contracts on individuals in personal feuds, but not against the general staff of an army."

"But it would be so easy," I insisted.

"Look at it this way, kid," Aahz put in. "If you could do it, they could do it. The way things are now, you're exempt from Assassins. Would you really want to change that?"

"What do I say in a war council?" I asked.

"I'll brief you on that when the time comes," Aahz reassured me. "Right now we have other things to plan."

"Such as what?" Tanda asked.

"Such as what to do about those signal towers," Aahz retorted, jerking his head at one of the distant structures.

"We probably won't have time to break their code, so the next best thing is to disrupt their signals somehow. Now, you said you picked up some special effects items

back at the Bazaar. Have you got anything we could use
on the signal towers?"

"I'm not sure," Tanda frowned thoughtfully. "I wish you
had said something about that before I went shopping."

"What about Ajax?" I suggested.

"What about him?" Aahz countered.

"How close would he have to be to the towers to disrupt things with his archery?"

"I don't know," Aahz shrugged. "Why don't you ask
him?"

Eager to follow up on my own suggestion, I squatted
down next to the dozing bowman.

"Um . . . Ajax," I called softly.

"Whatcha need, youngster?" the old man asked, coming instantly awake.

"Do you see those signal towers?" I asked, pointing at
the distant structures.

Ajax rose to his feet and squinted in the indicated direction. "Sure can," he nodded.

"We . . . um . . . I was wondering," I explained, "can
you use your bow to disrupt their signals?"

In response, Ajax drew an arrow from beneath his
cloak, cocked it, and let fly before I could stop him.

The shaft disappeared in the direction of the nearest
tower. With sinking heart, I strained my eyes trying to
track its flight.

There was a man standing on the tower's platform, his
standard leaning against the railing beside him. Suddenly,
his standard toppled over, apparently breaking off a handspan from its crosspiece. The man bent and retrieved the
bottom portion of the pole, staring with apparent confusion at the broken end.

"Any other targets?" Ajax asked.

He was leaning casually on his bow, his back to the
tower. He hadn't even bothered watching to see if his
missile struck its mark.

"Um . . . not just now, Ajax," I assured him. "Go back
to sleep."

"Fine by me, sonny," Ajax smiled, resettling himself. "There'll be plenty of targets tomorrow."

"How do you figure that?" I asked.

"According to that signal I just cut down," he grinned, "the army's fixin' to move out tomorrow."

"You can read the signals?" I blinked.

"Sure," Ajax nodded. "There're only about eight different codes armies use, and I know 'em all. It's part of my trade."

"And they're moving out tomorrow?" I pressed.

"That's what I said." The bowman scowled. "What's the matter, are you deaf?"

"No," I assured him hastily. "It just changes our plans is all. Go back to sleep."

Returning to our little conference, I found Aahz and Tanda engrossed in a conversation with Brockhurst.

"Bad news, kid," Aahz informed me. "Brockhurst here says the army's going to move out tomorrow."

"I know," I said. "I just found out from Ajax. Can you read the signal flags too, Brockhurst?"

"Naw," the Imp admitted. "But the Gremlin can."

"What Gremlin?" Aahz bared his teeth.

"He was here a minute ago," Brockhurst scowled, looking around.

"Well, handsome," Tanda sighed, eyeing me, "I think we just ran out of planning time. Better call your dragon. I think we're going to need all the help we can get tomorrow."

Gleep had wandered off shortly after our arrival, though we could still hear him occasionally as he poked about in the underbrush.

"You go get the dragon, Tanda," Aahz ordered.

"Though it escapes me how he's supposed to be any help. The 'boss' here and I have to discuss his war council tomorrow."

Any confidence I might have built up listening to Aahz's grand plan earlier fled me. Tanda was right. We had run out of time.

# XVII:

*"Diplomacy is the delicate weapon of
the civilized warrior."*

—HUN, A. T.

We waited patiently for our war council. The two of
us, Aahz and me. Against an army.

This was, of course, Aahz's idea. Left to my own devices, I wouldn't be caught dead in this position.

Trying to ignore that unfortunate choice of words, I
cleared my throat and spoke to Aahz out of the corner of
my mouth.

"Aahz?"

"Yeah, kid?"

"How long are we going to stand here?"

"Until they notice us and do something about it."

Terrific. Either we'd rot where we stood, or someone
would shoot us full of arrows.

We were standing about twenty yards from one of the
encampments, with nothing between us and them but
meadow. We could see clearly the bustle of activity within
the encampment and, in theory, there was nothing keeping
them from seeing us. This is why we were standing where

we were, to draw attention to ourselves. Unfortunately, so far no one had noticed.

It had been decided that Aahz and I would work alone on this first sortie to hide the true strength of our force. It occurred to me that it also hid the true weakness of our force, but I felt it would be tactless to point this out.

At first, Brockhurst had argued in favor of his coming along with me instead of Aahz, claiming that as an Imp he had much more experience at bargaining than a demon. It was pointed out to him rather forcefully by Aahz that in this instance we weren't bargaining for glass beads or whoopie cushions, but for a war . . . and if the Imp wanted to prove to Aahz that he knew more about fighting. . . .

Needless to say, Brockhurst backed down at that point. This was good, as it saved me from having to openly reject his offer. I mean, I may not be the fastest learner around, but I could still distinctly remember Aahz getting the best of Brockhurst the last time the two of them had squared off for a bargaining session.

Besides, if this meeting went awry, I wanted my mentor close at hand to share the consequences with me.

So here we stood, blatantly exposed to the enemy without even a sword for our defense. That was another of Aahz's brainstorms. He argued that our being unarmed accomplished three things. First, it showed that we were here to talk, not to fight. Second, it demonstrated our faith in my magical abilities to defend us. Third, it encouraged our enemy to meet us similarly unarmed.

He also pointed out that Ajax would be hiding in the tree line behind us with strung bow and cocked arrow, and would probably be better at defending us if anything went wrong than a couple of swords would.

He was right, of course, but it did nothing to settle my nerves as we waited.

"Heads up, kid," Aahz murmured. "We've got company."

Sure enough, a rather stocky individual was striding briskly across the meadow in our direction.

"Kid!" Aahz hissed suddenly. "Your disguise!"

"What about it?" I whispered back.

"It isn't!" came the reply.

He was right! I had carefully restored his "dubious character" appearance, but had forgotten completely about changing my own. Having our motley crew accept my leadership in my normal form had caused me to overlook the fact that Klahds are harder to impress than demons.

"Should I—" I began.

"Too late!" Aahz growled. "Fake it."

The soldier was almost upon us now, close enough for me to notice when he abandoned his bored expression and forced a smile.

"I'm sorry, folks," he called with practiced authority. "You'll have to clear the area. We'll be moving soon and you're blocking the path."

"Call your duty officer!" Aahz boomed back at him.

"My who?" the soldier scowled.

"Duty officer, officer of the day, commander, whatever you call whoever's currently in charge of your formation," Aahz clarified. "Somebody's got to be running things, and if you're officer material, I'm the Queen of the May."

Whether or not the soldier understood Aahz's allusion (I didn't), he caught the general implication.

"Yeah, there's someone in charge," he snarled, his complexion darkening slightly. "He's a very busy man right now, too busy to stand around talking to civilians. We're getting ready to move our troops, mister, so take your son and get out of the way. If you want to watch the soldiers, you'll have to follow along and watch us when we camp tonight."

"Do you have any idea who you're talking to?" I said in a surprisingly soft voice.

"I don't care who your father is, sonny," the soldier retorted. "We're trying to—"

"The name's not 'sonny,' it's *Skeeve!*" I hissed, drawing myself up. "Court magician to the kingdom of Possiltum, pledged to that kingdom's defense. Now I advise you to call your officer . . . or do you want to wake up tomorrow morning on a lily pad?"

The soldier recoiled a step and stood regarding me suspiciously.

"Is he for real?" he asked Aahz skeptically.

"How's your taste for flies?" Aahz smiled.

"You mean he can really—"

"Look," interrupted Aahz, "I'm not playing servant to the kid because of his terrific personality, if you know what I mean."

"I see . . . um . . ." The soldier was cautiously backing toward the encampment. "I'll . . . um . . . I'll bring my commanding officer."

"We'll be here," Aahz assured him.

The soldier nodded and retreated with noticeably greater speed than he had displayed approaching us.

"So far, so good," my mentor said with a grin.

"What's wrong with my personality?" I asked bluntly.

Aahz sighed. "Later, kid. For the time being, concentrate on looking aloof and dignified, okay?"

Okay or not, there wasn't much else to do while we waited for the officer to put in his appearance.

Apparently, news of our presence spread through the encampment in record time, for a crowd of soldiers gathered at the edge of the camp long before we saw any sign of the officer. It seemed all preparations to move were suspended at least temporarily while the soldiers lined up and craned their necks to gawk at us.

It was kind of a nice feeling to have caused such a sensation, until I noticed several soldiers were taking time to strap on weapons and armor before joining the crowd.

"Aahz!" I whispered.

"Yeah, kid?"

"I thought this was supposed to be a peaceful meeting."

"It is," he assured me.

"But they're arming!" I pointed out.

"Relax, kid," he whispered back. "Remember Ajax is covering us."

I tried to focus on that thought. Then I saw what was apparently the officer approaching us flanked by two soldiers, and I focused on the swords they were all wearing.

"Aahz!" I hissed.

"Relax, kid," Aahz advised me. "Remember Ajax."

I remembered. I also remembered we were vastly outnumbered.

"I understand you gentlemen are emissaries of Possiltum?" the officer asked, coming to a halt in front of us.

I nodded stiffly, hoping the abruptness of my motion would be interpreted as annoyance rather than fear.

"Fine," the officer smirked. "Then as the first representative of the Empire to contact a representative of Possiltum, I have the pleasure of formally declaring war on your kingdom."

"What is your name?" Aahz asked casually.

"Claude," the officer responded. "Why do you ask?"

"The historians like details," Aahz shrugged. "Well, Claude, as the first representative of Possiltum to meet with a representative of your Empire in times of war, it is our pleasure to demand your unconditional surrender."

That got a smile out of the officer.

"Surrender?" he chortled. "To a cripple and a child? You must be mad. Even if I had the authority to do such a thing, I wouldn't."

"That's right." Aahz shook his head in mock self-admonishment. "We should have realized. Someone in charge of a supply company wouldn't swing much weight in an army like this, would he?"

We had chosen this particular group of soldiers to approach specifically because they were a supply unit. That meant they were lightly armed and hopefully not an elite fighting group.

Aahz's barb struck home, however. The officer stopped smiling and dropped his hand to his sword hilt. I found myself thinking again of Ajax's protection.

"I have more than enough authority to deal with you two," he hissed.

"Authority, maybe," I yawned. "But I frankly doubt you have the power to stand against us."

As I mentioned, I did not feel as confident as I sounded. The officer's honor guard had mimicked his action, so that now all three of our adversaries were standing ready to draw their swords.

"Very well," Claude snarled. "You've been warned. Now we're going to bring our wagons across this spot, and if you're on it when we get here you've no one to blame but yourselves."

"Accepted!" Aahz leered. "Shall we say noon tomorrow?"

"Tomorrow?" the officer scowled. "What's wrong with right now?"

"Come, come, Claude," Aahz admonished. "We're talking about the first engagement of a new campaign. Surely you want some time to plan your tactics."

"Tactics?" Claude echoed thoughtfully.

". . . and to pass the word to your superiors that you're leading the opening gambit," Aahz continued casually.

"Hmm," the officer murmured.

". . . and to summon reinforcements," I supplied. "Unless, of course, you want to keep all the glory for yourself."

"Glory!"

That did it. Claude pounced on the word like a Deveel on a gold piece. Aahz had been right in assuming supply officers don't see combat often.

"I . . . uh . . . I don't believe we'll require reinforcements," he murmured cagily.

"Are you sure?" Aahz sneered. "The odds are only about a hundred to one in your favor."

"But he *is* a magician," Claude smiled. "A good officer can't be too careful. Still, it would be pointless to involve too many officers . . . er . . . I mean, soldiers in a minor skirmish."

"Claude," Aahz said with grudging admiration, "I can see yours is a military mind without equal. Win or lose,

I look forward to having you as an opponent."

"And you, sir," the officer returned with equal formal-ity. "Shall we say noon then?"

"We'll be here," Aahz nodded.

With that, the officer turned and strode briskly back to his encampment, his bodyguard trudging dutifully beside him.

Our comrades were bristling with questions when we reentered the tree line.

"Is it set, boss?" Brockhurst asked.

"Any trouble?" Tanda pressed.

"Piece of cake," Aahz bragged. "Right, kid?"

"Well," I began modestly, "I was a little worried when they started to reach for their swords. I would have been terrified if I didn't know Ajax was . . . say, where is Ajax?"

"He's up in that clump of bushes," Gus informed me, jerking a massive thumb at a thicket of greenery on the edge of the tree line. "He should be back by now."

When we found Ajax, he was fast asleep curled around his bow. We had to shake him several times to wake him.

# XVIII:

*"Just before the battle, Mother, I was
thinking most of you . . ."*

—SONNY BARKER

A long, slimy tongue assaulted me from the darkness,
accompanied by a blast of bad breath which could
have only one source.

"Gleep!"

I started to automatically cuff the dragon away, then
had a sudden change of heart.

"Hi, fella," I smiled, scratching his ear. "Lonely?"

In response, my pet flopped on his side with a thud
that shook the ground. His serpentine neck was long
enough that he managed to perform this maneuver without
moving his head from my grasp.

His loyal affection brought a smile to my face for the
first time since I had taken up my lonely vigil. It was a
welcome antidote to my nervous insomnia.

I was leaning against a tree, watching the pinpoints of
light that marked the enemy's encampment. Even though
the day's events had left me exhausted, I found myself
unable to sleep, my mind awash with fears and anticipa-

tion of tomorrow's clash. Not wishing to draw attention
to my discomfort, I had crept to this place to be alone.

As stealthy as I had attempted to be, however, apparently Gleep had noted my movement and come to keep
me company.

"Oh, Gleep," I whispered. "What are we going to do?"

For his answer, he snuggled closer against me and laid
his head in my lap for additional patting. He seemed to
have unshakable faith in my ability to handle any crisis
as it arose. I wished with all my heart I shared his confidence.

"Skeeve?" came a soft voice from my right.

I turned my head and found Tanda standing close beside me. The disquieting thing about having an Assassin
for a friend is that they move so silently.

"Can I talk to you for a moment?"

"Sure, Tanda," I said, patting the ground next to me.
"Have a seat."

Instead of sitting at the indicated spot, she sank to the
ground where she stood and curled her legs up under her.

"It's about Ajax," she began hesitantly. "I hate to
bother you, but I'm worried about him."

"What's wrong?" I asked.

"Well, the team's been riding him about falling asleep
today when he was supposed to be covering you," she
explained. "He's taking it pretty hard."

"I wasn't too wild about it myself," I commented bitterly. "It's a bad feeling to realize that we really were
alone out there. If anything *had* gone wrong, we would
have been cut to shreds while placidly waiting for our
expert bowman to intercede!"

"I know." Tanda's voice was almost too soft to be
heard. "And I don't blame you for feeling like that. In a
way, I blame myself."

"Yourself?" I blinked. "Why?"

"I vouched for him, Skeeve," she whispered. "Don't
you remember?"

"Well, sure," I admitted. "But you couldn't have known—"

"But I should have," she interrupted bitterly. "I should have realized how old he is now. He shouldn't be here, Skeeve. That's why I wanted to talk to you about doing something."

"Me?" I asked, genuinely startled. "What do you want me to do?"

"Send him back," Tanda urged. "It isn't fair to you to endanger your mission because of him, and it isn't fair to Ajax to put him in a spot like this."

"That isn't what I meant," I murmured, shaking my head. "I meant why are you talking to me? Aahz is the one you have to convince."

"That's where you're wrong, Skeeve," she corrected. "Aahz isn't leading this group, you are."

"Because of what he said back on Deva?" I smiled. "C'mon, Tanda. You know Aahz. He was just a little miffed. You noticed he's called all the shots so far."

The moonlight glistened in Tanda's hair as she shook her head.

"I do know Aahz, Skeeve. Better than you do," she said. "He's a stickler for chain of command. If he says you're the leader, you're the leader."

"But—"

"Besides," she continued over my protest, "Aahz is only one member of the team. What's important is all the others are counting on you, too. On you, not on Aahz. You hired 'em, and as far as they're concerned, you're the boss."

The frightening thing was she was right. I hadn't really stopped to think about it, but everything she said was true. I had just been too busy with my own worries to reflect on it. Now that I realized the full extent of my responsibilities, a new wave of doubts assaulted me. I wasn't even that sure of myself as a magician, and as a leader of men. . . .

"I'll have to think about it," I stalled.

"You don't have much time," she pointed out. "You've got a war scheduled to start tomorrow."

There was a crackling in the brush to our left, interrupting our conversation.

"Boss?" came Brockhurst's soft hail. "Are you busy?"

"Sort of," I called back.

"Well, this will only take a minute."

Before I could reply, two shadows detached themselves from the brush and drew closer. One was Brockhurst, the other was Gus. I should have known from the noise that the gargoyle was accompanying Brockhurst. Like Tanda, the Imp could move like a ghost.

"We were just talking about Ajax," Brockhurst informed me, squatting down to join our conference.

The gargoyle followed suit.

"Yeah," Gus confirmed. "The three of us wanted to make a suggestion to you."

"Right," Brockhurst nodded. "Gus and me and the Gremlin."

"The Gremlin?" I asked.

The Imp craned his neck to peer around him.

"He must have stayed back at camp," he shrugged.

"About Ajax," Tanda prompted.

"We think you should pull him from the team," Gus announced. "Send him back to Deva and out of the line of fire."

"It's not for us," Brockhurst hastened to clarify. "It's for him. He's a nice old guy, and we'd hate to see anything happen to him."

"He is pretty old," I murmured.

"Old!" Gus exclaimed. "Boss, the Gremlin says he's tailed him for over two hundred years . . . two hundred! According to him, Ajax was old when their paths first crossed. It won't kill him to miss this one war, but it might kill him to fight in it."

"Why is the Gremlin tailing him, anyway?" I asked.

"I've told you before, kid," a voice boomed in my ear, "gremlins don't exist."

With that pronouncement, Aahz sank down at my side, between me and Tanda. As I attempted to restore my heartbeat to normal, it occurred to me I knew an awful lot of light-footed people.

"Hi, Aahz," I said, forcing a smile. "We were just talking about—"

"I know, I heard," Aahz interrupted. "And for a change I agree."

"You do?" I blinked.

"Sure," he yawned. "It's a clear-cut breach of contract. He hired out his services as a bowman, and the first assignment you give him, he literally lies down on the job."

Actually, it had been the second assignment. I had a sudden flash recollection of Ajax drawing and firing in a smooth, fluid motion, cutting down a signal standard so distant it was barely visible.

"My advice would be to send him back," Aahz was saying. "If you want to soothe your conscience, give him partial payment and a good recommendation, but the way he is, he's no good to anybody."

Perhaps it was because of Tanda's lecture, but I was suddenly aware that Aahz had specifically stated his suggestion as "advice," not an order.

"Heads up, boss," Brockhurst murmured. "We've got company."

Following his gaze, I saw Ajax stumbling toward us, his ghostlike paleness flickering in the darkness like . . . well, like a ghost. It occurred to me that what had started out as a moment of solitude was becoming awfully crowded.

"Evenin', youngster," he saluted. "Didn't mean to interrupt nothin'! Didn't know you folks was havin' a meetin'."

"We . . . ah . . . we were just talking," I explained, suddenly embarrassed.

"I kin guess about what, too," Ajax sighed. "Well, I was goin' to do this private-like, but I suppose the rest o' you might as well hear it, too."

"Do what, Ajax?" I asked.

"Resign," he said. "Seems to me to be the only decent thing to do after what happened today."

"It could have happened to anyone," I shrugged.

"Nice of you to say so, youngster," Ajax smiled, "but I kin see the handwriting on the wall. I'm just too old to be any good to anybody anymore. 'Bout time I admitted it to myself."

I found myself noticing the droop in his shoulders and a listlessness that hadn't been there when we first met on Deva.

"Don't fret about payin' me," Ajax continued. "I didn't do nothin', so I figger you don't owe me nothin'. If somebody'll just blip me back to Deva, I'll get outta your way and let you fight your war the way it should be fought."

"Well, Ajax," Aahz sighed, rising to his feet and extending his hand. "We're going to miss you."

"Just a minute!" I found myself saying in a cold voice. "Are you trying to tell me you're breaking our contract?"

Ajax's head came up with a snap.

"I expected better from a genuine Archer," I concluded.

"I wouldn't call it a breach of contract, youngster," the old bowman corrected me carefully. "More like a termination by mutual consent. I'm jes' too old—"

"Old?" I interrupted. "I knew you were old when I hired you. I knew you were old when I planned my strategy for tomorrow's fight around that bow of yours. I knew you were old, Ajax, but I didn't know you were a coward!"

There was a sharp intake of breath somewhere nearby, but I didn't see who it was. My attention was focused on Ajax. It was no longer a defeated, drooping old man, but a proud, angry warrior who loomed suddenly over me.

"Sonny," he growled, "I know I'm old, 'cause in my younger days I would have killed you for sayin' that. I never ran from a fight in my life, and I never broke a contract. If you got some shootin' fer me to do tomorrow,

I'll do it. Then maybe you'll see what havin' a genuine Archer on your side is all about!"

With that, he spun on his heel and stalked off into the darkness.

It had been a calculated risk, but I still found I was covered with cold sweat from facing the old man's anger. I also realized the rest of the group was staring at me in silent expectation.

"I suppose you're all wondering why I did that," I said, smiling.

I had hoped for a response, but the silence continued.

"I appreciate all your advice, and hope you continue to give it in the future. But I'm leading this force, and the final decisions have to be mine."

Out of the corner of my eye, I saw Aahz cock his eyebrow, but I ignored him.

"Everyone, including Ajax, said if I let him go, if I sent him back to Deva, there would be no harm done. I disagree. It would have taken away the one thing the years have left untouched . . . his pride. It would have confirmed to him his worst fears, that he's become a useless old man."

I scanned my audience. Not one of them could meet my eye.

"So he might get killed. So what? He's accepted that risk in every war he's fought in. I'd rather order him into a fight knowing for certain he'd be killed than condemn him to a living death as a washed-up has-been. This way, he has a chance, and as his employer, I feel I owe him that chance."

I paused for breath. They were looking at me again, hanging on my next words.

"One more thing," I snarled. "I don't want to hear any more talk about him being useless. That old man still handles a bow better than anyone I've ever seen. If I can't find a way to use him effectively, then it's my fault as a tactician, not his! I've got my shortcomings, but I'm not

going to blame them on Ajax any more than I'd blame
them on any of you."

Silence reigned again, but I didn't care. I had spoken
my piece, and felt no compulsion to blather on aimlessly
just to fill the void.

"Well, boss"—Brockhurst cleared his throat getting to
his feet—"I think I'll turn in now."

"Me, too," echoed Gus, also rising.

"Just one thing." The Imp paused and met my gaze
squarely. "For the record, it's a real pleasure working for
you."

The gargoyle nodded his agreement, and the two of
them faded into the brush.

There was a soft kiss on my cheek, but by the time I
turned my head, Tanda had disappeared.

"You know, kid," Aahz said, "you're going to make a
pretty good leader someday."

"Thanks, Aahz," I blinked.

". . . if you live that long," my mentor concluded.

We sat side by side in silence for a while longer. Gleep
had apparently dozed off, for he was snoring softly as I
continued petting him.

"If it isn't prying," Aahz asked finally, "what is this
master plan you have for tomorrow that's built around
Ajax?"

I sighed and closed my eyes.

"I haven't got one," I admitted. "I was kind of hoping
you'd have a few ideas."

"I was afraid you were going to say that," Aahz grumbled.

# XIX:

*"What if they gave a war and only one side came—"*

—LUCIFER

"**W**ake up, kid!"
I returned to consciousness as I was being forcefully propelled sideways along the forest floor, presumably assisted by the ready toe of my mentor.

After I had slid to a stop, I exerted most of my energy and raised my head.

"Aahz," I announced solemnly, "as leader of this team, I have reached another decision. In the future, I want Tanda to wake me up."

"Not a chance," Aahz leered. "She's off scouting our right flank. It's me or the dragon."

Great choice. I suddenly realized how bright it was.

"Hey!" I blinked. "How late is it?"

"Figure we've got about a minute before things start popping," Aahz said casually.

"How long?" I gasped.

Aahz's brow furrowed for a moment as he reflected on his words. Klahdish units of time still gave him a bit of trouble.

"An hour!" he smiled triumphantly. "That's it. An hour."

"That's better," I sighed, sinking back to a horizontal position.

"On your feet, kid!" Aahz ordered. "We let you sleep as late as we could, but now you're needed to review the troops."

"Have you briefed everybody?" I yawned, sitting up. "Is the plan clear?"

"As clear as it's going to be, all things considered," Aahz shrugged.

"Okay," I responded, rolling to my feet. "Let's go. You can fill me in on any new developments along the way."

Aahz and I had been up most of the night formulating today's plan, and I found I was actually eager to see it implemented.

"You should be thankful you aren't on the other side," Aahz chortled as we moved to join the others. "Old Claude's been making the most of the time we gave him."

"Keeping them busy, is he?" I smiled.

"Since sunup," Aahz confirmed smugly. "Drilling, sharpening swords, never a dull moment in the Empire's army, that's for sure."

I wasn't sure I shared Aahz's enthusiasm for the enemy's spending lots of time sharpening their swords. Fortunately, I was spared the discomfort of replying as Gus lumbered up to us.

"You just missed Brockhurst's report," he informed us. "Still nothing on the left flank."

"Wouldn't we be able to tell from their signals if they were moving up additional support?" I asked.

"If you believe their signals," Aahz countered. "It wouldn't be the first time an army figured out the enemy had broken their code and started sending misleading messages."

"Oh," I said wisely.

"Speaking of signals," Aahz said with a grin, "you know the messages they were sending yesterday? The ones that went 'encountered minor resistance'?"

"I remember," I nodded.

"Well, it seems Claude has decided he needs to up the ante if he's going to get a promotion out of this. Overnight we've become 'armed opposition . . . must be subdued forcefully!' Neat, huh?"

I swallowed hard.

"Does that mean they'll be moving in reinforcements?" I asked, trying to sound casual.

"Not a chance, kid." Aahz winked. "Claude there has turned down every offer of assistance that came down the line. He keeps insisting he can handle it with the company he's commanding."

"I'd say he's got his neck way, way out," Gus commented.

". . . and we're just the ones to chop it off for him," Aahz finished.

"Where's Ajax?" I asked, changing the subject.

"Down at the forest line picking out his firing point," Gus replied. "Don't worry, boss. He's awake."

Actually, that wasn't my worry concerning Ajax at all. In my mind's eye, I could still see his angry stance when I called him a coward the night before.

"Mornin', youngster," the bowman hailed, emerging from the bush. "Think I got us a place all picked out."

"Hi, Ajax," I replied. "Say . . . um . . . when you get a minute, I'd like to talk to you about last night."

"Think nothin' of it," Ajax assured me with a grin. "I've plum fergot about it already."

There was a glint in his eye that contradicted his words, but if he was willing to pretend nothing had happened, I'd go along with it for now.

"I hate to interrupt," Aahz interrupted, "but I think friend Claude's just about ready to make his move."

Sure enough, the distant encampment was lining up in a marching formation. The hand-drawn wagons were packed and aligned, with the escort troops arrayed to the front and sides. The signal tower, despite its appearance, was apparently also portable and was being pushed along at the rear of the formation by several sweating soldiers.

"Late!" Ajax sneered. "I tell ya, youngster, armies are the same in any dimension."

"Okay, kid," Aahz said briskly. "Do your stuff. It's about time we got into position."

I nodded and closed my eyes for concentration. With a few strokes of my mental paintbrush, I altered Gus's features until the gargoyle was the mirror image of myself.

"Pretty good," Ajax commented critically, looking from Gus to me and back again.

I repeated the process, returning Aahz to his "dubious character" disguise.

"Well, we're off," Aahz waved. "Confusion to the enemy!"

Today's plan called for Gus substituting for me. The logic was that should anything go wrong, his stone flesh would not only keep him from harm, but also serve as a shield to defend Aahz.

Somehow it didn't seem right to me, to remain behind in relative safety while sending someone else to take my risks for me. It occurred to me that perhaps I had called the wrong person "coward" last night when speaking with Ajax.

The bowman seemed to accept the arrangement without question, however.

"Follow me, youngster," he cackled. "I don't want to miss any of this!"

With that, he turned and plunged into the brush, leaving me little choice but to trail along behind.

Fortunately, Ajax's chosen vantage point wasn't far. Old or not, I found he set a wicked pace.

Stringing his bow, he crouched and waited, chuckling softly in anticipation.

Settling in beside him, I took a moment to check the energy lines, the invisible streams of energy magicians draw their power from. There were two strong lines nearby, one air, one ground, which was good. While Aahz had taught me how to store the energies internally, with the amount of action scheduled for the day, I wanted all the power I could get.

We could see Aahz and Gus striding with great dignity toward the selected combat point. The opposing force watched them in frozen silence as they took their places.

For a moment, everyone stood in tableau.

Then Claude turned to his force and barked out an order. Immediately a half dozen archers broke from the formation and fanned out on either side of the wagons. Moving with slow deliberation, they each drew and cocked an arrow, then leveled the bows at the two figures blocking the company's progress.

I concentrated my energies.

Claude shouted something at our comrades. They remained motionless.

I concentrated.

The bowmen loosed their missiles. Gus threw up one hand dramatically.

The arrows stopped in mid-air and fell to the ground.

The bowmen looked at each other in amazement. Claude barked another order at them. They shakily drew and fired another barrage.

This one was more ragged than the first, but I managed to stop it as well.

"Nice work, youngster," Ajax exclaimed gleefully. "That's got 'em going."

Sure enough, the neat ranks of soldiers were rippling as the men muttered back and forth among themselves. Claude noted it, too, and ordered his bowmen back into the ranks.

Round one to us!

My elation was short-lived, though. The soldiers were drawing their swords now. The two groups assigned to guarding the sides of the wagon pivoted forward, forming two wings ready to engulf our teammates. As further evidence of Claude's nervousness, he even had the troops assigned to pulling the wagons leave their posts and move up to reinforce the center of his line.

That's what we were waiting for.

"Now, Ajax!" I hissed. "Arch 'em high."

"I remember, youngster," the archer grinned. "I'm ready when you are."

I waited until he raised his bow, then concentrated an intense beam of energy at a point a few inches in front of his bow.

It was like the candle-lighting exercise, and it worked as well now as it had when we had tried it last night.

As each shaft sped from Ajax's bow, it burst into flames and continued on its flight.

Again and again with incredible speed the bowman sent his missiles hissing through my ignition point. It required all my concentration to maintain the necessary stream of energy, moving it occasionally as his point of aim changed.

Finally, he dropped his bow back to his side.

"That oughta do it, youngster," he grinned. "Take a look."

I did. There in the distance, behind the soldiers' lines, thin plumes of smoke were rising from the wagons. In a few moments, Claude's supply company would be without supplies.

If we had a few moments! As we watched, the men began to advance on Aahz and Gus, their swords gleaming in the sun.

"Think we'd better do something about that!" Ajax muttered, raising his bow again.

"Wait a second, Ajax!" I ordered, squinting at the distant figures.

There had been a brief consultation between Aahz and Gus, then the gargoyle stepped back and began gesturing wildly at his companion.

It took me a moment, but I finally got the message. With a smile, I closed my eyes and removed Aahz's disguise.

Pandemonium reigned. The soldiers in the front ranks took one look at the demon opposing them and stampeded for the rear, half trampling the men behind them. As word spread through the formation, it became a rout, though I seriously doubt those in the rear knew what they were running from.

If anyone noticed the burning wagons, they didn't slow once.

"Whooee!" Ajax exclaimed, thumping me on the back. "That did it. Look at 'em run. You'd think those fellers never seed a Pervert before."

"They probably haven't," I commented, trying to massage some feeling back into my shoulder.

"You know," the bowman drawled, squinting at the scene below, "I got me an idea. Them fellers ran off so fast they fergot to signal to anybody. Think we should do it for 'em?"

"How?" I asked.

"Well," he grinned. "I know the signals, and you're a magician. If I told you what signal to run up, could you do it? Without anybody holdin' it?"

"Sure could," I agreed. "What'll we need for the signal?"

"Lemme think," he frowned. "We'll have to get a skull, and a couple of pieces of red cloth, and a black ball, an—"

"Wait a minute, Ajax," I said, holding up a hand. "I think there's an easier signal they'll understand. Watch this."

I sent one more blast of energy out, and the tower platform burst into flames.

"Think they'll get the message?" I smiled.

Ajax stared at the burning tower for a moment.

"Yer pretty good at that, youngster," he murmured finally. "Throwin' fire that far."

"Well," I began modestly, "we magicians can—"

" 'Course," he continued. "If you can do that, then you didn't really need me and Blackie to handle those wagons, did you?"

Too late I realized my mistake.

"Ajax, I—"

"Kinda strange, you goin' to all that trouble jes' to convince me I'm not useless."

"You're not useless," I barked. "Just because sometimes you're not necessary doesn't mean you're useless. I may be young, but I'm old enough to know that."

Ajax regarded me for a moment, then he suddenly smiled.

"Danged if you aren't right, youngst . . . Skeeve," he laughed. "Guess I knew it, but plum fergot it there fer a while. Let's go get some wine from that cask strapped to your dragon. I'd like to thank you proper fer remindin' me."

We headed back to camp together.

# XX:

*"Chain of command is the backbone of military structure and must be strictly obeyed."*

—F. CHRISTIAN

The mood back at the camp was understandably celebratory. If I had had any hopes for joining in the festivities, however, they were dashed when Aahz hailed me.

"Over here, kid!" he waved. "We've got some planning to do!"

"That's the other side o' bein' a general, youngster," Ajax murmured sympathetically. " 'T'aint all speeches and glory. You go on ahead. I'll do my drinkin' with the boys."

With a jerk of his head, he indicated Gus and Brockhurst who were already at the wine. Tanda was waiting for me with Aahz. That made my choice a little easier.

"Okay, Ajax," I smiled. "I'll catch up with you in a little bit."

"Congratulations, handsome!" Tanda winked as I joined them. "That was as neat a bit of work as I've seen in a long time."

"Thanks, Tanda," I blushed.

"I see you and Ajax are on speaking terms again," Aahz said, regarding me with cocked eyebrows. "That's not a bad trick in itself. How did you do it?"

"We . . . um . . . we had a long talk," I replied vaguely. "You said we had some planning to do?"

"More like a briefing," Aahz admitted. "Tanda here brought along a few special effects items I think you should know about."

I had completely forgotten about Tanda's errand which had left me alone at the Bazaar. Now that I had been reminded, my curiosity soared.

"Whatcha got, Tanda?" I asked eagerly.

"Nothing spectacular," she shrugged. "Knowing Aahz was involved, I figured we'd be on a tight budget so I stuck to the basics."

"Just show him, huh?" Aahz growled. "Spare us the editorial comments."

She stuck her tongue out at him but produced a small cloth sack from her belt.

"First off," she began, "I thought we could use a little flash powder. It never fails to impress the yokels."

"Flash powder," I said carefully.

"You set fire to it," Aahz supplied. "It burns fast and gives you a cloud of smoke."

"I've got about a dozen small bags of it here," Tanda continued, showing me the contents of her sack. "Various colors and sizes."

"Can I try one?" I asked. "I've never worked with this stuff before."

"Sure," Tanda said. She grinned, extending the sack. "They're yours to use as you see fit. You might as well know what you've got."

I took the sack and carefully selected one of the small bags from its interior.

"Better toss it to the ground, kid," Aahz cautioned. "Some folks can set it off in their hand, but that takes practice. If you tried it that way now, you'd probably lose a few fingers."

I obediently tossed the bag on the ground a few feet away. Watching it curiously, I focused a quick burst of energy on it.

There was a bright flash of light accompanied by a soft *pop*. Blinking my eyes, I looked at where the bag had been. A small cloud of green smoke hung in the air, slowly dissipating in the breeze.

"That's neat!" I exclaimed, reaching into the sack again.

"Take it easy," Aahz warned. "We don't have that much of the stuff."

"Oh! Right, Aahz," I replied, feeling a little sheepish. "What else do you have, Tanda?"

"Well," she said, smiling, "I guess this would be a pièce-de-résistance."

As she spoke, she seemed to draw something from behind her back. I say "seemed" because I couldn't see anything. From her movements, she looked to be holding a rod about three feet long, but there was nothing in her grasp.

"What is it?" I asked politely.

For a response, she grinned and held whatever it was in front of her. Then she opened her grip and disappeared into thin air.

"Invisibility," Aahz exclaimed. "A cloak of invisibility!"

"Couldn't afford one," came Tanda's voice from somewhere in front of us. "I had to settle for one of these."

What "one of these" was, it turned out, was a sheet of invisibility. It was a sheet of stiff material about three feet by seven feet. Tanda had been carrying it rolled up in a tube, and her disappearance had been caused by the sheet unrolling to its full size.

As she and Aahz chatted excitedly about her new find, I had an opportunity to further my knowledge in the field of invisibility.

Invisible sheets, it seems, were made of roughly the same material as invisible cloaks. Since the sheets were carried, not worn, they did not require the flexibility and softness necessary for a cloak. Consequently, they were considerably cheaper than the cloaks.

The effect was sort of like one-way glass. When you were on the right side of an invisible sheet, you could see through it perfectly well to observe whatever or whoever was on the other side. They, however, could not see you.

We were still discussing the potential uses of the new tool when Brockhurst hastened up to our group.

"Hey, boss!" he called. "We've got company!"

"Who? Where?" I asked calmly.

"Down on the meadow," the Imp responded, pointing. "The Gremlin says there's some kind of group forming out there."

"What Gremlin?" Aahz snarled.

"C'mon, Aahz," Tanda called, starting off. "Let's check this out."

There was indeed a group on the meadow, Empire soldiers all. The puzzling thing was their activity, or specifically their lack of it. They seemed to be simply standing and waiting for something.

"What are they doing, Aahz?" I whispered as we studied the group form the concealment of the tree line.

"They're standing and waiting," Aahz supplied.

"I can see that," I said. "But what are they waiting for?"

"Probably for us," my mentor replied.

"For us?" I blinked. "Why?"

"For a war council," Aahz grinned. "Look at it, kid. Aren't they doing the same thing we did when we wanted to talk? They're even standing in the same spot."

I restudied the group in this light. Aahz was right! The enemy was calling for a war council!

"Do you think we should go out there?" I asked nervously.

"Sure," Aahz replied. "But not right away. Let 'em sweat a little. They kept us waiting the first time, remember?"

It was nearly half an hour before we stepped from the tree line and advanced across the meadow to where the soldiers stood waiting. I had taken the precaution of outfitting Aahz in his "dubious character" disguise for the conference. Myself, I was bearing the invisibility sheet before me, so that though I was walking along beside Aahz, to the soldiers it appeared he was alone.

There were more soldiers at the meeting point than there had been at our first meeting with Claude. Even to my untrained eye, it was apparent that there were more than half a dozen officers present among the honor guard.

"You wish a meeting?" Aahz asked haughtily, drawing to a halt before the group.

There was a ripple of quick consultation among the soldiers. Finally one of them, apparently the leader, stepped forward.

"We wish to speak with your master!" he announced formally.

"He's kinda busy right now," Aahz yawned. "Anything I can help you with?"

The leader reddened slightly.

"I am the commander of this sector!" he barked. "I demand to see Skeeve, commander of the defense, not his lacky!"

I dropped one of the bags of flash powder on the ground at my feet.

"If you insist," Aahz growled, "I'll get him. But he won't be happy."

"I'm not here to make him happy," the leader shouted. "Now be off with you."

"That won't be necessary," Aahz leered. "He's a magician. He hears and sees what his servants hear and see. He'll be along."

That was my cue. I let drop the sheet of invisibility and simultaneously ignited the bag of flash powder.

The results were spectacular.

The soldiers, with the exception of the leader, fell back several steps. To them, it looked as if I had suddenly appeared from thin air, materializing in a cloud of red smoke.

For me, the effect was less impressive. As the bag of flash powder went off, it was made apparent to me that watching a cloud of smoke from a distance was markedly different from standing at ground zero.

As I was enveloped in the scarlet billows, my feeling was not of elated triumph but rather a nearly over-whelming desire to cough and sneeze.

My efforts to suppress my reactions caused me to con-tort my features to the point where I must have borne more than a faint resemblance to Gus.

"Steady, Master!" Aahz cautioned.

"Aahz. Ah!" I gasped.

"Do not let your anger overcome your reason," my mentor continued hastily. "They don't know the powers they trifle with."

"I . . . I did not wish to be disturbed," I managed at last, regaining my breath as the smoke dissipated.

The leader of the group had held his ground through the entire proceedings, though he looked a bit paler and less sure of himself than when he had been dealing with just Aahz.

"We . . . um . . . apologize for bothering you," he be-gan uncertainly. "But there are certain matters requiring your immediate attention . . . specifically the war we are currently engaged in."

I eyed him carefully. He seemed to be of a different cut than Claude had been.

"I'm afraid you have me at a disadvantage, sir," I said cagily. "You seem to know me, but I don't recall having met you before."

"We have not met before," the officer replied grimly. "If we had, be assured one of us would not be here cur-rently. I know you by reputation, specifically for your recent efforts to resist the advance of our army. For my-self, I am Antonio, commander of the right wing of the left flank of the Empire's army. These are my officers."

He indicated the soldiers behind him with a vague wave of his hand. The men responded by drawing themselves more erect and thrusting out their chins arrogantly.

I acknowledged them with a slight nod.

"Where is Claude?" I asked casually. "I was under the impression he was an officer of this sector."

"You are correct," Antonio smirked. "He *was*. He is currently being detained until he can be properly court-martialed . . . for incompetence!"

"Incompetence?" I echoed. "Come now, sir. Aren't you being a little harsh? While Claude may have overstepped his abilities a bit, I wouldn't say he's incompetent. I mean, after all, he *was* dealing with supernatural powers, if you know what I mean."

As I spoke, I wiggled my fingers dramatically at Aahz and removed his disguise.

The jaws of the attending officers dropped, ruining their arrogant jut. Then Aahz grinned at them, and their mouths clicked shut in unison as they swallowed hard.

Antonio was unimpressed.

"Yes, yes," he said briskly, waving a hand as if at an annoying fly. "We have had reports, many reports, as to your rapport with demons. Claude's incompetence is in his disastrous underestimation of the forces opposing him. Be assured, I will not be guilty of the same error."

"Don't count on it, Tony," Aahz leered. "We demons can be a pretty tricky lot.

The officer ignored him.

"However, we are not here for idle pleasantries," he said, fixing me with a stern gaze. "I believe we have a dispute to settle concerning right of passage over this particular piece of terrain."

"We have a dispute concerning your right of passage over the kingdom of Possiltum," I corrected.

"Yes, yes," Antonio yawned. "Of course, if you want to stop us from gaining Possiltum, you had best stop us here."

"That's about how we had it figured," Aahz agreed.

"Not to belabor the point, Antonio," I smiled, "but I believe we *do* have you stopped."

"Temporarily," the officer smiled. "I expect that situation to change shortly . . . shall we say, a few hours after dawn? Tomorrow?"

"We'll be here," Aahz nodded.

"Just a moment," I interrupted. "Antonio, you strike me as being a sporting man. Would you like to make our encounter tomorrow a little more interesting? Say, with a little side wager?"

"Such as what?" the officer scowled.

"If you lose tomorrow," I said carefully, "will you admit Claude's defeat had nothing to do with incompetence and drop the charges against him?"

Antonio thought for a moment, then nodded.

"Done," he said. "Normally I would fear what the reaction of my superiors would be, but I am confident of my victory. There are things even a demon cannot stand against."

"Such as?" Aahz drawled.

"You will see," the officer smiled. "Tomorrow."

With that, he spun on his heel and marched off, his officers trailing behind him.

"What do you think, Aahz?" I murmured.

"Think?" my mentor scowled. "I think you're going soft, kid. First Brockhurst, now Claude. What is this 'be kind to enemies' kick you're on?"

"I meant about tomorrow," I clarified quickly.

"I dunno, kid," Aahz admitted. "He sounded too confident for comfort. I wish I knew what he's got up his sleeve that's supposed to stop demons."

"Well," I sighed, "I guess we'll see tomorrow."

# XXI:

*"It takes a giant to fight a giant."*

—H. PRYM

Our pensiveness was still with us the next day.

Our opponents were definitely up to something, but we couldn't tell exactly what it was. Tanda and Brockhurst had headed out on a scouting trip during the night and had brought back puzzling news. The Empire's soldiers had brought up some kind of heavy equipment, but it was hidden from sight by a huge box. All our scouts could say for sure was that whatever the secret weapon was, it was big and it was heavy.

Gus offered to fly over the box to take a quick peek inside, but we vetoed the idea. With the box constantly in the center of a mass of soldiers, there was no way the gargoyle could carry out his mission unobserved. Even if he used the invisibility sheet, the army was so far flung that someone would see him. So far we had kept the gargoyle's presence on our team as a secret, and we preferred to keep it that way. Even if we disguised him as Aahz or myself, it would betray the fact that someone in our party was able to fly. As Aahz pointed out, it looked as if this campaign would be rough enough without giving the opposition advance warning of the extent of our abilities.

This was all tactically sound and irrefutably logical. Nonetheless, it did nothing to reassure me as Aahz and I stood waiting for Antonio to make his opening gambit.

"Relax, kid," Aahz murmured. "You look nervous."

"I *am* nervous," I snapped back. "We're standing out here waiting to fight, and we don't know who or what we're supposed to be fighting. You'll forgive me if that makes me a trifle edgy."

I was aware I was being unnecessarily harsh on my mentor. Ajax and Gus were standing by, and Brockhurst and Tanda were watching for any new developments. The only team member unaccounted for this morning was the Gremlin, but I thought it wisest not to bring this to Aahz's attention. I assumed our elusive blue friend was off somewhere with Gleep, as my pet was also missing.

Everything that could have been done in preparation had been done. However, I still felt uneasy.

"Look at it this way, kid," Aahz tried again. "At least we know what we *aren't* up against."

What we weren't dealing with was soldiers. Though a large number of them were gathered in the near vicinity, there seemed to be no effort being made to organize or arm them for battle. As the appointed time drew near, it became more and more apparent that they were to be spectators only in the upcoming fray.

"I think I'd rather deal with soldiers," I said glumly.

"Heads up, kid," Aahz retorted, nudging me with his elbow. "Whatever's going to happen is about to."

I knew what he meant, which bothered me. There was no time to ponder it, however. Antonio had just put in his appearance.

He strolled around one corner of the mammoth box deep in conversation with a suspicious-looking character in a hooded cloak. He shot a glance in our direction, smiled, and waved merrily.

We didn't wave back.

"I don't like the looks of this, kid," Aahz growled.

I didn't either, but there wasn't much we could do except wait. Antonio finished his conversation with the stranger and stepped back, folding his arms across his chest. The stranger waved some of the onlooking soldiers aside, then stepped back himself. Drawing himself up, he began weaving his hands back and forth in a puzzling manner. Then the wind carried the sound to me and I realized he was chanting.

"Aahz!" I gasped. "They've got their own magician."

"I know," Aahz grinned back. "But from what I can hear he's bluffing them the same way you bluffed the court back at Possiltum. He probably doesn't have any more powers than I do."

No sooner had my mentor made his observation than the side of the huge box which was facing us slowly lowered itself to the ground. Revealed inside the massive container was a dragon.

The box had been big, better than thirty feet long and twenty feet high, but from the look of the dragon he must have been cramped for space inside.

He was big! I mean, really big!

Now I've never kidded myself about Gleep's size. Though his ten-foot length might look big here on Klah, I had seen dragons on Deva that made him look small. The dragon currently facing us, however, dwarfed everything I had seen before.

He was an iridescent bluish-green his entire length, which was far more serpentine than I was accustomed to seeing in a dragon. He had massive bat wings that he stretched and flexed as he clawed his way out of the confining box. There was a silver glint from his eye sockets which would have made him look machinelike were it not for the fluid grace of his powerful limbs.

For a moment, I was almost overcome by the beautiful spectacle he presented, emerging onto the battlefield.

Then he threw his head back and roared, and my admiration turned icy cold within me.

The great head turned until its eyes were focused directly on us. Then he began to stalk forward.

"Time for the better part of valor, kid," Aahz whispered, tugging at my sleeve. "Let's get out of here."

"Wait a minute, Aahz!" I shot back. "Do you see that? What the keeper's holding?"

A glint of gold in the sunlight had caught my eye. The dragon's keeper had a gold pendant clasped in his fist as he urged his beast forward.

"Yeah!" Aahz answered. "So?"

"I've seen a pendant like that before!" I explained excitedly. "That's how he's controlling the dragon!"

The Deveel who had been running the Dragon stall where I acquired Gleep had worn a pendant like that. The pendant was used to control dragons . . . unattached dragons, that is. Attached dragons can be controlled by their owner without other assistance. A dragon becomes attached to you when you feed it. That's how I got Gleep. I fed him, sort of. Actually, he helped himself to a hefty bit of my sleeve.

"Well, don't just stand there, kid," Aahz barked, interrupting my reverie. "Get it!"

I reached out with my mind and took a grab at the pendant. The keeper felt it start to go and tightened his grip on it, fighting me for its possession.

"I . . . I can't get it, Aahz," I cried. "He won't let go."

"Then hightail it outta here, kid," my mentor ordered. "Tell Ajax to bag us that keeper. Better tell Gus to stand by with Berfert just in case. I'll try to keep the dragon busy."

An image flashed in my mind. It was a view of me, Skeeve, court magician, bolting for safety while Aahz faced the dragon alone. Something snapped in my mind.

"You go!" I snapped.

"Kid, are you—"

"It's my war and my job," I shouted. "Now get going."

With that I turned to face the oncoming dragon, not knowing or caring if Aahz followed my orders. I was Skeeve!

But it was an awfully big dragon!

I tried again for the pendant, nearly lifting the keeper from his feet with my effort, but the man clung firmly to his possession, screaming orders at the dragon as he did.

I shot a nervous glance at the grim behemoth bearing down on me. If I tried to levitate out of the way, he could just. . . .

"Look out, kid!" came Aahz's voice from behind me.

I half turned, then something barreled past me, positioning itself between me and the oncoming menace.

It was Gleep!

"Gleep!" I shouted. "Get back here!"

My pet paid me no mind. His master was being threatened, and he meant to have a hand in this no matter what I said.

No longer a docile, playful companion, he planted himself between me and the monster, lowered his head to the ground, and hissed savagely, a six-foot tongue of flame leaping from his mouth as he did.

The effect on the big dragon was astonishing. He lurched to a stop and sat back on his haunches, cocking his head curiously at the mini-dragon blocking his path.

Gleep was not content with stopping his opponent, however. Heedless of the fact that the other dragon was over four times his size he began to advance stiffly, challenging his rival's right to the field.

The large dragon blinked, then shot a look behind him. Then he looked down on Gleep again, drawing his head back until his long neck formed a huge question mark.

Gleep continued to advance.

I couldn't understand it. Even if the monster couldn't flame, which was doubtful, it was obvious he had the sheer physical power to crush my pet with minimal effort. Still he did nothing, looking desperately about him almost as if he were embarrassed.

I watched in spellbound horror. It couldn't last. If nothing else, Gleep was getting too close to the giant to be ignored. Any minute now, the monster would have to react.

Finally, after a final glance at his frantic keeper, the big dragon did react. With a sigh, one of his taloned front paws lashed out horizontally in a cuff that would have caved in a building. It struck Gleep on the side of his head and sent him sprawling.

My pet was game, though, and struggled painfully to his feet, shaking his head as if to clear it.

Before he could assume his aggressive stance, however, the big dragon stretched his neck down until their heads were side by side, and he began to mutter and grumble in Gleep's ear. My dragon cocked his head as if listening, then "whuffed" in response.

As the stunned humans and nonhumans watched, the two dragons conversed in the center of the battlefield punctuating their mutterings with occasional puffs of smoke.

I tried to edge forward to get a better idea of exactly what was going on, but the big dragon turned a baleful eye on me and let loose a blast of flame which kept me at a respectful distance. Not that I was afraid, mind you; Gleep seemed to have the situation well in hand . . . or talon as the case might be. Well, I had always told Aahz that Gleep was a very talon-ted dragon.

Finally, the big dragon drew himself up, turned, and majestically left the field without a backward glance, his head impressively high. Ignoring the angry shouts of the soldiers, he returned to his box and dropped his haunches, sitting with his back to the entire proceeding.

His keeper's rage was surpassed only by Antonio's. He screamed at the keeper with purpled face and frantic gestures until the keeper angrily pulled the control pendant from around his neck, handed it to the officer, and stalked off. Antonio blinked at the pendant, then flung it to the ground and started off after the keeper.

That was all the opening I needed. Reaching out with my mind, I brought the pendant winging to my hand.

"Aahz!" I began.

"I don't believe it," my mentor mumbled to himself. "I saw it, but I still don't believe it."

"Gleep!"

My pet came racing up to my side, understandably pleased with himself.

"Hi, fella!" I cried, ignoring his breath and throwing my arms around his neck in a hug. "What happened out there, anyway?"

"Gleep!" my pet said evasively, carefully studying a cloud.

If I had expected an answer, it was clear I wasn't going to get one.

"I still don't believe it," Aahz repeated.

"Look, Aahz," I said, holding the pendant aloft. "Now we don't have to worry about that or any other dragon. We've shown a profit!"

"So we did," Aahz scowled. "But do me a favor, huh, kid?"

"What's that, Aahz?" I asked.

"If that dragon, or any dragon, wanders into our camp, don't feed it! We already have one, and that's about all my nerves can stand. Okay?"

"Sure, Aahz," I smiled.

"Gleep!" said my pet, rubbing against me for more petting, which he got.

# XXII:

*"Hell hath no fury like a demon
scorched."*

—C. MATHER

Our next war council made the previous ones look
small. This was only to be expected, as we were dealing with the commander of the entire left flank of the
Empire's army.

Our meeting was taking place in a pavilion constructed
specifically for that purpose, and the structure was packed
with officers, including Claude. It seemed Antonio was
true to his word, even though he himself was not currently
present.

In the face of such a gathering, we had decided to show
a bit more force ourselves. To that end, Tanda and Brockhurst were accompanying us, while Gleep snuffled around
outside. Gus and Ajax we were still holding in reserve,
while the Gremlin had not reappeared since the confron-
tation of dragons.

I didn't like the officer we were currently dealing with.
There was something about his easy, oily manner that set
me on edge. I strongly suspected he had ascended to his
current position by poisoning his rivals.

"So you'd like us to surrender," he was saying thought-fully, drumming his fingers on the table before him.

". . . or withdraw, or turn aside," I corrected. "Frankly, we don't care what you do, as long as you leave Possiltum alone."

"We've actually been considering doing just that," the commander said, leaning back in his chair to study the pavilion's canopy.

"Is that why you've been moving up additional troops all day long?" Brockhurst asked sarcastically.

"Merely an internal matter, I assure you," the com-mander purred. "All my officers are assembled here, and they're afraid their troops will fall to mischief, if left to their own devices."

"What my colleague means," Aahz interjected, "is we find it hard to believe you're actually planning to accede to our demands."

"Why not?" the commander shrugged. "That *is* what you've been fighting for, isn't it? There comes a point when a commander must ask himself if it won't cost him more dearly to fight a battle than to pass it by. So far, your resistance utilizing demons and dragons has shown us this battle could be difficult indeed."

"There are more where they come from," I interjected, "should the need arise."

"So you've demonstrated," the commander smiled, waving a casual hand at Tanda and Brockhurst. "Witches and devils made an impressive addition to your force."

I deemed it unwise to point out to him that Brockhurst was an Imp, not a Deveel.

"Then you agree to bypass Possiltum?" Aahz asked bluntly.

"I agree to discuss it with my officers," the commander clarified. "All I ask is that you leave one of your . . . ah . . . assistants behind."

"What for?" I asked. I didn't like the way he was eye-ing Tanda.

"To bring you word of our decision, of course," the

commander shrugged. "None of my men would dare enter your camp, even granted a messenger's immunity."

There was a mocking tone to his voice I didn't like.

"I'll stay, Skeeve," Aahz volunteered.

I considered it. Aahz had demonstrated his ability to take care of himself time and time again. Still I didn't trust the commander.

"Only if you are willing to give us one of your officers in return as a hostage," I replied.

"I've already said none of—" the commander began.

"He need not enter our camp," I explained. "He can remain well outside our force, on the edge of the tree line in full view of your force. I will personally guarantee his safety."

The commander chewed his lip thoughtfully.

"Very well," he said. "Since you have shown an interest in his career, I will give you Claude to hold as a hostage."

The young officer paled but remained silent.

"Agreed," I said. "We will await your decision."

I nodded to my comrades, and they obediently began filing out of the pavilion. Claude hesitated, then joined the procession.

I wanted to tell Aahz to be careful but decided against it. It wouldn't do to admit my partner's vulnerability in front of the commander. Instead, I nodded curtly to the officers and followed my comrades.

Tanda and Brockhurst were well on their way back to the treeline. Claude, on the other hand, was waiting for me as I emerged and fell in step beside me.

"While we have a moment," he said stiffly, "I would like to thank you for interceding in my behalf with my superiors."

"Don't mention it," I mumbled absently.

"No, really," he persisted. "Chivalry to an opponent is rarely seen these days. I think—"

"Look, Claude," I growled, "credit it to my warped sense of justice. I don't like you, and didn't when we first met, but that doesn't make you incompetent. Unpleasant, perhaps, but not incompetent."

I was harsher with him than I had intended to be, but I was worried about Aahz.

Finding himself thus rebuked, he sank into an uncomfortable silence which lasted almost until we reached the trees. Then he cleared his throat and tried again.

"Um . . . Skeeve?"

"Yeah?" I retorted curtly.

"I . . . um . . . what I was trying to say was that I am grateful and would repay your favor by any reasonable means at my disposal."

Despite my concern, his offer penetrated my mind as a potential opportunity.

"Would answering a few questions fall under the heading of 'reasonable'?" I asked casually.

"Depending upon the questions," he replied carefully. "I am still a soldier, and my code of conduct clearly states—"

"Tell you what," I interrupted. "I'll ask the questions, and you decide which ones are okay to answer. Fair enough?"

"So it would seem," he admitted.

"Okay," I began. "First question. Do you think the commander will actually bypass Possiltum?"

The officer avoided my eyes for a moment, then shook his head briskly.

"I should not answer that," he said, "but I will. I do not feel the commander is even considering it as a serious possibility, nor does any officer in that tent. He is known as 'the Brute,' even among his most loyal and seasoned troops. May I assure you he did not acquire that nickname by surrendering or capitulating while his force was still intact."

"Then why did he go through the motions of the meeting just now?" I queried.

"To gain time," Claude shrugged. "As your assistants noted, he is using the delay to mass his troops. The only code he adheres to is 'Victory at all costs.' In this case, it seems it is costing him his honor."

I thought about this for a moment before asking my next question.

"Claude," I said carefully, "you've faced us in battle, and you know your own army. If your prediction is correct and the Brute attacks in force, in your opinion, what are our chances of victory?"

"Nil," the officer replied quietly. "I know it may sound like enemy propaganda, but I ask you to believe my sincerity. Even with the additional forces you displayed this evening, if the Brute sets the legions in motion, they'll roll right over you. Were I in your position, I would take advantage of the cover of night to slip away, and not fear the stigma of cowardice. You're facing the mightiest army ever assembled. Against such a force there is no cowardice, only self-preservation."

I believed him. The only question was what should I do with the advice.

"I thank you for your counsel," I said formally. "And will consider your words carefully. For now, if you will please remain here in the open as promised, I must consult with my troops."

"One more thing," Claude said, laying a restraining hand on my arm. "If any harm befalls your assistant, the one you left at the meeting, I would ask that you remember I was here with you and had no part in it."

"I will remember," I nodded, withdrawing my arm. "But if the Brute tries to lay a hand on Aahz, I'll wager he'll wish he hadn't."

As I turned to seek out my team, I wished I felt as confident as I sounded.

Tanda came to me readily when I caught her eye and beckoned her away from the others.

"What is it, Skeeve?" she asked as we moved away into the shadows. "Are you worried about Aahz?"

I was, though I didn't want to admit it just yet. The night was almost gone with no signs of movement or activity from the pavilion. Still, I clung to my faith in Aahz. When that failed, I turned my mind to other exercises to distract it from fruitless worry.

"Aahz can take care of himself," I said gruffly.

"There's something else I wanted your opinion on."

"What's that?" she asked, cocking her head.

"As you know," I began pompously, "I am unable to see the disguise spells I cast. Though everyone else is fooled, as the originator of the spell, I still continue to see things in their true form."

"I didn't know that," she commented. "But continue."

"Well," I explained, "I was thinking that if we actually have to fight the army, we could use additional troops. I've got an idea, but I need you to tell me if it actually works."

"Okay," she nodded. "What is it?"

I started to resume my oration, then realized I was merely stalling. Instead, I closed my eyes and focused my mind on the small grove of trees ahead.

"Hey!" cried Tanda. "That's terrific."

I opened my eyes, being careful to maintain the spell.

"What do you see?" I asked nervously.

"A whole pack of demons . . . oops . . . I mean Perverts," she reported gaily. "Bristling with swords and spears. That's wild!"

It worked. I was correct when I guessed that my disguise spell could work on any living thing, not just men and beasts.

"I've never seen anything like it," Tanda marveled. "Can you make them move?"

"I don't know," I admitted. "I just—"

"Boss! Hey, Boss!" Brockhurst shouted, sprinting up to us. "Come quick! You'd better see this!"

"What is it?" I called, but the Imp had reversed his course and was headed for the tree line.

A sudden fear clutched at my heart.

"C'mon, Tanda," I growled and started off.

By the time we reached the tree line the whole team was assembled there, talking excitedly among themselves.

"What is it?" I barked, joining them.

The group fell silent, avoiding my eyes. Brockhurst lifted a hand and pointed across the meadow.

There, silhouetted against a huge bonfire was Aahz, hanging by his neck from a crude gallows. His body was limp and lifeless as he rotated slowly at the end of the rope. At his feet, a group of soldiers were gathered to witness the spectacle.

Relief flooded over me, and I began to giggle hysterically. Hanging! If only they know!

Alarm showed in the faces of my team as they studied my reaction in shocked silence.

"Don't worry!" I gasped. "He's okay!"

Early in my career with Aahz, I had learned that one doesn't kill demons by hanging them. Their neck muscles are too strong! They can hang all day without being any the worse for wear. I had, of course, learned this the hard way one day when we. . . .

"At least they have the decency to burn the body," Claude murmured from close beside me.

My laughter died in my throat.

"What?" I cried, spinning around.

Sure enough, the soldiers had cut down Aahz's "body" and were carrying it toward the bonfire with the obvious intention of throwing it in.

Fire! That was a different story. Fire was one of the things that could kill Aahz deader than. . . .

"Ajax!" I cried. "Quick! Stop them from—"

It was too late.

With a heave from the soldiers, Aahz arched into the roaring flames. There was a quick burst of light, then nothing.

Gone! Aahz!

I stood staring at the bonfire in disbelief. Shock

numbed me to everything else as my mind reeled at the impact of my loss.

"Skeeve!" Tanda said in my ear, laying a hand on my shoulder.

"Leave me alone!" I croaked.

"But the army . . ."

She let the word trail off, but it made its impact. Slowly I became conscious of the world around me.

The legions, having given us our answer, were massing for battle. Drums boomed, heralding the rising sun as it reflected off the polished weapons arrayed to face us.

The army. They had done this!

With deliberate slowness I turned to face Claude. He recoiled in fear from my gaze.

"Remember!" he cried desperately. "I had nothing to—"

"I remember," I replied coldly. "And for that reason only I am letting you go. I would advise, however, that you choose a path to follow other than rejoining the army. I have tried to be gentle with them, but if they insist on having war, as I am Skeeve, we shall give it to them!"

# XXIII:

*"What is this, a Chinese fire drill?"*

—Sun Tzu

I didn't see where Claude went after I finished speaking with him, nor did I care. I was studying the opposing army with a new eye. Up to now I had been thinking defensively, planning for survival. Now I was thinking as the aggressor.

The legions were in tight block formations, arrayed some three or four blocks deep and perhaps fifteen blocks wide. Together they presented an awesome impression of power, an irresistible force that would never retreat.

That suited me fine. In fact, I wanted a little insurance that they would not retreat.

"Ajax!" I called without turning my head.

"Here, youngster!" the bowman replied from close beside me.

"Can Blackie send your arrows out beyond those formations?"

"I reckon so," he drawled.

"Very well," I said grimly. "The same drill as the first

battle, only this time don't go for the wagons. I want a half circle of fire around their rear."

As before, the bowstring set up a rhythmic "thung" as the bowman began to lose shaft after shaft. This time, however, it seemed the arrows burst into flame more readily.

"Ease off, youngster," Ajax called. "Yer burnin' em up before they reach the ground."

He was right. Either I was standing directly on a force line, or my anger had intensified my energies. Whatever the reason, I found myself with an incredible amount of power at my disposal.

"Sorry, Ajax," I shouted, and diverted a portion of my mind away from the ignition point.

"Tanda!" I called. "Run back and get Gleep!"

"Right, Skeeve," came the reply.

I had a hunch my pet might come in handy before this brawl was done.

The front row of the army's formation was beginning to advance to the rhythmic pounding of drums. I ignored them.

"Brockhurst!"

"Here, boss!" the Imp responded, stepping to my side.

"Have you spotted the commander yet?"

"Not yet," came the bitter reply. "He's probably buried back in the middle of the formation somewhere."

"Well, climb a tree or something and see if you can pinpoint him," I ordered.

"Right, boss! When I see him, do you want me to go after him?"

"No!" I replied grimly. "Report back to me. I want to handle him myself."

The front line was still advancing. I decided I'd better do something about it. With a sweep of my mind, I set fire to the meadow in front of the line's center. The blocks confronted by this barrier ground to a halt while the right and left wings continued their forward movement.

"Gleep!" came a familiar voice accompanied by an even more familiar blast of bad breath.

"We're back!" Tanda announced unnecessarily.

I ignored them and studied the situation. Plumes of white smoke rising from behind the Empire's formation indicated that Ajax was almost finished with his task. Soon, the army would find itself cut off from any retreat. It was time to start thinking about our attack. The first thing I needed was more information.

"Gus!" I said thoughtfully, "I want you to take a quick flight over their formations. See if you can find a spot to drop Berfert where he can do some proper damage."

"Right, boss," the gargoyle grunted, lumbering forward.

"Wait a minute," I said, a thought occurring to me. "Tanda, have you still got the invisibility sheet with you?"

"Right here!" she grinned.

"Good," I nodded. "Gus, take the sheet with you. Keep it in front of you as long as you can while you're checking them out. There's no sense drawing fire until you have to."

The gargoyle accepted the sheet with a shrug.

"If you say so, boss," he muttered. "But they can't do much to me."

"Use it anyway," I ordered. "Now get moving."

The gargoyle sprang heavily into the air and started across the meadow with slow sweeps of his massive wings. I found it hard to believe anything that big and made of stone could fly, but I was seeing it. Maybe he used levitation.

"All set, youngster," Ajax chortled, interrupting my thoughts. "Anything else I can do for ya?"

"Not just now, Ajax," I replied. "But stand by."

I was glad that portion of my concentration was free now. This next stunt was going to take all the energy I could muster.

I focused my mind on the grass in front of the advancing left wing. As testimony to the effectiveness of my efforts, that portion of the line ground to an immediate halt.

"Say!" Tanda breathed in genuine admiration. "That's neat."

The effect I was striving for was to have the grass form itself into an army of Imps, rising from the ground to confront the Empire's troops. I chose Imps this time instead of demons because Imps are shorter, therefore requiring less energy to maintain the illusion.

Whatever my efforts actually achieved, it was enough to have the soldiers react. After several shouted orders from their officers, the troops let fly a ragged barrage of javelins at the grass in front of them. The weapons, of course, had no effect on their phantom foe.

"Say, youngster," Ajax said, nudging me lightly. "You want me to do something about those jokers shootin' at our gargoyle?"

I turned slightly to check Gus's progress. The flying figure had passed over the center line troops, the ones my fire was holding in check. The soldiers could now see the figure behind the invisible sheet, and were reacting with enviable competence.

The archers in their formation were busy loosing their shafts at this strange figure that had suddenly appeared overhead, while their comrades did their best to reach the gargoyle with hurled javelins.

I saw all this at a glance. I also saw something else.

"Wait a minute, Ajax," I ordered. "Look at that!"

The various missiles loosed by the center line were falling to earth in the massed formations of the troops still awaiting commands. Needless to say, this was not well received, particularly as they were still unable to see the actual target of their advance force. To them, it must have appeared that by some magik or demonic possession, their allies had suddenly turned and fired on them.

Now a few blocks began to return the fire, ordering their own archers into action. Others responded by raising their shields and starting forward with drawn swords.

The result was utter chaos, as the center line troops
tried to defend themselves from the attacks of their own
reinforcements.

Mind you, I hadn't planned it this way, but I was quick
to capitalize on the situation. If the presence of a gargoyle
could cause this kind of turmoil, I thought it would be a
good idea to up the ante a little.

With a quick brush of my mind, I altered Gus's appearance. Now they had a full-grown dragon hovering
over their midst. The effect was spectacular.

I, however, did not allow myself the luxury of watching. I had learned something in this brief exchange, and
I wanted to try it out.

I dissolved my Imp army, then reformed them, not in
front of the troops, but in their midst!

This threw the formations into total disorder. As the
soldiers struck or threw at the phantom figures, more often
than not they struck their comrades instead.

If this kept up, they would be too busy fighting each
other to bother with us.

"Boss!" Brockhurst called, darting up to my side. "I've
got the commander spotted!"

"Where?" I asked grimly, trying not to take my concentration from the battle raging in the meadow.

The Imp pointed.

Sure enough! There was the Brute, striding angrily
from formation to formation, trying to restore order to his
force.

I heard the telltale whisper of an arrow being drawn.

"Ajax!" I barked. "Hold your fire. He's mine . . . all
mine!"

As I said this, I dissolved all the Imps in the Brute's
vicinity, and instead changed the commander's features
until he took on the appearance of Aahz.

The dazed soldiers saw a demon appear in their midst
brandishing a sword, a demon of a type they knew could
be killed. They needed no further prompting.

I had one brief glimpse of the Brute's startled face

before his troops closed on him, then a forest of uniforms blotted him from my view.

"Mission accomplished, boss!" Gus announced, appearing beside me. "What next?"

"What . . . did you . . ." I stammered.

I had forgotten that on his return trip, the invisibility sheet would shield the gargoyle from our view. His sudden appearance had startled me.

"Berfert'll be along when he gets done with their siege equipment," Gus continued, waving toward the enemy.

I looked across the meadow. He was right! The heavy equipment which had been lined up behind the army was now in flames.

Then I noticed something else.

The army wasn't fighting each other anymore. I realized with a start that between settling accounts with the Brute and Gus's reappearance, I had forgotten to maintain the Imp army!

In the absence of any visible foe, the Empire troops had apparently come to their senses and were now milling about trying to reestablish their formations.

Soon now, they would be ready to attack again.

"What do we do next, boss?" Brockhurst asked eagerly.

That was a good question. I decided to stall while I tried to work out an answer.

"I'll draw you a diagram," I said confidently. "Somebody give me a sword."

"Here, kid. Use mine," Aahz replied, passing me the weapon.

"Thanks," I said absently. "Now, this line is their main formation. If we . . . *Aahz!?*"

"Ready and able," my mentor grinned. "Sorry I'm late."

It *was* Aahz! He was standing there calmly with his arms folded as if he had been part of our group all along. The reactions of the others, however, showed that they were as surprised as I was at his appearance.

"But you . . ." I stammered. "The fire . . ."

"Oh, that," Aahz shrugged. "About the time I figured what they were doing, I used the D-Hopper to blink out to another dimension. The only trouble was I hadn't gotten around to relabeling the controls yet, and I had a heck of a time finding my way back to Klah."

Relief flooded over me like a cool wave. Aahz was alive! More important, he was here! The prospects for the battle suddenly looked much better.

"What should we do next, Aahz?" I asked eagerly.

"I don't know why you're asking me," my mentor blinked innocently. "It looks like you've been doing a fine job so far all by yourself."

Terrific! Now that I need advice, I get compliments.

"Look, Aahz," I began sternly. "We've got a battle coming up that—"

"Boss!" Brockhurst interrupted. "Something's going on out there!"

With a sinking heart, I turned and surveyed the situation again.

A new figure had appeared on the scene, an officer from the look of him. He was striding briskly along the front of the formation alternately shouting and waving his hands. Trailing along in his wake was a cluster of officers, mumbling together and shaking their hands.

"What in the world is that all about?" I murmured half to myself.

"Brace yourself, kid," Aahz advised. "If I'm hearing correctly, it's bad news."

"C'mon, Aahz," I sighed. "How could things get worse than they already are?"

"Easy," Aahz retorted. "*That* is the supreme commander of the Empire's army. He's here to find out what's holding up his left flank's advance."

# XXIV:

*". . . and then I said to myself, 'Why should I split it two ways—' "*

—G. MOUSER

The supreme commander's name was Big Julie, and he was completely different from what I had expected.

For one thing, when he called for a war council, he came to us. Flanked by his entire entourage of officers, he came all the way across the meadow to stand just short of the tree line, and he came unarmed. What was more, all of his officers were unarmed, presumably at his insistence.

He seemed utterly lacking in the arrogance so prevalent in the other officers we had dealt with, inviting us into the large tent he had had erected in the meadow for the meeting. Introducing him to the members of my force, I noticed he treated them with great respect and seemed genuinely pleased to meet each of them, even Gleep.

Our whole team was present for the meeting. We figured that if there was ever a time to display our power, this was it.

In a surprising show of generosity, Aahz broke out the

wine and served drinks to the assemblage. I was a little suspicious of this. Aahz isn't above doctoring drinks to win a fight, but when I caught his eye and raised an eyebrow, he responded with a small shake of his head. Apparently he was playing this round straight.

Then we got down to business.

Big Julie heard us out, listening with rapt attention. When we finished, he sighed and shook his head.

"Ah'm sorry," he announced. "But I can't do it. We've got to keep advancing, you know? That's what armies do!"

"Couldn't you advance in another direction for a while?" I suggested hopefully.

"Aie!" he exclaimed, spreading his hands defensively. "What do you think I got here, geniuses? These are soldiers. They move in straight lines, know what I mean?"

"Do they have to move so vigorously?" Aahz muttered. "They don't leave much behind."

"What can I say?" Big Julie shrugged. "They're good boys. They do their job. Sometimes they get a little carried away . . . like the Brute."

I had hoped to avoid the subject of the Brute, but since it had come up, I decided to face it head on.

"Say . . . um . . . Julie," I began.

"Big Julie!" one of the officers growled out of the corner of his mouth.

"Big Julie!" I amended hastily. "About the Brute. Um . . . he was . . . well . . . I wanted . . ."

"Don't mention it," Julie waved. "You want to know the truth? You did me a favor."

"I did?" I blinked.

"I was getting a little worried about the Brute, you know what I mean?" the commander raised his eyebrows. "He was getting a little too ambitious."

"In that case. . . ." I smiled.

"Still . . ." Julie continued, "that's a bad way to go. Hacked apart by your own men. I wouldn't want that to happen to me."

"You should have fed him to the dragons," Aahz said bluntly.

"The Brute?" Julie frowned. "Fed to the dragons? Why?"

"Because then he could have been 'et, too'!"

Apparently this was supposed to be funny, as Aahz erupted into sudden laughter as he frequently does at his own jokes. Tanda rolled her eyes in exasperation.

Big Julie looked vaguely puzzled. He glanced at me, and I shrugged to show I didn't know what was going on either.

"He's strange," Julie announced, stabbing an accusing finger at Aahz. "What's a nice boy like you doing hanging around with strange people? Hey?"

"It's the war," I said apologetically. "You know what they say about strange bedfellows."

"You seem to be doin' all right for yourself!" Julie winked, then leered at Tanda.

"You want I should clean up his act, Boss?" Brockhurst asked grimly, stepping forward.

"See!" Julie exploded. "That's what I mean. This is no way to learn warfare. Tell you what. Why don't you let me fix you up with a job, hey? What do you say to that?"

"What pay scale?" Aahz asked.

"Aahz!" I scowled, then turned back to Julie. "Sorry, but we've already got a job . . . defending Possiltum. I appreciate your offer, but I don't want to leave a job unfinished."

"What have I been telling you?" Julie appealed to his officers. "All the good material has been taken already. Why can't you bring me recruits like this, eh?"

This was all very flattering, but I clung tenaciously to the purpose of our meeting.

"Um . . . Jul . . . I mean, Big Julie," I continued. "About defending Possiltum. Couldn't you find another kingdom somewhere to attack? We really don't want to have to fight you."

"*You* don't want to fight?" Julie erupted sarcastically.

"You think *I* want to fight? You think I *like* doing this for a living? You think my boys like killing and conquering all the time?"

"Well . . ." I began tactfully.

Big Julie wasn't listening. He was out of his seat and pacing up and down, gesturing violently to emphasize his words.

"What kind of ding-bat *wants* to fight?" he asked rhetorically. "Do I look crazy? Do my boys look crazy? Everybody thinks we got some kind of weird drive that keeps us going. They think that all we want to do in the whole world is march around in sweaty armor and sharpen swords on other people's helmets. That's what you think too, isn't it? Eh? Isn't it?"

This last was shouted directly at me. By now I was pretty fed up with being shouted at.

"Yes!" I roared angrily. "That's what I think!"

"Well," Julie scowled. "You're wrong because—"

"That's what I think because if you didn't like doing it, you wouldn't do it!" I continued, rising to my own feet.

"Just like that!" Julie shouted sarcastically. "Just stop and walk away."

He turned and addressed his officers.

"He thinks it's easy! Do you hear *that*? Any of you who don't like to fight, just stop. Eh? Just like that."

A low chorus of chuckles rose from his assembled men. Despite my earlier burst of anger, I found myself starting to believe him. Incredible as it seemed, Julie and his men didn't like being soldiers!

"You think we wouldn't quit if we could?" Julie was saying to me again. "I bet there isn't a man in my whole army who wouldn't take a walk if he thought he could get away with it."

Again there was a murmur of assent from his officers.

"I don't understand," I said, shaking my head. "If you don't want to fight, and we don't want to fight, what are we doing here?"

"Did you ever hear of loan sharks?" Julie asked. "You know about organized crime?"

"Organized crime?" I blinked.

"It's like government, kid," Aahz supplied. "Only more effective."

"You'd better believe 'more effective,' " Julie nodded. "That's what we're doing here! Me and the boys, we got a list of gambling debts like you wouldn't believe. We're kinda working it off, paying 'em back in land, you know what I mean?"

"You haven't answered my question," I pointed out. "Why don't you just quit?"

"Quit?" Julie seemed genuinely astonished. "You gotta be kidding. If I quit before I'm paid up, they break my leg. You know?" His wolfish grin left no doubt the thugs in question would do something a great deal more fatal and painful than just breaking a leg.

"It's the same with the boys here. Right, boys?" He indicated his officers with a wave of his hand.

Vigorous nods answered his wave.

"And you ought to see the collection agent they use. Kid, you might be a fair magician where you come from. But"—he shuddered—"this, believe me, you don't want to see."

Knowing how tough Big Julie was, I believed him.

Giving me a warm smile, he draped his arm around my shoulders.

"That's why it's really gonna break my heart to kill you. Ya know?"

"Well," I began, "you don't have to . . . KILL ME?"

"That's right," he nodded vigorously. "I knew you'd understand. A job's a job, even when you hate it."

"Whoa!" Aahz interrupted, holding one flattened hand across the top of the other to form a crude T. "Hold it! Aren't you overlooking something, Jules?"

"That's 'Big Julie.' " one of the guards admonished.

"I don't care if he calls himself the Easter Bunny!" my mentor snarled. "He's still overlooking something."

"What's that?" Julie asked.

"Us." Aahz smiled, gesturing to the team. "Aside from the minor detail that Skeeve here's a magician and not that easy to kill, he's got friends. What do you think we'll be doing while you make a try for our leader?"

The whole team edged forward a little. None of them were smiling, not even Gus. Even though they were my friends who I knew and loved, I had to admit they looked mean. I was suddenly very glad they were on my side.

Big Julie, on the other hand, seemed unimpressed.

"As a matter of fact," he smiled, "I expect you to be dying right along with your leader. That is, unless you're really good at running."

"Running from what?" Gus growled. "I still think you're overlooking something. By my count, we've got you outnumbered. Even if you were armed—"

The supreme commander cut him short with a laugh. It was a relaxed, confident laugh which no one else joined in on. Then the laugh disappeared, and he leaned forward with a fierce scowl.

"Now, I'm only gonna say this once, so alla you listen close. Big Julie didn't get where he is today by over-looking nothin'. You think I'm outnumbered? Well, maybe you'd just better count again."

Without taking his eyes from us, he waved his hand in a short, abrupt motion. At the signal, one of his guards pulled a cord and the sides of the tent fell away.

There were soldiers outside. They hadn't been there when we entered the tent, but they were there now. Hoo boy were they. Ranks and ranks of them completely sur-rounding the tent, the nearest barely an arm's length away. The front three rows were archers, with arrows nocked and drawn, leveled at our team.

I realized with a sudden calm clarity that I was about to die. The whole meeting had been a trap, and it was a good one. Good enough that we would all be dead if we so much as twitched. I couldn't even kid myself that I could stop that many arrows if they were all loosed at once. Gus might survive the barrage, and maybe the others could blip away to another dimension in time to save themselves, but I was too far away from Aahz and the D-Hopper to escape.

"I . . . um . . . thought war councils were supposed to be off limits for combat." I said carefully.

"I also didn't get where I am today by playing fair," Big Julie shrugged.

"You know," Aahz drawled, "for a guy who doesn't want to fight, you run a pretty nasty war."

"What can I say?" the supreme commander asked, spreading his hands in helpless appeal. "It's a job. Believe me, if there was any other way, I'd take it. But as it is . . ."

His voice trailed off, and he began to raise his arm. I realized with horror that when his hand came down, so would the curtain.

"How much time do we have to find another way?" I asked desperately.

"You don't," Big Julie sighed.

"AND WE DON'T NEED ANY!" Aahz roared with sudden glee.

All eyes turned toward him, including my own. He was grinning broadly while listening to something the Gremlin was whispering in his ear.

"What's that supposed to mean?" the supreme commander demanded. "And where did this little blue fella come from? Eh?"

He glared at the encircling troops, who looked at each other in embarrassed confusion.

"This is a Gremlin," Aahz informed him, slipping a comradely arm around the shoulders of his confidant, "And I think he's got the answer to our problems. *All* our problems. You know what I mean?"

"What does he mean?" Julie scowled at me. "Do you understand what he's sayin'?"

"Tell him, Aahz," I ordered confidently, wondering all the while what possible solution my mentor could have found to this mess.

"Big Julie," Aahz smiled, "what could those loan sharks of yours do if you and your army simply disappeared?"

A nd so, incredibly, it was ended.
Not with fireworks or an explosion or a battle. But like a lot of things in my life, in as crazy and off-hand a way as it had started.

And when it had ended, I almost wished it hadn't.

Because then I had to say good-bye to the team.

Saying good-bye to the team was harder than I would have imagined. Somehow, in all my planning, I had never stopped to consider the possibility of emerging victorious from the war.

Despite my original worries about the team, I found I had grown quite close to each of them. I would have liked to keep them around a little longer, but that would have been impossible. Our next stop was the capital, and they would be a little too much to explain away.

Besides, as Aahz pointed out, it was bad for morale to let the troops find out how much their commander was being paid, particularly when it was extremely disproportionate to their own wages.

Following his advice, I paid each of them personally. When I was done, however, I found myself strangely at a loss for words. Once again, the team came to my aid.

"Well, boss," Brockhurst sighed. "I guess this is it. Thanks for everything."

"It's been a real pleasure working for you," Gus echoed. "The money's nice, but the way I figure it, Berfert and I owe you a little extra for getting us out of that slop chute. Anytime you need a favor, look us up."

"Youngster," Ajax said, clearing his throat, "I move around a lot, so I'm not that easy to track. If you ever find yourself in a spot where you think I can lend a hand, jes' send a message to the Bazaar and I'll be along shortly."

"I didn't think you visited the Bazaar that often," I asked, surprised.

"Normally I don't," the bowman admitted. "But I will now . . . jest in case."

Tanda was tossing her coin in the air and catching it with practiced ease.

"I shouldn't take this," she sighed. "But a girl's gotta eat."

"You earned it," I insisted.

"Yea, well, I guess we'll be going," she said, beckoning to the others. "Take care of yourself, handsome."

"You will be coming back?" I asked hurriedly.

She made a face.

"I don't think so," she said wryly, "If Grimble saw us together . . ."

"I meant, ever," I clarified.

She brightened immediately.

"Sure," she winked. "You won't get rid of me that easily. Say good-bye to Aahz for me."

"Say good-bye to him yourself," Aahz growled, stepping out of the shadows.

"There you are!" Tanda grinned. "Where's the Gremlin? I thought you two were talking."

"We were," Aahz confirmed, looking around him. "I don't understand. He was here a minute ago."

"It's as if he didn't exist, isn't it, Aahz?" I suggested innocently.

"Now look, kid!" my mentor began angrily.

A chorus of laughter erupted from the team. He spun in that direction to deliver a scathing reply, but there was a blip of light and they were gone.

We stood silently together for several moments staring at the vacant space. Then Aahz slipped an arm around my shoulder.

"They were a good team, kid," he sighed. "Now pull yourself together. Triumphant generals don't have slow leaks in the vicinity of their eyes. It's bad for the image."

# XXV:

*"Is everybody happy?"*

—MACHIAVELLI

Aahz and I entered the capital at the head of a jubilant mob of Possiltum citizens.

We were practically herded to the front of the palace by the crowd pressing us forward. The cheering was incredible. Flowers and other less identifiable objects were thrown at us or strewn in our path, making the footing uncertain enough that more than once I was afraid of falling and being trampled. The people, at least, seemed thoroughly delighted to see us. All in all, though, our triumphal procession was almost as potentially injurious to our life and limb as the war had been.

I was loving it.

I had never had a large crowd make a fuss over me before. It was nice.

"Heads up, kid," Aahz murmured, nudging me in the ribs. "Here comes the reception committee."

Sure enough, there was another procession emerging from the main gates of the palace. It was smaller than ours, but made up for what it lacked in numbers with the prestige of its members.

The king was front and center, flanked closely by Grimble and Badaxe. The chancellor was beaming with undisguised delight. The general, on the other hand, looked positively grim.

Sweeping the crowd with his eyes, Badaxe spotted several of his soldiers in our entourage. His dark expression grew even darker, boding ill for those men. I guessed he was curious as to why they had failed to carry out his orders to stop our return.

Whatever he had in mind, it would have to wait. The king was raising his arms, and the assemblage obediently fell silent to hear what he had to say.

"Lord Magician," he began, "know that the cheers of the grateful citizens of Possiltum only echo my feelings for this service you have done us."

A fresh wave of applause answered him.

"News of your victory has spread before you," he continued. "And already our historians are recording the details of your triumph . . . as much as is known, that is."

An appreciative ripple of laughter surged through the crowd.

"While we do not pretend to comprehend the workings of your powers," the king announced, "the results speak for themselves. A mighty army of invincible warriors vanished into thin air, weapons and all. Only their armor and siege machines littering the empty battlefield mark their passing. The war is won! The threat to Possiltum is ended forever!"

At this, the crowd exploded. The air again filled with flowers and shouting shook the very walls of the palace.

The king tried to shout something more, but it was lost in the jubilant noise. Finally he shrugged and reentered the palace, pausing only for a final wave at the crowd.

I thought it was a rather cheap ploy, allowing him to cash in on our applause as if it were intended for him, but I let it go. Right now we had bigger fish to fry.

Catching the eyes of Grimble and Badaxe, I beckoned them forward.

"I've got to talk to you two," I shouted over the din.

"Shouldn't we go inside where it's quieter?" Grimble shouted back.

"We'll talk here!" I insisted.

"But the crowd . . ." the chancellor gestured.

I turned and nodded to a figure in the front row of the mob. He responded by raising his right arm in a signal. In response, the men in the forefront of the crowd locked arms and formed a circle around us, moving with near military precision. In a twinkling, there was a space cleared in the teeming populace, with the advisors, Aahz, Gleep, myself, and the man who had given the signal standing alone at its center.

"Just a moment," Badaxe rumbled, peering suspiciously at the circle. "What's going on—"

"General!" I beamed, flashing my biggest smile. "I'd like you to meet the newest citizen of Possiltum."

Holding my smile, I beckoned the mob leader forward.

"General Badaxe," I announced formally, "meet Big Julie. Big Julie, Hugh Badaxe!"

"Nice to meet you!" Julie smiled. "The boy here, he's been tellin' me all about you!"

The general blanched as he recognized the Empire's top commander.

"You!" he stammered. "But you . . . you're—"

"I hope you don't mind, General," I said smoothly. "But I've taken the liberty of offering Big Julie a job . . . as your military consultant."

"Military consultant?" Badaxe echoed suspiciously.

"What's the matter," Julie scowled. "Don't you think I can do it?"

"It's not that," the general clarified hastily. "It's just that . . . well—"

"One thing we neglected to mention, General," Aahz interrupted. "Big Julie here is retiring from active duty. He's more than willing to leave the running of Possiltum's army to you, and agrees to give advice only when asked."

"That's right!" Julie beamed. "I just wanna sit in the sun, drink a little wine, maybe pat a few bottoms, you know what I mean?"

"But the king . . ." Badaxe stammered.

". . . doesn't have to be bothered with it at all," Aahz purred. "Unless, of course, you deem it necessary to tell him where your new battle plans are coming from."

"Hmm," the general said thoughtfully. "You sure you'd be happy with things that way, Julie?"

"Positive!" Julie nodded firmly. "I don't want any glory, no responsibility, and no credit. I had too much of that when I was workin' for the Empire, you know what I mean? Me and the boys talked it over, and we decided—"

"The boys?" Badaxe interrupted, frowning.

"Um . . . that's another thing we forgot to mention, General," I smiled. "Big Julie isn't the only new addition to Possiltum's citizenry."

I jerked my head at the circle of men holding back the crowd.

The general blinked at the men, then swiveled his head around noting how many more like them were scattered through the crowd. He blanched as it became clear to him both where the Empire's army had disappeared to, and why his men had been unsuccessful in stopping our return to the capital.

"You mean to tell me you—" Badaxe began.

"Happy Possiltum citizens all, General!" Aahz proclaimed, then dropped his voice to a more confidential level. "I think you'll find that if you should ever have to draft an army, these new citizens will train a lot faster than your average plow pusher."

Apparently the general did. His eyes glittered at the thought of the new force we had placed at his command. I could see him mentally licking his chops in anticipation of the next war.

"Big Julie!" he declared with a broad smile. "You and

your . . . er . . . boys are more than welcome to settle here
in Possiltum. Let me be one of the first to congratulate
you on your new citizenship."

He extended his hand, but there was an obstruction in
his way. The obstruction's name was J. R. Grimble.

"Just a moment!" the chancellor snarled. "There's one
minor flaw in your plans. It is my intention to advise the
king to disband Possiltum's army."

"What?" roared Badaxe.

"Let me handle this, General," Aahz said soothingly.
"Grimble, what would you want to do a fool thing like
that for?"

"Why, because of the magician, of course," the chancellor blinked. "You've demonstrated he is quite capable
of defending the kingdom without the aid of an army, so
I see no reason why we should continue to bear the cost
of maintaining one."

"Nonsense!" Aahz scolded. "Do you think the great
Skeeve has nothing to do with his time but guard your
borders? Do you want to tie up your high-cost magician
doing the job a low-cost soldier could do?"

"Well . . ." Grimble scowled.

"Besides," Aahz continued. "Skeeve will be spending
considerable time on the road furthering his studies . . .
which will of course increase his value to Possiltum. Who
will guard your kingdom while he's away, if not the
army?"

"But the cost is . . ." Grimble whined.

"If anything," Aahz continued, ignoring the chancellor's protests. "I should think you'd want to expand your
army now that your borders have increased in size."

"What's that?" Grimble blinked, "What about our borders?"

"I thought it was obvious," Aahz said innocently. "All
these new citizens have to settle somewhere . . . and there
is a lot of land up for grabs just north of here. As I understand it, it's completely unguarded at the moment. Possiltum wouldn't even have to fight for it, just move in and

settle. That is, of course, provided you have a strong army to hold it once you've got it."

"Hmm," the chancellor said thoughtfully, stroking his chin with his hand.

"Then again," Aahz murmured quietly, "there's all the extra tax money the new citizens and land will contribute to the kingdom's coffers."

"Big Julie!" Grimble beamed. "I'd like to welcome you and your men to Possiltum."

"I'm welcoming him first!" Badaxe growled. "He's *my* advisor."

As he spoke, the general dropped his hand to the hilt of his axe, a move which was not lost on the chancellor.

"Of course, General," Grimble acknowledged, forcing a grin. "I'll just wait here until you're through. There are a few things I want to discuss with our new citizens."

"While you're waiting, Grimble," Aahz smiled, "there are a few things we have to discuss with you."

"Such as what?" the chancellor scowled.

"Such as the Court Magician's pay!" my mentor retorted.

"Of course," Grimble laughed. "As soon as we're done here we'll go inside and I'll pay him his first month's wages."

"Actually," Aahz drawled. "What we wanted to discuss was an increase."

The chancellor stopped laughing.

"You mean a bonus, don't you?" he asked hopefully. "I'm sure we can work something out, considering—"

"I mean an increase!" Aahz corrected firmly. "C'mon, Grimble. The kingdom's bigger now. That means the magician's job is bigger and deserves more pay."

"I'm not sure I can approve that," the chancellor responded cagily.

"With the increase of your tax base," Aahz pressed, "I figure you can afford—"

"Now let's be careful," Grimble countered. "Our overhead has gone up right along with that increase. In fact, I wouldn't be surprised if . . ."

"C'mon, Gleep," I murmured to my pet. "Let's go see Buttercup."

I had a feeling the wage debate was going to last for a while.

# XXVI:

*"All's well that ends well."*

—E. A. POE

I was spending a leisurely afternoon killing time in my immense room in the palace.

The bargaining session between Aahz and Grimble had gone well for us. Not only had I gotten a substantial wage increase, I was also now housed in a room which was only a little smaller than Grimble's, which in turn was second only to the king's in size. What was more, the room had a large window, which was nice even if it did look out over the stables. Aahz had insisted on this, hinting darkly that I might be receiving winged visitors in the night. I think this scared me more than it did Grimble, but I got my window.

When I chose, I could look down from my perch and keep an eye on Gleep and Buttercup in the stables. I could also watch the hapless stable boy who had been assigned to catering to their every need. That had been part of the deal, too, though I had pushed for it a lot harder than Aahz.

Aahz was housed in the adjoining room, which was nice, though smaller than mine. The royal architects were scheduled to open a door in our shared wall, and I had a hunch that when they did, the room arrangement would change drastically. For the moment, at least, I had a bit of unaccustomed privacy.

The room itself, however, was not what was currently commanding my attention. My mind was focused on Garkin's old brazier. I had been trying all afternoon to unlock its secrets, thus far without success. It stood firmly in the center of the floor where I had first placed it, stubbornly resisting my efforts.

I perched on my windowsill and studied the object glumly. I could levitate it easily enough, but that wasn't what I wanted. I wanted it to come alive and follow me around the way it used to follow Garkin.

That triggered an idea in my mind. It seemed silly, but nothing else had worked.

Drawing my eyebrows together, I addressed the brazier without focusing my energies on it.

"Come here!" I thought.

The brazier seemed to waver for a moment, then it trotted to my side, clacking across the floor on its spindly legs.

It worked! Even though it was a silly little detail, the brazier's obedience somehow made me feel more like a magician.

"Hey, kid!" Aahz called, barging through my door without knocking. "Have you got a corkscrew?"

"What's a corkscrew?" I asked reflexively.

"Never mind," my mentor sighed. "I'll do it myself."

With that, he shifted the bottle of wine he was holding to his left hand, and inserted the claw on his right forefinger into the cork. The cork made a soft pop as he gently eased it from the neck of the bottle, whereupon the cork was casually tossed into a corner as Aahz drank deeply of the wine.

"Ahh!" he gasped, coming up for air. "Terrific bouquet!"

"Um ... Aahz?" I said shyly, leaving my window perch and moving to the table. "I have something to show you."

"First, could you answer a question?" Aahz asked.

"What?" I frowned.

"Why is that brazier following you around the room?"

I looked, and was startled to find he was right! The brazier had scuttled from the window to the table to remain by my side. The strange part was that I hadn't summoned it.

"Um ... that's what I was going to show you," I admitted. "I've figured out how to get the brazier to come to me all by itself ... no levitation or anything."

"Swell," Aahz grunted. "Now, can you make it stop?"

"Um ... I don't know," I said, sitting down quickly in one of the chairs.

I didn't want to admit it, but while we were talking I had tried several mental commands to get the brazier to go away, all without noticeable effect. I'd have to work this out on my own once Aahz had left.

"Say, Aahz," I said casually, propping my feet on the table. "Could you pour me some of that wine?"

Aahz cocked an eyebrow at me, then crossed the room slowly to stand by my side.

"Kid," he said gently, "I want you to look around real carefully. Do you see anybody here except you and me?"

"No," I admitted.

"Then we're in private, not in public ... right?" he smiled.

"That's right," I agreed.

"Then get your own wine, apprentice!" he roared, kicking my chair out from under me.

Actually, it wasn't as bad as it sounds. I exerted my mind before I hit the floor and hovered safely in thin air. From that position, I reached out with my mind and lifted the bottle from Aahz's hand, transferring it to my own.

"If you insist," I said casually, taking a long pull on the bottle.

"Think you're pretty smart, don't you!" Aahz snarled, then he grinned. "Well, I guess you are at that. You've done pretty well . . . for an amateur."

"A professional," I corrected with a grin. "A salaried professional."

"I know." Aahz grinned back. "For an amateur, you're pretty smart. For a professional you've got a lot to learn."

"C'mon, Aahz!" I protested.

"But that can wait for another day," Aahz conceded. "You might as well relax for a while and enjoy yourself . . . while you can."

"What's that supposed to mean?" I frowned.

"Nothing!" Aahz shrugged innocently. "Nothing at all."

"Wait a minute, Aahz," I said sharply, regaining my feet. "I'm Court Magician now, right?"

"That's right, Skeeve," my mentor nodded.

"Court Magician is the job you pushed me into because it's so easy, right?" I pressed.

"Right again, kid." He smiled, his nodding becoming even more vigorous.

"Then nothing can go wrong? Nothing serious?" I asked anxiously.

Aahz retrieved his wine bottle and took a long swallow before answering.

"Just keep thinking that, kid." He grinned. "It'll help you sleep nights."

"C'mon, Aahz!" I whined. "You're supposed to be my teacher. If there's something I'm missing, you've got to tell me. Otherwise I won't learn."

"Very well, *apprentice*." Aahz smiled, evilly emphasizing the word. "There are a few things you've overlooked."

"Such as?" I asked, writhing under his smile.

"Such as Gus, Ajax, and Brockhurst, who you just sent back to Deva without instructions."

"Instructions?" I blinked.

"Tanda we don't have to worry about, but the other three—"

"Wait a minute, Aahz," I interrupted before he got too far from the subject. "What instructions?"

"Instructions not to talk about our little skirmish here," Aahz clarified absently. "Tanda will know enough to keep her mouth shut, but the others won't."

"You think they'll talk?"

"Is a frog's behind watertight?" Aahz retorted.

"What's a frog?" I countered.

"Money in their pockets, fresh from a successful campaign against overwhelming odds ... of course they'll talk!" Aahz thundered. "They'll talk their fool heads off to anyone who'll listen. What's more, they'll embellish it a little more with each telling until it sounds like they're the greatest fighters ever to spit teeth and you're the greatest tactician since Gronk!"

"What's wrong with that?" I inquired, secretly pleased. I didn't know who Gronk was, but what Aahz was saying had a nice ring to it.

"Nothing at all." Aahz responded innocently. "Except now the word will be out as to who you are, where you are, and what you are ... also that you're for hire and that you subcontract. If there's any place in all the dimensions that folks will take note of information like that, it's the Bazaar."

Regardless of what my mentor may think, I'm not slow. I realized in a flash the implications of what he was saying ... realized them and formulated an answer.

"So we suddenly get a lot of strange people dropping in on us to offer jobs, or looking for work," I acknowledged. "So what? All that means is I get a lot of practice saying 'No.' Who knows, it might improve my status around here a little if it's known that I regularly consult with strange beings from other worlds."

"Of course," Aahz commented darkly, "there's always the chance that someone at the Bazaar will hear that the other side is thinking of hiring you and decide to forcibly remove you from the roster. Either that, or some young hotshot will want to make a name for himself by taking on this unbeatable magician everyone's talking about."

I tried not to show how much his grim prophecy had unnerved me. Then I realized he would probably keep heaping it on until he saw me sweat. Consequently, I sweated . . . visibly.

"I hadn't thought of that, Aahz," I admitted. "I guess I did overlook something there."

"Then again there's Grimble and Badaxe," Aahz continued as if he hadn't heard me.

"What about Grimble and Badaxe?" I asked nervously.

"In my estimation," Aahz yawned, "the only way those two would ever work together would be against a common foe. In my further estimation, the best candidate for that 'common foe' position is you!"

"Me?" I asked in a very small voice.

"You work it out, kid," my mentor shrugged. "Until you hit the scene there was a two-way power struggle going as to who had the king's ear. Then you came along and not only saved the kingdom, you increased the population, expanded the borders, and added to the tax base. That makes you the most popular and therefore the most influential person in the king's court. Maybe I'm wrong, but I don't think Grimble and Badaxe are going to just sigh and accept that. It's my guess they'll 'double team' you and attack anything you say or do militarily and monetarily, and that's a tough one-two punch to counter."

"Okay. Okay. So there were two things I overlooked," I said. "Except for that—"

"And of course there's the people Big Julie and his men owe money to," Aahz commented thoughtfully. "I wonder how long it will be before they start nosing around looking for an explanation as to what happened to an entire army? More important, I wonder who they'll be looking for by name to provide them with that explanation?"

"Aahz?"

"Yeah, kid?"

"Do you mind if I have a little more of that wine?"

"Help yourself, kid. There's lots."

I had a hunch that was going to be the best news I would hear for a long time.

# ABOUT THE AUTHOR

Robert (Lynn) Asprin was born in 1946. While he has written some stand-alone novels such as *Cold Cash War, Tambu, The Bug Wars,* and also the *Duncan and Mallory* illustrated stories, Bob is best known for his series: *The Myth Adventures of Aahz and Skeeve*; the *Phule* novels; and, more recently, the *Time Scout* novels written with Linda Evans. He also edited the groundbreaking *Thieves World* anthologies with Lynn Abbey. His most recent collaboration is *License Invoked*, written with Jody Lynn Nye. It is set in the French Quarter, New Orleans, where he currently lives.